PRETTY GIRLS DANCING

ALSO BY KYLIE BRANT

The Circle of Evil Trilogy

Chasing Evil
Touching Evil
Facing Evil

Other Works

Deep as the Dead
What the Dead Know
Secrets of the Dead
11
Waking Nightmare
Waking Evil
Waking the Dead
Deadly Intent
Deadly Dreams
Deadly Sins
Terms of Attraction
Terms of Engagement
Terms of Surrender
The Last Warrior
The Business of Strangers
Close to the Edge
In Sight of the Enemy
Dangerous Deception
Truth or Lies

Entrapment

Alias Smith and Jones

Hard to Tame

Hard to Resist

Born in Secret

Hard to Handle

Undercover Bride

Falling Hard and Fast

Heartbreak Ranch

Undercover Lover

Friday's Child

Bringing Benjy Home

Guarding Raine

An Irresistible Man

McLain's Law

Rancher's Choice

PRETTY GIRLS DANCING

KYLIE BRANT

This is a work of fiction. Names, characters, organizations, places, events, and incidents are either products of the author's imagination or are used fictitiously. Any resemblance to actual persons, living or dead, or actual events is purely coincidental.

Published by Thomas & Mercer, Seattle

www.apub.com

ISBN 13: 9781542049955 (hardcover)
ISBN 10: 1542049954 (hardcover)
ISBN-13: 9781477820155 (paperback)
ISBN-10: 1477820159 (paperback)

Cover design by David Drummond

Printed in the United States of America

First Edition

For Grady, whose smiles light up my world.

Whitney DeVries

October 30
11:48 p.m.

Whitney reached under her pillow for her buzzing cell phone, read the text on the screen, and smiled.

Are you coming?

A wash of excitement flooded her as she stared at the words. Was she? She'd changed her mind a dozen times since she and Patrick had come up with this plan. Had half expected that in the end, he would change his mind, too. Ride a moped twelve miles just so they could meet up for the first time in person? It had sounded thrilling when they'd started talking about it a couple of weeks ago. But now second thoughts dampened her excitement. Her dad would seriously kill her if she got caught.

The text alert sounded again. This time there was a cartoon pic of a sad-looking donkey sitting in a snowbank. Freezing my ass off here.

Delighted, she muffled a laugh in her pillow. Patrick's sense of humor was the thing she liked most about him. But it didn't hurt that he was hotter than any of the boys at her school. He was a sophomore, a year older than her, had blond hair and Liam Hemsworth blue eyes, with a majorly cute dimple when he smiled. She'd seen him only twice before when she'd visited Gram in Blackston. They'd gone to the grocery store, and he'd been stocking shelves. As they'd walked by, Gram had noticed her looking and whispered, "What a hottie." They'd laughed about that all the way home.

And then a few months later, out of the blue, he'd friended her on Facebook. Her bestie, Macy, had agreed that was clearly a sign. Two weeks later he'd messaged. Have I seen you in Blackston? Maybe at Moulders last summer with your Grandma? Moulders had the best iced chocolate mochas, and Gram could take Whitney there only when her disapproving mom wasn't around. Whitney had never seen *him* there, so the thought of Patrick Allen checking her out the way she had him at the grocery store was totally cool. Soon they were exchanging messages or texts every day. He'd told her about his football injury the year before and how depressed he'd been just sitting on the sidelines. She'd confided about the huge fight with her mom and dad over her quitting dance to spend more time on soccer, and then being stuck as third-string goalie. They'd bitched about their strict parents and pesky brothers (Patrick had two). She could talk to him—really talk to him—even though there had been no actual phone calls because Patrick had *zero* privacy at his house.

But tonight would be different. She could speak to him for the first time, face-to-face the way she hadn't had the guts to last summer. A surge of courage rose, and she texted back. Be there in a few. Before she could change her mind—again—Whitney slipped out of bed, setting the phone on the nightstand, and arranged the pillows on the center of the bed, covering them with the blankets. Dad had already checked in on her when he'd gotten home after second shift, which meant he'd be asleep by now. Quickly she changed into the clothes she'd set out just in case Patrick showed up. And in case she didn't chicken out of meeting him. She went to the dresser and dragged a brush through her hair.

She froze when she heard a small sound. Waiting, her breath tangled in her chest. When she heard nothing further, the breath hissed out of her silently. Her mom had been in bed for hours, and once Dad turned in, the only one who might wake up was Ryan. At ten, he still had the occasional nightmare, which was funny since *he* was a nightmare most of the time.

She put on the fuchsia peacoat she'd draped over her desk chair, grabbed her cell, and tucked it into a pocket before moving toward the window facing the side yard. Because this wasn't the first time she'd sneaked out, she knew exactly how to slide each of the clips on the screen to unlock them. She rolled the crank to open the window, then eased the screen down and leaned it against the wall. Sending one last glance toward her closed bedroom door, she threw a leg over the casement. Followed it with the other. A moment later, she was jumping nimbly to the ground and heading toward the backyard. It had been too risky to consider taking her bike. Her parents' bedroom was the closest to the garage, and her dad had superhuman hearing.

A chilly wind sent dry leaves swirling around her, and the sound they made crunching beneath her feet seemed abnormally loud in the surrounding silence. She shivered, buttoning her coat as she walked. The park where she was meeting Patrick was just a few blocks away. She'd spend an hour with him, max, before returning home and climbing back into her room. No one would be the wiser.

She had a sudden image of her dad in the window when she returned, and her step faltered. He was okay most of the time, but he could be completely unreasonable about some things. Curfew was one of them.

An alert sounded again, and she dug in her pocket for her cell. If I get caught, I'll be grounded for life. Then a picture of a prisoner behind bars. She smiled, her thumbs dancing over the keys in response. You? I'm the one with a cop for a dad. Solitary for me.

The Baxters' dog sent out a trio of barks as she hurried by the chain-link fence of her neighbors' yard. She kept a close eye on the windows of the house. But no lights snapped on, which had her breathing easier. Just another couple of blocks now.

There wasn't any traffic on the street when she crossed it. No surprise there. Nothing happened in Saxon Falls after dark, not that she ever got much of a chance to find out. Her mom and dad believed in Neanderthal parenting, because her curfew was still ten o'clock. She'd once asked if they'd found their rules in a cave somewhere chiseled on stone tablets, but neither had thought that was funny.

When her phone sounded, she looked at the text, expecting to see another from Patrick. Instead, it was from Macy. Is it on?

It's on.

Hot damn, girl! The accompanying emoji had a tongue hanging out, and Whitney's cheeks burned despite the brisk air. She hadn't considered much beyond actually meeting Patrick in the flesh. Just planning it had consumed their conversations over the last few weeks. His dad had been in the military and ran the family the way he had his platoon. From the sounds of it, he was stricter than Whitney's dad, whom she and Macy often referred to as Attila.

She could see the park's entrance from here, and she increased her pace. Would he be shy or try to kiss her? Other guys had, and a few of them she'd kissed back. Nothing more than that, although Macy laughed and called her a prude. Michael Feldman had tried to stick his hand under her shirt, and she'd given him a fat lip. Of course, Michael looked like an orangutan with glasses. Whitney wasn't sure what she'd do if Patrick tried the same.

Her cell pinged, and she slowed to look at the screen. I can't wait to see you.

Something warmed in the pit of her belly, and she texted back. I'm here. She strained her eyes to find him. Clouds streaked the sky overhead, obscuring the stars, but an occasional sliver of moon shone through before it was lost again. The WWII monument was in back of the fountain. That was the spot they'd decided on, but it was still too far for her to make him out.

Saxon Falls Park had never seemed spooky before, but she'd never been here at night. Alone. The city had gone cheap on the lighting, and there were only a few streetlamps dotting the area, all of which must turn off at midnight. She got a sudden chill and hunched farther into her coat, taking out her cell to switch on its flashlight app.

There. She could see Patrick now, or rather his moped parked next to the monument. Her stomach did flips. She'd walked just a few blocks in the biting wind, but he'd driven twelve miles in it, just for her. The knowledge put a spring in her step, and Whitney thought maybe—just maybe—if Patrick wanted to feel her up, she'd let him.

"Hey you," she called out softly as she closed the distance to the monument. "Froze solid yet?"

A shadow shifted behind the statue, but her gaze traveled beyond it to a hulking shape along the tree line fringing the park. The monument was near the rear of the area, and there was nothing else of size there. At least there shouldn't be. Comprehension filtered in a moment later. It was a vehicle. A van. She stumbled to a halt, a hot ball of panic forming in her belly. The figure that stepped out from the cover of the statue was dressed all in black. Face. Hands. Clothes.

Whitney didn't waste time screaming. She whirled. Bolted. He might know the park, but he wouldn't be familiar with the woods surrounding it. It was there she headed, fear giving her feet wings. If she could make it, she had a chance. She could lose him among the trees. Find the path he wouldn't . . .

A mighty weight tackled her to the ground. She rolled, kicking and punching wildly. Two dark-clad arms grabbed her shoulders, pinning them to the ground. She latched her teeth into one arm, heard a vicious oath. Then a sharp needle of pain shot through her arm. She opened her mouth to shout. A gloved hand clapped over her lips.

Whitney continued to struggle, but her limbs grew leaden. The black-hooded creature loomed above her. Panic still pounded through her veins, but her thoughts were scattered. She saw herself as if from afar, an insect struggling on a collector's pin.

Her vision blurred as waves of unconsciousness threatened. The weight was removed. Freedom! The thought was a bolt of adrenaline. But when she commanded her legs to move, they remained unresponsive. She tried to raise a hand. Only could twitch her fingers. She felt herself being lifted. Carried by that hated person in black. It was getting harder to think, but one nebulous thought formed. Swam across her mind.

Leaving her room tonight had been the biggest mistake of her life.

Janie Willard

November 1
11:30 a.m.

"Janie, out front, please. We're about to get busy."

There was a quick hitch in Janie's throat, a spreading heaviness in her chest as she reluctantly turned away from the fryers and grills. Making her way from the kitchen to the Dairy Whip's front counter, she concentrated on the slow and steady breathing that could usually keep the deep-seated anxiety at bay. The medication in her purse would make speaking to people a bit easier, but for the last few months she'd been trying to curtail her dosage. She didn't want to end up like her mother, reliant on chemicals just to get through the day.

A gaggle of high schoolers was crowding toward the front door, and she took her place next to a register, order pad ready. A quick scan of the faces revealed that she knew them all, at least by sight. They were only acquaintances because Janie didn't make friends. Except for Alyvia Naughton, who'd steamrollered into her life in kindergarten and hadn't seemed to care that it had been nearly nine months before Janie had spoken a word to her. Apparently, "give me back that damn truck" had cemented whatever attraction Janie held for Alyvia because they'd been best friends ever since.

The crowd at the counter separated into two lines, and Janie picked up a pen before saying automatically, "May I help you?"

"Yeah, um." The girl stared up at the posted menu as if entranced, seemingly oblivious to the people waiting behind her. "I think . . . a chocolate-dipped cone. Medium. No, wait. What's the name of the one with sprinkles? I want that one."

It was simpler when Janie kept her head down, writing the orders, turning her back to make the treats. More difficult when she had to announce the amount, take the money, and count back change. To *interact.* The place seemed to swell with bodies. With noise. So many . . . *words* were floating in the air, demanding responses, although fortunately not from her. She'd perfected the art of flipping a switch—robot mode, her therapist called it—and focused on the tedium while attempting to disregard the snippets of conversation floating around her.

". . . see her costume last night? Sort of skanky, don't you . . ."

". . . gone for two days already . . ."

"Cade seemed to like it."

". . . probably ran off with a guy. I heard her dad was super strict . . ."

"He's a total player, what guy wouldn't . . ."

"That's three twenty-eight." The words came in a rush but were steady enough. She collected the money and counted back the change. The girl—Ellie Breitbach—sat behind her in third-period calculus. They'd never exchanged a word.

Cone in one hand, change in the other, she turned away and picked up the conversation where she'd left off with her friend. "Still, she's just so obvious. She's gonna get a rep if she doesn't . . ."

"May I help you?" Janie focused on the next customer. And then the next. The two lines dwindled. So thoroughly had she blocked the chatter that when the piercing words rang out, they took a moment to sink in.

"What do you think about it, Janie?"

She stilled. Squelched the panic that threatened to surge and searched for the speaker. Recognizing her, Janie's stomach clenched. "About what?"

In a carefully studied move, Heather Miller gathered up her long, blonde hair in one hand before letting it cascade again, probably for the benefit of the slack-jawed boy glued to her side in the booth. "That girl that disappeared in Saxon Falls a couple of days ago. Surely you've heard. It's been on the news. She might even have been a victim of the Ten Mile Killer, like your sister. Don't you just think that's awful?"

Responses raced across her mind and remained unuttered. She thought a lot of things, actually. Like how Heather was a bitch and the only person Janie knew whom she actively disliked. That she realized when she was being baited and would never give the girl the satisfaction of a reaction.

Because even the mention of the Ten Mile Killer made Janie want to scream in ineffectual rage.

But, of course, she said none of these. "I think they're wrong," she responded flatly. Doris, the manager, hurried over from the other register, protective as always.

"That's enough nonsense," she said loudly. Pitching her voice lower, she murmured, "I've got the rest of this. You can go on back."

Janie turned blindly, Heather's voice following her as she headed toward the kitchen. "What? She's bound to hear about it. It's on the local channel. Some people are saying it's just like Janie's . . ."

She walked straight through the kitchen to the hook by the back door where she'd left her things. She grabbed her purse before heading out the door, already digging into it for something to calm the nerves that were suddenly raw and quivering.

With not-quite-steady hands, she found the package of cigarettes and shook one out. It took three attempts to light it. She drew deeply on the cigarette and let the smoke fill her lungs.

But it did nothing to calm the riot in her blood. A girl was missing. And this time from nearby. It would start again. The instant hysteria. The inevitable comparisons. Janie's family history would be rehashed over coffee cups and dinner tables. Because her sister's kidnapping seven years ago had been the most sensational thing that had happened in West Bend, Ohio, since its last lynching, more than a century ago.

She'd been ten when Kelsey had disappeared. *Vanished into thin air.* The news stories had been titled with clickbait clichés. *Without a trace.* There'd been a media firestorm. It'd seemed as though each time the TV had been switched on, there was a story about the Kelsey Willard kidnapping.

Janie leaned her head against the siding of the building and blew out a thin stream of smoke. It was unseasonably cool, but she felt like a furnace had torched beneath her skin. A vise of dread tightened in her chest as the memories rushed in. Her house had been full of people for weeks after it happened. The local cops and then more from the state. Pastors, neighbors, relatives, friends . . . it seemed like everyone they'd ever known was in and out of their home at some point. As a kid, her social anxiety had manifested as selective mutism, and the crowds filling their home were almost as terrifying as the disappearance of her sister. When she hadn't been able to escape to her room, she'd learned how to fade into the woodwork. But that didn't mean she didn't see—and hear—what was going on.

She inhaled again, then considered the cigarette in her hand. At the time, her mom had said tragedy brought out the best in people, but Janie wasn't so sure. People had said the right things, but she'd sensed a furtive look of excitement in their eyes layered under the sympathy. As if they were thrilled and even a little bit scared to be on the fringe of the most horrible thing that could happen to a family. Like adrenaline-seeking kids sneaking up to the town's haunted house on a dare, slapping a hand on its siding, and then racing back to safety just for the bragging rights. *We were this close!*

A car door slammed, and her spine shot with tension. But Matt Thorson—another employee several years older than Janie—just hurried through the parking lot toward the back door. He passed within a foot of her but never even glanced at her as he entered the building.

She relaxed again as the screen door slammed behind him. It was inevitable, she supposed, taking another puff, for any missing female in the state under nineteen to elicit the media hysteria that always led back to the Willards' door. And probably to the killer's previous victims' families, too, now that she thought about it. Worse still were the times when unidentified female human remains were discovered. The inevitable calls about testing the remains and comparing the results to Kelsey's DNA always had her mother in bed for days. The aftermath of Kelsey's kidnapping was a carousel of horrors they could never escape.

She sank along the chilly siding to sit on the frigid cement sidewalk. A better person would be concerned about the unknown girl from Saxon Falls. And maybe Janie would have been if she hadn't experienced this so many times. The idiot would show up eventually, after running away, joyriding with a friend, or shacking up with a boyfriend. They always did. But not before reporters started dredging up the past, leaving her mom an emotional basket case and her dad just a little more detached than before.

It'd be easy to hate journalists for that alone. She brought the cigarette to her lips again. They'd been all too quick to forget the Willards when leads on Kelsey's case started drying up. When the police came by less and less frequently. That was about the time her mom and dad's friends—the ones who hadn't started avoiding them altogether—started wearing this totally fake cheerful expression when they talked about anything and everything other than Janie's sister. Finally, the cops just stopped returning phone calls. More than a year went by, and still no

Kelsey. Even at eleven, Janie had realized what that meant. Kelsey wasn't coming back, no matter what her parents said. Her life was divided into a Before and After, two chapters in the same book. First, she had a sister. Then she didn't.

She ground her cigarette out on the cement next to her. Then lit another. *You can't consider the meds a crutch and not realize cigarettes are serving the same purpose.* Dr. Drake's words echoed in her brain. Sometimes what he said made sense, whether she wanted to hear it or not. But some things he just didn't have a clue about. Like how she was always going to be defined by Kelsey's disappearance.

And how that could ruin her memories of her sister if she let it.

A mental image floated across her mind. She and Kelsey when they were kids, arms out to their sides, twirling in endless circles across the yard, pretending to be butterflies. *Fly high, Janie! Fly high.* Their mom had even bought them matching butterfly necklaces for Christmas that year. She smiled a little at the memory. Abruptly sobered when she recalled that Kelsey had been wearing hers when she vanished.

She exhaled, and like the stream of smoke, the memory dissipated to be replaced with thoughts of the unknown teen from Saxon Falls. No matter that she was likely off on a lark; her disappearance was doing a number on those she left behind. It was hard to summon sympathy for a girl who intentionally churned emotional waters in her wake. She didn't know what Janie did. That tragedy changed a family. Sometimes it shattered it. Parents split up. The surviving kids developed coping mechanisms. She smiled grimly. *Coping mechanisms.* A $200-an-hour phrase that meant searching for normal. God knew that was what she'd spent too many years doing before she was old enough to realize that "normal" was unattainable because it didn't exist. At least not for the Willards. Not anymore.

The chimney stack on the restaurant next door belched a thin thread of smoke not unlike the one she expelled. Her sister's kidnapping hadn't destroyed them. Not totally. But it was as if someone had taken an eraser to her family. Smudge, smudge, smudge. One fraction at a time, Kelsey had faded away until there was just the slightest shadow. And the rest of them were a bit fainter around the edges. Still there, but they were all a little . . . less.

She flicked the ash off the end of the cigarette into the graveled parking lot that hemmed the walk. Watched the embers glow. Knew she'd have to keep a close eye on her mom for the next few days. Turn off the phone. Try to keep her away from the TV. Lose the morning paper. Because it didn't take much these days to spin Claire Willard off her carefully constructed orbit. Janie knew just how fragile her mother was beneath her elegant, stylish exterior. Claire played bridge with friends twice a month, volunteered at church, and had her city clubs—the ultimate suburban housewife. If anyone else knew how much time she spent sitting on Kelsey's bed with a glass of vodka, they didn't talk about it, not even Janie's dad.

Especially not her dad. Janie's mouth tightened. Years ago her parents used to have some pretty ugly fights about her mom's drinking, about his work and, God, why couldn't Claire just put the damn past behind her? But somewhere along the line, they must have called a truce. Sometimes Janie missed the fighting. At least that emotion had felt real.

She watched the traffic on the road in front of the business without really seeing it. Life had a way of moving forward from even the worst circumstances. Eventually, everyone resumed their roles. Janie thought her parents deserved awards for theirs. They came to school conferences; they told her how proud they were of her grades. Getting up in front of the class for a speech could still turn her into a quivering case of nerves, but there was nothing wrong with her brain. Which was why, now that college acceptance letters had started rolling in, she finally had her ticket out. Until graduation, though, she was content enough with the part she played: the quiet loner everyone overlooked. Because most of the time that suited her just fine.

"Is Janie back here?"

She scrabbled to her feet as Doris's words traveled through the open back door. Dropping the cigarette, Janie stepped on the butt and leaned down for her purse.

"Janie?" The manager stuck her head outside, swiveling it to either side.

She opened her mouth to answer but then heard Matt's voice. "I just came in, and I didn't see her."

"Well, where in heaven's—" The door shut on the rest of the woman's words.

A resigned laugh escaped her as Janie walked back to the entrance. If that wasn't the perfect summary of her existence for the last seven years.

Her sister was a ghost. But it was Janie who was invisible.

Claire Willard

November 2
12:00 p.m.

"I know spring is months away, but it's never too soon to start planning. I'd love to see us do the county park beds in purple and red salvia. Petunias are so . . ."

". . . I swear the boy got that lazy gene from his father. He doesn't even shower some days, and forget about asking him to lift a . . ."

". . . Quinn's three-day sale. Don't you just love their shoes?"

Claire Willard sipped from her vodka martini and let the snippets of luncheon conversation swirl around her. The second drink of the day always softened the edges a bit, made it worth the painstaking care she took with her appearance. By the third or fourth glass, the difficulty she'd had getting out of bed that morning would be long forgotten. She coveted the blessed numbness. Guarded it closely. Like the collection of rainbow-colored pills she kept secreted inside a tiny drawer at the base of an antique clock in her bedroom.

Monday luncheon at the West Bend Country Club was a weekly mainstay, except around the holidays, when most people were frantically busy with preparations. The participants varied slightly from week to week, as the other women had appointments, prior commitments, or God knew what else to keep them busy. Sometimes Claire purposefully stayed away, to keep up the pretense that she, too, had a life so full that it was a struggle to fit it all in.

"Claire, what do you think? You always have such lovely taste."

She blinked and, with an accuracy honed by long practice, refocused. "You know me, I'm all about the perennials. I'd love to see Central Park's beds in a blanket of tulips. Go with daylilies for the summer and mums in the fall. Then we only need to plant a tenth of the annuals, just as borders. More expensive in the short term, but it will save the organization money in the long run."

The suggestion required little thought, as it was one that got bandied about yearly. At times, she wondered if these women really cared about the colors of the flower beds they tended for the city, the latest fashions, or minor family conflicts. Or if, like her, they immersed themselves in trivialities in a frantic effort to avoid a yawning inner emptiness that sometimes threatened to swallow them whole.

Occasionally, she found such minutiae soothing. Normal, even. But at other times—when she was having a particularly dark day—it made her want to shriek at these women for wasting their time on such silliness when there were far more important things to think about.

Like missing children. Kidnapped girls. Her Kelsey.

One day at a time. That's what she'd heard endlessly at that worthless support group she and David had attended for a while. She'd taken it one day at a time for 2,592 days. They'd said it would get easier.

They'd lied.

"You're so clever, Deirdre." She leaned back slightly as the twenty-something waitress laid a white-on-white-patterned china plate down in front of her. Artful bits of lettuce were adorned with baby tomatoes under a sprinkling of blue cheese that masqueraded as salad. "You always find the best sales. I swear I'm going to plant a GPS on your car and tail you whenever you go shopping."

The women laughed, and Claire smiled serenely. Witticisms and pleasant chatter kept her a welcome member of the group. After Kelsey had been taken, she'd quickly learned that people had a finite tolerance for the suffering of others. Empathy went only so far before their personal comfort levels maxed out, and they started backing away from displays of grief. No one wanted to be reminded that tragedy befell without warning, striking at random. It was easier to believe that people bounced back from the most unimaginable heartbreak possible to once again care about five-inch heels and city-beautification efforts. And that was possible only when others kept their pain to themselves.

Claire had grown quite adept at keeping secrets.

Once the salads had all been served, the clink of metal on china provided a melodious backdrop for the ebb and flow of conversations that entwined and detoured like garden paths. As usual, she was seated next to Barbara Hunt, who used to be her dearest friend back when Claire had the energy to sustain such a relationship. She remained the closest thing to a friend Claire had, and if Barbara suspected there was far more going on than what Claire allowed to show on the surface, she had the grace not to pry and to try to protect her from those who would.

"Becca says Janie aced the chemistry exam last week. Naturally." Barbara looked up from her plate with a quick smile. "She's a bit jealous. Science comes so easily to Janie. I wish we could find a tutor with her knowledge next semester. The girl is barely scraping by with a C minus."

"Poor dear." The sympathy was automatic, but Claire's mind was elsewhere. Had Janie told her about the chemistry test? It was difficult to recall, but she thought not. David was the one who checked the school's online grades to keep tabs on Janie's academic progress. Claire focused on making sure her daughter went to her appointments with Dr. Drake and took the medication the man prescribed—a task she'd been failing miserably this school year. No one outside the family realized just how stubborn her socially reticent daughter could be. "Maybe we could work a trade, and Becca could help Janie with English. She's having an awful time with Mr. Latham." Mostly because the man was an absolute sadist who was lax about accommodating for Janie's social anxiety disorder.

"Oh, everyone has a terrible time in his class." This from Mimi Swenson, a small dark-haired woman who pecked at her salad like a finicky wren. "When I was in high school, he had me in tears weekly. I'm going to make sure Lizbeth doesn't have him when she's a senior. I hear he's turned into something of a lech."

"Kelsey was a whiz in science, too, if I recall." Claire stiffened slightly as Barbara continued to chatter. "Of course, she excelled at most things."

On some level, Claire realized what her friend was doing and was grateful for it. She was one of the few people who wasn't afraid to mention Kelsey's name. Most people acted as if she'd never existed, carefully avoiding a mention of her so as not to bring up unpleasantness. Barbara understood that it was like sharing a treat with someone starving.

But the gratitude was filtered by pain. As always, it was the verb that stopped her. Kelsey *was*. Not Kelsey *is*. Not Kelsey *will be*. For the first few years, every time she'd heard her baby referred to in the past tense, it had been like a knife to the heart. And the first time she'd unthinkingly uttered it herself, Claire had cried for days.

Because talking about Kelsey in the past tense meant that she'd finally given up hope. That she no longer believed that someday, somehow, her daughter would come home to them. Occasionally, she'd see a news show about a reunited family. And the mother would always say, "I never stopped believing. I always felt like I'd know if my child wasn't still out there." After seven years, Claire hadn't given up hope, either. But she hated that it was getting more and more difficult to summon.

"Yes," she said belatedly, her hand reaching for her glass again. "Both the girls must have gotten their math and science acumen from their father. Heavens knows neither subject was my best."

"How fortunate that Janie shows an aptitude for science," Karla Ferin chimed in. "In that field, she might be able to avoid public speaking altogether."

There was a nervous titter around the table at the comment, and Claire hid her quick burst of indignation behind a rueful smile. "I know it's hard to believe, but she shows no qualms about debating household rules at great length. Maybe I should insist our discussions take place outside the school building. I might just win an argument once in a while."

Laughter alleviated the tension. Karla was a relative newcomer to the group, having moved to West Bend to take a Realtor's job a couple of years ago. Claire had never cared for her. She had a sly manner of faintly couching criticisms in humor. Just minutes earlier, she'd been complaining about her son's laziness, although from what Claire had heard, lack of ambition was the least of the boy's sins. He'd dropped out of school and had been in and out of trouble with the law.

"Is Josh looking at getting a GED, Karla?" This from Barbara, as she pushed aside her salad plate with a sigh. "I think he can do part of the work online these days so it wouldn't interfere with his job." It was a well-orchestrated dance; Claire defusing hurtful words with self-deprecating humor and Barbara following up with a jab at the offender, cloaked in solicitude. Claire felt a sudden burst of affection for her friend. David often complained about the dog-eat-dog world of marketing, but these weekly luncheons required skilled verbal thrust and parry that was its own type of warfare.

Two faint spots of color rode high on Karla's cheekbones. "Yes, of course, we have a school psychologist looking into it."

"At least you know where he is," Susan Prescott put in from across the table. "Isn't it horrible about that missing girl over in Saxon Falls? They still haven't found her, and it's been all over the news."

Susan's words yanked Claire from humor to dread with whiplash speed. And for the first time that afternoon, all the snippets of conversation congealed into the same topic.

"It was Helen DeVries's granddaughter. My hairdresser does Helen's hair, and she's just distraught."

"Probably took up with some boy . . ."

"She's been gone three days already . . ."

"I hear the Ohio Bureau of Criminal Investigation was called in. The locals aren't wasting any time, especially after what happened to—ow! That's my toe!"

"I'm so sorry, Mimi. How clumsy of me." Barbara made a production of fussing over the other woman, seated on the other side of her. "I had such a cramp in my foot, but I didn't mean to set it down on you. Are you all right? I swear I'm such a klutz sometimes. Why, just the other day . . ."

Claire became belatedly aware that her fork was suspended in midair and had been since the topic had been introduced. Slowly, as if disconnected from her body, her hand lowered it to her plate. Released it.

Her chest constricted, making it an effort to breathe normally. It seemed as if news like this reared up to ambush her every few months. Something would appear in the papers or on TV that would cause the past to rage to the surface, every slice of pain and fear fresh again, hot and pulsing with new life. As if a stranger's tragedy belonged to her in some way because she'd lived through it, too. And this . . . this wasn't even a stranger. She knew Helen DeVries. Claire and the woman used to attend the same church. Whitney, the girl's name was. She'd be about the same age Kelsey had been when she was taken.

"I'm so sorry, Claire." Mimi looked shaken, whether from her verbal faux pas or her throbbing toe, it was difficult to tell. "I'm sure the girl will be found safely."

"Yes." Because the word came out husky, Claire cleared her throat. "But her poor parents . . ."

Barbara's hand snaked out to capture hers under the table. Gave it a brief squeeze.

Claire felt like a fraud. Because her words had been automatic. A sound of empathy when, in fact, she possessed none. Dealing with the loss of Kelsey should have made her more attuned to the agony of others, but too often it felt like a contest of who had suffered more.

Whitney is probably alive! She'll eventually return unhurt and happy, not gone forever . . . dead or as good as . . .

The waitress began clearing the salad plates. Claire fought an overwhelming urge to excuse herself. David. She needed to call David. It was a habit she'd tried to break herself of because her husband had grown weary of it years ago. Each instance when she heard details of a missing child on the news . . . every time she learned of some atrocity inflicted on a young girl, the details would take up residence in her brain and lodge there like a burrowing parasite spreading its poison until it was all-consuming. Certainty would grow that the case mirrored Kelsey's fate. She'd been murdered by her kidnapper. Forced into child prostitution. The victim of a pedophile.

There had been a time, a long while ago, when her husband had tried to calm her when she'd worked herself into a state over news like that. When they'd embrace tightly to form a human shield, a fragile defense against an unimaginably cruel fate.

Those days were long past. Claire couldn't remember the last time David had touched her in any but the most casual of ways. And still, the familiar urge burned hotly within her, demanding a release.

"Claire, your entree looks delicious. You have to tell me if it's as good as it looks. For the sake of my waistline, please lie to me."

At Barbara's words, she realized their lunches had been served. Like an automaton, she picked up her fork. The first bite was tasteless. So was the second.

She was thinking of Whitney DeVries's parents. She always thought of the parents when she heard news like this. Not what they were feeling. Not sympathy for what they were going through.

No, Claire always found herself wondering what *they* hadn't told the police.

David Willard

November 2
2:54 p.m.

"Great news on the Turnbull account, Willard." Steve Grayson stopped David in the hallway, flashing his toothpaste-ad smile. "You pulled that one out of the fire. Sometime over drinks you'll have to tell me how you kept them from following through on their threat to go with Samuels' Marketing."

The man stepped closer, lowered his voice. "I'm hearing murmurs of corporate espionage."

"Espionage? That's water-cooler gossip, Steve," David said easily. "Although I did discover some interdepartmental errors that almost cost us the client."

His cell phone vibrated. Checking the screen, he saw that it was another call from Claire. He held the phone up. "I have to take this." With a wave, he headed toward his office. His *corner* office and the symbol of everything he had that Steve Grayson wanted. There had been times in the last few days when he'd been certain that the man was finally going to get it. But yesterday he'd finally prevented Turnbull from jumping ship, and today his world was right again.

David stopped by his assistant's desk and plucked the fistful of blue while-you-were-gone notes from her outstretched hand.

"Mr. Schriever called and wants you in his office at three thirty." David checked his watch. He had half an hour. "Everything else there"—Traci gave a nod to the messages he'd taken from her—"can wait until tomorrow. Except for Claire. She called twice. She sounded upset, David. She said you weren't answering your cell. But when I asked, she said it wasn't an emergency."

"Really?" He frowned at the phone he still held, making a show of thumbing through his call log. "Nothing here. I swear I'm getting another carrier. This one drops calls all the time. I'm sure that's what happened with hers." He shoved the cell back in his pocket and headed toward his inner office.

David dropped the messages on his desk to deal with later and crossed to his private bathroom. Figuring he had time for a shave and to change his shirt, he unknotted his tie, already planning strategy. Kurt Schriever would have heard about the near debacle with the Turnbull account—Grayson would have made damn sure of that. Which underscored David's suspicion that the younger man was behind the screw-ups. Kurt would be livid, David figured as he quickly shaved his five o'clock shadow and turned toward the closet. Taking a fresh white shirt from a hanger, he slipped it on. But Kurt would calm down after they discussed the interest Bonner Nursery was showing following a meeting David had had with them.

Still plotting strategy, he reentered his office, shoving his shirttails into his unzipped pants and then started. "Jesus, Claire!"

His wife rose from the edge of the couch she'd been perched on. "Did I startle you? Traci showed me in. Why didn't you call me back?"

"I just got into the office myself." He zipped up and grabbed his suit jacket from the chair he'd draped it over. Donning it, he added, "I had my cell turned off during my meetings today, so I missed your calls. But I'm afraid I've got to meet with Kurt in a few minutes. What do you need?" He stopped, a sudden stab of concern piercing his impatience. "Is Janie okay?"

"Yes, of course." She made a face. "Still insisting on Stanford after she's already been offered a full ride at OSU, and quite vocal about it. She actually made a list of her reasons for attending a university halfway across the country. I swear, under different circumstances she'd make an excellent trial lawyer. One conversation with her, and I feel like I've gone three rounds in the ring."

He felt a flash of relief. "She's a teenager. She's supposed to be argumentative." That behavior, at least, was normal, a description that didn't always fit their youngest.

"Yes, but she's particularly good at it."

They shared a rueful smile, and he looked, really looked at his wife for the first time . . . in a while, he realized. She was impeccably dressed, still a damn fine-looking woman. But she could no longer completely hide the shadows beneath her eyes, and despite the subtle plastic surgery she'd had last year, there were stress lines that creased her mouth when she was worried, like she clearly was now.

"There's a girl missing. And David, she lives just a few miles away. Do you think . . . could it be . . ."

His gut knotted. Skirting her gaze, he strode to the briefcase he'd laid on his desk and opened it, reexamining the contents to make sure he'd have everything he needed for the upcoming meeting. "Claire." His voice was as soft as he could manage. "Don't do this."

"I know the girl's grandmother. We both attended Trinity Baptist in Saxon Falls. How can that happen here again? You don't think Kelsey's kidnapper . . . that he's *back*?"

The last two words had his shoulders slumping. God, he was tired of this. Tired of being the strong one, tired of replaying this scene every damn time some girl forgot to tell her parents where she was going for a few hours. "No, I don't." Snapping the briefcase shut, he turned to face her.

"But what if it *is*?" His wife's voice was getting that strident tone he recognized. And damn it, he didn't have time for a scene.

"Claire!" His tone was sharper than he meant it to be. "This has nothing to do with Kelsey. Every bad thing that happens to a child in this country isn't connected to her." He had to draw a breath, difficult to do when his chest felt hollowed out. "It was seven years ago. You have to get some . . . distance." God knew it was the only thing that had kept him sane. He'd spent months after his daughter's disappearance on the edge of a yawning black and roiling precipice before he'd made a conscious decision to move away from it. With every passing year, he took another step back.

Claire remained teetering on the brink, arms wheeling. One wrong move would have her free-falling into that darkness. He'd given up thinking he could save her from it. Some days he thought she wanted to leap into the abyss.

Because he wasn't willing to provide that push, he crossed to her, and she flung herself at him. His arms, stiff and wooden, were slow to slip around her.

Helplessness rose up inside him as he felt the shudder shake her frame. Every time he touched her, he was reminded of his failures. A better man would have found a way to help her heal from the trauma of losing their daughter. Instead, somehow he'd managed to lose both his daughter and his wife. He was a louse of a husband and not much better than a part-time father to Janie. But those weren't the character flaws that kept him awake at night.

It was the spectacular way he'd failed Kelsey seven years earlier.

Special Agent Mark Foster

November 2
4:02 p.m.

Sleet pinged off the window behind Mark as he shifted awkwardly in the front of the interview room. As miserable as the weather had become outside, given the chance, he'd switch locations in a heartbeat. The crowd of journalists danced and bobbed before him as the reporters jockeyed for position.

"We're here at the request of Saxon Falls Chief of Police Don Masterson to assist in the investigation in any way we can." The booming voice of Ben Craw, senior agent with the Ohio Bureau of Criminal Investigation, required no amplification to carry across the conference room inside the police headquarters. "Our first concern is to see that Whitney DeVries returns home safely."

"Is this in any way tied to Halloween?"

"Will there be an Amber Alert?"

"Does she have a history as a runaway?"

"Did the girl have a boyfriend?"

Mark stood stoically at Craw's side, grateful he wasn't the one having to answer the questions lobbed at them like live verbal grenades. He did his best work in the field. Thrusting a microphone in his face was an open invitation for him to say something stupid, one he usually obliged. Craw was an old hand at this. He'd been with the state's top investigative agency for nearly thirty years. Every day of it showed on his face.

"We have no evidence to suggest foul play at this time." Craw raised his hands to halt the frenzy of voices before continuing. "All signs point to the girl leaving her home willingly. At seven forty-five Saturday morning, Mrs. DeVries woke up after tending to her ill son all night. She went to her daughter's room to check on her. The inside screen on the girl's bedroom window had been removed, and the window was open. She immediately woke her husband, a deputy with the local sheriff's office, who commenced searching for her. Mrs. DeVries stayed home with her son, who was still sick."

The reporters had quieted, all furiously scribbling. Mark figured they realized that further interruptions at this point were useless.

"Deputy DeVries alerted the police and spent the next few hours contacting several of Whitney's friends from school, none of whom admitted knowledge to her whereabouts," Craw continued. He was consulting no notes. The man's memory for detail was uncanny. "At two o'clock p.m., a canine unit was brought in from Cleveland. The dog followed the girl's scent to the Saxon Falls City Park, where it ended. That indicates to us that she may have gotten into a vehicle with someone. That's a lead we're actively investigating."

Mark caught a glimpse of Shannon and Brian DeVries at the back of the crowd and mentally cursed. He'd specifically advised the parents against attending the press conference, as their presence was guaranteed to turn the event into a media free-for-all. He caught Chief Masterson's eye across the dais, and the man's brow furrowed. He'd seen them, too. All they could do now was brace themselves for the fallout. Craw was going to be pissed.

But even given his irritation with the couple, he couldn't altogether blame them. His son, Nicky, was three, and Mark only could imagine how he'd feel if the boy disappeared. It was bad enough that his wife kept extending her and Nicky's visit with her parents in Bowling Green. A one-week stay had already stretched into two. He missed the kid like crazy. If they caught a quick break in this case, he'd take a couple of days' leave and drive over there to see him.

Imperceptibly, he shifted his weight. And while he was at it, he'd deal with his wife, Kelli. He had no idea what was going on in her head. He damn well hoped this stay was still just a visit. Getting a straight answer from her was getting increasingly difficult. For the last several months, their conversations had had a habit of degenerating into accusations and tears. Family life was never smooth sailing.

His attention wandered back to the DeVrieses. Mark knew from personal experience that in every marriage, there was always something going on beneath the surface. Which was why he and Craw were going to have to take a closer look at the DeVries family dynamics.

"Anyone with knowledge of Whitney's whereabouts, or who may have seen or heard from her recently, is encouraged to call this number." Craw indicated a large card Masterson held up bearing a toll-free number in bold-block print. "That's all we have for you today."

There was an instant tumult. No one believed the press would be dismissed that easily. But as planned earlier, Craw handed off the microphone to Masterson, who would do his best to respond to questions without revealing any more details. Mark didn't envy the man his task, but he and the other agent were already heading out of the room. Other than a shouted question or two tossed their way, most of the attention remained on the chief.

"You're about thirty seconds from being the center of a media circus," Mark murmured to Brian DeVries when he reached his side. Craw flanked Mark, shielding their exchange from the reporters in the room. If the older agent was the master of the press, Mark's forte was dealing with distressed parents. "If that's what you want, we can't prevent it. But open that door, and they'll never give you a moment's peace."

DeVries jutted his jaw. "We have a right to be here." He was a slight man, maybe five-six with a vaguely antagonistic attitude. As a law-enforcement officer, he should know enough to cooperate with the investigation. But instead, he seemed to think he knew best how to handle it. It was going to be a test of Mark's patience to maintain a civil relationship with him.

"You do." He gave a nod. "It's your choice. But if it's one you're going to make, you'll make it alone. We're not going to run interference for you."

Shannon DeVries's dark eyes were worried as she looked to her husband for reassurance. "Maybe we should leave. I don't want them following us home. What if they try to talk to Ryan?"

Mark could have told her that the longer her daughter remained missing, the more likely it was that she would have unwanted company camped in front of her home, but that was a conversation for later. If the weather didn't improve, they might get a reprieve for the time being, regardless.

"I don't need anyone running interference." But Brian DeVries scanned the crowd of reporters again and looked uncertain. "We just wanted to hear if you had any details to release."

Inching toward the door, Mark imperceptibly herded the two along with him. "When we do, you'll hear about it before the press does." Craw reached for the knob, and Mark felt a spark of relief when the couple slipped through it ahead of him.

Outside the conference room, he motioned to a young police officer. "Show Mr. and Mrs. DeVries the back exit and follow them home. Make sure they don't get hassled." The man nodded, and after a short pause, the couple turned to follow him.

"Now why can't you be that smooth in front of a microphone?" Ben Craw searched inside his suit jacket pockets for some gum. He fought a continually losing battle against smoking. He'd quit at least a dozen times in the last year. Mark had kept track. Craw found a piece and unwrapped it, popping it into his mouth as he scanned the open space outside the room.

"Then what would you do?"

"Put out fires before they start." He jerked a thumb at the door they'd just exited. "Did you hear the question shouted out there at the end by the loudmouth from KKXT?" At Mark's head shake, he continued. "Wanted to know if this was the work of the Ten Mile Killer. Christ on a cracker." He shook his head in disgust. "We've got no forced entry, evidence that the girl left the house of her own accord, and some bozo already has her the victim of a serial killer."

"One who's probably died of old age by now."

It was the wrong thing to say. Craw's blue eyes narrowed, and he jabbed a finger at Mark's chest. "There's no evidence linking this girl to the TMK. That case over in West Bend deep-sixed Tom Hannity's career. He's a damn fine agent and a good friend of mine. It's always easy to second-guess, but the guy did everything right near as I could tell but couldn't catch a break in the investigation. And because of it, every runaway, every Amber Alert, every kid who gets lost in the tristate area has the press dragging that case out again. Anything for a story, right? But mark my words, when the DeVrieses hear it brought up—and they will—they're going to make your life a living hell."

He started off toward Masterson's office. Mark followed more slowly. "Me? Why me?"

"Because you're good with parents, remember? I'm the guy who handles the media."

Whitney DeVries

November 2
5:32 p.m.

He was back. She could hear him breathing.

Whitney guiltily scrambled off the blow-up mattress, the chain attached to the manacle on her wrist jangling. Her prison was a large shadowy room with a raised stage at one end, where she was shackled to a long barre attached to the back wall. The place was nearly dark. The only light came from a computer screen and a projector, centered somewhere in the middle of the room. And the flickering, illuminated scene it cast on the white cement-block wall behind her.

"Whitney, dear."

She hugged her arms around her middle, feeling chilly and exposed in the thin leotard. His voice made her feel that way. Like a fingernail lightly running down her spine. Quickly she made her way to the center of the stage.

"What are rules one and seven?"

Her mind went blank like it did whenever Mrs. Zaner called on her in math because Whitney and a friend were whispering. But this time she knew the answer. She did! But there were so very many rules . . .

"Not to . . . not to . . . ," she stuttered, buying time. And then her mind cleared, and a spasm of relief shook her. "Not to stop practicing before the film is over."

"Very good. And rule number one?" The voice was deep and slow and sort of hollow sounding. Maybe it seemed freakier because it always came from the dark. No matter how hard she peered, she could never make out more than a shadow.

Or maybe it was because it never changed. Happy? Angry? Who knew with the freak. It was always even. "I may use the bed from nine p.m. to seven fifteen a.m."

"Well, now I'm confused. It's only five thirty. You do seem to know the rules. You just didn't obey them."

The flesh on her arms rose. She began to shake.

"I want to be fair, Whitney. I really do. If you have a logical reason for your disobedience, now's your chance to tell me."

How could crazy sound so *normal*? He could have been her dad, telling her for the tenth time to turn off her iPod and do her chores. Except her dad didn't have that creepiness in his voice. That wet, syrupy evil.

"I . . ." Her throat dried out. When the projector was on, it was impossible to see beyond its beam to the darkness beyond. It was like having a conversation with a psycho ghost.

"I . . . got tired. I couldn't sleep last night." Couldn't because she'd been crying for her mom and dad. For her little brother, Ryan, and her cat, Freckles. She wanted her family. She wanted her room. She wanted her friends. She even wanted witchy Mrs. Zaner.

"Is there anything else?"

"I want to go home!" She stomped her foot, the words tumbling out of her as rage shoved aside fear for the moment. "Let me go!" She yanked at the chain securing one wrist to the steel barre. It clanked in rhythm with her shouts. "Take me home! Take me home now, you fucking freak!" The demand ended on a shriek.

"I'm afraid you've made your situation worse." The voice was mild, but disapproval threaded through it. "Now you've broken rules four and five, as well. I can only assume that you're willfully disobeying."

The fury that had welled up inside her vanished as if it had been sucked away by a vacuum. Fear did a fast sprint up her spine. "I didn't mean to." What would he do now? Would he come up here? Would he touch her? Would he make her do disgusting things with him? Her mind scrambled away from that thought. *Please, no. Please, God, no.*

"I'm sorry."

"I know you are, dear. But with every choice comes a consequence. However, I've always felt that each misbehavior is an opportunity for reteaching. So let's go over those rules again."

"I have them memorized! I just got tired." Consequences? At home, a consequence was being grounded. Having to do Ryan's chores when she was mean to him. One time she had to make dinner all by herself because her mom had gotten tired of her complaining about what they were having, but that hadn't been bad. She could make spaghetti and garlic bread just as well as her mom. And afterward it'd even been sort of fun, with her dad making a big deal out of being scared to taste it, and Ryan pretending he was choking. Her mom had eaten three bites and smiled at her, calling her my little chef. Whitney's eyes filled with tears. She'd make dinner every night. She'd do all of Ryan's chores forever, if she could just go home again.

"I'm waiting."

The voice had gone stern. She wet her lips. "Rule number one: I may use the bed from nine p.m. to seven fifteen a.m. Rule number two: shower from seven fifteen to seven twenty. Brush teeth, comb hair, and get dressed from seven twenty to seven thirty. Breakfast from seven thirty to seven fifty-five. Practice begins sharply at eight." She was alerted to each of the times by a loud buzz from the computer. And she'd already discovered what happened when she slept through the morning alarm. The water ran only during that time, so she'd had to go without a shower or water to brush her teeth. Food for the daily meals was waiting on the opposite side of the stage when she woke up each morning. A couple of pieces of fruit, two small plastic bottles of milk, a pair of wrapped peanut-butter sandwiches, granola bars, and a small box of dry cereal. The thought of him sneaking the food in here without her being aware, maybe watching her sleep, made her want to puke.

She'd even tried to stay awake so she could see him putting it there. It seemed important that she knew what he looked like. When she got out of here, she might have to give a description so the police could arrest him and let him rot in prison. She hoped bad things happened to him there. She hoped someone *killed* him in prison.

"Rule number three . . ." Whitney paused, wondered if he'd hear the hatred in her voice. "Toilet use at seven fifteen a.m. and every four hours precisely until bedtime." She'd almost peed her pants that first night, waiting for morning. But she hadn't dared to break one of his stupid rules until just now. And had been busted for it.

"Number four: no shouting, arguing, or pouting. Five: no rudeness, name-calling, profanity, or vulgarity of any sort." It was a good thing he couldn't read her mind. A really good thing. Because he was a fucking asshole, and she wished he was dead!

She started then, backed an inch closer to the wall. She still couldn't see him. But he *felt* closer. The bravado left her, and she began to tremble like a leaf in a windstorm. "Rule number . . . number . . ."

"Six."

Dread snaked and twisted nastily in her stomach. His voice did sound nearer. Why was it so dark in here? She strained to see even as her mind grappled for the next rule. "Never give less than my best effort at practice." God, he was worse than her dance instructor had ever been, and she'd taken lessons from Tami Jae for ten years before she'd finally quit a few months ago.

"You may skip number seven since you already repeated it. Rule number eight?"

Yeah, she'd like to skip number seven. She had to follow the routine on the same film every day. Hour after hour of warming up, practicing the positions, one through five. Then barre exercises. The metal barre on the stone wall behind her ran three-quarters of the way across the stage. Her chain was attached to a sliding mechanism on it that let her move its length. Lucky her. Then it was demi-pliés and arabesques until her muscles were like Jell-O. *Tendu* and *rond de jambe* until she wanted to scream. It was all beginner stuff she'd learned when she was a little kid. And always at the end, there was a simple dance routine that combined all the movements. Mind-numbing monotony that gave her way too much time to think.

Was that the scrape of a shoe? Was he coming up here? Whitney stumbled backward until she felt the barre at her back. "Rule number eight: privileges are earned for good behavior and punishment for bad." Like being lied to, kidnapped in the middle of the night, and kept in a dungeon wasn't punishment enough? "Rule number nine: never try to escape." Fat chance. She spent every waking moment trying to figure a way out of here. But so far she'd come up with nothing. She repeated the rest of the damned rules like an automaton, hating the unseen man more with every word.

"Excellent. Let's go back to rule number eight, shall we?"

Fear fisted in her belly. She wanted to go home. Oh, God, why couldn't she go home? "I said I was sorry."

It was like she hadn't spoken. "Strip naked, folding your clothes neatly. As I told you before, if you refuse, I'll come up and do it for you."

No, no, no, no, NO! A silent scream of protest howled through her. He'd given her the leotard and tights to put on and taken her clothes that first day. Only the threat that he'd change her himself had had her stripping before him then, awkward with haste, wanting to bare as little as possible. One sleeve of the leotard unfastened at the seam with

Velcro, which allowed for the chain. How long had he been planning this?

The thought of his hands on her made her body convulse in revulsion. Slowly, fingers stiff with resistance, she took off the clothes, piece by piece. Ballet slippers, scuffed and barely white anymore. Leotard. Tights. Everything in her size, or close enough. Her body racked with trembling as she hesitated on her bra.

"You have ten more seconds."

That had her moving. She could slide the released garment down her secured arm only to the length of chain. And when she removed the panties, shame and disgust crawled over her skin. Knowing he was out there, looking at her . . . but oh, God, if he touched her . . . she couldn't handle that. Every news show she'd ever seen about a missing kid flashed through her mind again, and she started to pray all the prayers that Pastor Mikkelsen had ever taught at Bible camp, and that was a lot.

"Now come to the front of the stage as far as the chain will allow, and get down on your hands and knees. Face the wall. Quickly now." She moved as directed, crouching to clasp her knees, trying to make herself as small as possible.

"The rules are ranked in ascending order, up to the most important." His voice sounded more distant now. Something had shut down inside her. She was going far away. "And of course, breaking the most important rules result in more serious consequences. A lash for each one broken. That's five, in case you lost track."

Alarm filtered through her numbed mind as she heard the snap. She raised her head, tried to look over her shoulder when the first flick of the whip cut through her skin. Searing agony exploded across her back. All thought vanished as the whip fell again and again, slashing skin, bruising muscle.

On the third blow, Whitney started to scream.

Janie Willard

November 4
10:43 a.m.

"Janie?" Mr. Latham folded his arms across his chest, resting them on top of the pudge of his belly that strained the buttons on his sweat-stained shirt. "We don't have all day. Name one comparison and one contrast between the Greek god Ares with his Roman counterpart, Mars."

It wasn't that she hadn't heard him. Of course she had. And she knew the answer. But as soon as he'd called her name the first time, her heart had sped up until its pounding rocketed in her chest. She tried to moisten her lips, but her mouth was dry. Knots tightened in her stomach as she felt everyone in the room looking at her. Mocking her. *So stupid. She doesn't know anything. Weirdo.*

That's your imagination. It isn't real. Dr. Drake's words sounded in her mind as she struggled to lasso her careening thoughts. *No one is judging you.* No one but the sadist in front of the room, his ample ass hitched on a corner of the desk. "Ares . . ." The violent hammering of her heart sounded in her ears. Her palms felt like a flash flood had struck. "They're . . . they're both . . ."

"Mr. Latham, you know Janie doesn't talk." A few titters followed Heather's interruption. "It's just mean to try and make her. It's like punishing a dog that can't learn to shake hands." Outright laughter now, from more than a few. "It's really not fair to the dog."

The teacher's indulgent smile defused his next words. "Heather, that's not appropriate."

The burning inside Janie's chest turned to anger. No real weight behind the reprimand, not for Heather Miller. Because when Latham "accidentally" pushed books off his desk, Heather was one girl who was always willing to go up front and pick them up for him, usually making certain he got an excellent look at her cleavage when she bent down to retrieve them. Heather had never said no when asked, as Janie had, in an automatic, emphatic explosion of sound that had left Latham red-faced and her classmates howling with laughter.

Sometimes pride could come to her rescue, beating back the waves of panic. She battled for it now, the words coming out of her in a rush. "Ares and Mars . . . they were both considered gods of war, but the Greek god Ares wasn't revered by the people, where the Roman god Mars was given a more dignified . . ." The bell rang, and there was an instantaneous shuffling of feet, of possessions being gathered.

Latham got up to circle his desk and peer down at his lesson plan. "Quiz tomorrow, and you'll be asked to compare and contrast Greek and Roman gods. Make sure you bone up on them."

"Boner exam," some guy in the back muttered, and laughter burst out again.

Latham looked up, frowning. "Who said that?"

Everyone was crowding toward the front in a wall of people that always had Janie remain glued to her chair until they'd passed. She could feel someone at her side. Knew without looking who it would be. "I hear the most prestigious school scholarships value communication more even than test scores." Heather's voice sounded in her ear.

"I hope you realize you'll have to do a verbal presentation. The days of you getting a free pass because of your poor dead sister are almost over."

"Shut! Up!" As comebacks went it ranked at about first-grade level, but it was all Janie could manage. Impotent fury was welling, most of it directed inward. She hated the anxiety that could still grip her, but even more, she hated allowing herself to be victimized by it. Stuffing her laptop in her backpack, she stood suddenly, and Heather stumbled back a few steps, only to be brought up short by a desk. She placed her hand on it as if bracing herself from falling.

"Don't push me!" Her voice rang out.

"What? What's going on?" As the last cluster of students headed through the doorway, Latham looked their way, frowning again.

"Nothing, Mr. Latham." Heather winced, cradling her wrist in her other hand. "I'll be fine."

He marched down the aisle toward them, his dark mustache twitching in irritation. "What's wrong with your hand? Are you hurt?"

Janie's gaze bounced between Heather and the teacher incredulously. He was actually buying this farce?

"Not really. I banged it on the desk when Janie shoved me, but—"

"I didn't."

It was as if Janie hadn't spoken. "To the office, both of you. Heather, have the nurse look at your wrist. Janie, see Mrs. Rimble."

"What?" The scene was taking on a cartoonish aspect. "Why?"

"Because I said so. Now go." He'd already turned away. Students for the next period were straggling in.

Temper nearly choking her, Janie strode toward the door. In light of Heather's words, it was somehow worse being sent to Rimble, the counselor, and not Templeton, the dean of students. She stopped, waiting impatiently for a couple of girls to stop talking and then followed them through the doorway. But Heather was full of shit if she thought Janie hadn't earned every grade and test score on her own. And she'd managed it without flashing her boobs at that creeper Latham.

Behind her she heard, "Oh, that's such a good call, Mr. Latham. Janie is probably a little on edge because of that missing girl from Saxon Falls. I'm sure it reminds her of her sister . . ."

Janie shouldered her way through the jammed hallways, her free hand clenched at her side. She'd figured out the Heather Millers of the world long ago. They were experts at sizing up people's vulnerabilities and then pressing the right button every chance they got. Heather was more accomplished than most because somehow she always managed to be the wounded party.

Anger scorched Janie's stomach as she made her way toward the office. Latham wouldn't cut her the slightest slack when it came to making a speech in front of the class, but he lacked the balls to send her to Templeton. And she knew exactly what was behind his sudden solicitousness. *The days of you getting a free pass because of your poor dead sister are almost over.*

There was a kernel of truth in the taunt. Between the accommodations required for her social anxiety and her family tragedy, there were few teachers in the school who didn't treat her just a little bit differently from other students. Barely perceptible, but the kid gloves were there. Which was another reason she was determined to attend college as far away from West Bend, Ohio, as possible. There was nothing that burned quite as much as pity. Kelsey would have despised it even more than Janie did.

She was jostled again by the wall of students, this time harder. Janie tried to right herself but tripped over something and fell to all fours. A knee to her back sent her sprawling face-first.

"Oh, goodness, Janie, are you hurt?"

The voice ringing through the hallway was instantly recognizable. A moment later, Heather crouched gracefully down beside her, her hand extended. "Let me help you."

It was unplanned. Automatic. Janie reached out a hand to grasp Heather's before yanking her down, hard. Off balance, the other girl toppled to the floor, rapping her face smartly on the edge of the laptop she clutched. On cue, the perfect nose her parents had bought for her two summers earlier began to gush.

Heather stemmed the flow with her fingers, looking at the bright-red blood with disbelief quickly followed by rage. "You . . . bitch!" Her hand flew out, slapping Janie with enough force to snap her head to the side. She dropped her things and launched herself toward Janie, fingers curled.

She clamped her hands around Heather's wrists, struggling to keep the other girl's nails from raking her face.

"Cat fight!"

"Throw a punch!"

"Lose the clothes!" The crowd around them began to swell. Then was abruptly parted.

"That's enough! Heather! Enough!"

One moment Janie was dangerously close to losing an eye. The next, the other girl was gone, lifted away and held tightly by—Janie's heart took a nosedive—Susan Booker, the principal. *Shit.*

"She started it! I was just trying to help her up, and she . . ." Predictably, Heather dissolved into tears. "She hit me! Look at my nose!"

Slowly Janie gathered her things and got up. As she rose, she glanced at the crowd of students being dispersed by a couple of teachers and felt everything inside her go to ice. Her lungs clogged. Anxiety balled in her chest, spreading its tentacles to curl around her heart. Squeeze. She was the center of attention and for a moment couldn't move. Speak. Breathe.

"Janie!" The principal's voice cracked like a whip as she moved Heather away with a hand at her back. "To the office! The rest of you, get to class!"

◆ ◆ ◆

"I don't know whether to be baffled at this turn of events, or proud."

Janie's surprised gaze met Rimble's for the first time since entering her office moments ago. She'd sat outside the counselor's door for a couple of hours. She hadn't seen Heather, but that was unsurprising. The outer offices were a rabbit warren of exits, inside hallways, and smaller rooms. The nurse's room was next to the principal in the interior space. Rimble had just appeared moments ago. Janie could guess where she'd been.

"On the one hand, I'm disappointed that you engaged in violence, which is never the answer to solving problems. But I've known you for four years, Janie." Lori Rimble clasped her hands on the table separating them and leaned forward. "And I realize what it cost you to stand up for yourself this way when you're being bullied at school."

Eyes widening in shock, Janie could only stare. This was definitely not the conversation she'd expected to hear after bloodying Heather Miller's nose. "I'm not bullied." *Bullied* implied victimhood, and she'd never allow herself to be that vulnerable. She might have been powerless to prevent what happened to her sister and the toll it took on her and her parents, but she'd fought for years against the diagnosis that could control her life if she let it. She was nobody's victim.

"You didn't let yourself be." A smile flickered at the corners of the woman's lips before she firmed them. "But as I mentioned, your response was ill advised. That said, there were several witnesses to the altercation in the hallway and in Mr. Latham's class before that. I believe Mrs. Booker has been quite thorough in talking to all of them and has a clear picture of what transpired. Would you like to tell your side of things?"

Wary, she remained silent. She was vaguely familiar with the progressive-discipline policy at the school, although she'd never thought to find herself on this end of it.

Rimble smiled wryly. "I thought not. Mrs. Booker has decided—and I agree—that this matter would best be handled at the minimal level of consequences. Neither you nor Heather has ever been in trouble before, and both have distinguished academic records. I will warn you that if there's another occurrence of this behavior, it will be dealt with more severely. And as your friend, I want to caution you that by allowing yourself to be manipulated into a reaction, you're playing into Heather's jealousy of you."

Manipulated. The arrow hit its mark. It was another moment before the rest of the counselor's words registered. "Jealousy?" Janie was incredulous. Heather? The idea that anyone would be jealous of her was hard to fathom. That Heather would be was downright unbelievable.

For the first time, the counselor's expression looked stern. "Don't sell yourself short, Janie. You and Heather are at the top of your class. Don't give her an edge." Without allowing Janie time to digest her advice, she went on. "Heather will serve her after-school suspension tomorrow. Yours will be Friday." Her smile was back. "Now, is there anything you'd like to say?"

Janie shook her head, still mentally reeling.

"Then you can go. Your father is here and will take you home for the day. But don't forget what I said. Given the recent news stories, I know this is going to be a difficult time for you and your family. I'm here to help if you'll let me."

Blindly, Janie rose, went to the door. She could have told the woman that there was nothing she could do. Nothing anyone could do.

The longer Whitney DeVries remained missing, the worse it was going to get for the Willards.

Claire Willard

November 4
11:35 a.m.

As she sat on the edge of Kelsey's unmade bed, Claire could feel the tight fist in her chest loosen for the first time since she'd heard the news of Whitney's disappearance. David had done his usual pulling away after she'd appeared at his office. She'd known better but had been unable to stop herself.

Sipping from her third drink since Janie left that morning, she fingered the pills in the pocket of her robe. She didn't take them indiscriminately because it was getting harder and harder to find doctors who would prescribe them. Claire still recalled her shock and fury three years ago when her family doctor, Dr. Schultz, had refused to renew the prescription of antidepressants and sedatives he'd begun prescribing after Kelsey had been kidnapped.

His words had slashed like jagged little daggers, even cloaked as they'd been in a kindly manner. The upshot of that appointment had been that even the medical profession placed parameters on suffering. And apparently, she'd hit hers the fourth year after Kelsey was taken.

She squeezed the glass in a grip that made her knuckles ache. Before this, she hadn't known that grief came with an unwritten statute of limitations. There should be a handbook documenting them for families of victims, so they wouldn't be blindsided when hit with one. A one-year maximum for a messy divorce, maybe two for the passing of a spouse. Surely the death of a child deserved an extra year or so. No matter. She'd out-grieved the limits, and then she'd been cut off. Claire had been reduced to doctor shopping, like some common junkie desperate for a script. She resented that almost as much as she had Dr. Schultz's final words.

Claire, you need help that you aren't going to get from the pills. Why not try therapy again?

She'd listened to enough psychologists jabbering about the seven stages of grief to know that David had worked his way through them all, moving along to acceptance and hope at what medical professionals would approvingly call a healthy pace. Claire brought the glass to her lips and drank deeply. She also knew that David had left her at a distant stage four—depression, reflection, and loneliness—while he'd made his laps. That was, perhaps, the greatest betrayal of all.

"Mrs. Willard, I'm leaving for the day. Unless there's anything else?"

Claire looked up, summoned a smile. Marta stood framed in the doorway, wearing jeans, a T-shirt, and a concerned expression. Her apparel was a vast improvement over the ridiculous gray dress and apron their former cleaning service had required of their employees. David frowned whenever he saw the maid—he was a stickler about appearances. But he was rarely here during the day, so Claire had ignored his objections.

After years together, she thought the maid knew her better than her husband did.

"Nothing, Marta, thank you. I'll see you on Monday. But if your daughter isn't better by then, give me a call, and we'll adjust your hours." For a moment, she wondered why they clung to the outdated notion that their home still required a maid twice a week. David spent more time at the office than he did in the oversize house he'd insisted they buy a decade ago in the ritzy neighborhood. Janie had always been relatively neat, and it wasn't like Claire didn't have the time to clean.

But in the next instant, it occurred to her that without Marta, some weeks she would go days on end without anyone other than family to talk to. Mostly because making the effort with others seemed just that. With David away so much and Janie well ensconced in her high school world, the other woman's presence was sometimes a welcome distraction from her own moods.

It wasn't that Marta was or had ever been a confidant, but it was impossible to keep the family dynamics from the help. And after all these years, she and Marta had developed a sort of verbal shorthand.

"I've got your recyclables. We've got pickup tomorrow." The other woman lifted a white trash bag clutched in her hand that Claire knew would contain vodka bottles. She kept them beneath the bathroom sink in the guest bathroom, behind the cleaning supplies. Without it ever being mentioned, every week Marta disposed of the empties.

There had been a time when the unspoken knowledge inherent in the exchange would have shamed Claire, but she'd come to embrace it with a weary sort of gratitude. "Thank you, Marta. I don't know what I'd do without you."

"You won't have to find out. See you next week." She disappeared down the hallway, and Claire sat silently, listening to the sound of the maid's receding footsteps.

The house phone rang in their bedroom. She ignored it, lying down on the bed, cradling the glass against her chest, her face pressed into Kelsey's pillow. She could no longer smell her daughter's shampoo on it, but she drew some small comfort in curling up on the mattress the way Kelsey used to, her eyes on the room that had stayed precisely the same since the day her daughter had left it.

Janie had always been the tidier of the two girls. She never needed reminding to hang up her things, to put her shoes in the closet, or to put her book bag away. Even now that she'd taken up smoking—she thought Claire didn't know—there were no signs of her habit in her room. Kelsey had been a dervish, rushing from one activity to the next. The blue sweater she'd worn on her last night home still lay on the floor. A pair of scruffy sneakers sat exactly where Kelsey had toed them off. A couple of books were carelessly tossed on the bed. Marta replaced each item precisely in the same spot when she cleaned.

Claire's gaze wandered to the bookcase against one wall. The shelves were jammed with trophies and plaques from Kelsey's earliest years on the child beauty-pageant circuit. If Claire had to choose, those years would stand out as her favorite memories with her daughter. David hadn't wholly approved of the entire scene and had rarely accompanied them. So it had just been Claire and Kelsey going to dance lessons, singing lessons, photo shoots, and of course, the weekend contests themselves. She'd loved the time so much that she'd put off having a second child, even lying to David about trying to conceive when in reality, she'd still been taking the pill. She'd reveled in the glamor of it, the camaraderie and competition with other mothers, the time alone with her daughter, who'd done quite well in the pageants. It wasn't until David had suggested they see a fertility specialist that she'd reluctantly gone off birth control. She'd been pregnant within three months, and as she'd feared, Kelsey's pageant days were over a couple of years later. David had quickly grown tired of being left with Janie while Claire took Kelsey to lessons and competitions. And having Janie along had given Claire her first inkling that something was wrong with her youngest daughter. Even as a baby, her oldest had been sociable, holding out her arms to people who stopped to speak to her. Janie had been just the opposite, screaming with fear when strangers appeared, whether they spoke to her or not.

David had never understood her love for those experiences with Kelsey. Just as he hadn't understood her reaction to losing her. Four years after their child had been taken, Claire had come home to find every single thing in her daughter's bedroom boxed up. The bed had been stripped. The closet emptied. Walls and shelves bare. It's time, David explained in that infuriatingly logical tone he had, as if an unseen clock had tolled the exact hour when all should be ready to accept the unacceptable.

They'd had the worst fight of their lives then. For a long time, Claire hadn't been certain their marriage would survive it. She'd said hurtful things, horrid things. Some she'd meant, but others she hadn't. Just as she'd hoped that David hadn't meant all the invectives he'd hurled her way. After he'd slammed from the house, she'd set about like a woman possessed, returning the room to normal. Every article of clothing was replaced in dresser drawers and on hangers. Every item to its place on the shelf. The same books positioned just so on the carefully mussed bed.

She'd looked up once to see Janie framed in the doorway, watching her silently, an anxious expression on her face. That had shaken her. Although diagnosed in kindergarten with selective mutism, Janie had come a long way with the anxiety disorder, rarely showing symptoms at home, and only then if they had visitors. But Claire hadn't been able to go to her, to reassure her. How could she tell her daughter that everything would be all right when Claire knew nothing would be? Not ever again.

Hours into her task, Marta had joined her without a word. Kelsey was a clever artist and each of her drawings had been rehung on the wall. Every trophy precisely positioned on the shelves. The other woman had known even better than Claire where each object belonged. That single act had cemented a relationship between them that had never been acknowledged verbally. It never needed to be.

Her cell rang then. Claire considered not answering it. But withdrawing it from her robe pocket, she saw it was Barbara. Her friend had been known to come over if there was no answer, to check on Claire personally. It was a habit forged in those early days after Kelsey was taken.

"Barbara." She forced a note of cheer she wasn't feeling into her voice. "Hello. I'm afraid you've caught me in the middle of something. What's up?"

"Nothing much." Claire could imagine her friend sitting in her sunroom, with her second oversize mug of coffee and the morning paper. "I haven't talked to you since the luncheon and thought I'd check in."

Her earlier sense of contentment vanished. Claire rose to sit on the bed again and brought the glass to her lips, taking care so her friend wouldn't hear the ice cubes clinking together. "I'm just fine." The lie tasted bitter on her lips. "Trying to summon the ambition to go grocery shopping. I swear Janie inhales everything I bring home and never seems to gain an ounce. If I could clone her metabolism, I'd be set for life."

Barbara laughed, as expected, but seemed distracted. "That's good then. I was afraid . . . after the talk at the luncheon . . . I was just hoping you weren't worrying yourself over the DeVries girl."

Claire clutched the phone so tightly, the sides of it cut into her palm. "Oh, well . . ." Not even Barbara knew the extent of the state of panic and emotional turmoil she went through whenever she heard news like that. It was important to Claire that she didn't. Better to keep up at least the pretense that she'd moved on, rather than the rest of the world passing her by while she remained frozen in the past. "Hearing news like that is always difficult. How are the parents holding up? Have you heard anything?"

"You can imagine, I expect. Helen said Shannon is beside herself. I'm not sure how much support Brian is for her. I always thought he was sort of a hard man. Not that I'm judging," her friend hastened to say. "But you and David . . . all through your ordeal, I was just so thankful you were there for each other. That you pulled each other through the worst experience parents can endure and came out closer than ever."

Claire stared hard at the melting ice in her glass. "Yes." Her voice was flat. "We're very lucky that way." She should be grateful that the farce she worked so hard to present to the world was readily accepted. But the knowledge just made her feel empty. People saw what they wanted to see. Whatever was most comfortable to believe.

That tightness was back in her chest. Setting the glass on the bedside table, she fumbled in the pocket of her robe for a pill. After a moment's hesitation, she withdrew a second and swallowed them both, chasing them down with a gulp of vodka.

"I know this is terribly presumptuous of me. But I was wondering . . . if you feel up to it . . ." Something in Claire stilled in anticipation of Barbara's next words. "Maybe if it wouldn't be too terribly painful for you, could you talk to Shannon? I'd come along, of course. But I'm sure she'd take a great deal of comfort in discussing things with you. As I said, I'm not sure how helpful Brian is, emotionally speaking, and of course, he's going through hell, too. Perhaps even David . . ."

There was more, but Claire stopped listening. The phone was still clutched in her hand. Still pressed against her ear. But Barbara's voice was very far away.

Other noises had intruded. Supplied by memory, honed excruciatingly sharp by years and pain. The sound of voices, Claire's raised, Kelsey's shouting. The anger and contempt, so hot and pulsing that it seemed to reverberate in the air. The stomp of her daughter's feet down the stairs, the slam of the door. And then the quiet. The awful, echoing silence that had enveloped Claire, as she was left to replay the hideous scene over and over, grappling with shock and sorrow while her mind frantically searched for comprehension. For options.

Memory was sly that way. It had gotten harder and harder to cling to the exact sound of her daughter's laugh, the smell of her hair. But that final scene was branded indelibly in her mind. It often sprang forth unsummoned, an emotional ambush.

Dimly, she was aware of the cell vibrating in her hand. She didn't remember disconnecting the call. The screen didn't show Barbara's number this time but Janie's school.

Claire made no move to answer it. She couldn't. The past was rising up again, rushing in and dragging her back into the darkness.

David Willard

November 4
2:48 p.m.

"Janie? David?" Claire gathered her robe around her and hurried down the stairway. "What are you two doing home?"

David glared at her as he ushered his daughter through the front door. "A better question would be, where the hell have you been? The dean of students tried calling you. I tried calling. I had to leave work to go to the high school. Have you been home all this time?"

His wife put a hand to her hair as she crossed the hall to them. "I was just about to get into the shower. I've been sick all day and sleeping. I must not have heard the phone."

His gaze narrowed. He couldn't recall the last time he'd seen his wife not immaculately groomed and attired by 8:00 a.m. She did look ill. Pale and a little shaky.

"What happened? Janie, are you sick?" She pressed her hand to their daughter's forehead, only to have the girl duck away from her touch. Claire turned to David. "Are you going to tell me what's going on?"

"I'll let Janie do that." His daughter remained silent, and David suppressed a surge of impatience. He'd had to reschedule the creative-content meeting on the Bonner campaign. He put his hand on Janie's shoulder and guided her into the family room. She tolerated his touch only slightly better than she had Claire's, but then she rarely showed him the obstinate side that she sometimes displayed to his wife. Something about mother-daughter relationships he'd heard about but didn't pretend to understand.

Janie shrugged out of her backpack and dropped into the tan-leather recliner that matched the couch. Claire stood before her uncertainly, swaying a little bit. David sent her another look, considering. Sick could look a lot like hungover, and the vodka she favored always seemed plentiful in the cupboard. But he took out the garbage, and he knew for a fact that there were only empty bottles in it after they'd entertained. He shook his head, banishing the half suspicion, and focused on his daughter again.

Claire reached out a hand to her, fingered the ugly scratch on the girl's neck. "Janie, what happened here?"

Janie reached up to touch the mark where her mother's fingers lay as if surprised by it. "I guess Heather must have scratched me. She was trying hard enough. Glad now that I bloodied her nose for her."

"Janie Lyn!" Claire's concern turned to shock. "You . . . hit her?"

"Not exactly," David put in. "Sit down, Claire." She looked like a stiff wind would blow her over. She walked unsteadily to perch on the edge of the nearby couch. He sat in a chair next to it. "I got a call because Janie got into an altercation with another girl at school."

His wife looked baffled. "An altercation. Janie? At school?"

He couldn't blame her for her disbelief. He'd reacted similarly when Templeton had called his office. Throughout Janie's school career, the ongoing concern had been her lack of participation. Her anxiety with verbal communication. Never getting physical with another student. Voice dry, he answered. "Yes, to both questions. And after my meeting with the Millers and the school personnel, I do believe she was provoked." He didn't miss the grateful look his daughter sent him. By the time he'd finished dealing with Lucy and Hal Miller, he'd been feeling more than a little violent himself. He'd wanted to kick Hal's ass, and it hadn't been the first time.

Still looking stunned, Claire asked, "Who? Who did you hit, Janie?"

"Heather Miller. I didn't exactly hit her, although I'm sure she told a completely different story." Janie shrugged. "She pushed me down, so when she offered her hand to help me up, I pulled her down, too. She cracked her face on her laptop." A look of satisfaction fluttered across her expression. "It was like a faucet pouring out blood."

"Oh, Lord." If anything, his wife went paler. "Not . . . not Lucy Miller's daughter."

Janie lifted a shoulder. "I don't know. I've never met her mother. If Lucy Miller covers mean-spirited bitchiness under a fake-sweet phony façade, I'm guessing they're related."

David's mouth twitched. "That's enough, Janie." The description fit Lucy Miller to a tee. His daughter's situational-communication problems aside, she was perceptive as hell. Maybe it came from all the time she spent listening rather than talking. Sometimes he worried that she was a little too observant.

He sneaked a surreptitious look at his watch. The last thing he needed was to miss the rescheduled team meeting, too. "The girl is Lucy Miller's daughter," he affirmed. "Lucy and *Hal* Miller." The man was West Bend's chief of police now, but seven years ago, he'd been the lead investigator in Kelsey's case. And yeah, he'd been shoved aside when the BCI had been called in, but he'd still been involved.

His inflection wasn't lost on his wife. She slumped deeper into the couch, as if it had swallowed her up, and David knew in that moment that he was going to have to give Claire a carefully abbreviated account of the conference.

"Heather is using the whole Whitney DeVries thing to get in my head. Mrs. Rimble thinks she's trying to get an edge in grades and scholarships." Janie looked vaguely surprised at the idea. "I didn't even figure Heather realized we were competing. Maybe she thought if she could provoke me, I'd do something bad enough to disqualify myself from honor society or teacher recommendations or something."

"God." Claire's voice was faint, her hand at her throat in that way she had when she was distressed. "I knew it. David, I told you, I knew that the DeVries girl—"

"Janie, you can go to your room." From the sounds of things, the girl had been through enough today, and he didn't want this scene to deteriorate into another one of his wife's meltdowns. He could control it, maybe, but not in front of his daughter. She'd been through a lot, too, in her young life. Sometimes he thought he and Claire forgot about how their tragedy had been Janie's tragedy, too.

This afternoon had reminded him.

Janie didn't need a second invitation. She was out of the room like a shot and headed for the stairs. He gave Claire an edited version of what had gone on with Janie at school that day, although the counselor, Mrs. Rimble, had been quite detailed about the things Heather had been overheard saying. Whoever said kids could be cruel had made a gross underestimation. Bunch of young cannibals was more like it.

"Who was at the conference?" With a flicker of relief, David noted that Claire had revived a little. She was at least sitting up straighter, one hand jammed into a pocket of her robe, fingers fiddling with something.

"Booker; that counselor, Mrs. Rimble; the dean of students, Templeton; the Millers; and me."

"It must have seemed odd that I wasn't there. How did you explain my absence?"

"Claire, try to focus!" David leaned back in his chair, loosened his tie, and reached for calm. "I covered, all right? Templeton is a bit of a weasel, and Lucy Miller was going on and on about her perfect daughter's soft heart and how she was probably just so concerned for Janie's state of mind. How she didn't mean any harm, and how awful Janie was for causing Heather's injury." If Heather was half as annoying as her mother, David could easily understand why Janie had lost her cool. It had been the first time he'd met Lucy Miller, and he'd felt a similar urge. "Templeton's got no backbone, so he may have backed the Millers, but Booker seemed fair. And that Rimble, I think she might be in Janie's corner. She was professional, but every time Templeton bent the Millers' way, she'd remind them of the emotional hurt that Heather had caused Janie."

"Well, I'm certainly glad they aren't just blaming Janie in this, then." He was relieved to see a spark of life return to Claire's expression. "It sounds like much ado about nothing. This is so unlike her, but she was obviously provoked. I've been on the receiving end of some of Lucy Miller's comments before, and if her daughter is anything like that witch, she's probably a nasty little piece."

Tired of the whole mess, David rubbed the back of his neck, eager to get back to work. "They both got off pretty lightly. Each will serve an after-school suspension. The Millers objected, but the principal was adamant that their daughter had violated the school's antibullying policy." And the memory of that particular part of the meeting was satisfying. The other parents' angry protests, and the counselor providing moral support to keep that wimp Templeton standing firm. "Heather serves hers tomorrow, and Janie will do so Friday. The girls are to stay the hell out of each other's way, and if there's more trouble, the repercussions will get more serious." He rose, straightened his suit coat, and reknotted his tie. "You might want to impress that bit of information on Janie."

"I will." Claire rose, too, looked anxiously toward the doorway Janie had disappeared through. "Hopefully, she's in the mood to listen."

"She will be if you use the right approach. Be supportive. We have no idea what she's been going through since that girl disappeared from Saxon Falls." He expected the sharp swivel of his wife's head, but plowed on, intent on making his point. "For all we know, that Miller girl is the tip of the iceberg. Kids talk, just like adults do. This is hard on Janie, too. It's easy to lose track of that." The reminder was as much for himself as his wife. He felt a fresh stab of guilt for not keeping better tabs on what was going on in his daughter's life.

But the introduction of the DeVries girl had a predictable effect on his wife. Her chin trembled. "I know you don't want to hear this, but the papers . . . one of the stories has already mentioned a possible link between Whitney DeVries's and Kelsey's disappearances. If there is . . . maybe the investigation this time around will—"

"Claire! For once think about the daughter we have, and not the one we lost!" Out of patience and out of time, David walked through the door. The last thing he wanted to think about right now was Kelsey's investigation. He'd already had memories of it rubbed in his face, sitting in the principal's office facing that prick Hal Miller. He'd been an arrogant son of a bitch at their first meeting and hadn't improved in the time since.

When it had become apparent that the two girls were going to serve the same consequence, Miller had tried to throw his weight around. And when that hadn't worked, he'd transferred his attitude to David. He'd had plenty of the man's bullshit after Kelsey's kidnapping. There was no love lost between them, and time hadn't diminished the level of animosity. Evidenced by Miller's last muttered remark to David as he'd brushed by him to leave the office.

Your performance of concerned father isn't any more convincing today than it was in my interview room seven years ago.

Bastard.

Special Agent Mark Foster

November 4
5:34 p.m.

"No! We've been through this a dozen times!" Shannon DeVries plucked at the arm of the couch with quick, nervous movements. "Why aren't you doing something?" Her voice grew louder. A little wild. "Why aren't you finding my daughter instead of asking us the same questions over and over like a broken record?" She sprang up from the couch on that last word as if propelled and paced agitatedly. "It's like being stuck in that movie *Groundhog Day*. We just keep reliving the same horrific hours, and nothing changes. You people are useless!"

Mark glanced at Brian DeVries to gauge his mood. The man made no move to calm his wife and looked one step away from having his own outburst.

Dealing with parents was always a minefield. Managing one who was law enforcement required a degree of diplomacy that Mark feared he hadn't yet acquired in his twelve years as an agent. Normally, the trick was to soothe and elicit information at the same time. To rewrap what they already knew with any new facts that could be shared to give them a sense of progression. DeVries saw through those efforts. And despite being a cop, he was as impatient as any other parent would be with less-than-lightning-speed results on his daughter's investigation.

Mark couldn't totally blame him. If he were in the man's position, he'd be chewing glass by now.

"Don't think that because I'm here talking to you that nothing is being done for Whitney. Agent Craw is conducting more interviews as we speak. We've got local officers manning the tip line and investigators following up on every single lead that comes in. We've submitted details of your case to federal databases, and we follow up on each hit we get. We've got more personnel back at BCI headquarters chasing down details they don't have to be on scene for." He gave Shannon a reassuring smile. "You've got a regular battalion working on your behalf, even if you don't see most of them."

It was impossible for a civilian to understand the myriad paths this investigation had already explored. Or the way each path would branch off for each of the tiniest facts. But he'd gotten Shannon's attention, and that was step one. She returned to the couch, sank down, seeming calmer.

He felt a stab of empathy. When he became irritated, he just thought of Nicky, and how he'd feel if he were in the parents' place. The investigators would be ready to shoot him by now. Maybe that's why he was better suited than Craw to deal with the families. Thrice-divorced, Ben had never had kids. He was still a hell of an agent but had a harder time having his decisions constantly questioned by the victims' families.

"I can't think of anything more difficult than what the two of you are going through now. But we're making progress." He sat on the edge of the ottoman in front of the couch. "The reason I asked again about boyfriends is that our warrants went through. We've gotten the cell phone data back for Whitney's cell, as well as preliminary forensic information from her social media sites. We've focused on speaking to everyone she was friends with online that we haven't already interviewed. We found an irregularity in one of the Facebook accounts."

"An irregularity?" Brian leaned forward, his dark gaze intense. "What does that mean?"

Mark kept his voice conversational. "There was a boy from Blackston that she was friends with online. She was communicating with him regularly, at first using Facebook chats before they started text messaging."

Shannon looked at her husband helplessly. "I don't understand. The only time Whitney is in Blackston is when we're at my mom's."

Her husband didn't spare her a glance. "So, who's the boy?"

"His name is Patrick Allen." Mark watched the two carefully. "Does that ring a bell?"

Shannon shook her head. She was a petite blonde woman, nearly dwarfed by the oversize sofa. "I grew up in Blackston, but I don't recognize the name. Do you think he had something to do with Whitney's kidnapping?"

"We're not sure yet." Mark shifted his gaze to Brian. "We've interviewed the boy, and he denies knowing your daughter. Said he's been locked out of his Facebook account for months and hasn't been able to resolve the issue. He finally gave up and established a new one, and Whitney isn't a contact on it."

"And you believe him?"

Ignoring the belligerence in the other man's tone, Mark replied, "We have no reason not to at this point. His father agreed to surrender the boy's cell and the family electronics. We also have Patrick's school-issued laptop. But the Allens were in Columbus visiting relatives the weekend Whitney went missing. Their alibi will be easy to verify." In fact, the team was in the process of doing that right now.

"Relatives could cover up for him. Did he have access to a vehicle? Maybe he was luring Whitney on behalf of someone else. I wouldn't be so quick to write off this kid's involvement." Brian's words came in short, staccato bursts.

"We aren't." Mark's look encompassed both parents. "We won't."

"What . . ." Shannon's voice broke on the word, and she paused as if to steady herself before going on. "What did the messages say?"

"The chats were pretty innocuous. We're unable to get the content of the text messages, just the dates and times when they occurred. There were no phone calls, and although kids seem to favor Snapchat and Instagram over Facebook these days, there's no indication that they were communicating through those sites." Mark could tell from Brian's expression that the import of those facts wasn't lost on the man. But Shannon's brow furrowed.

"I know Whitney has Snapchat because once in a while she shows me a picture she . . ." Comprehension dawned, and she looked stricken. "That's why, isn't it? He never called . . . he avoided sites that regularly used pictures because . . . he isn't Patrick Allen at all." Her words ended on a sob, and she buried her face in her hands.

"We're investigating that possibility." Mark noted how long it took Brian DeVries to move from his chair, go to his wife, and put his arm around her. Something about the act seemed awkward. Not for the first time, Mark wondered what they'd discover down the road about the couple's marriage.

He didn't like this aspect of the investigation. The most delicate balancing act of his job was to show empathy for the hell they were going through even before he could discount them as suspects. But statistics didn't lie, and a significant percentage of crimes against juveniles were committed by the parents. So one of the things he wasn't telling the DeVrieses was the number of hours he and Craw were spending corroborating their statements. Looking into their backgrounds. Their financials. Their relationship.

Inwardly, he squirmed at the thought. Scratch the surface, and many marriages would show flaws and weaknesses. Even his own.

Especially his own.

Pushing aside the thought, he continued. "That's why I asked again about a boyfriend. Do you recall Whitney ever mentioning a new friend? Hinting that she was communicating with someone different?"

"She wouldn't do that. Tell us, I mean." Brian's voice was flat. "She's fourteen. She isn't allowed to date for another two years. She knows that's nonnegotiable with us. And if I had heard there was a boy she was talking to, she would have had to answer a lot of questions. Part of having a cop for a father."

"Maybe she mentioned something to your son."

"Ryan?" Shannon raised her head, wiping away tears. "Doubtful. He's a thorn in her side most of the time . . . totally normal sibling dynamics," she hastened to add. "If he suspected anything, he'd have taunted her, probably at the top of his lungs. Believe me, I'd have heard about it."

"I'd still like to talk to him."

"He's napping." And from the tone of Brian's voice, the kid would be undisturbed this evening. "Ryan is still a bit under the weather, and as you can imagine, he's pretty worked up about his sister. He isn't sleeping well at night."

Mark nodded. "Another time, then. When he's feeling better."

"Have you traced the devices that the communications to Whitney were coming from?" Brian asked.

"He knew how to hide his tracks online. There are a number of ways he could have hacked the boy's Facebook account. A phishing scam. Sending him a link to click on. He probably used a VPN so his IP address couldn't be traced." All this was supposition. It all boiled down to the fact that there'd be no leads from the offender's computer. "His phone was a burner."

DeVries uttered an ugly oath and looked away, his throat working. He obviously grasped the significance of that detail. Disposable phones came without contracts. Without identified users. There were legitimate reasons to buy them. But they were difficult to trace, and that fact would appeal to someone with something to hide.

Mark continued. "We got the phone number for the burner from your daughter's cell records. We've discovered the network provider of the offender's phone, and obtained a dump of all the transmissions to and from that number. It was used only to communicate with Whitney. We've installed a trap in the system. If he uses the phone again, we'll get the time and tower location." Mark looked at Shannon. "Your neighbor called the tip line yesterday. The lady who lives to the left of you?"

"Cyb Gladstone," Brian muttered. His fingers flexed on the arm of the chair. Relaxed.

"We spoke to her before, of course, but she thinks she remembers hearing a garage door being raised the night Whitney disappeared. Do you recall hearing anything like that?"

"No." Her voice certain. "We would have heard if it had been ours. Our bedroom is nearest to the garage. The last time we called Ask a Nurse about Ryan's fever was, what . . . two fifteen or so." Mark knew this was true. Shannon had phoned into the hospital's question line at 12:21 a.m. and Brian at 2:14 a.m. Those facts in their statement had already been verified with the hospital's call logs.

"By four, we were both dead to the world," Brian continued. "Ryan's fever broke around three, and his bed was soaked. We changed him, and he crawled into bed with us. That was the only sleep we got that night after he finally conked out for good."

"Cyb's a sweetheart, but I don't know how reliable she is," Shannon said doubtfully. "Last summer she swore she heard a gunshot in front of her house. It was just the garbage collectors clanging around. She takes a lot of medication . . ." Her voice drifted off, but her meaning was clear.

If the older woman wasn't reliable, it might put into doubt her claim that Brian and Shannon DeVries had violent arguments sometimes on their back deck late at night. Money problems, the woman had confided. Mark put a mental question mark on the neighbor's input. "Mind if I look around again? In the garage, and in Whitney's room?"

"Why? It's clear Whitney left—or was taken—through her bedroom window." Brian's voice bordered on combative.

Mark had already learned that Shannon reacted with tears, her husband with anger. Under the circumstances, both responses were normal in a situation that was anything but. "Probably so," he agreed. The only prints on the window and casing belonged to family members. Nor had dusting in the garage or the other exits resulted in other latent prints. "But the last thing we want to do is to accept anything at face value. This case is too important to overlook anything."

"Fine." Brian shot up, striding out of the room, his spine stiff.

Shannon watched him go, her soft, dark eyes worried. "It's all right. Let us know if you need anything." Before Mark could rise, she'd scurried after her husband, disappearing into the kitchen.

Left to his own devices, Mark exited the room and walked down the hallway, walking past the kitchen. Next to what would be the master bedroom, there was a small foyer, with a coat closet on one wall and the entry from the garage on another. The house's security system was rigged to the front and back entrances but not to this door, although it did boast a dead bolt. In Mark's experience, most people felt garage entries were already secure. After all, the automatic door was also locked.

He pulled a pair of latex gloves out of one pocket of his leather coat. The evidence team was done with the scene, but old habits were hard to break. He unlocked the inner door to the double garage, flipped the dead bolt, and pushed it open. The space bore no windows or extra outside exit. Two midsize vehicles would be a tight squeeze. It was kept neat enough to give him a flicker of guilt about the boxes he'd never gotten around to unpacking in his, though he and his wife had been in their house for almost five years. A pegboard kept the tools organized over a small workbench on one wall. Four bikes hung from hooks suspended from the ceiling. He'd already ascertained that Whitney's was among them. The lawn mower and snowblower were wedged into one corner. Just inside the automatic door was a double-door metal cupboard. Crossing to it, Mark pulled open one side, peered in. It contained bats, balls, basketballs, gloves . . . the type of sports equipment kids accumulated.

He let himself back into the house, resecuring the door behind him, and headed toward Whitney's room. Criminals had ways to exploit weaknesses in garage-door security. It was even possible, he supposed, for an intruder to wait until Brian DeVries returned from work after dark and roll into the garage while the man drove inside, or get his hands on a master garage-door opener and find the same frequency the DeVries had. The plausibility ratio ratcheted downward when factoring in the dead bolt on the door leading into the house. The first cops on the scene had found it secured, and the parents had sworn it was locked every night. If true, it meant Whitney hadn't left that way, no matter what the neighbor claimed to have heard.

The most obvious answer was usually the right one. He stopped in the doorway of Whitney's room. The window was closed, but the interior screen still leaned against the wall. He went to it, craning his neck to look out, following the path she'd taken with his gaze. The trail the dogs had picked up was beneath this window, through the yard between the DeVries and Gladstone houses. Across the backyard and the neighbors' yards to the south. No way to tell from that whether she'd been walking or had been carried. The dogs would alert either way.

But what they'd discovered on the girl's Facebook account pretty well cemented the theory that she'd left of her own accord. Pervs haunted social media sites for opportunities to make contact with kids, but Mark was struck by the amount of planning evident with the use of Patrick Allen's account. The kidnapper hadn't aimlessly trolled for young girls; he'd targeted Whitney. Mark knew Brian had guessed that, too.

Turning back to the room, he studied it again. He'd been on the scene before, of course. More than once. It was a typical teenage girl's room, if a bit on the messy side. The floor was so littered with clothes, shoes, books, and empty hangers that it took a careful scan to discern the color of the carpeting. Beige. The crime-scene team had been thorough, but there'd been nothing of note under the mattress, behind the posters, or squirreled away in the dresser drawers. Certainly nothing as telling as what they'd found in her Facebook account.

There was a hooded sweatshirt hanging from the blade of the overhead ceiling fan and a white ballet slipper in the center of the closet doorway. The door couldn't be closed without shoving it aside. Something about that slipper nagged at his memory, but Mark couldn't put it in context.

Stepping carefully, he wandered about the room. The set of shelves held books and notebooks, framed photos of Whitney and friends. All had been identified in the file. Each one had been questioned, with the exception of Macy Odegaard, whom they'd been unable to reach. Shannon had thought they were out of state for the girl's grandma's funeral. Hopefully, they'd have a line on the family tomorrow. Maybe Macy would know more about Whitney's relationship with the supposed Patrick Allen. The other friends all had denied any knowledge of a boyfriend, although Mark had accumulated a lengthy list of boys who were supposedly interested in the girl, which they were checking out.

Next to the window, a poster of Justin Bieber shared wall space with one of Nicki Minaj, each hung with neon-pink poster putty. There was a huge bulletin board covered with overlapping photos, concert-ticket stubs, sports clippings of the local high school teams, and a couple of selfies of Whitney with friends. All had been identified and spoken to. There was an empty spot on the cluttered desk where her school-provided laptop had sat. Cyber forensics had found nothing on it so far. Social media sites were blocked, and the only e-mail accessed on it was a school account. It appeared that she used her phone and the family computer for personal communications.

"To be honest, it almost always looks like this."

Swiveling, Mark saw Shannon standing in the doorway, her gaze scanning the space. "Drives me nuts. I make her clean it every Saturday, so I can get in here with a vacuum. I always tell her, 'Whit, it'd be so much less work just to keep it clean.' But Brian says we have to pick our battles, and a clean room and made bed are pretty trivial in the grand scheme of things." She fell silent, her eyes welling with tears. "I guess he was right."

"I don't know much about raising teenagers, but that sounds like a good idea." And he was sort of surprised to hear that it came from her husband. It reflected an indulgence and understanding that he wouldn't expect from the man. He pointed to the area next to her bed. "Is that where she usually kept her school bag?"

Shannon nodded, her gaze riveted on it. "After fifty reminders to carry it to her room, yeah." A little smile played across her lips before disappearing. "She's got a million great qualities, but organization isn't one of them."

"Are she and her dad close?" Other than the original statement taken by the chief of police when BCI got called, Shannon had never been questioned without Brian at her side. Mark couldn't get a read on whether that was the woman's choice or her husband's.

Eyes misting, Shannon nodded. "She's his little girl." Her voice cracked a little on the words. "He was thrilled when Ryan was born, of course, but I never got the idea that he was disappointed when we had a daughter first. Some men . . . it matters to them, you know? But not to Brian. She was his world. And it's killing him. He doesn't let anyone see, but he's dying inside. Because he's her daddy, and he didn't protect her." She was crying now, silent tears tracing paths down her cheeks, and Mark took a handkerchief from his pocket, handed it to her. Being good at dealing with parents meant he always had a clean one ready.

He waited for her to compose herself, studying the room again, his gaze lingering on the slipper, the sense of familiarity stronger. Crossing to it, he picked it up. Let it dangle from the end of one gloved index finger. "Did she dance?" He tried to recall if they'd listed dance as one of her activities. He didn't think so.

Shannon leaned against the doorjamb as if the strength had suddenly streamed out of her, the damp handkerchief clutched in her fingers. "She took jazz and ballet from the time she was three. I was so upset when she quit. She nagged me about it for six months before she finally wore me down. Guess I loved it more than she did. I have a scrapbook of all the recital pictures and newspaper stories about her group. They were pretty good."

"How long ago did she stop taking lessons?"

"It was May. I made her go through the recital and everything. Maybe a little part of me was hoping once she did, she'd change her mind, but she didn't."

"Almost six months then." He sent her an easy smile, but something was still niggling at him. "Why would she have her dance shoes lying around if she hadn't had lessons for six months?"

"For the same reason she has a teddy bear she hasn't touched in years under her bed. I don't know how she gets the place in such a shambles in the space of a few days. She goes searching for something, and anything in her way gets tossed aside and pretty soon . . ." She gestured to the room.

Mark smiled. "Sounds like my son when he's going through his toy box. Most things go right over his shoulder." He turned the slipper over. Size seven, which matched the description they had of the girl. And he was bothered more than he should have been that the parents had forgotten to include Whitney's former interest in the background they'd given the BCI. You never knew what might be important . . . The thought splintered as another intruded.

"What?" Distracted, he glanced at Shannon, who was regarding him closely. "You looked . . . I don't know." She gave an uneasy laugh. "Like something just occurred to you."

"I just remembered I was supposed to call Agent Craw fifteen minutes ago," he lied. "I appreciate your time tonight. You and your husband's. Feel free to contact me if you have questions. And I'll keep you apprised of developments."

Suddenly in a hurry, Mark headed through the door and down the hall, with Shannon on his heels. Moments later, he was hunching against the wind's bitter bite as he hastened to his car. If he did speak to the other agent tonight, he knew better than to share the thought that had struck him as he had contemplated that ballet slipper. The older man would chew his ass. Probably rightly so.

He slipped into the vehicle. Started it. The memory of the dance shoe refused to be shunted aside. It looked like thousands of others worn by girls across America.

It also looked like those worn by the dead victims of the Ten Mile Killer.

Mark pulled away from the curb, noting the neighbor watching him through her front window.

There were few agents in the BCI who hadn't checked out the TMK case file at one time or another. The case was the most notorious one in the agency's recent history. The fact that it had remained unsolved made it all the more bitter. All the victims had been found in a ten-mile radius deep in the Wayne National Forest. He remembered from his reading that many of the TMK's victims had taken dance. And when their bodies had been discovered, each victim had been clad in leotard, tights, a tutu, and ballet slippers. It was the most notable commonality in the crimes. The memories of the photos of their posed, decomposing bodies had acid churning in his gut.

Without a body, Craw hadn't been convinced that Kelsey Willard had been victimized by the Ten Mile Killer, no matter what the locals thought. But the cases of two teenage girls missing from towns twelve miles apart—even with seven years between the occurrences—had enough surface similarities to be examined for links before they could be dismissed as coincidence.

Kelsey Willard's bike had been found abandoned seven years ago, with no trace of the girl. Whitney DeVries also appeared to have left her home voluntarily, but they had evidence she'd been targeted. They'd been close in age at the time of their disappearances. Both had once taken dance.

Keeping an eye on the oncoming headlights spearing through the darkness, he reached into his pocket, thumbed Ben's number into his cell.

"Where you at?" the other agent asked. "I'm ready to head out and get something to eat."

"Just leaving the DeVrieses. Have you gotten the agency file yet?"

"It was delivered a couple of hours ago."

"I'll pick up some sandwiches." Mark slowed the vehicle as the brake lights on the car ahead of his flashed. "We can eat while we work. I'm eager to get a look at the Willard investigation."

Whitney DeVries

November 5
5:37 p.m.

The movie flickered on the white-painted concrete wall. Fear kept Whitney's gaze glued to it. The final scene was playing, the one where the stupid beginning ballet moves she'd practiced all day were strung together in a simple sequence. When it finished, it would start over again, an endless cycle.

The arabesque stretched the barely healed wounds on her back and hips, sending fiery jolts of agony through her system. Each pirouette had sore muscles screaming. If she moved too far from one side to another, a scab on her back would break open. Blood would drip down her spine, soak through the leotard, and make it stick to her. She hadn't been given a change of clothes. She'd just gotten *these* back.

Demi-plié, demi-plié, *relevé*, *tendu*. Her arm arched up, the skin on her shoulders stretching and pulling. She could hear Tami Jae's voice in her head: *Graceful, graceful, the hand movements tell a story. You're not swinging a bat, Whitney!*

For a moment she pretended she was in Tami Jae's studio. That she had to get through only an hour and a half before she could go home.

Forty-five minutes for ballet, and then the last half of the class spent on jazz, her favorite. She imagined her mom sitting with the other moms in the corner, all talking and laughing quietly among themselves. The image became so real for an instant that she glanced to the side, half expecting to see Susan Paulus practicing next to her, as she had during the weekly lessons for years. They'd smile and roll their eyes as Tami's voice grew crosser. She always got pissy when they didn't have a good lesson.

But Susan wasn't there. Whitney's mom wasn't in the corner. She squeezed her eyes shut tight. When she opened them again to fix her gaze on the film, they were blurry with tears.

She wanted to rest. She wanted to curl up in a little ball and sleep until this nightmare was over. But when she was allowed to sleep, she'd be on her stomach because every other part of her body ached.

Whitney had never been in so much pain in her life.

The worst thing that had ever happened to her was when she'd fallen off her bike when she was six or so and broke her arm. That had hurt. Until now she would have said it was the most agonizing thing in the world. But that was before she knew much about pain. Or about the world.

She was learning more than she'd ever wanted to about both.

The *cambré* had her leaning backward. The movement had fresh tears springing to her eyes. She was lucky the dance sequence was so easy because after her punishment, it had been a struggle just to complete these routines. Maybe that's why the freak had chosen it. Maybe he'd just been waiting to use that whip on her.

Maybe he was waiting to do it again.

Panic scampered up her spine, and she renewed her efforts. She felt stiff and wooden, but her hands were uninjured. She let them tell a story like Tami Jae had said, wrists cocked, fingers held just so, graceful and delicate. And the next time her mind wandered, she'd imagine them wrapped around the freak's throat.

It hadn't just been the beating, although she'd wondered for hours afterward if she was dying. No, the worst had been moments later, when she'd heard him coming up on the stage. She hadn't been brave then. She hadn't tried to look up to see his face. At the sound of his footsteps, she'd crawled away, as fast as the pain would allow.

Remembering that had a hot burn of shame spreading in her chest. Because he hadn't used his whip on her again. He'd taken her clothes instead.

If your behavior improves, you may earn your clothes back, Whitney. But tomorrow you'll practice without them. Clothes are a privilege earned by good behavior. You haven't earned any privileges.

The words had been only noise, delivered in that low, hollow voice. She'd just been relieved he wasn't going to hurt her again. But the next day had been worse than the actual beating.

She'd been *naked* all day. The bra was hanging on the chain that attached to her wrist cuff, but she hadn't dared reach for it. She'd had to stand up there in the light afforded by the computer screen and projector, knowing he could see her. Watching her bending and stretching in a way that exposed her body. What made it even worse was that she was having her period. The humiliation of it all still made her stomach lurch. There had been tampons in the meager supplies by the shower, but having to practice all day completely nude, the telltale string hanging down between her thighs . . . nothing in her life had been worse than that. Not the broken arm. Not her first *real* physical with Dr. Baylor. Not the whipping.

She didn't dream of being rescued anymore. Not after that day. Now her mind was filled with images of hurting the freak herself. Of breaking free and finding a bat or heavy metal bar and whaling on him, over and over until he screamed and bled and begged. She, who caught ladybugs that had wandered into the house and set them free outside rather than flushing them like her mom did, wanted to hurt another human being.

Except he wasn't human. He was a monster. The kind her dad had always told her didn't exist when she'd been a little kid and hadn't wanted to go to bed at night. Together they'd look under the bed, in the closet, and behind the door to prove that nope, no monsters there.

Now she knew better. Monsters didn't live in your bedroom. They lived in your town or one just like it. They probably had jobs and neighbors and maybe waved to people passing by as they mowed their lawns. Monsters weren't the frightening, fanged creatures in the stupid horror movies she watched at sleepovers with her friends.

Even though she hadn't seen the freak's face yet, she knew. Monsters looked just like the rest of us. And somehow, that made them even scarier.

She ended the routine with a plié in the fifth position, *tendu* to second, and *assemblé*. The simple jump had her bruised muscles screaming. The deep bow at the end pulled at the healing scars on her back. But it wasn't pain that filled her thoughts; it was dreams of revenge.

"Bravo! Bravissimo!"

The sound of his voice turned her insides to ice. Whitney had to fight an urge to scurry to the corner, cower there, shaking, arms wrapped around herself protectively. She hated that her brain couldn't control the reactions of her body. She should slouch right now, cross her arms, and give him the "whatever" attitude that always drove her dad nuts. She should do something, anything, to prove that he hadn't broken her. To show she wasn't afraid.

But she merely straightened slowly, returned to demi-pointe, hands at rest. Because her body *was* still afraid. And as much as she despised herself for it, Whitney couldn't overcome that.

"You mastered the first film in the series in record time." The freak's voice was almost jovial. "That's quite an accomplishment. How long did you take lessons?"

"Ten years. I quit in May." Her voice sounded meeker than she would have liked, but in her head, where she was stronger, she was filing away details. He knew she'd taken lessons. That meant he was from around her town, right? Or maybe he'd been at her recital last spring. Seen the picture of her group in the paper.

Another thought intruded, and her stomach plummeted. Because he wouldn't have had to learn that by stalking her. She'd *told* him. At least, she'd told someone she'd thought was Patrick Allen.

"Yes, you quit." The pleasant tone had vanished. Now it held an edge that had her inching closer to the wall. "And that disappoints me, Whitney. It really does. Children need to be taught to follow through on whatever they undertake. I'm not a fan of this modern permissive parenting."

Who gives a rat's ass what you're a fan of? The mutinous thought hovered on the tip of her tongue, remained unuttered. It wasn't brave to just invite another beating for no reason. If it happened again, it was going to be for something that mattered. Like being punished for trying to find a way out of here.

"As a reward for your swift progress, you've earned a privilege."

She remained silent. Unless it was a key out of her dark, shadowy prison, she wasn't interested.

"You'll now be allowed a half hour of television before bedtime."

A ribbon of hope unfurled within her, only to wither at his next words. "Nick at Nite will be programmed to show on the back wall, just as your practice films are."

A laugh almost escaped her. She'd hoped at first that she'd be allowed out of this room. Maybe through that door—there had to be a door—behind him and allowed somewhere she'd have a better chance of escape. But . . . Nick at Nite? Really? Did he think she was *eight*?

His expectant pause had the flesh on her arms raising. "That would be . . . nice," she said. Enthusiasm was impossible to muster, especially in light of her disappointment.

"You've earned it, dear. Good behavior should be recognized, just as certainly as bad behavior is punished."

His voice sounding in the near darkness had the barely healed wounds on her back and shoulders throbbing as if in response.

"Now, please sit down."

Ignoring an inner urge to bolt at the command, she sank to the wooden floor. Pulled up her knees and wrapped her arms around them.

"I'm afraid I have some troubling news, and it's understandable that you'll be upset. Your family was killed yesterday morning. It was a plane crash. There were no survivors. I'm so sorry, Whitney, for your loss."

Her first reaction was shock. Then bewilderment. "No, they weren't. You're wrong. They wouldn't have been on a plane. They're *looking* for me."

"They aren't looking for you, Whitney. No one is. I told you that before. Everyone thinks you ran away. Ungrateful children often do, you know. There was a family vacation scheduled, was there not? You were all going to California and planned to leave yesterday."

Her heart started thudding in her ears. A greasy tangle of nerves knotted in her stomach. How could he know that? How could he? Unless . . . Aunt Julie was in the hospital, but they wouldn't have gone without Whitney. They wouldn't! Had she told Patrick about the trip? Her thoughts were scattered. She couldn't remember. But she must have. And now the freak was using his knowledge to mess with her. She didn't care now what reaction her words would bring. The denial was surging through her, demanding release. "You're lying. Just to be mean and cruel and . . . and an asshole! You're *lying*!"

"We'll suspend the rules, just for now, because of your terrible loss." How could he spew those *lies*, those vicious untruths, and sound so fucking reasonable? "I know you don't want to believe it. Both your parents and Ryan, poor boy, so very young. I realize it's a shock. But you aren't alone, Whitney, dear. You still have me."

Those words highlighted the horror of it all. She didn't believe him. She didn't! Her family would never believe she ran away. They wouldn't go to California with her missing. No matter how worried they were about her aunt or how much Ryan may have begged because he was looking forward to seeing Disneyland.

"I don't believe you." The tears streaming down her face made it difficult to see, but there was nothing to look at, anyway, beyond the stage except for the glow of the computer screen and projector. It was like staring into an inky pit. Horrible words were being tossed from the shadows like poisonous pebbles. Did he think she was a child? That he could say anything and make her believe it? "I'm not stupid. You're trying to manipulate me." That's what monsters did, didn't they? Break you down, body, spirit, and mind? That's all he was trying to do. Because it wasn't true. It wasn't. It wasn't . . . it wasn't!

Logic ruled one part of her, emotion the other. Because even as the denials came, an overwhelming flood of loneliness swept over her, snatching the sobs from her breath, worming deep inside her and radiating from within, icy tendrils of fear. "I'll never believe you."

She could hear him moving closer, and for once, it didn't matter. There was something she feared far more than him, after all. Like discovering that maybe, just maybe, he was telling the truth.

"Look at the wall."

Whitney wiped her face on the sleeve of her leotard as she turned. Saw nothingness on the white brick. Then a blank Internet search page with a URL to the *Columbus Dispatch*. A story filled the screen, zoomed in on the headline.

Fiery Plane Crash Kills 120

The screen changed to a story for the *Cincinnati Daily News*.

California-Bound Plane Crashes

It was dated November 4.

"No." But the word was a sob now. A plea. "Please, God, no."

Now there were just headlines on the page. All of them blurred together.

Crash of New Plane Baffles Airline
Fiery Crash Shuts Down Cleveland-Hopkins Airport

Cleveland. They were going to leave from Cleveland. She might have told Patrick that, too. But when a picture of her brother came up on the screen, followed by each of her parents, with their names under the heading *Deceased*, a howl of despair tore up from her belly. The hard, racking sobs left her throat jagged and raw. All her doubts, all her sorrow balled up in one huge boulder of grief and demanded a release. And when it was over, when she'd cried herself dry and could produce nothing more than a whimper, she lay crumpled on the floor, her face pressed to the gritty boards, the sense of desolation overwhelming.

"That's good. It's best to let grief out, so it doesn't fester. That's healthy."

She'd forgotten the freak. He was still out there somewhere. Watching her breakdown with the same cold scrutiny he'd probably had when observing her practicing naked. That's what she was left with. Only him.

"This is your home now. I'm the only family you have remaining. Our connection was so quick. So strong. You already feel like my daughter, and if you let yourself, soon you'll feel the same way about me. Why don't you try? Call me Daddy."

An hour ago, she would have laughed at him, at least in her mind. Been repulsed by the obscenity of his suggestion. But now she felt nothing. There was only emptiness and a yawning sense of despair. Because he hadn't lied. It was true, all of it. Her family was dead. She wanted to be dead, too. Instead, she was alone. At the freak's mercy. And even that didn't seem to matter anymore. Nothing did.

"Daddy," she repeated dully.

Janie Willard

November 6
3:48 p.m.

She'd sneaked into the bathroom for a quick smoke before showing up to suspension, which under the circumstances was probably smart. Janie had initially planned to use the time as a study hall. They didn't get much for homework over the weekend, but she had an AP physics test Monday because Fredericks was a sadist. And her government project was due in a week. She had to work Sunday, so it'd be nice to have everything done before then.

It'd taken less than ten minutes, however, to discover that nothing productive was going to occur in suspension. Once she'd given up, she'd started a long e-mail to Alyvia updating her on "the experience in captivity," as her friend had put it. Alyvia had been wildly pumped about the whole Heather Miller fiasco. Janie suspected missing the scene had been a major disappointment for her friend.

Her laptop pinged quietly, signaling an incoming e-mail. She read the name, studiously avoiding looking at the sender, who was seated two rows away. Instead, Janie stared hard at Mike Humphries, the supervisor, who was tipped back in his chair behind the desk in the front of the room, buried deep in the sports pages of the *Cincinnati Daily News*. He'd looked up only once since they'd filed in to take attendance and issued a warning against talking and cell phone use before retreating behind the wall of newspaper. The man wasn't a teacher but did some assistant coaching and study hall supervision. If he had another job outside the school she'd never heard of it. From the looks of him, he spent his other waking hours working on his heavily muscled gym-rat physique.

Her laptop pinged again. Same sender. Just like the last five e-mails. She reached out to tap the key that would mute the computer.

"No cell phones, guys." Humphries didn't even look up as he turned a page. Neither did four of the other occupants of the room. One boy was asleep, slouched low in his chair, his head tipped back, jaw gaping. Two others were amusing themselves by rolling tiny spit wads and attempting to throw them in the dozing boy's mouth. The floor around her desk was littered from the bombardment they'd aimed her way earlier. She was glad they'd turned their juvenile attentions elsewhere.

But it was the final guy in the room who was proving to be the biggest source of annoyance. Cole Bogart. He'd just moved to their school last year. Janie knew him only by sight, but she'd heard of him. Everyone had. He'd gotten caught hacking the school's server last winter and been kicked out for his efforts. Apparently, he was back this fall. She'd never exchanged so much as a glance with him. Which made the barrage of e-mails he'd been sending to her school e-mail since she'd sat down hard to explain. Janie hadn't opened any of them. She knew just enough about him to be certain she had nothing to say to him.

She was just about to push "Send" when the content of her message to Alyvia blanked. Words began to appear in the empty space.

Why are you ignoring me????

What the hell? Janie stared at the screen, dumbfounded.

We have a common nemesis. You should read my messages.

She looked over at Cole. He never glanced up, his head bent over his computer. When she returned her gaze to her laptop, another message had appeared.

Heard about you punching Heather Miller in the face.

The line of words was followed by an animated graphic of a champagne bottle's cork popping off and liquid bubbling down the side of the bottle.

"Knock it off, assholes!"

Janie started. The dozer had awakened and was scowling at his two tormentors. Humphries lowered his newspaper enough to glare over it. "That's enough! I said no talking!"

Unable to restrain herself, she typed, How are you doing this? Somehow he'd gotten inside her e-mail and was using it like an Instant Messaging system. She would have sworn it was impossible if she wasn't watching it happening in front of her.

This?

A moment later, Humphries's face appeared on top of a baboon's backside. She ducked her head to hide her smile.

Nice trick, she wrote.

> I have a lot of them. Unfortunately, I got caught practicing mine. Shit happens. But not to everyone, ever notice that? Some people get away with far worse than changing grades online. Check out the last e-mail I sent you.

She hesitated, glanced at the clock. Another hour left. Dozer appeared to have gone back to sleep. The other two jerks were engrossed in what appeared to be a rousing and totally silent game of flick football. Janie went to her inbox. Scrolled to the last of the half dozen messages Bogart had sent. Opened it.

Her heart did a slow free-fall. Hastily, she closed out of the message, but the image in it was burned into her brain. A teenage girl, clad only in a thong, arms crossed over her bare chest, shooting a sultry look over her shoulder.

And not just any girl. Heather Miller.

Is that how you get your kicks? She returned to the message page, typing furiously, fueled by an irrational rage that had nothing to do with Heather. Splicing pictures or whatever the hell you did. It's cyberbullying, and you're an asshole. You should have been kicked out for more than a semester.

> Calm down. I didn't do anything. Stumbled on this pic and plenty more on a site I found. Deep web has some nasty corners. Imagine my surprise when I found HM in one of them. Why do you care, anyway?

The cursor blinked accusingly, punctuating Cole's final sentence. Why *did* Janie care? She didn't. Not about Heather Miller, anyway. She wasn't even shocked. Beneath that golden-girl surface, Heather had a wild side. Janie had heard the girl was hooking up with Josh Ferin, who was a total loser with a rep for supplying any illegal substance anyone wanted. So, no, she wasn't totally surprised by the picture.

Her reaction was rooted in something much more personal.

> Look for yourself if you want. Maybe neither of us would be too sad if this pic went viral.

The message was followed by a web address. The text on the page began to delete under her gaze until only the image and address remained. Although she couldn't look away, it wasn't Heather Miller's picture she was thinking about.

It was Kelsey's.

◆ ◆ ◆

"I've only got, like, an hour." Alyvia Naughton bounded up the steps behind Janie and followed her through the bedroom door, flinging herself down onto Janie's neatly made bed. "FPs are on my case big time, and with conferences next week, I need to do some serious sucking up because chances are they'll be even less happy when they see my grades. That means spending the weekend with them visiting their relatives, who are even more boring than they are."

FPs. Alyvia-speak for foster parents. Rarely did she call any of them by name. Janie slid her backpack off and set it on the desk. Maybe, she reflected as she flopped onto the futon next to it, Alyvia didn't bother to learn names anymore. This had to be at least the seventh home she'd been placed in. The second in six months. "Still trying to ride it out until the end of the school year?"

Alyvia propped herself on an elbow facing Janie. "I have to. The caseworker warned me I'd go residential if this one didn't work out." She shrugged as though she didn't care. Janie knew otherwise. "This place isn't as bad as some. And it sounds like they're getting another kid soon, so the focus will be off me for a while." She folded her hands in false reverence. "Thank God."

Janie smiled, for the first time in days feeling like a weight had lifted. Alyvia could do that for her. Her friend had been on a short leash lately since she'd skipped school to nurse a killer hangover at a friend's. In some ways, the two of them were polar opposites. But since Kelsey died, Janie had often found herself feeling as adrift as Alyvia was, for far different reasons.

Kelsey. Thoughts of her sister had her smile vanishing.

"So I thought you were going to text me while you were in lockup."

"No phones. Tried to e-mail you." She gave her friend a condensed version of the events after school. When she got to the image Bogart had sent her of Heather Miller, Alyvia bolted upright on the bed.

"Are you kidding me? Heather Fucking Miller has nudies floating around on the Internet? Are they real or Photoshopped? Doesn't matter," she decided a moment later. "We can use them either way."

"*We* aren't using anything." Janie knew that would be Alyvia's first thought. "Although I get the feeling that's exactly what Bogart wanted. To hurt Heather. And that he was trying to manipulate me into being the one to do it."

Alyvia twirled a lock of her currently pink hair around an index finger. "Why would he? He's the computer genius. You know he was kicked out last year for . . . oh."

"Yeah, oh." Janie leaned back and toed off her shoes. "He can't afford to get caught for anything again. They can trace IPs where e-mails originate." Although after his display this afternoon with her e-mail, she wasn't so sure Bogart wasn't capable of circumventing discovery.

"Just as a matter of discussion . . . all it would take is stealing someone's phone to text the pic of the bitchacrite to a couple of guys, who could be counted on to share widely." Something on Janie's face must have warned her because she shrugged. "Just sayin'."

"But see, he wouldn't even have to do that. He can . . ." Unable to come up with the terminology, Janie waved a hand. "He was in my e-mail. I mean, he took it over and was writing to me on a message I started to you. He could do that from anyone's account. Send the picture to the whole student body and make it look like it came . . . I don't know, from Templeton, even."

"And they'd know who had the skills to pull that off. Bogart would be the first they'd look at."

The scorch of anger that had settled in her chest the moment she'd seen that image of Heather burned hotter now. "He's an asshole."

"Maybe." Alyvia's tone was contemplative. "He's no fan of hers, apparently. You know, he got thrown out for changing grades last year. Do you think he changed some of hers?"

"Why would he, if he doesn't like her? I'm sure they made the teachers double-check the grades after he was caught."

"But how long had he been at it? How far back would they have looked? She might have been cheating to stay neck and neck with you academically all year."

Janie contemplated her friend, all too aware of how her mind worked. "I'm not using the picture. And neither are you."

"Fine." Alyvia's pout was quickly replaced by a calculating expression. "At least let me see the nudie."

Figuring it was the least she could do after dashing the rest of her friend's hopes, Janie got up and fetched her laptop from her book bag and turned it on. Joining her on the bed, she brought up her e-mail and showed her the photo, which Alyvia surveyed with a critical eye.

"Do you think that's touched up? Because I have a hard time believing she can have an ass like that without working out. It's been a year since she quit volleyball."

Drolly, Janie responded. "I guess you've given it more thought than I have."

Lifting a shoulder, her friend said, "It's not as skanky as I was hoping for. Like something she took for Ferin. Or maybe he was the one behind the camera."

"And then posted it on a site in the deep web?" Janie was skeptical. "He doesn't strike me as tech-savvy enough to manage that."

Alyvia's cell chirped. She looked at it and rolled her eyes theatrically. "God almighty, I can hardly breathe. The FPs are yanking the chain already." Rising, she added, "He could have sold the pics. He's that much of a loser. Check out the site Bogart gave you."

"The site is probably blocked on the school computer." Janie got up and typed the URL that Cole had sent her into a search engine on her personal laptop. It was old, since the school had issued each student a laptop when she was in ninth grade and her dad had said they wouldn't be updating her computer until she was heading off to college. Which couldn't be soon enough. As she carried the computer back toward her friend, she made a mental note to check the mail to see if she'd heard from Stanford yet. She'd taken the SATs for the final time in August, and the colleges she'd targeted would have her test scores by now.

"Wow." The screen successfully diverted her attention from thoughts of college admissions. The address Bogart had given her didn't direct her to the entrance of a site. Rather, once she clicked on it, she was deep into a page with hundreds—no, make that thousands—of thumbnail photos. All of scantily clad or completely nude teenage girls.

"Holy shit." Alyvia was momentarily taken aback. "Cole said he got Heather's picture off this? What *is* this?"

Without clicking on any of the thumbnails, Janie scrolled slowly to the bottom, where she saw there were more than two hundred pages. "I don't know." There was a greasy tangle of nausea in her stomach. Again, she was struck by a nagging sense of familiarity.

Alyvia rose. "*That* is creepy as fuck. But I gotta go. I'll text you from Bumfuck, Indiana, or wherever the hell the FPs are dragging me to." Alyvia zipped up her coat and strode to the door. "Call me later.

Especially if you find Heather's picture on there. Maybe there are more. You think the cops know about that site?"

All too glad to set the computer aside, Janie walked her friend downstairs to the front door. "If they don't, they should." Because it *was* creepy. Perverted and demeaning and . . . a chill worked down her spine at the thought of looking more closely at it and seeing someone she recognized on the site.

Someone much closer to her than Heather Miller.

Claire Willard

November 6
6:30 p.m.

"Where's Dad?"

"Working late."

"He worked last weekend."

Claire set the last dish on the table with deliberate care and pulled out a chair. Sank into it carefully. Was it Friday? Of course it was. She'd forgotten that when David had called earlier. The mind fog was so thick today, like sticky strands of gossamer that she couldn't seem to quite brush away. It hadn't been until Janie and her friend had bounced into the house that she'd even considered the time. David's call minutes later had been met with relief; she wouldn't have to come up with an excuse for the late dinner preparations. Because even she couldn't explain where the day had gone.

She sent her daughter an overly bright smile. "Something came up. He'll be home later, but it's just the two of us for dinner. What are your plans for the long weekend?" Parent-teacher conferences were Monday. She wondered if David remembered. On the heels of that thought came another, and she searched her daughter's expression carefully. There had been a time when just an upcoming weekend would have sparked a burst of anxiety from her daughter. The thought of all those hours to fill would have had her making note after copious note, each more heartbreaking than the next.

Watch two hours of TV.

Homework four hours.

Read one hundred pages in library book.

Talk to Alyvia . . . two hours total.

Send two e-mails.

To the unknowing, the lists would look like plans. Things to check off during a busy weekend before the days got away from her. But Claire knew they'd served to stave off her daughter's anxiety about all that empty time to fill. Claire didn't recall running across one of those notes for at least a year. Maybe it was better these days.

Or maybe Janie was just getting more adept at hiding it. Like she was with the cigarettes that she must smoke in her car, the faint stench of which clung to her clothes. Whatever her daughter's plans for the weekend, Claire could be fairly certain that they wouldn't include leaving the house. Janie didn't have a social group. She had a longtime friendship with Alyvia that Claire had never pretended to understand. Their relationship had troubled her for years, until she realized that Janie wasn't interested in making other friends. Now she accepted Alyvia gratefully, one constant in her daughter's otherwise turbulent life.

Janie picked up the bowl of rice and helped herself to a heaping serving that she then topped off with the sweet-and-sour pork that Claire had prepared. David despised the dish, but with any luck the roast she'd thrown in the oven after he'd called would be ready when he did come home later that evening.

"Nothing special." It took Claire a moment to realize that Janie was responding to her question. "I have to work Sunday, and Alyvia's gone until then. I've got a test to study for tonight, and sometime tomorrow

I need to watch a documentary on civil liberties for my government paper."

"Maybe we can go to a movie tomorrow night." The suggestion was impulsive, and from Janie's expression, Claire had managed to surprise her daughter. "After all, in a few short months, you'll be off to college." Not in California, if Claire had anything to say about it, but in nearby Columbus. Even so, the thought brought a flicker of nerves. Today's fuzziness aside, she was all too aware that Janie's presence in the house brought a much-needed focus to Claire's days. Worries about how her daughter would fare in a different city, on a campus of tens of thousands, were outweighed by the prospect of the yawning emptiness that stretched before Claire with her gone.

"Okay. Sure."

"I'll look up what's showing. You can pick. But nothing too scary."

A rare smile from her daughter. "As long as it doesn't have subtitles, I'm good."

Claire took a small serving of everything and took a bite. Swallowed. "You seem to have survived after-school suspension relatively unscathed."

A shrug. "It was lame. Humphries is worthless. I couldn't get anything done because the other guys there were screwing around. So it was a waste of time."

"Well," Claire injected a note of false cheer into her voice, "at least it's over. And that Miller girl got the same consequence, which makes me feel a bit better about the whole thing."

Janie set her fork on the edge of her plate. And something in her level gaze had Claire's stomach jittering. "I've been wondering . . . remember that envelope I found after Kelsey went missing? Whatever happened to it?"

The words reverberated in her ears, echoing like a Chinese gong. Everything inside Claire went to ice. "Envelope?" she managed, and scooped a tiny bit of rice onto her fork. Guided it to her lips. "I really don't recall."

"You don't recall? I gave it to you, remember? I found it under my mattress two days after she was gone. There was a thousand dollars inside. And pictures. Those pictures of Kelsey."

Not now, not now, after all this time, not now! "Oh, that envelope," she tried lamely. "There was some cash . . . it certainly wasn't a thousand dollars. You were a child. I'm sure it seemed like a lot . . ."

"I thought you didn't remember? And it *was* a thousand dollars. I was ten. Old enough to count money."

That tone, the direct stare were so like David's that they took Claire's breath away. At least they would have, if her lungs weren't already gasping.

"I . . ." She cursed her mental fuzziness. "It was so long ago . . ."

"Do you still have it, then?"

"No." The sliver of truth calmed her frenzied thoughts. "Of course not. I gave it to the investigators. There was a rumor going around at the time that someone in the area was taking pictures of teenage girls." Because she couldn't meet her daughter's probing gaze, she pretended to eat. But the food had gone to ash in her mouth.

"Did they . . . were they ever able to—"

"Janie, enough!" The lash of her voice had her daughter's expression closing, but Claire couldn't think about that now. "They never told us anything. Ever. You were young. We kept you away from it as much as we could, but the agents . . . it was just questions, questions, questions but never any answers." She was distantly aware that her voice had risen. Was helpless to steady it. "They told us almost nothing. Weeks and months went by, and they gave us so little. And now there's this new girl. I can't stop wondering if she was taken by the same person who took Kelsey. And what that means, if he took another one. It means your sister is almost certainly . . ." She choked on the final word, and for one horrible moment, she thought she was going to lose what little she'd managed to eat, right there on her plate.

"Forget it. I shouldn't have said anything." Janie got up to come around the table, pressing Claire's water glass into her hand. Urging it to her lips. "It doesn't matter. Drink. More," she demanded when Claire could manage only a tiny sip. She stayed at her side until the glass was half-empty.

Scrambling for some semblance of calm, Claire waved Janie away. "I'm fine. Finish your meal."

"Jax Martinson let a dog into the school this morning." Her daughter reseated herself. "A big, goofy-looking thing. It was pretty funny. Templeton was trying to catch it and fell on his butt, and the dog jumped on top of him, licking him like crazy . . ."

Aware of what her daughter was doing, Claire was nonetheless thankful for the change of subject. The story segued into talk of their Thanksgiving plans. With a mental start, Claire realized the holiday was less than three weeks away. They planned to spend it in Colorado skiing, but for the life of her, she couldn't recall if David had selected a specific location yet. She half listened to Janie chat about bringing Alyvia along—that much she remembered agreeing to—as she searched her memory. Could come up with nothing.

"I'll probably have to rent stuff once we get to Breckenridge." Janie pushed her plate away and looked expectantly at Claire. "I mean, I'm sure my skis are okay, but my boots and ski pants were too small when we went last year."

Breckenridge. Of course, she remembered now. They'd tried Vale and Aspen. David and Janie had wanted to try somewhere different. "We may as well buy you new." She managed a smile for her daughter. "You can start looking online, but you'll have to hurry in order to get it delivered in time." Shopping was something Claire had once adored, but Janie had never been a fan of going store to store, browsing. Overly pushy sales clerks could send her daughter's social anxiety into overdrive.

"Okay." Rising, Janie started to collect the dishes. "I'll clean up, Mom."

"No, you go ahead." Claire shooed her away. "There isn't much, and afterward I'm going to watch a little TV until your dad gets home." The chore would give her something tangible to focus on.

As her daughter left the room, Claire quickly cleared the table and carried dishes to the kitchen. Her inability to remember where they were heading to ski had rattled her more than a little. That was happening more and more frequently these days. That, and the time slipping away from her. How much had she drunk today? Not much, she concluded as she loaded the dishes in the dishwasher. She was always careful about drinking when she took the pills, and she'd taken two of those today. Or was it three?

The mental question had her sagging against the counter. When had she become so weak? So dependent? The easy answer lay in Kelsey's disappearance, but with a rare flash of self-honesty, Claire knew it had begun far sooner. She'd always been the strong one in her family. Capable. She'd needed to be after her father left, with her mother working all the time to support Claire and her two younger brothers. She'd been in charge of meals and babysitting the boys. Bath time, homework, laundry, packing lunches . . . it had all fallen to Claire. And she'd handled it along with high school and junior college with an ease she envied now.

David had seemed like a white knight when she met him. Strong and confident. So sure of his place in the world. And so attentive. After years of being the caretaker, maybe she'd enjoyed being pampered a bit. She'd worked right up until the time she'd had Kelsey, but David had suggested she not go back to her job afterward. They hadn't needed the extra income by then, and Claire had been all too happy to immerse herself into making a home for them. The part-time nanny had been a present that Christmas, so she could have some time to herself and with her friends. The bigger house and Marta had come later. And with each new acquisition, there had been less and less for which Claire had to be responsible.

Maybe that had started the slow leak of her former independence. And at the time when she'd most needed strength, she'd found her reservoir nearly depleted. She pushed away from the counter, angered at the thought, slammed the dishwasher closed, and crossed to the oven. When Kelsey had vanished, she'd leaned on David. That had been natural, hadn't it? But he'd been able to draw on the well of resolve he'd always possessed, while she'd been left clinging to the remnants of who she used to be.

The roast looked lovely; the glaze she'd added was browning the top nicely. Claire covered it again and busied herself tidying up the kitchen, trying—and failing—to silence the thoughts buzzing in her head like angry little bees.

She wasn't proud of who she'd become since Kelsey had disappeared. Any more than she was proud of lying to her daughter this evening. For years, she'd been dodging the memory of that envelope. And when she couldn't avoid it, she convinced herself she'd done the right thing at the time.

Finally, out of things to clean, Claire carefully folded the damp dishcloth she'd been using over the faucet. There were times, blessedly infrequent, when she couldn't avoid second-guessing herself. Couldn't evade the one nagging question that had never gone away.

What would have happened if she *had* been completely honest with the investigators?

David Willard

November 6
6:48 p.m.

"Agent Foster." David let the man in the rear entrance to the office building, his gaze going over the agent's shoulder to scan the darkened back lot. It was vacant, save the two vans that would belong to the cleaning crew. The sight had a measure of tension seeping from his muscles. "I appreciate your flexibility. I don't imagine you normally keep these kinds of hours."

Mark stepped inside and gave a slight shake, sending drops from the light mist falling outside flying from his leather jacket. He followed David through the dimmed lobby to the bank of elevators. "You keep late hours yourself, especially for a Friday night."

"Hazard of the job." David managed a tight smile as they walked into the elevator and turned as the doors closed noiselessly.

They rode up to the fifth floor in silence. Once they stepped out of the elevator, Mark looked around. "Nice place."

"We just had our offices renovated last year." David led him past the front desk, through his darkened outer area, past Traci's space and into his office. He immediately regretted inviting the man here. His presence tainted the space. Awakened memories of Kelsey's investigation—memories he'd sought to bury. But he'd had no choice. The man wouldn't be put off. "Almost makes up for the hours I have to keep sometimes. Something to drink?" He crossed to the mini fridge.

"I'll take a water. Thanks." David could hear the man moving around the room as he withdrew two bottles from the fridge. When he rose and turned around, he found the agent studying the long, polished mahogany table, littered with the products of his current project. "Here you go." He crossed to Mark and handed him a bottle, then led him to the couch and chairs near the windows.

"Thanks again for shoehorning me into your schedule." Mark sank into the chair as he opened the bottle, took a swig. "I really didn't want to wait until Monday to talk to you."

"Better here than at my home," David said candidly. "This DeVries girl's disappearance has my wife pretty upset. She's been . . . emotionally fragile for the last few years."

"I can imagine anyone would be after what you both endured." The sympathy in the agent's expression looked sincere. "We're taking another look at your daughter's case. I hate to remind you of that time again, so I'll be as brief as I can." The agent took a notebook out of his coat pocket, flipped it open. It didn't escape David's notice that he didn't promise not to speak to Claire.

"The report indicates that Kelsey left home on her bike."

"Yes. She and Claire had argued, and Kelsey stormed out. It was unusual for her, but she was fourteen. All hormones, you know? Up one minute, down the next." David stopped and took another drink of water, the next words hard to summon. "We never saw her again."

"Had she mentioned any new friends? Someone she'd met online?"

Impatient, David shook his head. "Nothing like that, and Kelsey probably would have. She was always the talkative one."

"Except there had been a change in her behavior recently."

Mark's words were like a dash of ice water, and acted like a wake-up call. David cursed himself mentally for lowering his guard. The man's congenial attitude might be the polar opposite of Hal Miller's years ago, but he was cut from the same cloth. And who knew what was included in Kelsey's investigative file? If it had included Miller's biases, that would put this visit in a whole different light.

"Like I said, Kelsey was fourteen." He slid the nail of his thumb under the label of the bottle, loosening it. "Bubbly one minute, moody the next." He manufactured a smile. "I'm told teenage daughters and drama go hand in hand." He spoke more from practice than memory. Seven years had chipped away at his recollections of his eldest daughter. Sometimes a sliver of recall would filter through, and he could hear her laughter, see her smile as vividly as if all the intervening years had disappeared. But in the next moment, it would slip away like a wisp of fog. And he'd be left with pictures, videos, and oft-repeated memories to fill in the shadows left by her absence.

"Your daughter's school counselor was concerned about her change in behavior." The agent tipped the bottle to his lips, his gaze watchful over it. "Her grades had slipped a bit. Her teachers noted the moods, too."

"But they weren't able to suggest what might be causing it." David knew that because several of them had sought them out after Kelsey's disappearance to tell them as much. "None of her friends could shed any light on where she might have been heading, what might have been on her mind . . ." His voice tapered off, a familiar guilt flickering. As Kelsey's father, it had been his responsibility to make his daughter's world right. But family life was always far more complicated than any parenting books would lead one to believe.

Driven to move, he surged to his feet, drank the rest of the water and then crossed to the trash can in the corner to drop it in. When he shoved his hands into his pants pockets, his fists were clenched. "You think the missing girl has something to do with Kelsey's case?"

Mark cocked a brow. "Two girls of a similar age disappear from smallish towns twelve miles apart, we have to look for possible connections. I realize this is difficult for you." The concern in his voice sounded genuine. David didn't buy it. "Bringing up the past is painful. But maybe they knew some of the same families. Or you and the other parents had similar acquaintances."

David's shoulders slumped slightly as he experienced an overwhelming sense of déjà vu. There was a special type of hell reserved for parents who'd lost a child. An infinite invitation to suffering. "Claire and I both provided exhaustive lists of everyone we'd ever met. As did Janie. I was told the people checked out."

"Would you be willing to fill out another?" Mark asked. "Of anyone you've met since then, either socially or through work? And your wife and daughter, as well."

Wearily, David nodded, though he was uncertain about mentioning this to Claire. The last thing his wife needed was verification that her fears had been realized, and they were looking for similarities between the DeVries girl and Kelsey.

"I can promise that we're following up on every single link we find, no matter how remote. Which is why I'm asking if you knew Whitney DeVries." At David's head shake, the man continued. "Brian DeVries? He's a deputy for Fenton County."

"No."

"Shannon DeVries?"

David started to shake his head again, then stopped. "Claire knew . . . her mother-in-law, I think. My wife attended church over there for a period of years." He lifted a shoulder. "I'm not religious, so Claire would take the girls, when she could force them to go."

"So she'll be on the list your wife filled out seven years ago." Foster was scribbling in his notebook.

"She might be. We both did as well as we could, but we were pretty shell-shocked at the time."

"Of course." The agent nodded, then looked up expectantly. "Mr. Willard, I'm dotting all my *i*'s here. That's why I'm going to ask where you were last week on the night of October 30."

The words seemed to hang in the air, as if coming from a distance. Then they hurtled closer to slam into him with the force of an oncoming locomotive. "Where was I? I can tell you where I wasn't. I wasn't in Saxon Falls. I wasn't ripping another family's daughter away from them. I wasn't condemning the DeVrieses to the same hell my wife and I have been in for seven fucking years." His voice cracked, and he stopped, aware that he'd been shouting. "God almighty, you people never let up."

The agent was watching him with a calm, gray gaze that seemed to miss nothing. "I don't blame you for your reaction, but I want you to think about something. If this girl's disappearance *is* related to Kelsey's, we've got fresh leads. New sets of eyes. Solving Whitney DeVries's case might mean solving your daughter's. We'll be talking to every single person mentioned in Kelsey's investigation, as well as in the new case." He paused for a moment before going on. "And I'll be putting that same question to dozens more before it's over."

David turned half-away, tried to bring himself under control. No doubt the agent considered his response damning, but good God, how much would ever be enough?

What do you mean you can't recall what your last conversation with your daughter was about? Seems like at a time like this, Mr. Willard, a father would be playing those words over and over in his mind.

Forty minutes? You waited forty minutes after your wife called you to go look for your daughter? Pretty concerned, were you?

Funny, you say you drove around looking for Kelsey for hours, but no one recalls seeing your vehicle . . .

"I was in Columbus." He forced the words out, aware the other man was staring at him. "I'm there for a long weekend every other week with either the CEO or accounts director, meeting with clients. Socializing. The firm uses the Fairview on North Sixteenth." He strode to the file cabinet tucked next to his desk. Pulled open a drawer and rummaged through it, bringing out a folder. Flipping through the papers inside, he drew some out. Walked back to the agent and thrust them at him. "Here are copies of the receipts we turned in to accounting for the hotel and meals. We hosted six guests at Morton's Steakhouse Saturday night. I can make duplicates if you need them."

"No need." The man closed his notebook and tucked it away, drawing his phone out of his pocket. He took the sheets and snapped pictures of each before peering more closely at the signature on the receipts. "Kurt Schriever. Is he the CEO or the accounts director?"

"Schriever owns the company," David said shortly. "He's the CEO." He took the receipts that Mark handed back to him. Barely managed not to wad them into a tight ball and hurl them at the man.

"I appreciate your cooperation, Mr. Willard. If you give me your e-mail address, I'll send you the lists of acquaintances your family filled out so you can update them and e-mail them back."

He turned and walked to his desk, setting the receipts on top of it, and grabbed a business card and pen. At the moment, he would have promised the man anything to get rid of him. He scrawled his home e-mail address on the card and went back to hand it to the agent.

"Thank you." Mark slipped it into the pocket of his coat as he rose. "And I apologize for dredging up memories of your family's tragedy." He headed for the door. "I can show myself out."

The company's security protocol dictated that David should have seen him downstairs and out the rear entrance. But he was frozen in place, buried under an avalanche of the past. Mark was full of shit. Like he could summon memories that never really were gone to begin with, no matter how hard David tried to lock them away.

Finally able to move, he strode to the mini bar, poured three fingers of Scotch into one of the heavy, leaded glasses. The first scorch of liquor burned all the way down. He drained the glass, welcoming the hot pool it made in his stomach.

God, how he hated that this time Claire was actually right, or close to it. The cops were considering whether the two cases were related. And it would start over again, *had* started over again, and this time, it might completely consume them both.

He considered the empty glass in his hand. *Claire.* He couldn't face her now, not after what just happened. He needed time to consider just how he was going to prepare her for the visit she would undoubtedly receive from Agent Foster. Despite the man's attempts at sympathy, David knew there was no chance Mark wouldn't follow up with her.

A familiar need was flooding through him, for escape, for *distance.* He needed time. Time to tuck the guilt away, to feel normal again. To distract himself from the stark and gray world that his life here had become. Claire inhabited that world every day. Sometimes David thought she didn't want to leave it.

But he did. And he had.

As if propelled, he went to the closet and took out the bag of extra clothes he kept here. Slipping into his wool overcoat, he went back to his desk, picked up his cell, and shut off the lamps. He was dialing a familiar number as he walked out of his office, pausing to lock the door with his free hand.

"Yes, Claire. Something's come up. No, it's work." He secured the door leading into the outer office and strode to the elevator. "A major wrinkle with one of the Columbus accounts. I'm on my way there now. Probably all weekend, I'm afraid. Yes. I know. Tell Janie I'll call her later."

The elevator pinged, and he walked into it as he slipped the cell into his pocket, relief filling him. Turning, he fixed his gaze on the panel, willing the lift to move faster.

And tried not to think about what a son of a bitch he was.

Special Agent Mark Foster

November 6
7:30 p.m.

At Mark's entrance, Ben Craw looked up from the long table he'd had brought into his motel room and grunted. "I gave up on you hours ago and went out for a bite."

Setting the pizza box down on the desk tucked in the corner of the room, Mark unzipped his coat and slipped out of it, hanging it on the back of the desk chair. "It took longer than I thought it would to get David Willard to make time for an interview today. But no worries. I'm hungry enough to eat the whole pie myself." He flipped open the lid of the box and placed a wedge of pizza onto one of the paper plates the restaurant had included. Turning, he strolled back to the table, studying the papers strewn across it as he lifted the piece of pizza to his mouth and bit into it. "Oh, my God." The explosion of taste had his eyes closing in ecstasy. He took another greedy bite. "This is amazing."

Craw slid a glance at him. "Get a hold of yourself, Foster."

Both he and the other agent resided in London, about a half hour from Columbus and an hour and a half away from West Bend. As long as there were active leads to follow in this case, they'd be working it from here. The senior agent had had one of the beds removed from the room to make space for the table. On the wall behind it were notes and graphs relating to the case. The information posted there was evolving by the day. Mark hooked the free folding chair with his foot, pulled it out, and sank into it. "Seriously. I'm having a foodgasm. You know how long it's been since I've had pizza? Kelli's had me on the healthy eating kick for months. And as a former pizza connoisseur, this rates among the best I've ever had."

The other agent's look became more assessing. "What is that? Sausage?"

"Three meat, double cheese with mushrooms." Mark wolfed down the rest of the slice, rose, and went back for more. "You'll be sorry you didn't wait."

"I could eat. Bring me a slice."

Mark returned with a second plate and handed one to Ben. "You sure? It's got pepperoni on it. I thought that gave you indigestion."

"Everything gives me indigestion these days. This case is no exception."

They ate in silence for several minutes as Mark unabashedly scanned the screen of Craw's open laptop, which displayed new case details. Craw finished first, belched indelicately, then went for a second slice, unceremoniously dumping another on Mark's plate when he returned. "So, how was Willard?"

"About what you'd expect." Polishing off his second piece, Mark turned his attention to the third. "Visibly unhappy to see me and far unhappier by the time we were through." It was part of the job, but the task had given him no pleasure.

Craw grunted as he set his slice down, half-eaten, and rubbed at his chest.

"Is he alibied this time around?"

According to the Kelsey Willard file, her father had been working late when his wife had called to tell him the girl was missing. "Time will tell." Mark set his plate down and wiped his fingers with a napkin before he pulled his cell from his pocket. Finding the pictures of the receipts Willard had shown him, he handed the cell to Craw. "He spends a four-day work weekend twice a month on firm business in Columbus."

The other agent flipped through the photos before handing the phone back. "Gives us a place to start. The hotel shows a check-in time of six o'clock Thursday night and a checkout time of eight a.m. Monday. Columbus is only ninety minutes away, so that doesn't eliminate him by any means. How'd he seem to you?"

"Tense. Frustrated. Defensive. Sad." Mark punctuated the words with bites of the pizza. "All in all, about what you'd expect, having the worst trauma of his life brought up again. He's not eager to have us talk to his wife. Got the feeling she hasn't recovered from her daughter's loss." That sparked another thought, and he peered more closely at the poster he'd constructed and taped to the wall that detailed the connections between the Willard and DeVries disappearances. Even after four days, it was depressingly scanty. "He did say Claire Willard used to attend the same church as Brian DeVries's mother."

Craw looked interested. "The grandmother, huh? Brian and Shannon said they didn't attend any church regularly."

"Neither does David Willard. But he mentioned that his wife took the girls with her sometimes."

The other agent nodded. "Gives you something to follow up with the families. I finally got the chance to interview Whitney's best friend, Macy Odegaard. She knew about the supposed online romance between Whitney and Patrick Allen from the beginning. But I didn't get much that we didn't already know. The girl did mention a couple of times that Brian DeVries was pretty strict." The man lifted a beefy shoulder. "Again, we got that from their communications. But it's obvious why the victim might have been easily convinced to keep the relationship under wraps." He reached into the breast pocket of the suit coat he still wore and thumbed a Tums out of its wrapper, popped it into his mouth. "Far more interesting information from the DeVrieses' financials. Brian DeVries has made an annual cash withdrawal on his credit card in the amount of five thousand dollars for the last three years. Still has nearly that much in the outstanding balance. That happens when you make only the minimum payment. The interest on those advances is outrageous."

Mark straightened. "And you asked him about that." It wasn't a question.

Craw folded the edges of the paper plate over the rest of his slice and leaned down to stuff it in the wastebasket below. "Swung by to see him on my way to dinner. Guess it would be fair to say he wasn't happy to see me. Less happy when I left, I'm guessing. Said he was paying off a bet to a friend. Guy by the name of Dane Starkey."

"Think he's got a gambling problem?" That would open up a whole host of leads to follow up on. A cop with a vice exposed himself to lots of complications, the most damaging of which would be his vulnerability to blackmail.

"Swore he isn't. Bet on a game when he had too many beers and got in way over his head. Says it's paid in full now. I'll follow up with the other guy. He's out of Columbus."

"Bookies don't extend installment plans."

"But maybe a friend did so he could pay a bookie. Or maybe it's exactly the way he said."

The two exchanged a look. *Nothing's ever exactly as it seems.* It was one of Craw's favorite sayings. So they'd tug on that string and see where it led.

"Why is DeVries paying the minimum on a credit-card debt that size every month? They have money issues?"

"Wondered how long it'd take you to come up with that." The agent looked pleased with himself. "They live paycheck to paycheck from the looks of it. The younger kid, Ryan, had issues when he was born. Ended up in the NICU for a couple of weeks and had three heart surgeries before he was two. Insurance barely covered half. Their monthly hospital payment is bigger than the one for their house."

Sympathy flickered. There wouldn't be much a parent wouldn't do to save a child, even going into massive debt. "So we'll follow up. See if the Willards had a link to the hospital or to DeVries's bet buddy."

His mind went to the moments he'd spent in Whitney's bedroom talking to her mother. "The DeVries girl took dance lessons," he said abruptly. Craw swiveled his head to stare at him. "They didn't think to include that fact in their original statement because she'd quit months ago." Omissions like that were a constant frustration and could stymie an investigation. "I've got the teacher's name, and I'll talk to her, the kids in her classes, and their parents. Maybe there were local competitions that both victims had been involved in, too." He hadn't gotten that far with Shannon DeVries, but he would.

He paused, searched carefully for his next words. "You said the Willard case was investigated as if linked to the Ten Mile Killer." Sensing the other agent was about to protest, he hurried on. "You also seemed to think that was a mistake. You probably heard how it all went down at the time, with your buddy working it. What made them think Willard was a TMK victim?"

Craw glowered at him for a moment, then grimaced. "They found his last victim four months before Kelsey Willard came up missing. That vic had been kidnapped two years earlier. Been exposed to the elements for months, but I can't say for how long. You ever hear of Luther Sims?" The name rang a distant bell. After trying and failing to retrieve the memory, Mark shook his head. The other man went on. "The closest thing to a profiler BCI had at the time. A senior special agent who'd probably taken a couple of classes at Quantico that got him elevated to expert status in the agency." His tone bore his disdain. "He's the one who worked on a victimology profile for the TMK victims."

"That wouldn't be rocket science, would it, given the way the killer dressed them at the end?"

"Exactly. But this Sims figured there were girls that hadn't been found." Craw tugged at his tie, which was already loosened. "The agency brought him in as a consultant on the case, and he was the one who said Willard fit the TMK's victim profile. Once that news got out, the media circus hampered every step of the investigation."

The same was true about many of the cases they worked. Mark kept that thought to himself. Media coverage could taint potential witnesses, or worse, lead to a flood of "tips" that proved to be a waste of legwork. Craw might be letting his friendship with the lead agent on the case color his view of how it played out.

As if reading his thoughts, the other agent insisted, "The focus of an investigation has to be free of preconceived ideas. You have someone inserted in the case that points the needle in a certain direction . . . you start looking at leads differently."

"So the agency pressured Hannity about how he handled the case."

"Not at first. But you can bet the postmortem on yet-another unsolved case was filled with finger-pointing."

Failure to capture the most notorious serial killer in recent Ohio history would have that result, Mark knew. Hannity might have been the latest scapegoat to sacrifice his career to that end. "But Kelsey Willard's body was never found. That should shed doubt as to whether she was ever a victim of the TMK at all." Mark's cell gave a familiar ring. He grabbed it from his pocket and rose to walk to the adjoining door. "I'll be back in a few. FaceTiming with my . . . hey, buddy!" Delight filled him as his son's face filled the screen.

"Dad! Guess what I saw! A fire truck. Firemen were cleaning it, and Dad, there was a dog! It had spots, and . . ."

Given Nicky's excitement about the events of his day, there was little required of Mark beyond an exclamation or occasional question. He was content to listen to his son's voice, see his chubby face alight with excitement. A bittersweet pang lodged deep in his heart. God, he missed everything about the kid. Tucking him in at night and the hilarious schemes the boy concocted to avoid sleep. Walking into his room later and sitting on the edge of the bed, watching him sleep. Longing swept over him. He missed his family.

"Have you caught the bad guy yet, Dad?"

"Not yet."

"You could have Spider-Man help you." Nicky's freckled expression was earnest. "He's got Spidey senses, and he'd know who was lying."

Something in Mark lightened. "Spider-Man?" He pretended to consider the suggestion. "I don't know. Seems like Daredevil is the better detective."

"You could get both of them! They could work together. And hey! Wolverine could help, too, because he could sniff out—"

"Time to tell Daddy good night, Nicky." He could hear Kelli's voice in the background. "Grandma's got your bath running with all your superheroes in it."

Mark's muscles went tight as his wife and son negotiated over how much time Nicky would be allowed to play. Glancing at his watch, he noted that it was already past the boy's normal bedtime. Apparently the schedule she adhered to so closely at their home in London was more flexible at her parents' house.

"Okay, bye, Dad. Love you!"

In a contest between further conversation and the prospect of a watery superhero battle, Mark was unsurprised to find himself on the losing end. "Bye, big guy. Kelli?"

His wife's face came on the screen. She looked good, as always, but her smile was strained, and the blue smudges under her eyes were darker than they'd been a couple of days ago. "Dad took him to the fire station today. He was pretty impressed."

"Sounded like it." He kept his voice carefully neutral. Conversations with his wife had turned into a minefield the last several months. A casual misstep could set off a detonation. "Is he being good for you?"

"He misses you." Mark drew in a breath at her admission. Her smile went wry. "He tells everyone we meet that his dad is a superhero with the NBC." They both laughed. Nicky had yet to master the acronym for Ohio's Bureau of Criminal Investigation. "How's the case?"

"Just starting to come together." Full days followed by evenings spent going over reports from different investigators—agency and local police entities—who were pursuing avenues as assigned by Craw. "How much longer are you planning to stay in Kentucky?"

"You wouldn't be home much if we were there, anyway."

He recognized the evasiveness in her answer for what it was. Mark *had* been home when Kelli and Nicky had left. But reminding her of that was one of those mines to be avoided, so he continued to step gingerly. "Have you given any more thought to going back to work?"

She'd mentioned it on and off for the last eighteen months, and he was starting to think it might be a good idea. It'd give her something to do besides sit home and brood all day, manufacturing paranoid doubts about their relationship. "You used to enjoy your work for the nonprofit before Nicky was born."

"My going back to work isn't going to magically solve our problems."

"It might be a good first step."

Kelli's mouth tightened. "Like my seeing Dr. Brewer again would be a good first step?"

That familiar feeling was back, carving a furrow in his chest. "He helped you with your emotions before . . ."

"When I had postpartum depression! This isn't a *me* problem, Mark. It's an *us* problem. You're never home, and when you are . . . there's such distance between us. Are you . . ." Her lips compressed as her throat worked for a moment. "Are you having an affair?"

A familiar feeling of helplessness swept over him, tinged with guilt. "No, of course not. God, how can you even ask me that? All I do is work and spend time with you guys. At least I did, before you hauled my son five hours away and refused to come home."

"Nicky's calling me. I have to go." His cell screen went dark when she disconnected.

"Fuck," he whispered viciously and whirled to kick at the bed. "God damn it." Kelli's accusation was a punch in the gut. But she was right about the distance between them. There'd been a time when they'd told each other everything, but somehow over the last year and a half, the words had dried up. There was a chasm between them, one he was helpless to breach. Every time he tried, he said the wrong thing, and the conversation ended before it really began. Their marriage was in trouble and had been for a while. The admission had his chest going tight. Maybe he'd handled it all wrong from the beginning. Hell, yes, he had. Things had gotten so uncomfortable that he'd delayed going home as soon as he could have some nights. They had to find a way to communicate, or Mark could predict exactly where his marriage was heading.

He stared at the phone clutched in his hand without really seeing it. Nothing brilliant occurred to him. Maybe when things wrapped up here, they should see a counselor. A professional might be able to steer them back to each other.

But first, there was a case awaiting him in the next room where he could make some forward progress. Slipping the phone into his trouser pocket, he turned on his heel, striding to the adjoining door, and reentered Craw's room. "Sorry, that took—" He stopped short, eyes widening. "Was it something I said?" Craw was dumping the contents of the dresser drawers into a suitcase open on his bed.

"Just got a call from Special Agent in Charge Bennett. An interagency task force has been formed to investigate the deaths of those Cincinnati police officers killed last week. I'm being reassigned."

"Now?" The gang-related shooting of three law-enforcement officers was big news in the state. Bigger, apparently than that of another missing girl.

Ben crossed to the closet and took out his shirts and suits. "Don't worry, another agent will take my place here soon. Until then, you'll have to juggle all the details yourself." The man winked at him as he folded the garments into the bag. "Consider this a learning opportunity."

"That shouldn't be a problem, as long as they get the new agent . . ." Comprehension dawned. "Aw, shit." Mark jammed a hand through his hair. "This means I have to handle the press." The older man's laughter did nothing to dissipate Mark's dismay.

"You've heard of the old public-speaking trick, haven't you?" The older man's tone was amused. "Just picture them all naked."

Whitney DeVries

November 8
5:53 p.m.

The music was all that saved her. When Whitney followed the films, she didn't have to think; didn't have to *feel.* There was only muscle movement. And by putting every ounce of effort into the activity, maybe later tonight she'd be exhausted enough to sleep.

Hands graceful in the air, she completed the double *en dehor* pirouettes and added her own twist at the end with a double piqué turn and came to a stop, chest heaving.

"*Very* nicely done. But that last bit wasn't part of the routine, was it?"

She barely started at the voice coming from the shadows. No longer wondered why she never heard him come in. A tiny frisson of fear started at her nape. She hadn't followed the film exactly. Would he punish her for that?

It seemed selfish to worry about herself when her mom, dad, and Ryan might be . . . *Don't think about that. Don't think don't think don't think!*

"I've been practicing my double piqués." It was a lie. The addition had been spontaneous, but talking was another form of distraction.

"For some reason, they've always been harder for me than the *en dedans* or *en dehors*." Some of the movements were particularly awkward with one of her wrists shackled to the barre. She had to move closer to it to effect enough slack in the chain to move more freely.

"Remember, the piqué is a turn, not a spin. And spot where you want to end. You must spot the front to finish *en face*."

It could have been Tami Jae lecturing her. Whitney peered out into the shadows, but as usual, the glare from the projector and computer screen prevented her from seeing anything. For the first time, the curtain of fear and misery parted enough to allow a sliver of curiosity. "Did you dance?" There had been a couple of boys in her classes over the years. Dweebs, both of them. Tami had shown them articles of football players taking ballet to help with their footwork, but those were definitely not the type Whitney had ever noticed around the dance studio.

"My mother was a ballerina with the New York City Ballet. That's her in the films. She was a rising star. When she had her family, she took up teaching."

"Did she teach you?"

"No." He sounded sort of mad now, and Whitney's newfound curiosity shriveled. Her body was healing from the beating, but only on the outside. Inside, she found herself reacting to every inflection in that hated voice. "She did instruct my sister, though. She was a quick learner, like you. Perhaps you'll end up being better than both of them."

Who the fuck cares! The words were a mental scream, stifled inside her. While the dancing had served as diversion, now, standing motionless, the seething knot of emotions were tangling and tightening inside her again. Ever since he'd shown her those news stories, she'd been on an emotional roller coaster, whipping from the pit of despair to climb the peak of hope once more. The stories had looked so real . . . was it even possible to fake something like that? Logically, Whitney knew that if it were, the freak had every reason to do it. He'd want her to feel alone, wouldn't he? She'd be easier to manipulate if she believed she had only him. That was why he made her call him Daddy. Out of some sick and twisted game he was playing where she was the pawn.

The thought had her fear solidifying into anger. She could beat him only if she stayed strong. Smart. If she kept him out of her head, where his words had taken up residence ever since he'd told her that her family was dead.

Her pulse jittered. He was lying about that. She had to believe that he was. Had to, or there would be no point in continuing to live.

"I've told you something personal." His words jerked her attention back to him. "I want to know you better. Tell me something about yourself."

Whitney stood paralyzed, her mind going blank for a moment.

"I . . . I broke my arm once. Fell off my bike."

"A broken arm? How unfortunate. That's a common childhood injury. I suffered one myself, although not from bike riding."

Maybe someone had broken it for him. Whitney found herself hoping that was the case. "It was pretty painful for a while. I had to have surgery to get pins in it."

"That's regrettable, but pain can provide us an opportunity to grow. As I believe you have in the last couple of days. I want you to realize, Whitney, that your hard work recently has not gone unnoticed. There will be an extra fifteen minutes of television allowed this evening. Unless there is another reward you'd prefer?"

Silently, she shook her head. What would she ask for? Her freedom? Her family back? Nothing else mattered.

"Tomorrow will be a hard day for you . . . the funerals of your family will be held. I'll do whatever I can to help you get through this. I hope knowing that you have me now will make it easier."

Like yanking a plug from a drain, her earlier inner defiance swirled away. *No.* A sob lodged in her throat, choking her. No, it couldn't be true. He was still lying. Trying to hurt her. Make her weak.

But despite the logic, her legs buckled, and she sank into a graceless heap on the floor. Anguish and disbelief revived their inner war, threatening to tear her apart.

"A loss like this is too much to bear alone. You must pray for acceptance and understanding. And gratitude that God, in his infinite wisdom, has provided you with a new family even as yours is laid to rest."

The sharp cry that wrenched from her then was unrecognizable to her ears.

"Pray with me now, Whitney." That voice. Relentless. Without mercy. "Our Father, who art in heaven . . ."

◆ ◆ ◆

She was incapable of thought. Like an automaton, she followed the guidelines that were already embedded after just a few days. Although she wanted nothing more than to collapse on the mattress, she sat cross-legged on the stage, blinded by tears and grief, staring at the TV shows that flickered on the wall in back of the stage. She hadn't eaten. She would have choked if she tried. And she couldn't bring herself to care what the freak might do to her when he found the leftover food.

Maybe he would kill her. She almost wished he would.

The tug-of-war of hope and desolation had been won for the moment. It was difficult to stir the ashes of her soul and find even a sliver of optimism. If he wasn't lying . . . *He had to be lying. He had to be!* But if he wasn't . . . she didn't want to live, either. And maybe she'd be in control of that. Because she'd caught a break even he didn't know about.

It had happened two nights ago as she'd lain awake, thoughts too much like these tumbling around in her head. A tiny clink had sounded nearby, metal on metal. The noise hadn't been unusual. The links on the chains that connected the handcuff on her wrist to the barre made a racket with the slightest movement.

She'd found the source of the sound the next morning when she showered. A screw had worked free of the base holding the showerhead in place. Whitney had picked it up and examined it, all the while looking over her shoulder, half expecting the freak to be there. Ready to punish her.

It had a flat head. It wouldn't take a Phillips screwdriver. She knew that much from helping her dad fix stuff in the garage when she was little, handing him the tools he needed. When she'd gotten older, they'd built stuff together, like birdhouses and window boxes. The screw was about two inches long with a pointed end. She'd tested the point on the skin inside her wrist. Broke skin. And in that moment, she had her first secret from the freak. A weapon, to be used either on him or on herself. The future would decide which.

It hadn't been until last night that a lightbulb had gone off in her head. The screw could be more than a weapon. It could also be used as a tool.

The show abruptly halted. Rubbing her swollen eyes, Whitney unfolded herself and rose, unable to recall what she'd been watching. There would be only a few minutes to brush her teeth and undress for bed before the computer and projector would switch off.

There was just enough laxity in the chain to allow her to move to the corner of the stage. It had dark curtains hanging along the front for about five feet, which provided a semblance of privacy. She brushed her teeth and then peeked into the shower.

The screw was still lying on the floor, where she'd left it after using it last night. She'd decided that leaving it in plain sight was the best defense. If it were found in her possession, she'd be punished, but she could always claim she hadn't seen it. *Plausible deniability.* Her dad's voice sounded in her head so clearly when she'd found it that he could have been standing beside her. He always said that when she and Ryan were arguing over which of them was at fault for some accident in the house. *If you're going to make up a story, make it a good one.*

The lights turned off. The darkness was broken only by the splinter of moonlight bordering the black curtain that covered the lone, small horizontal window near the ceiling in the back corner of the stage. It didn't matter. The task Whitney had begun the previous evening could be accomplished by touch alone.

The walls surrounding the stage were brick. Solid. But the flooring was two-inch wooden strips. If she could pry up one of those slats, she'd be armed with something far more formidable than a screw.

She wasn't yet sure if she wanted to die. But there wasn't a doubt that she wanted *him* to.

"He could be lying. He's a liar," she whispered. It did little to push aside her fog of grief, but the sound of her voice comforted her. "I'd know if they were gone. I'd feel it." The screw tightly clasped in one fist, she exited the shower stall and got down on her hands and knees beneath the window. Painstakingly, she counted each seam over to the sixth strip, where she'd left off last night. With her fingernails, she felt along each edge of wood, searching for the slightest opening. When she found one, she'd stop, wedge the point of the screw in it, and try to leverage the board upward.

Mindless activity. Like the dancing today, the task kept her brain occupied with something other than the awful thoughts that wanted to intrude. She already knew she'd be unable to sleep. So instead, she spent the night hours in a blind, tactile dance. Each time she was unsuccessful, she moved on.

"You just never give up, Whit—do you?" It was her mother's voice in her head this time. "You get your mind made up, and nothing and no one can change it." Whitney didn't remember what had brought on her mother's exasperation that time, but it was true. Once she'd settled on something, she didn't give in. Like when she was convincing her parents to let her quit dance. Or fighting for a later curfew. *That* had been a battle she hadn't won. The memories had her pausing for a moment to wipe her eyes on the sleeve of her leotard.

She had to move the mattress in order to check the flooring beneath it. Her movements were getting clumsier now with exhaustion. After this section she'd put the screw and the mattress back in place and try to sleep. Tomorrow night she'd start again. And the night after that.

The crack she found between the boards was the fourth slat inside the area where her mattress normally sat. Fumbling for the screw, she stuck its tip into the crack and pried upward. When the board came loose without friction, the screw slipped and sliced into her palm. She couldn't prevent a sound of pain, which she quickly bit off.

A long breath shuddered from her. She'd lost track of time, but it had to be the middle of the night, and the freak wasn't near. She didn't know where he went after he visited her, but he had never returned before morning. The tension eased from her spine, and she wiped the blood she could feel welling on her hand on her tights. Then she lifted the board completely out of the floor. Examined it.

It was no more than two feet in length and a half inch thick. As a club, it wouldn't do much damage, but there were wicked nails on the interior of either end that might. Whitney sat back on her heels and considered her unexpected success. Now that she had one slat loose, it should be easier to loosen another. And where one board might not be a lethal weapon, two together would be.

Setting the strip down, she slipped her fingers into the two-inch crack she'd discovered. And immediately touched something foreign.

She yanked her fingers back. That small sliver of light around the curtain didn't spread this far. The hole she'd uncovered was shrouded in darkness, like most of the rest of the stage. Swallowing hard, she shoved her fingers back inside the fissure, ran them along the object inside. It felt like . . . paper.

Drawing it out, she scooted with it back over to the window, uncaring for the moment that the movement had the links of chain clanking. Once at the wall, she could see the paper was white and rolled up like a scroll. When she unrolled it, she realized it wasn't one sheet. It was several. And they were covered with writing.

She could read only the part lit by the tiny slice of light, so she had to painstakingly move the sheet from left to right along the concrete bricks to make out the words.

My name is Kelsey Willard.

If someone's reading this, I'm probably dead.

Janie Willard

November 9
3:33 p.m.

A distant sound in the house had Janie's gaze jerking up from the laptop, her body stilling as she strained to make it out. It had come from downstairs. The sudden tension seeped from her shoulders. Her mom's note had said she had gone to one of her do-gooder church activities. It was probably just Marta leaving.

She took a moment to straighten the pile of pillows she'd been propped against. Stretched out on the bed, Janie had her old computer before her, a notebook at her side. The desk would have been more comfortable, but sitting at it would have given a person coming in her room a clear view of the screen. And she didn't want anyone to see the site she was on.

She didn't want to be seeing the site she was on.

Setting her jaw, she returned to her chore. Clicking on each thumbnail, studying the face of the girl—they were all girls—closely before moving on. Since Friday, she hadn't been able to forget the picture Cole Bogart had shown her from this site. The image had replayed over and over in her brain, intertwining with the conversation she'd had with her mom. Something had compelled her to set aside the homework she'd planned and take a closer look at the site. And she'd made a discovery then that kept her returning to the task over and over throughout the weekend.

Heather Miller wasn't the only girl she recognized on the web page.

Compared with the tiny sound she'd heard moments ago, the next was a sonic boom. And instantly recognizable. The peal of the doorbell, followed by voices and footsteps thundering up the stairs to her room. Alyvia barreled inside like a cotton-candy-haired Tasmanian devil, laptop clutched to her chest.

"Oh, my God, you have a devious mind. I think I'm rubbing off on you. Except this never would have occurred . . . move over."

Obligingly, Janie made space on the bed, and her friend sat beside her, her legs stretched out next to Janie's. "Whose computer did you borrow?"

"Tank's." At Janie's expression, Alyvia's face went angelic. "What? I knew he had his own and that he'd loan it to me, no questions asked."

Tank Morgan was a loser, a fifth-year senior, who spent far too much time hanging around Alyvia. Janie knew he was the one her friend had gotten drunk with last week. He appealed to the other girl's worst instincts and was the single biggest impediment to her getting the diploma she claimed she wanted. As if life didn't throw enough obstacles in her path, Alyvia had a habit of hauling in more to trip over.

"He doesn't do anything without expecting something in return."

"Story of my life, girl. Look here . . ." She shifted to dig into the pocket of her oversize army surplus jacket and pulled out a folded sheet of paper. "I spent four hours online last night after you called. I came up with eight numbers."

"Eight?" Her stomach clenching, Janie picked up the notebook at her side and compared the names and numbers she'd jotted down with the ones her friend had noted. "I recognized these six." She stabbed a finger at each of Alyvia's entries in turn. Each model in the pics on the site was assigned a number. Subsequent pictures of the same girl had a letter affixed after them. "From what I can figure out, the owner of this site must charge by the download. You can even buy credits to use on it at a slightly cheaper rate."

"Sure." Alyvia bobbed her head. "For the pervert bargain hunters. Makes sense. Okay, let's see." She studied the two pages aligned together. "How did you guess that Heather's bosomy buddies would be on here, too?"

"I didn't." Because her voice was husky, Janie cleared it. "I really thought Ferin probably uploaded some personal pics. But I thought it was worth checking to see if I knew anyone else on there. I mean, the list of girls he's hooked up with would fill volumes." From what she'd heard, the guy was a walking STD. "If he'd done it to Miller, it figured that he would have to others, too."

"Good thought, but it doesn't appear likely. Unless you think he's also banging Molly Stabe and Erin Forwith." The two girls were usually inseparable from Miller. "Which I'm sure he'd be into, but I doubt the bitchacrite would approve. I about shit myself when I saw them on there. Do you know Stabe is still in Girl Scouts? At her age? But that definitely wasn't a Scout sash covering her hoo-ha."

Janie's mouth quirked. Alyvia could always make her smile. "Kaylee Cross is on there. She graduated three years ago. And these two." She tapped a couple of other names on her page. "I recognize them but don't remember their names. They're older, too. Maybe graduated with Cross or the year after."

"Tabitha Downing and what's-her-face. Babs, I think they called her. Huntsman. Yeah, I think you're right. Three years ago. These other two on my list? One is Deedee Bakker. She was in the Kisser's foster home with me for a few months. Remember when I had to live in Akron?"

Janie did. Two years ago, there had been no home available in West Bend, and Alyvia had been placed across the state. That had lasted for a few months until she'd been returned to her mother's care—for the last time. In a drug-induced frenzy, Sheila Naughton had stabbed her daughter for eating the last frozen pizza, and authorities had removed Alyvia for good after that. "Where is she now?"

Alyvia gave her a look. "Like we're pen pals? Who the hell knows? And this last one I recognized . . . I don't know her name. But I'm pretty sure I've seen her before. Last summer, at a party at the lake house."

The lake house was a home outside of town built on a wooded lot edging a man-made lake. The most elaborate home in the vicinity, it had stood vacant for years since its owners had gone through a bitter divorce. The story Janie had heard was that the husband refused to sell it because he'd have to split the proceeds with his ex. It was more likely that no one around here could afford it. At any rate, the small beach behind it was a frequent site for keggers, and every year someone at the high school seemed to acquire a key to the place and hosted parties until the cops shut it down again.

Alyvia went silent then for a moment before saying, "So . . . what do we do with this? I mean, it's interesting and all, especially finding Miller and her posse on it, but unless you want to make her pics public . . ." She held up a hand to squelch Janie's protest. "Not arguing—much—but if not, it's a big nothing burger."

Avoiding her friend's gaze, Janie returned her attention to the screen in her lap. "I don't know," she admitted. "I thought . . . maybe that girl might be on here. Whitney DeVries."

Her friend's head swiveled toward her. "Why would you think that?"

Janie's shrug was defensive. "I didn't really . . . I just wondered if I'd see anyone else I knew. Someone might have stolen these from the cloud or whatever. That's a crime."

"Yeah. And that someone might have been Bogart. Which makes him a douchebag, but we already knew that, and again, who cares?"

A familiar anxiety spread through her. "I figure between the two of us, we're more than halfway through. You know me. When I start something, I have to finish it." Not exactly a lie, especially now.

Alyvia sighed. "I don't have much time. The FPs went to conferences, and I figure when they get back, I'm going to get grounded, no matter how much ass I kissed last weekend. I thought maybe we could go to the mall. Hang out."

"I have an appointment with Dr. Drake at four forty-five." The thought was accompanied by dread. After a prolonged battle with her mother, she'd graduated to telephone appointments for the most part in the last few months. But the deal they'd struck meant Janie still had to visit with him in person a few times a year, and this was one of those times.

"Fine." Alyvia scowled. "I'm probably living on borrowed time, anyway. I'll go to the last number on the site and work toward you. How's that?"

Janie sent her a quick look, touched. "It's okay. You've helped enough."

Bending her head over the keyboard, Alyvia said, "Not as much you're going to help me with my chemistry homework. Pretty sure I have at least a half dozen late assignments. Also sure I'm going to hear about it shortly."

"I will. Promise." They worked in silence for forty-five minutes, until Janie's eyes started to burn. Her phone vibrated. That would be the alarm she'd set up to remind herself of the appointment. The dread pooling in her stomach was an outsize response to the upcoming meeting. She didn't mind Dr. Drake. Not really. What she minded was still having to see the man after fourteen years of therapy. She minded the niggling feeling she had that she was as cured as she was ever going to get. And Janie wasn't at all certain how cured that actually was.

"I gotta go." She lowered the lid of her laptop and looked at her friend. "Thanks a lot, Liv. I owe you. More than six chemistry assignments, probably." Her friend was staring at the laptop balanced on her knees as if transfixed. "I can throw in a study jam for the chemistry semester final, how's that?"

Only then did Alyvia look at her. And the expression on her face was terrible to see. "Liv?"

"I'm sorry. I wish I hadn't . . . oh, shit, Janie."

Her heart began to pound on cue. Following the direction of her friend's gaze, Janie leaned over and peered more closely at the screen. The world did a slow, nauseating spin. The girl in the picture was pretty. Dark-haired with a pout that showed she was comfortable in front of a camera. One hand was strategically placed in front of her crotch. The opened baby-blue sweater she wore was positioned to skim the edges of her nipples.

Janie recognized the photo. She'd seen it seven years ago.

It was her sister, Kelsey.

◆ ◆ ◆

"Did you drive here? Or get dropped off?"

Dr. Drake's question yanked Janie's attention back to him. "I drove. I told you last month, driving is going well. No anxiety." None, at least, that she couldn't overcome with a little self-talk and some deep breathing. She'd waited until she was sixteen and a half to take the state-mandated driver's education course, a full year later than most of her peers. But for her, tackling new experiences could come with unique challenges.

The mustache he was sporting was new. She wondered if he'd grown it to make up for the fact that his hair had thinned in the time since she'd begun seeing him. He smiled conspiratorially, showing a glimpse of very white teeth. "And how many cigarettes does it take before you start the car?"

He had her there. She lifted a shoulder. "Depends." And smiled back at him. She might have spent a great deal of her life resenting the need for therapy, but Janie had always liked him. And she was honest enough to admit that he'd gotten her through the worst time in her life.

His expression sobered. "I've wondered how the disappearance of the girl from Saxon Falls is affecting your family. It can't be easy to have the past dredged up again."

Her chest went tight. "It never is."

"I want you to remember the ways we've discussed coping during times like these. Insulate yourself as much as possible from the news. Find distractions. Focus on your future plans. And above all, reach out if it becomes too much." She had to look away from the intensity in his gaze. "There's no shame in any of that, Janie. You've come so far. The last thing we want at this point is for you to have—"

"I'm not going to have a *setback*." God, she hated that word and the memories that accompanied it.

"I wasn't going to say that." But she knew that he'd been thinking it. "Something so similar happening nearby is bound to summon memories of the most painful time in your life. There are healthy and unhealthy ways to deal with that. Use the healthy tools we've worked on over the years."

There was little she wouldn't do to avoid that topic. Searching for a change of subject, she asked, "Can I get your advice on something?"

Looking pleased, the doctor nodded. Before she could change her mind, she ran a carefully edited version of the pictures and the website by him. "Have you seen sites like that? Can the owner be traced, like if the police knew about it?"

"I'm familiar with sites like you describe. Some are actually fronts for some pretty dark stuff. Child prostitution, sex trafficking, you name it. Or the person behind the site might be gathering these images through illegal means, like hacking. There may be a chance some of these girls were coerced."

She thought about the pictures of Kelsey. There had been at least half a dozen photos in the envelope she'd found seven years ago. After one shocked glance through them, she'd focused on the money. "I think . . . I mean, I wonder if they're getting paid to do it."

Dr. Drake looked skeptical. "It's possible, of course, but sites like these are usually exploitive in nature. They exist for the gratification of others. It's doubtful they'd be paid at all or at least no more than a pittance."

A thousand dollars wasn't a pittance. A greasy tangle of nerves knotted in her belly, not unlike the feeling she'd gotten when she'd found that envelope under the mattress in her bedroom. She'd known immediately that Kelsey had hidden it there. It hadn't been the first time her sister had stashed something she wanted to keep from her mother's eyes in Janie's room. It had been a joke between them. The way Kelsey kept her bedroom was a guarantee there would always be someone poking around in it. Cleaning or just checking on the condition of the space before nagging Kelsey to pick it up. Janie's room was pristine by comparison.

"You seem really bothered by this." She refocused on the therapist. "The police should be alerted. With the girls you've already identified, they'd have a place to start by talking to the known victims and their families to see if they can get a lead on how the pictures ended up online. And more important, if any of the girls pictured were victimized in any way."

Her pulse went to ice. And abruptly, the mental scenarios she'd been working through for the last couple of days clarified. If her mother had been telling the truth about turning that envelope over to the state agents seven years ago, none of this would be new information. It would have all been part of the investigation.

But in the last few years, Janie had become an expert on Claire Willard's moods. And she knew when her mother was lying.

Claire Willard

November 9
4:40 p.m.

"Honestly," Barbara said with a sigh. "I think the citywide rummage sale is such a great fund-raiser, but is it my imagination or does the organization and pricing get more complicated every year?"

"It's not your imagination at all." Claire smiled at Barbara. "I struggled with how to even group some of the donations. I mean, a cardboard animal head?"

Barbara chuckled as she turned onto the private drive leading to Claire's neighborhood. "It's an eye-opener to realize what some will spend their money on."

"It'll probably be more so when we see how quickly those items go at the sale." The two laughed as Claire's house came into sight. She was feeling more than a bit pleased with herself. For the entire weekend, she'd been unable to shake the thoughts of the Claire who had existed prior to marriage. Everyone changed over the years, so it should be equally possible for her to shift back to that independent woman she'd once been. The one who had deftly juggled so many balls with little help from her overworked mother. This morning, Claire had taken a baby step toward that end when readying for the day. Just one yellow pill and the busyness of the subsequent hours had kept her engaged and focused. As successes went, it was miniscule. But it represented an accomplishment for her. Like developing long unused muscles, rebuilding her inner resolve would take time. The road to change would be paved with tiny steps just like these.

The fact that she was even considering the need to make adjustments was a monumental leap forward.

"I'm thinking of getting a job." The barely formulated thought somehow melded into words. "Maybe just something part-time at first. Certainly, I have the time." There'd be even more hours to fill next year. Before foreboding could form, she shoved the thought aside. Visions of how empty the house would be with Janie away could shatter her fledgling strength.

Barbara looked delighted. "That's an excellent idea. Volunteering can be fulfilling, but a job—especially one you enjoy—can really provide one with a sense of purpose. What do you think you'd be interested in?"

"I haven't gotten that far." Her pulse skipped a little just considering it. Maybe—hopefully—from anticipation as much from trepidation. "There's no rush. I'm just in the reflection stage at the moment."

"Well, I, for one, am all for . . ." Barbara's words trailed off as she swung into the drive. "That's not Janie's car out front, is it?"

Claire turned to look. "No. Janie would park in the garage, at any rate." At the thought of her daughter, she dug out her cell phone and checked to see if she'd received a recent text from her. But there was nothing since the one she'd gotten earlier, informing Claire that she'd gone to her appointment with Dr. Drake.

"Maybe just a salesman then. He's getting out of his car, see?"

As the two women exited the vehicle, Claire saw a dark-haired man rounding the hood of a gray sedan and heading for the drive. Inexplicably, nerves clutched in her belly.

"I'm looking for Claire Willard."

She could feel Barbara moving closer to her side and felt a moment's gratitude for her friend's ever-vigilant protectiveness. "I'm Claire Willard."

The man's smile made him look boyishly attractive. "I called a couple of times, but your maid said you were gone. I was on my way out of town and thought I'd swing by to see if you'd returned." He pulled off one glove and reached inside his coat to hand her something, which she took numbly. An official ID badge. "Special Agent Mark Foster, BCI. Is it okay if we go inside? I have a couple of questions for you."

Fifteen minutes later, Claire was seated on the edge of the sofa in the family room. Had she asked Barbara to stay? She couldn't recall. But the woman had accompanied them into the house, retrieved coffee from the kitchen, and was handing out mugs. Claire's fingers wrapped tightly around hers. Marta must have left for the day. The distant thought flickered. She always made a fresh pot before leaving. David liked coffee after dinner. He never seemed to suffer the side effects of drinking caffeine before bedtime.

"Mrs. Willard?" Belatedly, she became aware that both Mark and Barbara were looking at her. "I asked if it was okay to speak freely in front of your friend."

"Oh. Yes." She glanced at the woman by her side. "Of course. What's this about?"

The agent took some folded sheets from the interior pocket of his jacket. "I can't tell you how sorry I am to bring up difficult memories. But I'm sure you've heard of Whitney DeVries's disappearance. As I told your husband, we're looking at any connections to your daughter's case."

His words seemed to come from a distance. "My . . . husband?"

"Yes, when we spoke Friday. I'm sure he told you about our conversation." The man's smile was probably meant to be reassuring. "He was very helpful."

"Oh, yes, of course. I'm sorry." Managing a laugh, she brought the coffee to her lips. Forced herself to take a sip. She hadn't spoken to David since he'd called to say he would be away for the weekend again, although she knew he'd FaceTimed Janie. "The weekend can be so busy. I'd completely forgotten."

We're looking at any connections to your daughter's case . . .

The words bounced around in her head like an internal echo. The world seemed to tilt on its axis. After all this time. All the news stories she'd been so certain were linked in some way to Kelsey, it hardly seemed possible . . .

"This is something you filled out for the agents seven years ago." Somehow, he was in front of her. He opened the pages he carried and handed them to her before returning to his seat. "It lists all your relatives, friends, acquaintances . . . everyone you knew even peripherally at the time your daughter went missing. I'd like to ask you to look it over and update it."

She stared at the papers in her hand uncomprehendingly. "I don't understand. How would it help?"

"They'll check for names that appear on your and David's lists and those that Shannon and Brian filled out."

Barbara touched her arm. "This can be a good thing, Claire. It means looking at Kelsey's case, as well as this new one."

Her eyes filled. *A good thing.* Her mind was buzzing, her thoughts a jumble. But one thought rang through, clear as a bell. If the two cases were connected, finding Whitney DeVries might also mean finding Kelsey. The rapid surge of hope left her weak.

"Of course." Her voice was husky, so she took another drink. "Of course I'll update it." She'd do anything. Everything. Whatever it took for them to start looking into Kelsey's disappearance again. They'd have to, wouldn't they? If the agents were looking for links, that must mean they would comb through Kelsey's investigation. Maybe see something the other agents hadn't. Or chase a lead that hadn't been examined seven years ago. It had been a long time since she'd allowed herself to feel this sort of wild, burgeoning joy.

"Thank you. I know this is painful. What about your daughter? Janie? Is she home?"

Her mind abruptly blanked. "What? Why?"

Mark leaned forward in his chair, his hands clasped around the mug. "I've been reading through Kelsey's file. Janie was a child seven years ago. And her . . . disability . . . meant the agents weren't able to speak to her at the time. I thought now she might be in a better position to—"

"No!" As suddenly as the joy had come, it was replaced with rage, a hot, pulsing river of it. "No, you will not be talking to my daughter. She's still a minor. We can prevent you from speaking to her." Could they? Surely so. "You have no idea what she went through after Kelsey—" Her voice broke then, and she could feel Barbara slipping an arm around her shoulders. "The trauma was too much for her. She had a setback. Couldn't leave the house for almost two years. Couldn't go to school. We had to hire tutors." She shuddered at the memory of the double-edged tragedy: the one that had befallen the daughter they'd never seen again, and the other targeting the one who'd survived. "This can't affect her. I won't allow it."

"Janie still suffers from social anxiety," Barbara said from her side. "She's back in school, doing extremely well academically. But I'm sure her therapist would agree that drawing her in to the middle of this wouldn't be beneficial for her."

The man's expression was somber. "I didn't realize the ongoing nature of Janie's disorder. It's fine. I can get by without talking to her."

Until Barbara's arm tightened around her, Claire didn't realize she was shaking. In the last five years, Janie had made incredible strides. Had slowly transitioned into public school again. Then had gradually improved her attendance. Her participation and vocal responses. With her grades, it would be easy to forget that as far as she'd come, she still had miles to go to adjust to a socially interactive world. From Claire's conversations with Dr. Drake, she knew her daughter's anxiety would always remain with her, in some fashion.

They couldn't protect her from that. But Claire could, and would, guard her from anything that threatened to disrupt the growth she'd made.

"You've been through the hardest thing a parent could endure," the agent said. "My being here . . . bringing it up again is difficult. Believe me, I know that. Just a couple of questions, and I'll be out of your hair. Whitney DeVries disappeared October 30. That was a Friday night." He paused expectantly. "Do you recall where you were that evening?"

Claire raised a trembling hand to her forehead. Rubbed at an ache that had appeared there. "I . . . home, I guess."

"That would have been our Auxiliary Trick or Trunk night," Barbara put in. "Remember, Claire? Before the football game, in the high school parking lot."

Of course. "Now, I do. I left here . . . about three?" She looked at her friend for agreement. "We decided to buy more candy, although in the end, we had more than enough . . ." Her voice trailed off. "It was over by seven. I was home shortly after that."

"Who was here with you?"

"Ah . . ." Her thoughts were scrambled. "Just Janie. That was David's weekend in Columbus. My daughter's friend stayed the night. They were having a horror-show marathon. The *Halloween* ones, I think." She'd made herself scarce for the duration. Claire didn't need Hollywood's rendition of horror. She lived with her own.

He nodded. "Your husband mentioned that you had once attended the same church as Brian DeVries's mother."

"Yes, years ago." Claire couldn't recall the last time she'd been to church. The faith that she'd been raised with had seemed to slip from her grasp after Kelsey was gone. Just one more thing that had vanished with her daughter.

"And you took the girls?"

"Um . . . Kelsey more often than Janie, probably, but certainly both of them at times. Kelsey is the only one who attended any youth activities. That would have been very difficult for Janie back then." And wouldn't be a favored activity even now.

"What sort of activities?"

Claire tried to recall. Her mind was a hopeless jumble of thoughts. She sent a beseeching look to her friend, who put in smoothly, "There were youth church nights on Wednesdays. Bible school on Sundays, and I know our kids attended church camp at least a couple of summers together."

Seizing on the information, Claire nodded. "Yes, Kelsey refused to go back to camp after the second time. By twelve, she'd outgrown it, I think. The following year I switched to a church here in town. I wasn't really a fan of the new pastor who'd taken over a couple of years earlier. Even less of a fan of his wife." She sent an apologetic look to her friend. Barbara had been on the church board that had hired the Reverend Mikkelsen.

Mark looked at Barbara. "What about you, Ms. Hunt? Are you still a member of that church?"

"I am, yes. While I don't always agree with some of Reverend Mikkelsen's more conservative views, the church does a lot of good work for the community. I know Helen DeVries well and am acquainted with her daughter-in-law."

"And Whitney DeVries?"

"She's attended church occasionally with Helen. I've met her a time or two."

"Did she ever take part in the youth activities that your families did?"

Barbara smoothed her slacks with her free hand and took a sip from the mug she held. "I wouldn't know. I don't have children that age anymore, and I haven't been on the church board for years."

The man stared at her for a moment before snapping his fingers. "Barbara Hunt. I knew that name sounded familiar. You gave a statement after Kelsey Willard disappeared."

Claire stilled. She shouldn't be surprised. Anyone connected to their family would have been questioned. And as much time as she'd spent with Claire, Barbara had known her family well.

But something in the woman's face had needles of caution stabbing through her. "Yes."

Mark used his free hand to check both his coat pockets before finding a notebook and drawing it out. Expertly, he flipped it open and thumbed through it. Stopped for a moment to read before glancing up again. "You were the last on record to report seeing Kelsey Willard the day she disappeared."

Claire swayed in her seat. "You . . . you saw Kelsey? When? Where?" Barbara reached for her hand. She snatched it away. "You never told me that. Never. How could you not have told me that?"

Her expression tortured, the woman said, "I didn't see how it would help you to hear it. It was on Baltimore Street, about three miles from here. She was on her bike. I saw her for only an instant."

Kelsey's bike had been found much farther away than that. On Gilbert, just around the corner and down the block from the fire station. Which had been empty, because it was staffed by volunteers on an as-needed basis. Six miles from her house. The one Claire had forbidden her to leave. The one Kelsey had stormed out of, anyway.

You're not going anywhere, young lady. Not with that attitude. And not on a school night.

I wouldn't have an attitude if you weren't on my back about every little thing. She'd shoved her arms through the sleeves of her jacket, her jaw jutted in a way that was becoming all too familiar.

Honestly, you're just so mercurial these days. I don't see—

That's just it, Claire, *you don't see. You don't see anything, because you're blind!*

The slam of the door like a rifle shot sounding through the house. Her frantic calls to David, because of course, they had to go after her. Find her. But no one had ever found Kelsey. And Claire had been left to replay that final scene over and over in her mind, picking it apart for clues to a puzzle she'd never solved.

"Do you have anything to add to your original statement, Ms. Hunt?"

Barbara shook her head, looking miserable. The agent consulted his notes again. "One thing you said struck me. That you glimpsed Kelsey well enough to be certain it was her. And that she looked anguished."

The walls were pressing in on her, squeezing the air from the room. Claire bolted to her feet with a suddenness that had the coffee sloshing over the edge of the mug. "How could you?" The words were a furious hiss. "How could you keep that from me?" She and David had clung to every bit of information the agents had shared with them. Going over and over every word, wringing each detail to sift for precious news of their daughter. They'd certainly been told where Kelsey had last been seen.

But not by whom.

She looked anguished . . .

"Mrs. Willard, I don't think—"

"You have to leave now." It was an effort to put one foot in front of the other. The floor felt like quicksand shifting beneath her feet. Unsteady, she set the mug down on the end table as she went by. "Both of you. Go."

"Claire." Barbara rushed after her, catching up with her at the staircase. "It didn't change anything. And I was trying to spare you, that's all. You didn't need . . ."

With great effort Claire turned her head to look at the other woman. "You knew how desperate we were for every detail. Not sharing this with us . . . it was cruel. I told you how it felt for us to be kept in the dark by the police. The agents. For you to do the same thing, knowing that . . ." The taste of betrayal was bitter.

"I didn't. At least . . . I mean, David knew. He . . . we decided there was no use burdening you with it. It doesn't change anything."

There was a part of her that knew that was true. Kelsey had been so angry when she left the house. A sudden temper that had seemingly bubbled out of nowhere and escalated into inexplicable fury. Maybe that temper had fueled her energy to ride six miles across town. In God's name, what had happened to her normally sunny-dispositioned daughter?

"Maybe not." She turned, grasping the railing for the support she desperately needed and started upstairs. "But that wasn't your decision to make. Or David's. You should have told *me*."

David Willard

November 9
4:38 p.m.

David nosed his car out of the company parking lot, still riding a sense of euphoria. A coworker honked at him, and he lifted a hand in acknowledgment. A group of colleagues was heading to a nearby pub for celebratory drinks. They'd allowed him to beg off when he'd cited parent-teacher conferences that evening, only on the condition that he'd join them the following night. With the news they'd just gotten, David had no doubt that spirits would still be high the next day.

It was rare to leave one of Kurt's meetings with a glow, but learning that David and his team were up for no fewer than three awards on two different ad campaigns was enough to send his spirits skyrocketing. And not just any awards—one was for an EIA, the first such nomination in the history of the company. The showing was unprecedented.

It was a career-making achievement for him as creative director for each of the ads.

He stopped at a light, his fingers drumming lightly on the steering wheel. Even a very subdued Steve Grayson had congratulated him. The man knew as well as David did what the nominations would do for his clout with the agency and for his résumé. With Janie off to college next year, there was nothing stopping him from looking for a job with a bigger agency. Higher-profile clients. A more attractive salary package.

The light switched to green, and he pressed on the accelerator. A nomination wasn't a win, but a man in his position could daydream, couldn't he? He let himself do exactly that for the entire drive across town. Pulling into his drive, he parked in the garage and, grabbing his suitcase from the back seat, headed for the house, a spring in his step.

It was about damn time something in his life started going right.

◆ ◆ ◆

"Claire." He stopped dead in the doorway of their bedroom, his bag in hand. Irritation flickered. The room was dark. She was sitting on the edge of the bed, unnaturally still. "I thought you'd be ready. We have conferences tonight."

"You didn't tell me you'd spoken to Agent Foster."

Foster. His stomach plummeted. *Shit.* "I'd planned to tonight. Why, did he call?"

"He was here. When Barbara and I returned from setting up for the church rummage sale."

Son of a bitch. David strode to the bed, lifted the suitcase on it, and unzipped it. He'd told the man he hadn't wanted him at the house, hadn't he? Had informed him of Claire's fragile state. Apparently, that hadn't been direct enough. His earlier elation fading, he lifted two suits from the suitcase and carried them to the closet. "Did he ask about the church you used to go to in Saxon Falls?" When she didn't answer, he turned toward her. "Claire?"

"He said he was looking for connections between the two cases. Kelsey's and Whitney's. I knew. I've always known. I told you that day in your office."

She had. The same way she'd insisted that every news story in the nation about a missing teen was somehow linked to Kelsey. He supposed, given the law of averages, at some point she was bound to be right. "They *might* be," he emphasized. "But at least they'll be taking a look at Kelsey's case again." Although he couldn't say he was any more impressed with Mark than he'd been with the cops and BCI agents seven years ago. "It doesn't mean they'll find anything new. Or that they'll keep us abreast of developments as they arise." That observation was tinged with bitterness, honed by experience.

"You think they'll keep things from us." Her voice sounded faraway, despite her proximity. "The way you and Barbara kept something from me."

He paused in his task. "What are you talking about?" She sounded *off*. Looked . . . vacant, somehow. As if she were here but not. He walked over to peer at her more closely. Was she on something? For a while, she'd had an issue with sedatives and God knows what else the doctors had been giving her. But there had been no new prescription bottles in the medicine cabinet for years. David knew; he checked regularly.

"Barbara was the last one to report seeing Kelsey alive." Her voice hitched once, then steadied. "She saw her on Baltimore on her bike. Looking anguished. She told you. Neither of you shared that with me."

The accusation that sounded in her words was familiar. But she wasn't teetering on her usual hysteria. At least, not yet. He dropped heavily down on the bed beside her. "Because it would upset you, and for what? It wasn't news. It didn't change anything."

"I used to have this dream." Her utter motionlessness was almost eerie. As if he were conversing with a statue. "Still do sometimes. It's the day Kelsey disappeared. I know that somehow, although all I see is a huge, poster-size picture of her. And suddenly it rips down the middle. I run to it and try to patch it, but I can't find any tape. And it tears again. Then again. Over and over until all that's left are tiny little bits swirling around in a wind that's come up. I chase the pieces, because I know if

I can patch them all back together, Kelsey will be whole again. She'll be back. And I do somehow. But even with the repair, there are pieces gone. They blew away and were lost. Now she'll never return because some of the parts are missing forever." For the first time, she looked at him. "Do you understand?"

"Yes." God help him, he did. "I think it's the same way I felt when we thought the police were withholding details from us. Like if we had a complete picture of the case, we'd somehow see something they hadn't. But it's a feeling, Claire. It's not true. Us knowing every fact wouldn't change anything. Just like you having completed the image in your dream wouldn't bring Kelsey back." His excitement on the drive home had been replaced by melancholy. Conversations with his wife too often had that effect on him. "I couldn't protect my daughter when she needed me the most. I couldn't shield you from the hell we were plunged into. Janie started having more problems, and I couldn't change that, either. But I could shelter you from some things that I knew only would hurt you. So yeah, I told Barbara to keep the information to herself."

He braced himself for the outburst he was certain was coming. But she remained unnaturally still. "It does," she whispered. "Hurt. Six miles she rode. She was last seen thirty minutes after she left the house. And she still appeared every bit as upset as she was when she'd slammed out. My last conversation with her was an argument. How do I forgive myself for that?"

The words were like a knife slipped cleanly between his ribs, then twisted. "We can't change what happened," he said bleakly. "We only can go on. I'm attending Janie's conference. Why don't you stay home and lie down for a while? I'll fill you in when I get back."

She didn't answer. But after a moment, she rose and went to the adjoining bathroom. Closed the door. He shot from the bed as if launched. Strode out of the room. But try as he might, he couldn't leave her words behind.

Because he had dreams, as well. A nagging nightmare in particular that he couldn't seem to shake. He, too, would like to change that final day. But even more, David wished he could undo one particular scene with his oldest daughter. The one that had put unalterable events into motion.

In his dream, he relived those moments over and over, trying to edit the conversation that had changed everything between them. Sometimes Kelsey ran into his arms and called him Daddy like she had when she was a little girl. She'd lose that snarky teen tone and the too-knowing attitude. He'd gotten very good over the years at revisionist history.

Some of the time, he almost believed his own fabrication.

Special Agent Mark Foster

November 9
6:45 p.m.

"I appreciate you coming in." Mark showed Dane Starkey into the room. The man to whom Brian DeVries claimed to have lost a bet was slightly built, with slicked-back, thinning dark hair, a sharp nose, and receding chin. The truculence stamped on his expression gave him an unfortunate resemblance to a belligerent ferret.

"It's not like I had much choice." He grabbed a chair from the conference table, the legs scraping as he pulled it out enough to sink into.

"On the contrary," Mark said smoothly. "We discussed several options."

"And all of them sucked." The man's head swiveled as he examined the space. Mark had chosen a conference area rather than an interview room in the BCI's main office in London. "But this was better than you coming to my workplace. Or my house. Still not sure why we couldn't have done this on the phone."

"Because then I couldn't show you these." Mark flipped open the folder in front of him and took out copies of Brian DeVries's financial transactions with the man. He pushed them across the table. "Brian

DeVries paid you a lot of money over the last three years. I want to know why."

Not even a flicker of surprise. So DeVries had warned him. Mark had cautioned him against it but wasn't surprised to find the man hadn't listened. He hadn't yet shown a propensity for following directions. Which just made Mark more determined to discover what they were concealing.

"I think you've got me mixed up with someone else."

"It's been a long day." He slipped out of his suit coat and folded it over the back of his chair, watching the man's gaze go from the gun in his shoulder harness to the shield clipped to his belt. Leisurely he took his seat. Loosened his tie. "Can't say I'm at my most patient after putting in twelve hours. So I'm only going to ask you one more time to explain those cash payments DeVries made to you."

Starkey moistened his lips. Picked up the sheets and studied them more carefully. "Oh, yeah, I remember now. It was a bet. A stupid game we bet on. We'd both had a few, and one thing led to another . . . the stakes got pretty high. I felt bad about Brian losing, so I let him pay it off over three years."

"What game?"

"Ah . . ." Perspiration dotted the man's upper lip. "I don't really recall."

"You won a fifteen-thousand-dollar bet, and you don't remember what game?" Skepticism dripped from Mark's words. "Try again."

"Well, let me think. I guess it was the Bengals and the Vikings. Three seasons ago."

"And his memory clears." Mark smiled humorlessly. "When and where did you two first meet?"

"At a farewell party. A friend of a friend."

"Here's how this is going to go, Dane. The more you lie to me, the more I'm going to think you have something to hide." He raised a hand to silence the man's objection. "The more I think you're concealing something, the more I'm going to wonder what it is. That will get my imagination going. And I'm going to start imagining, hey, maybe this guy is lying because he had something to do with the kidnapping of Brian DeVries's daughter."

"That's bullshit!" Starkey shot out of his chair.

"Is it?" Mark reached for the water pitcher sitting on the table between them and poured himself a glass. Drank. "I don't think so. You guys being such good buddies and all, you probably know all about his family. Maybe met them."

The man was sweating in earnest now. "No. I haven't. I mean, I barely even know Brian."

"Well enough to meet up for drinks, though, right? Alone? Because I'm not hearing you mention others who witnessed this fifteen-thousand-dollar bet. Sit down." Mark waited for him to comply before saying, "Where were you the evening of October 30?"

"Man, I don't know, but I wasn't anywhere near Saxon Falls."

"Dane." Mark leaned forward. "I've already got investigators on you. They're sniffing around your job, your family, your friends . . . everyone's going to know that BCI is asking questions about you. Pretty soon, they'll begin asking why. They'll start looking at you differently. Because if we're interested in you, there's probably reason, right? And we're going to find out exactly what you're lying about, and then, because you forced me to waste manpower on your lying ass, I'm going to nail you to the wall for doing whatever it is that you don't want to tell me you did."

Starkey slumped back in his chair. "Fucking DeVries. And he comes out of this smelling like a rose, right? Walks away clean, just like always."

"When did he walk away? What did he walk away from?"

The man looked away, stubbornly silent.

"That's a whole lot of pent-up hostility you have against the man. Makes me consider whether it's enough to drive you to kidnap his daughter."

"I'm not the one that likes little girls, okay? You ask DeVries about that, why don't you?"

Adrenaline spiked. If Starkey had evidence to back up his claim, it could be a critical turning point. There was a reason investigators always first looked at the parents in cases like this. But DeVries had passed a background check prior to getting a job in law enforcement. If Starkey was telling the truth, how the hell had that happened? "I'll do that. But right now, I'm asking you. Why did DeVries pay you fifteen thousand dollars?"

"He owed a hell of a lot more." The man punctuated his words with a fist to the table. "He should have gone to juvie, the perverted little prick. My cousin was twelve. Twelve fucking years old when he molested her."

Everything inside him quieted. Twelve years old. Two years younger than Whitney DeVries. "And how old was he?"

A sulky shrug. "I don't know. Fifteen? Got it all swept under the rug. Went to counseling, but he sure didn't get sent away. Then I hear he's a cop now? There ought to be a damn law about that."

Paraphilia often started in the teen years. Mark thought quickly. If DeVries had a juvie record that had been sealed, possibly even expunged after a number of years, it wouldn't have shown up on a background check. Smaller police forces didn't use polygraph tests, so DeVries wouldn't have had to worry about trying to pass one en route to landing a job with the sheriff's office.

"So you decided to blackmail him."

"I thought it was time for him to pay. For once in his miserable life, he was going to know what it was like to be powerless. See how he liked it."

"What'd you do with the money?" When Starkey didn't answer, Mark pressed him. "You being so concerned about your cousin, I figure when she's asked, she'll say you gave it to her, right? For her emotional suffering."

The answer was written in the other man's expression. "Just because Shelley's moved on doesn't mean DeVries shouldn't have to suffer, finally. I'm the one who learned he got that job with the sheriff's office, so I laid the groundwork. I didn't suggest anything illegal. Plenty of people in my family in Columbus remember what happened, even if he didn't live around there for long. Wouldn't take much to plant a story about it in his local newspaper, and that's what I told him. DeVries is the one who mentioned making it worth my while not to do it."

"How'd you contact him?" They hadn't found anything on DeVries's home computer or cell that linked to Starkey.

"Used my day off to wait for him in the parking lot outside his office." A flicker of pride crossed Starkey's face. "He didn't remember me at first, but once I started talking, he couldn't wait to get me out of there. Had me meet him at some dive bar a few miles away. That was the only contact we had. He just mailed the checks on the yearly dates we agreed on."

"Ever late for a payment?"

The man swung his head back and forth. "A guilty conscience makes a man punctual."

"And how much did he agree to pay in total?"

"Twenty thousand. He still owes me another five. We agreed on a four-year payment plan."

"I wouldn't start spending the rest, if I were you." Mark nudged a legal pad toward the man. "Write it down. All of it. I want dates and names of anyone who can verify the story about your cousin. Phone numbers and addresses. Then write a full accounting of your meeting with DeVries. And while you're at it, include where you were the night of October 30."

The man picked up the pen. Tapped it restlessly on the pad. "I don't have to give the money back, right? It was a business transaction between two consenting parties."

"Yeah, extortionists often describe it that way." Catching the eye of his SAC through the small glass window in the door, Mark rose. "Don't leave anything out."

He left Starkey to the task and walked out of the room. Special Agent in Charge Todd Bennett jerked his head toward the man Mark had left behind. "Think he's good for the girl's kidnapping?" The SAC had been watching the interview in the next room on CCTV.

"He and DeVries just jumped to the top of my suspect list." Mark looked back to consider the door he'd just left. "There must be something to Starkey's story for DeVries to pay him that much money. I need to take a run at him. Craw talked to him about the money the first time, and he flat-out lied about it."

"Maybe the money is only the start." Bennett's voice was grim. "Could be our friend in there also planned for DeVries's daughter to suffer the same thing his cousin did."

As far as motivation went, revenge was the most solid one they'd encountered so far. Mark nodded grimly. "I'll be all over his alibi," he promised. "I've already done a preliminary check on him. He doesn't have a criminal history, but we'll dig deeper." If a cousin of the alleged victim could be driven to blackmail Brian DeVries, what might the girl's immediate family be capable of? Starkey wasn't the only family member that required investigation. "It's also possible that the guy's just an opportunist. He saw a chance to stick it to DeVries and make some money at the same time. And for all his professed indignation on his cousin's behalf, it doesn't sound like he shared the money with her."

The SAC's faded brown gaze was shrewd. "Interesting that the DeVries case never showed up in the law-enforcement background check."

Lifting a shoulder, Mark said, "It wouldn't if it had been sealed or expunged. But Starkey would have had to have been a teenager himself at the time. Maybe he doesn't know all the details. We don't even know at this point if it got reported. I'll find out."

Todd nodded. He couldn't be much over fifty, but his hair was prematurely white. It glistened under the florescent lights. "Agent Greg Larsen has taken over profiling duties for us in the last couple years. He's acquainted himself with the Kelsey Willard case, should you ever want his input."

This was news to Mark. He hadn't known the agency had replaced Luther Sims. "I might do that." Switching the subject, he said, "Ben mentioned you had another agent in mind to take his place on the case."

"Don't worry—I haven't forgotten you."

"Great. I've got so many loose threads on this case, I'm starting to feel like a cat chasing a laser pointer. When's he start?"

"Not he." Bennett took his vibrating cell from his pocket. Looked at the screen. "She. You've worked together before. Sloane Medford will be in West Bend the day after tomorrow."

The man had already turned to answer the call before he finished the sentence. Then he strode away. It was just as well. Mark wasn't sure he was a good enough actor to keep the dismay from his expression.

Sloane Medford. *God damn it.*

The clouds were charcoal smears across the sky, extinguishing every hint of light. Mark got turned around twice before finding the private drive he'd been directed to. It opened to a small clearing in front of a neatly built log cabin. From the twin spears of his headlights, he could see the front door open and someone step outside onto the porch.

Luther Sims, the retired BCI profiler who'd worked the Ten Mile Killer case.

Mark brought the vehicle to a halt. It had been pretty clear how Ben Craw had felt about Sims being brought in on the Willard disappearance seven years earlier, but for now, Mark was the lead on this investigation. And after spending hours the last several nights poring over the old case files, he knew he'd be remiss in not getting firsthand information from the BCI's expert on the TMK.

Getting out of the car, he zipped up his coat before walking toward the cabin. It was still chilly but without the torturous arctic wind from earlier that day. "Mr. Sims." There was a ramp leading up to the porch. He climbed the steps next to it and stuck out his hand. "Mark Foster. Thanks for agreeing to meet me. Sorry about the hour."

"Agent." Sims's handshake was firm. "Don't worry about the time. As I said on the phone, we just got home only a few hours ago ourselves." He jerked a thumb at a small SUV parked in front of a detached double garage. It still had a canoe fastened to the racks on top. "Still haven't completely unpacked. First matter of business when we arrived was to get Elizabeth, my wife, situated. Please come in."

Mark followed the older man through the cabin door. Wiped his boots thoroughly on the hooked rug just inside as he looked around. "This is cozy. How long have you lived here?"

"Since my retirement three years ago." Sims's tone was hushed. "We love it, although given the progression of Elizabeth's rheumatoid arthritis, I've been making some improvements to the place."

Two rooms opened off the hallway. On the right, dim light spilled through the half-open door. Mark could see a woman sitting upright in bed, holding a book in gnarled fingers, reading glasses perched on her nose. Her long, gray hair framed a face that from this distance seemed curiously unlined. Respectfully, he averted his eyes. On the left was a good-size family room with a small flat-screen TV and several photos adorning the walls. He recognized Sims and his wife in a dated wedding picture. A much younger Luther in an army uniform. The two of them holding up the respective fish they'd caught. And one that might be a somber Elizabeth Sims taken decades earlier.

"Let's go to the kitchen, where we won't disturb my wife."

Mark followed the man down the hall, where it opened onto a good-size kitchen with a center island and a table and chairs. Luther pulled out a chair, waved Mark to it. It was a moment before he sat. "Pretty view. Better during the day, I'm sure." The back wall was a bank of windows. The shades hadn't yet been drawn, showing a deep lawn that was hemmed on three sides by tree line.

"We like it. Both Elizabeth and I enjoy the outdoors. At least," the man said with a quick glance toward the bedroom, "she used to. She has to depend on the wheelchair more and more. And recently, she was diagnosed with early-onset Alzheimer's. It's frustrating for her." His smile held a tinge of sadness. "Still managed a couple canoe rides on our recent trip, though."

Mark sank into the chair. The woman's diagnosis would explain the locks discreetly placed below the handles on the kitchen drawers and cupboards. They'd done the same at his grandma's house before the disease progressed, and she'd been placed in a nursing home. "Where'd you go?"

"Spent three weeks at Berlin Lake. The fishing wasn't great this year, but the fall foliage was spectacular." He seemed to stop himself then, chuckling ruefully. "Listen to me. Three years out of the agency, and it's fishing, hiking, and canoeing that fill my thoughts. A far cry from my work days."

Mark shot him an easy smile. "That's what retirement is supposed to be about, isn't it?"

Sims nodded. He was late sixties, Mark figured, and had kept most of his hair, although silver had heavily encroached on the brown. At five-ten, maybe one sixty, he hadn't let himself go since leaving the agency.

"You look like you're a good way from retirement, so let's talk about what brought you here. You're working the kidnapping over in Saxon Falls."

"I am. Given its proximity to West Bend, we have to look for connections to the Kelsey Willard case, which you were involved in."

There was a subtle shift in Sims's demeanor. In his eyes. The relaxed look vanished from his expression, and he was a cop again. "Like you, I worked the special investigations unit, originally out of Athens. But the last dozen years or so, I was loaned out to any serial-crime investigation."

"Because of your profiling experience."

The man nodded. "My SAC asked me to attend the first couple of classes at Quantico. It was extensive training, and I studied even more on my own. The agency provided regular opportunities after that to keep up with it. It wasn't something I planned, but it ended up defining my career."

"You were the one who linked eight deaths. Attributed them to the same killer."

"Unofficially, I attributed twelve homicides to the Ten Mile Killer." The man's correction surprised Mark. "I believe that eight of the bodies found in the last twenty years could be linked to him. Another I dismissed as the work of a copycat. There were subtle differences in the bruising around the throat, the costuming, and the way the victims were positioned. The other four girls I suspect he's guilty of killing were never found. Kelsey Willard is one of them. At least, I haven't heard that her body was discovered."

Mark shook his head. "No. But it sounds like you were convinced the TMK was responsible from almost the beginning of her case. So there must be more than the final appearance of the bodies that link his victims."

The man turned a hand. "I identified some similarities, yes. All females, ranging from fourteen to sixteen when they disappeared. There were physical resemblances—they were dark-haired and slender. Attractive. The bodies that were found were clad in leotards, tutus, tights, and ballet slippers, although some of the girls had dancing experience while others hadn't. All had been manually strangled in the same way. The pattern of bruising on the throat was remarkably similar. None of them showed signs of sexual abuse, although not all of them were virgins. The body dumps were located in fairly remote areas within approximately ten miles of one another in the Wayne National Forest in the southeastern part of the state. And every one of them had a parent that was lacking in some way. Sometimes it was the mother, but most frequently the father."

He took a breath, then gave a wry smile. "Admittedly, the last link is the most subjective. And evaluating parents who are in the midst of trauma is hardly fair. But the more you dig into the family dynamics, the more you discover about the relationships before the kidnappings. I was still working on strengthening that premise when I retired from the agency."

A parent that was lacking in some way. Mark considered the words. If Starkey was to be believed, Brian DeVries had sex with a preteen girl when he was a teenager himself. If he'd carried a fetish for girls into adulthood, there had been nothing uncovered in his home or on his computer to suggest it.

But if Mark dug into that portion of Brian DeVries's life, he might find that this secret from the man's past had impacted his daughter in some less obvious way.

"Whitney DeVries's kidnapper posed as a teenage boy from a neighboring town and lured her to a meeting place. Does that match with any of the other disappearances you linked to the TMK?"

Sims thought for a minute. "No. In the first two cases, the killer snatched them out of their homes, from their beds. In the other instances, the girls disappeared when they were out of the house alone. But as you know, MOs change. They reflect opportunity, and the offender can adapt and polish his MO to better suit his purpose."

"The agent I was partnered with at the beginning of this case seemed to think there was some dissension about whether Kelsey Willard was a victim of the TMK."

"There was, yes. The lead agent working the case was rather dismissive of the theory." His shrug was almost imperceptible. "Forensic profiling is still regarded suspiciously by some in our profession. As I recall, the man was going to remain unconvinced until the body was found and definitively matched the physical similarities I just shared."

"But you don't think all of the TMK's victims were discovered."

The man shook his head decisively. "Have you seen the TMK files?"

Mark nodded. The files were stored in more than thirty boxes in the cold-case room. Much of the information had been uploaded, and he'd requested it, but even the computer files would take a week to go through. "I'm just starting."

A quick flash of a smile from Sims. "Be sure and take a close look at the photos from the dumps. You'll see how isolated the areas were. Many of the bodies had remained undiscovered for years."

"And he hunted within the state lines?"

"As far as we know. The way he left the bodies is a pretty distinctive detail. It would have popped up on CODIS if he'd emulated that elsewhere. It's probable that he hunted only within the state boundaries. That made us think he was a resident, or hailed from a surrounding state, close to the border. But we couldn't rule out someone who passed through on a frequent basis. Like a salesman or trucker."

"What was the closest proximity between victims?"

Sims shot him an approving glance. "You're thinking of the DeVries and Willard girls. Their towns are what . . . fifteen miles apart?"

"Twelve."

The man pulled at his lower lip, considering. "Dahlia Humphries and Iris Johnson. Victims four and eight. Their homes were around twenty miles apart. But there were three victims and approximately nine years between them."

Was Whitney DeVries the work of a copycat? Mark wondered. She'd been kidnapped using a very different process than any of the other victims. It could point to an offender who had perfected his strategy. Or it could mean a totally different offender altogether. "So you can't estimate how long the killer keeps his victims? Because of the amount of time some of the victims went undiscovered?"

"The shortest interval between linked kidnappings has been three years. Piecing together the forensic anthropologists' reports on the remains, I concluded he kept them all for months. Some for more than a year. But I don't have a lot of answers for you, Agent Foster." The man's tone was tinged with defeat. "I spent a third of my career studying those crimes, and I'm left with more questions than answers. You take some of these cases with you when you leave." He tapped a finger to his temple. "Up here. Especially the unsolved ones. This is the one that has always haunted me. I'm not ashamed to tell you that I used to have nightmares after another body was discovered. Didn't make for a peaceful sleep. It got so bad that I came home one day, and Elizabeth had hung a framed print on the wall above our bed. One by that famous artist . . . the guy who painted the ballerinas."

Mark shook his head. He knew nothing about art. The other man continued. "She used to tell me to focus on the picture before I went to sleep so I'd dream about it instead of the bodies. Darned if that didn't help." He stopped, looking a bit embarrassed about the admission before switching the subject. "The crime is about the offender. His wants. His needs. So what was it he wanted? And how did each of the victims 'fail' him? Because that's what their deaths represented. Their failure to satisfy whatever it was that he desired from them. If you can answer that question, you'll break this case."

Put like that, solving this thing seemed even more insurmountable. Mark saw the man glance at the kitchen clock. Following his gaze, he was shocked to find it was nearly 9:00 p.m. "I've kept you long enough."

He still had another forty miles to drive back to West Bend. Fortunately, he'd FaceTimed Nicky last night, because it was too late now. He had hours ahead of him with reports from local law enforcement and diving into the Willard file again. He rose. Sims didn't object as he got up and ushered him from the room and down the hallway.

When they reached the bedroom, the man reached out to close the door, but not before Mark's gaze was drawn involuntarily to the print on the wall. A dreamy picture of dancers in filmy pink tutus, hands posed gracefully over their heads. A stark contrast to the photos of victims taken at the dump sites.

The door clicked shut. "I always promised myself that picture would come down when the killer was behind bars," Sims said quietly. "That's up to you and your team now."

A tall order, Mark thought. He wondered what he'd use to ward off nightmares if they failed to find Whitney DeVries in time. They continued toward the door.

"Because of the proximity of the DeVries and Willard victims, we're looking hard for any connections to the Willard case." Mark pulled out the gloves he'd jammed in his pockets.

"As you should."

"Was there anything that stood out to you about it? Anything that never quite gelled?" That happened with every investigation, Mark knew. Unanswered questions. The kind Sims had alluded to.

The man rubbed his face, for the first time looking weary. "Every investigator has his bugaboos. The things he or she can really get hung up on. Me, I was never satisfied with the alibis given by two of the people questioned. Of course, we know that not everyone can account for every minute of their day. Others live alone with no convenient corroborating witnesses. But it always leaves me with questions."

"Do you remember who they were?"

Without hesitation Sims answered. "Of course. The Reverend Mikkelsen and Kelsey's father. David Willard."

Whitney DeVries

November 10
5:34 p.m.

"Whitney, dear."

Dread snaked down her spine. Oh, God, that voice. That tone. Her body recognized it. Instinctively knew she was in danger.

She sat cross-legged on the stage as she'd been instructed. As usual she couldn't see him in the darkness. He was little more than a shadow, standing well out of the way of the computer screen's glow.

"Tell me, Whitney. Did you do your best today?"

Rule number six. Never give less than your best effort. Panic scampered up her spine. Tiny frissons of ice formed in her veins.

"It's a harder routine," she began, surprised at how shaky her voice sounded. It was impossible to concentrate on her answer when her body was already reacting to his words. Would she be whipped again? Or did the punishment get even worse with each infraction?

She began to tremble. Because she already knew that excuses wouldn't work. They'd only make him madder. There was a whisper at the base of her skull. *Stay strong. Smart.* The next words formed without conscious thought. "But you're right. I can do better. I *will* do better tomorrow. Thank you for reminding me. We have to be made aware of our failures in order to improve, right?" That had been one of Tami Jae's sayings. She'd had a million of them when it came to critiquing her students' dancing.

"That's correct." Was there a note of surprise in his words? "And very mature, Whitney. We all need to be open to criticism, especially when learning something new. But it's not enough to say you'll do better; you have to make a plan. What will be different about tomorrow?"

Sensing the trap in the question, she felt her way carefully. "I'll have to focus more intently. And I can do that by emptying my mind and feeling the music." Whoever would have believed that all Tami Jae's bullshit would come in handy?

"And what was distracting you today?"

"I miss my family."

"And you will for a time."

For a time? For a time? Anger elbowed aside fear. Was this freak for real? Like after a while, she'd just forget her dad and mom and brother? Erase them from her heart the way he tried to erase them from her mind? Sometimes she was almost convinced that he was lying about their deaths.

Today hadn't been one of those days.

"We all have obstacles in our paths. Character is the way we choose to get over them. I lost my sister, Margaret, when I was just a few years older than you. It was very, very difficult. My mother never got over it. You might say it contributed to her breakdown a couple years later. So you need to decide now, Whitney. Are you going to let this hardship defeat you? Or are you going to rise above it?"

Her jaw clenched. "It won't defeat me." *He* wouldn't defeat her. She wouldn't let him win.

"That's an excellent sentiment. Tomorrow we'll see how well you do following through on it. Now, take off your leotard. Turn and face the wall."

Her bones went to water. "I'm sorry about my effort. Tomorrow will be better. I promise." Her muscles were already quivering in anticipation of what was to come.

"For your sake, I hope that's true. But failing at something is not the worst thing you can do, Whitney. It's letting people down. That requires a consequence. By breaking rule six today, you disappointed me greatly. Not following my instruction will break another rule and disappoint me even further."

That had her rising, but her knees buckled, and she nearly fell. Her hands were shaking so hard, it was difficult to undo the Velcro on the sleeve of the leotard. Drag it off her shoulders. Push the garment down her legs. She turned and bent to a crouch, her body tensing in anticipation. *He won't win*, she vowed. *He won't he won't he won't.*

The whip snapped, shattering her inner resolve. An instant later it cut into her flesh. Her scream echoed and rocketed about the room. The pain was a shredding agony. But it was mixed this time with a red-hot pulse of rage.

◆ ◆ ◆

Her eyes burned as she stared into the darkness. Her punishment hadn't been complete without the loss of TV privileges, too. A bitter laugh escaped her. As if not being able to watch a child's show was any match for being whipped.

She could feel the stickiness on her back. Knew the lash mark was oozing again. It would stick to the thick flannel nightgown she wore. Once a week she was instructed to leave her clothes at the edge of the stage to be laundered. Yesterday morning when she'd retrieved them, the nightdress had been with them. The garment was old-fashioned, and not new. The fabric was pilled from wear and frequent washings. She'd dutifully thanked her captor for it, even though it looked like something people wore a century ago. She'd even planned to ask for a blanket the next time she earned a privilege.

That was before she'd been reminded that the tiniest infraction led to a vicious result.

Anger and resentment were frothing inside her, diluting even the grief that had risen and ebbed in waves since he'd told her about her family. She'd spent the last few nights continuing her search of the rest of the stage floor, hoping to find another loose board. One would be useless against him, but two or three would make a club. So far she'd failed, and that failure had whittled away at her determination. If there were a way out of here, wouldn't Kelsey Willard have found it?

The girl that had been here before her might be dead now. The possibility had terrified Whitney for days. Made it difficult to hang on to a slender thread of hope.

But that was a coward's thinking. The throb of fury kept beat with the ache in her back. She had to be brave enough to face whatever else might be on those papers, because there might be something there that would help her get into the freak's head so she could beat him at his own game.

Something that might help her escape.

The thought tantalized her. Maybe Kelsey Willard had gotten away, and the papers would tell Whitney how she could, too. Her throat dried out. Or maybe it would tell her worse things . . . things she didn't want to know. Details that would make it harder for her to concentrate on staying strong. Beating the freak.

The mental tug-of-war hadn't stopped since she'd replaced those papers. Had nibbled at her thoughts even during her nightly search of the floorboards. The lashing she'd gotten today had solved her dilemma. Whatever she might discover in those pages, it had to be better than cowering in her bed, awash in pain and humiliation. *That* was letting him win.

Mind made up, Whitney threw off the thin cover and carefully got off the mattress, her gaze on the sliver of light hemming the curtain at the window high on the wall at the far end of the stage. The floorboards were cold beneath her feet as she scurried to the shower stall. After a sharp intake of breath from the pain, she lowered herself to her hands and knees and searched blindly for the screw on the floor. Some opportunities she was forced to earn. Others she'd take.

Her fingers closed around the screw, and she tiptoed back to the mattress. She probably didn't have to worry about being quiet. She'd figured out that he watched her somehow when the computer was on. He had to have fixed it so it streamed the old dance films and dumb-ass Nickelodeon channel through the projector. There must be some sort of camera app open on it because he'd known when she'd taken a nap that time. The memory had a shiver chasing down her spine.

She'd made a point of studying her prison while she stretched before dancing. There were no wires to be seen. No telltale red lights that suggested a hidden camera. And why would he bother? The chain attaching her wrist to the metal barre was inescapable.

Breath hitching at the thought, she carefully lowered herself to all fours, running her fingers over the floorboards. If he had some way to watch her here without the computer turned on, he'd have punished her again for her discovery a few nights ago. But he hadn't. Which meant he didn't know.

She found the rough edge of the board she'd pried up before and hesitated. It hadn't just been fear of her captor that had her rolling the papers up and jamming them back into their hiding place that first night. Whitney hadn't wanted to read more.

My name is Kelsey Willard.

The flesh on her arms rose. She wasn't the first the freak had taken. The knowledge had hammered inside her brain in the days since. Had twisted her guts into knots. It would be easier if it didn't make a terrible sort of sense. The clothes she was forced to wear that were clearly not new. The routine she was expected to keep. The security of her imprisonment. Even the hated rules she had to recite every evening before he left her. All spoke of planning.

He'd done this before. And maybe Kelsey Willard hadn't been the first. A shudder worked through her. Had he killed them? Why else had Kelsey expected to die? Had she tried to escape? There might be answers beneath Whitney's fingertips. The question was whether she was strong enough to accept them.

Did Whitney want to know more? The dread curling through her stomach was its own answer. It was hard enough to try to remain hopeful that the freak was lying about her family's death. Worse now that she'd found something that seemed to verify her worst fears about him and his intentions. She didn't know if she was strong enough to deal with more bad news.

If someone's reading this, I'm probably dead.

Would knowing be worse than uncertainty? She already knew the answer to that. It had driven her from the bed, finally. Maybe Kelsey hadn't died at all. Maybe she'd escaped this prison. And the only way Whitney was going to be sure was if she read the rest of the pages beneath the floorboard.

The breath she drew in then sliced through her lungs. Before she could second-guess herself again, she applied the screw to the floorboard. Levered it out of place and reached inside for the tightly rolled pages. Drew them out.

She moved toward the window. The tiny glow around the curtain provided the only light. Her hands were shaking so much, it was difficult to unroll the pages. And then it seemed to take longer than it should to flatten them against the wall. Reposition them an inch at a time until a slant of light made it possible to read what was on them.

I was on my bike the day he took me. At least, I guess the monster keeping me here is the driver of the black van that was following me. By the time I realized he'd been behind me for a while, he was trying to hit me. He knocked me off my bike, and the next thing I knew, I woke up in this dungeon.

It was laborious reading. Every few words Whitney had to slide the pages to a new spot into the light. She paused now, though, frozen in place. *A black van.* Was that the vehicle that had been at the park? That had been the moment when she'd realized something was horribly wrong. When she'd made out the hulking shape at the rear of the park. A van. Everything happened so fast after that. She hadn't noticed a color, but it had to have been a dark one to blend in with the shadows.

Something inside her howled at her to stop. To put the pages away and forget she'd ever found them. This wasn't helping. Reliving someone else's pain didn't make hers easier to bear.

Knowing there had been a girl before her—who might be dead now—didn't help, either.

But something made her go on. Even after a cloud must have shifted over the moon, blocking the tiny ray of light that poked through the curtain for long minutes. Her mom sometimes said she was as obstinate as a mule. Maybe that was the reason she didn't move away from the wall, even when everything inside her head told her she should.

He told me my family was dead. Killed by a home intruder who had broken in to rob the place and found them home. I wanted to die then, too. What's the point of surviving this place—him—if I have no one to go home to? Mom and Janie . . . my little sister. She needs me. She really does. She has a problem, and I can help her best. She listens to me, and sometimes I can help her with the fear that keeps the words locked up inside her. Hearing that was worse than anything else. Even the beatings. Oh, God, the beatings. Sometimes he'd whip me so bad, I thought I was dying, too.

And other times I'd break one of his damn rules just so he'd hurt me again. If my family was dead, shouldn't I be in pain, too?

Whitney pressed the back of one hand to muffle the sob on her lips. Kelsey Willard's family had died, too? *No.* There was no way it could have happened to them both. A tremulous ribbon of hope unfurled within her. Eagerly she repositioned the paper, squinting to see more.

He could be lying. That's the only thing that keeps me going. Maybe he thought I'd be easier to control if I thought I had no one but him. And if he'd lie about that, what else is he lying about? It's been a long time now since I was taken. Maybe over a year. I've decided I'm not going to give in. I'm not going to let him win. He can control everything about me except my mind. The way to beat him is to let him think he's broken me, so I'm letting him think that.

Some days it isn't even an act.

He knows so much about me. I didn't realize it for a while because I was so wrapped up in loneliness and grief. But he knows where I went to school, my parents' and sister's names, where my dad works. Is he an acquaintance of our family, or has he been watching us? And it made me think. His learning all about me is what got me into this chamber of horrors. Maybe learning all about him will get me out.

There must be a reason he never lets me see him. The same reason he uses that creepy voice changer to distort his voice to sound like a Darth Vader wannabe. Because he's careful, or maybe because he's afraid I'd recognize him. That's the thought that scares me the most.

The slant of light was extinguished again. And this time, although Whitney waited a long time, it didn't come back. A voice changer. Why hadn't she thought of that? The deep tones with the slightly hollow sound. She and her friends had voice-changer apps on their phones. They tried them all, sounding like grown men, robots, and aliens. She rolled up the papers. Retraced her steps to put them back in their hiding place. She replaced the screw on the floor of the rickety shower and made her way to the mattress, all the while trying to suppress the emotions careening inside her.

But huddled beneath her thin covers, hugging her knees close to her chest, the other girl's words washed over her again.

He told me my family was dead. He'd told Whitney the same thing. Shown her proof. Tortured her with pictures of the plane crash. Read her the obituaries in the paper. Even read some of the things people had written on the site at the funeral home. What were the chances that both Kelsey's family and hers had been killed after they were kidnapped?

Not good. Whitney smiled in the darkness, a tiny spark of anticipation igniting. Her mom and dad and Ryan were alive. She was almost sure of it.

And she was going to figure out a way to get back to them.

Janie Willard

November 11
7:20 a.m.

There was a light knock at her bedroom door. "Janie? You have a visitor."

"It's okay, Mom. Come in." When the door opened, she surveyed her mother carefully. Claire was, as usual, immaculately groomed in linen slacks, patterned blouse, and matching cardigan. Hair carefully fixed. Makeup subtle but effective. She could be going to one of her endless meetings or ready for a day of shopping. But she dressed the same way whether she was planning to leave the house or not. If her mother had clothes for lounging, Janie had never seen them. She'd rarely even seen her in a pair of jeans.

Her color was back. The pinched look was gone from her lips, and her brow wasn't furrowed. Something inside Janie relaxed. Whatever had been going on with her mother for the last couple of days, she seemed to have recovered.

"Is it Alyvia? I told her I'd pick her up." Sitting on the edge of the bed, Janie pulled on a pair of flat, black-leather boots that reached nearly to the knee of her denim-clad legs. Standing again, she pulled down the hem of her hooded tunic top. Her long, straight hair was still wet. She usually allowed it to dry over breakfast. There'd be no time wasted on styling it or applying makeup. That had been Kelsey's deal. It would never be Janie's. She crossed to her desk and picked up her backpack. Reached for her school laptop.

"No, it's not Alyvia." Claire came further into the room, lowering her voice conspiratorially. "It's a young man. He says his name is Cole."

Janie froze. "Cole Bogart?"

"I believe that's what he said, yes." Claire's expression became troubled, alerting Janie that she needed to temper her response. It took little to raise her mom's protective instincts. "He said he knew you from school. Should I send him away?"

Cole Bogart. Janie completed the act of stuffing her laptop into her bag, her mind racing. He'd tried to reach out by e-mail a few times since they'd been in after-school suspension. She'd deleted them, unopened. Since she wasn't on any social media sites—whom would she talk to?—he couldn't use that avenue.

Apparently, he'd found another way to contact her.

"I'll get rid of him." Claire turned to the door. "I won't have him coming here and upsetting you."

"No." The word burst from Janie's lips before she could consider it. "It's fine. He probably just wants to talk about the government project."

"Are you sure?" Claire hovered uncertainly. "I don't know why he couldn't wait and speak to you at school. I have breakfast ready."

"I'll be in to eat in a few minutes."

"I showed him to the family room."

Janie nodded. The family room was far enough away from the kitchen to be private. She'd get rid of him without any fear that her mother would overhear and ask more questions.

She zipped her backpack and slowly followed her mother downstairs. Unspoken between them was the fact that this was the first time a boy had come to the house to see Janie. They'd flocked around Kelsey, although their parents refused to let them date until they were fifteen.

It hadn't stopped guys from showing up to hang out, though, usually in a mixed group. Her sister had enjoyed the attention, but there hadn't been any one guy she'd been interested in. Janie would have known. Kelsey had shared stuff like that, chattering on about who was hot, who wasn't, and who liked whom.

She paused at the bottom of the stairway. But there had been one thing her sister hadn't shared. Something major. Which underscored the fact that Kelsey had had secrets Janie never knew about.

Taking a breath, she slid the backpack down one arm and left it next to the stairs before walking into the family room.

Cole was standing in front of the fireplace, hands shoved in the pockets of his Buckeyes jacket, studying the family pictures arranged on the mantel. Her chest constricted with a familiar tightness. She took a long, steady breath. Exhaled slowly. Repeated the exercise before asking, "What are you doing here?"

He turned. His smile flickered and then fell away. "Hey. Just wanted to talk to you for a minute."

"I don't know why." The words burned as she forced them out. Deep breathing didn't help. A thousand reasons for his presence here were racketing around her brain. The fact that most were ridiculous and paranoid didn't quell their formation. She knew better than to allow any one of them to settle and take hold. *Just get through it.*

"I figured it'd be easier for you to talk at home." For the first time, he looked uncertain. He reached up to push his shaggy brown hair from his eyes. "And I thought maybe you wouldn't want anyone to see us together at school."

The hint of uncertainty in the words had her studying him more carefully. It was unexpected. He'd seemed plenty sure of himself up until now. But they hadn't had a real conversation, she realized suddenly. Just online.

"I couldn't figure out why you were so mad," he continued. "You know. Before. But then I thought about it and figured maybe you thought I was trying to set you up. Give you the material to bring down Heather Miller and then have you take the fall for it."

She took a few more steps into the room. Came to a halt behind the couch. "Weren't you?"

He shook his head violently enough to have his hair flying. "No. I was . . . I dunno. Trying to apologize, I guess."

Janie blinked. This whole scene was getting more bizarre by the moment. "For changing Heather's grades?"

"What?" His puzzlement appeared genuine. "Shit, she's got the teachers at that school so buffaloed, all she has to do is show up and they give her a gold star. No, I . . ." His gaze slid away as his voice trailed off. After a moment, he tried again. "Last spring. I took her SATs for her."

Janie leaned against the couch, her knees going suddenly weak. "How? You were . . ."

"Kicked out. Yeah. Didn't mean I couldn't sign up to take it. Ferin put us in touch. You know the two of them are a thing?" She could only nod. "Humphries monitors the test. He's not exactly observant. Just took a little sleight of hand to switch answer forms."

Of all the possible reasons she'd imagined for his appearance here today, this one hadn't occurred to her. "Why tell me? I could turn you in."

"You won't." He cocked a brow at her expression. "You wouldn't use that picture against Heather, and I figure you hate her a lot more than you do me. When I switched schools last year . . . well, let's just say I was pissed off and not thinking things through. I did some dumb stuff."

"You were pissed about moving?" Most kids their age would be upset at being forced to switch schools so close to graduating.

He regarded her silently, as if trying to decide something. Finally, he responded. "My brother was killed almost two years ago. Half brother really, but we were raised together since we were eleven. Drunk driver who hit the car blew nearly three times the legal limit. Walked with no more than probation." Janie recognized the bitterness in his tone. She'd lived it. "I just wanted him to pay. But he never will. Guess you know about that."

She ignored the reference to Kelsey. "What do you want Heather Miller to pay for?"

His gaze met hers. "I've been doing some digging. Almost sure she's the one who tipped the school off about my operation last year. She could have found out from Ferin. He and I . . . ah . . . traded services for a while. Then she offered me two hundred bucks to take the SAT for her, because by then I was the safest bet in the world. I mean, who would believe me if I ever tried to rat her out? Assuming I could, without implicating myself. Anyway"—he shrugged—"the score I got her is a few points higher than yours. And I started thinking, that might mean the bitch beats you out of scholarships. Awards and whatnot, while she gets by scot-free. Just like the bastard who killed my brother."

Traded services. Meaning last year Ferin supplied illegals to him. She didn't ask how he knew her SAT score. From what she'd observed, he pretty well walked through the school server at will. There was a quick burst of temper, one that was short-lived when a snippet from her altercation with Heather floated across her mind.

I hope you realize you'll have to do a verbal presentation. The days of you getting a free pass because of your poor dead sister are almost over. Being certain that Heather was cheating her way into the university of her choice burned. But Janie couldn't argue with the truth. She'd be at a disadvantage in any case because of her anxiety. No amount of practice would magically gift her with an ease for social discourse. And that couldn't be blamed on Heather Miller.

"Sometimes cheaters win." Her voice was flat, her fingers clenched on the top of the couch. "Sometimes crimes aren't solved. And sometimes people don't pay for what they've done. Getting high doesn't change that." Janie was the last one to pretend she had the answers. But she knew that they weren't found in a vodka bottle. They didn't coincide with the number of pills popped. Her mother was living proof of that.

"Jesus, that's harsh."

Tired of this conversation—of him—she half turned away. "So's life." Her attitude didn't reflect the measure of sympathy she felt for him. He'd had two years to adjust to the loss of a sibling. She'd had seven. She could have told him it didn't get easier. Time—which was said to heal all wounds—was really a sneaky bitch. Because it also faded recollections that were once so sharp and clear. Until her sister's face was fuzzy. The sound of her laugh was more difficult to summon. Somehow the memories faded more than the pain ever would.

"Well." He shuffled his feet awkwardly. "Guess I should go."

She watched him head toward the doorway. Would never know what made her stop him. "Cole?" He turned to look at her. "Write down your memories of your brother. Every single thing, no matter how small. Later on you'll remember moments, but you won't recall the day-to-day stuff. What you both said. Normal stuff you'd do together. Silly stuff you'd laugh at." She stopped, suddenly tongue-tied again.

"Is that what you did?"

She shook her head. "I was too young." And her anxiety had only magnified her personal misery until both had taken over her life. "But I wish I had."

He nodded slowly. "Okay. Thanks. I still owe you. Seriously, you ever need a favor . . ." The offer dangled in the air between them. When she didn't respond, he headed for the door. She doubted very much that he'd apologized to every student impacted by his actions, and she had no illusions about why he'd singled her out. Pity. Similar tragedies. Shared pain.

She waited until she heard the front door close behind him before she headed toward the kitchen. Janie couldn't imagine what Cole Bogart could ever offer that she'd want.

And she had nothing to offer him, either.

◆ ◆ ◆

"Did your foster parents lift the ban for you riding in friends' cars?" Janie stubbed out the cigarette she'd lit after pulling out of her friend's driveway. It might take more than one to calm the tangle of nerves in her gut after Bogart's visit.

"As if." Her friend buckled her seat belt. "Apparently they think that punishment will prevent a repeat of my skipping school. Or getting drunk to begin with. Whatever. They had an early appointment at the family services' office. Probably to meet the new kid or sign papers or something. Anyway, once I knew they'd be gone, I texted you." She raised her brows meaningfully. "I've got big news."

"Light me another cigarette, will you?"

Alyvia dug in the dash compartment, unerringly coming up with the Band-Aid box hiding Janie's pack of cigarettes. Using the lighter on the dash, she lit it and drew deeply from it.

"Nothing beats nicotine in the morning. Unless it's tequila." She took another puff before handing it over. "Remember I said I recognized Deedee Bakker on that perv website? And how she was in a foster home with me for a while?"

Janie drew on the cigarette before placing it in the ashtray. "Did you get her contact information from your caseworker?"

"No, that uptight wench lives by the book. But there was another girl living with us at the time, Sarah, and I found her on Facebook. Anyway, she still kept in contact with Deedee, and I got a phone number."

A drumroll of anticipation started in Janie's chest. "Did she talk to you about the pictures?"

"Eventually." The smugness in Alyvia's expression matched her tone. "It took finesse, for sure. That bitch always hated me. But finally, I said I'd heard she'd had some 'artistic' pictures taken and said a friend of mine was interested and could she recommend the photographer, yadda yadda. She shut down real fast when I brought up the photos. I had to make a couple of threats before she gave in." She shrugged as if it had been no big deal, but Janie could imagine the conversation. Alyvia's shitty life had resulted in a streak of toughness that she could wield or tuck away, depending on the situation. "And you're never going to believe who the photographer was. Herb Newman."

Revulsion skated through her. "Mr. Newman from school?"

Alyvia reached for the cigarette again. "Only you would call the janitor *Mister*."

"He worked at the church I used to go to in Saxon Falls when I was a kid." He'd always been hanging around, sometimes talking to Reverend Mikkelsen, working on the lights, cleaning, or setting up the Christmas decorations. Janie tried to picture Kelsey trusting the pudgy, bearded custodian to take those pictures she'd hidden in Janie's room. Failed. There'd been $1,000 cash in the envelope. Herb Newman didn't look like he'd ever had that much money at one time in his life.

"Deedee said something like that, too. That she knew him from church camp or something."

Janie opened her mouth to ask about the money, then closed it again. It had been a huge leap for her to share the information about Kelsey's photos, but she hadn't mentioned the cash. Liv was her best friend, but some things were too raw. Too private. And she hadn't shared her suspicion that Claire hadn't given the information to the police. She had protective instincts of her own.

But it made her wonder what other secrets her family might have kept from her.

"What are you going to do?"

Braking for a stoplight, Janie considered the question. She'd had thoughts of giving the name to the BCI, but without the context of her sister's possible relationship to the photographer, the information would be meaningless to them. Did the pictures have anything to do with Kelsey's death? There was no way to be certain, short of thoroughly checking out Newman. And the people best prepared to do that were cops.

She'd been ten when her sister was taken. Helpless to do anything to assist. Too young, too disabled to talk to the BCI agents, even if she'd wanted to. And now she had her mother to consider. Janie had learned to read the signs, and experience told her that Claire Willard had been hitting the vodka hard for the last couple of days. No action could be taken that might end up pushing her mom over the edge.

The BCI finding out that she'd been less than open seven years ago would be a gigantic shove.

So Janie had to step carefully. Gather details herself, and then figure out how to share them if necessary in a way that wouldn't implicate her mother.

"Are you there?" Alyvia snapped her fingers in front of her face. "I asked—"

"I heard you." Nebulous bits clicked into place as the beginning of a plan began to formulate. One that had her heart and throat constricting simultaneously. "I'm going to talk to Newman. Set up a photo shoot."

Claire Willard

November 11
9:35 a.m.

The house's emptiness was always deafening after Janie left for school. Claire finished a bowl of oatmeal she didn't want and reached for coffee. Her fingers wrapped around the mug, absorbing the heat even as she lifted it to her lips and sipped. A corresponding stream of warmth slid down her throat. Spread. The sensation was pleasant. A splash of vodka in the coffee would be even more . . .

Determinedly she pushed the craving aside. The last two days had been spent in a haze of alcohol and pills, and the residue of self-loathing was even less palatable than the oatmeal had been.

She needed to call Barbara. She should offer an apology. Muscles tensing, she raised the mug again. But she wasn't sorry. Not really. And her friend would sense that. Barbara knew her better than anyone these days. Certainly better than David did. So she'd explain rather than apologize, but she wondered if she could make her friend understand. Could anyone truly empathize when they hadn't suffered the same loss? Losing a child made Claire jealous of every moment others had with

Kelsey that she hadn't shared. Life had dealt only a finite number of pieces of her daughter, and now, without her, Claire wanted to selfishly collect and hoard all those bits for herself.

She stared into the dark liquid in the mug blindly. Had she known what fate had in store, she would have guarded the last moments with her daughter more carefully. Now it was too late. Being jealous of her friend's final sighting of her daughter was completely unreasonable. She realized that. But she was helpless to feel differently.

Taking another long sip of coffee, Claire reached for the fledging threads of inner fortitude she'd pledged to rebuild only days earlier. She was going to slip sometimes. That was to be expected. But what mattered was restarting again. Stronger. More determined than ever to change.

The self-talk was meant to be a confidence booster. Instead, it felt more than a little depressing. Maybe Dr. Schultz had been right. Maybe she should try a therapist again. Especially now, when she was at least willing to—

A distant peal interrupted her thoughts. She blinked, looking toward the kitchen doorway, puzzled. It wasn't one of Marta's days, and even if it were, the woman let herself in. Claire froze for a moment, remembering the agent who'd stopped by a couple of days ago. She didn't want to face him again.

The doorbell rang a second time, more insistently. Claire didn't move. It could be Barbara. It probably was. It would be like her friend to give Claire time to calm down and then check in on her. The coffee splashed precariously close to the edge of the mug as she set it down hastily, lurching to her feet, and hurried to the front door.

A tremulous smile on her lips, she pulled the door open. "I was just thinking about . . ." The rest of the sentence tapered off as she stared in shock at the woman on her porch.

Shannon DeVries offered her a smile, one that quickly faded. "I'm sorry to show up like this. But . . . strange as it sounds, you're the only one I know who might understand."

◆ ◆ ◆

It felt surreal to be standing in her kitchen, a woman she barely knew ensconced in a chair at the table as Claire poured another mug of coffee. Distantly she noticed that her hand on the carafe was trembling. A ball of dread was knotting in her belly. There was no one she'd rather not talk to than the mother of Whitney DeVries. But the memory of the early days after Kelsey had been taken kept her from sending the woman away. Whatever Shannon had to say, Claire probably *would* understand.

That still didn't mean she wanted to hear it.

Turning, she crossed to the table and silently handed the woman the mug, then topped off her own. Finally, having run out of distractions, she slipped into her seat, bringing the coffee to her lips as if to ward off what was to come.

"Brian's been going in to work the last few days." Shannon took a cautious gulp of the steaming liquid, then lowered the mug to the table. "Not on active duty, of course, but first shift, at a desk. He says it's because we can't afford to lose the income. But my boss gave me time off, and I know his would, too." She looked away. When she continued, her voice was low. "The doctor thought it was better to have Ryan back in school. I think Brian just can't stand to be home alone with me. The silence . . . it's louder when it's just the two of us. I know it doesn't make sense, but . . ."

"It does." The words were out of Claire's mouth before she gave them a thought. Those first days had been spent in a fog of disbelief and grief. She and David had clung to each other at first, terrified and inconsolable. And even having Janie at home, her condition worsening, hadn't been enough to distract them from the widening void left by Kelsey's absence.

She felt a flicker of anger at Shannon's husband, whom she didn't know at all. What kind of man was he? David had been at her side constantly, at least at first. The sequence was fuzzy with the distance of time, but it had been after the agents had stopped returning calls that her husband had started drawing away, too. At least, that was the way it had seemed then. But if ever there was a time a couple should be supporting each other, it was now.

"You both need each other." Claire had to force the words out. She felt like a fraud, mouthing empty platitudes. She had no advice for this woman. Although Claire had been whole when Kelsey had been taken, she wasn't any longer. She couldn't advise Shannon on how to bear the unbearable. She'd never learned that lesson herself.

"It's so hard to be in the house alone when he and Ryan are gone. What am I supposed to be doing?" She raised a beseeching gaze to Claire, as if begging for answers. "How do I spend my days without going crazy wondering . . . the most horrible things go through my head, and I just sit in her room and cry, thinking about what could be happening to Whit. What might have already happened. I feel like I'm losing my mind."

The words lassoed Claire's heart. Squeezed it tightly. They perfectly described how she still spent too much of her time. "You shouldn't be alone. Do you have parents nearby? How do you get along with your mother-in-law? Or perhaps a friend could stay with you while he's at work." She couldn't even imagine how she would have coped if left on her own. David had been there. Barbara had been a mainstay, and there had been a steady stream of friends and neighbors. Time had reduced that stream to a trickle until it had finally stopped completely.

"Helen is wonderful," Shannon said quickly. "But it's almost harder to have her there, praying and quoting Bible verses that are supposed to make me feel better. They don't. They make me want to scream. What good does it do to pray to a God that allowed this to happen? Where was he when a stranger snatched Whitney away from us? After Helen leaves I feel wound so tightly that I'm going to snap at the least provocation. I find myself making excuses to keep her away. And most of our friends are Brian's acquaintances from work, or the gym." She ducked her head, as if ashamed. "I didn't really notice until now that I have no close friends of my own. With working and the kids, it just seemed like there was never enough time . . ."

Barbara had observed once that Brian DeVries was a hard man. Claire wondered now if he was also a controlling one. It was impossible not to feel compassion for the miserable younger woman sitting beside her. "That's natural in this day and age, isn't it? I haven't worked since the kids were born, so I had more time to cultivate those relationships. But with a job, husband, and kids . . . I'm sure it's a full-day's work just to cope with grocery shopping, household chores, dinner, and homework."

The other woman's blonde head bobbed in agreement. She lifted the mug to sip from it. "People stop over. But I realize they don't know what to say." Her smile was miserable. "*I* wouldn't know what to say to us. What am I supposed to be doing? Surely there's some way I could be helping them find Whitney. But how?"

The questions raked at Claire's nerves. Awakened memories from those early days that she'd regulated to the back of her mind. "The agents will ask you to make a list of everyone you know and their connection to your family."

"They've done that. I've thought of a couple of additions twice and updated it, but there has to be more. I feel like they aren't giving us all the information about what they've discovered. Because if they have, it doesn't seem like a heck of a lot."

Was it better to sugarcoat things or to be honest? Claire decided on a mixture of the two. "They don't. And that is terribly hard. There's so much that goes on in the investigation that doesn't lead anywhere. They told us only what could be proven to directly relate to Kelsey's disappearance. It's a long, frustrating process. That's why I suggest having someone with you until they bring Whitney home again." She'd added that last as a kindness. Shannon seized on it with a desperation that was heartbreakingly familiar.

"Do you think they will?" Her pretty face was alight with a hope that had something inside Claire withering. "It's been thirteen days. You always hear the first couple of days are the most important in these types of things, but they don't seem to have made that much progress."

Thirteen days? Claire swallowed the hot tide of bitterness that rose. What was thirteen days compared to seven years and counting? Engulfed in grief or not, the woman was incredibly tone deaf. Claire's earlier sympathy faded as she began to think of a way to gracefully usher Shannon out of her house.

And then felt like a complete curmudgeon when the woman's soft brown eyes filled with tears. "Oh, my God, listen to me. You've experienced everything I'm going through and for so much longer. Claire, I'm sorry. That's why I'm here. Tell me what to do. How do I get through this? It's like I'm disappearing myself, a little more each day. Like the outline of me is there, but everything of substance drained away when we woke up to find Whitney gone. I feel like I'm going crazy."

The misery in her voice, in her expression, had Claire's resentment draining away as suddenly as it had appeared. "You're not crazy." She was shocked by the fierceness in her tone. "Or if you are, I was the exact same kind of crazy. What's *normal* when faced with the worst tragedy of our lives? Who gets to make those guidelines? People who have never experienced the same thing? I got through every day like I was feeling my way in the dark. Nothing about my life was *normal* anymore. It was an unknown world, not one I ever asked to visit. Normal is whatever gets you through the day. I needed a doctor to prescribe sedatives. I still take them sometimes." A sliver of honesty, quickly glossed over as she went on. "And it does help to have someone around. Maybe if you told Brian how you felt . . ."

"He doesn't talk much when he's home, either." A curtain of hair shielded Shannon's face as she bent over the mug in her hands. "I know he's hurting, too, but he seems so angry all the time. I worry he blames me. And sometimes I'm angry with him, too. He's been so distant. We're having some money problems. He works so much overtime, but we never seem to get ahead. And all that gets in the way when we should be supporting each other."

"What about your parents?"

Shannon shook her head. "Mom's in Blackston. This has hit her so hard, she's taking something for her nerves. My sister is in California, and we talk every day. She'd come and stay for a while, but she just got out of the hospital and really can't afford the ticket, and neither can I."

Claire stared at her, a nebulous idea forming. "I could help with that." She had little to offer the other woman to ease the traumatic path she was on, but she had money. It would buy a tiny patch for the twenty-four-hour misery Shannon was engulfed in. "Call your sister. Set things up. Then I'll make the arrangements for the flight."

"Oh, no, I couldn't." Shannon looked simultaneously delighted and worried. "That's not why I came. And you barely know me."

"I know you're a member of a club neither of us wanted to join." Claire wasn't aware that tears had formed until one slid down her cheek. "And I understand the heartache you're feeling." Because it was still there. A pain that never eased.

There were more protestations, which Claire patiently dismissed. David's job paid very well. The money hadn't protected them from the awful, whimsical nature of tragedy. It hadn't provided them a way to heal in the aftermath. But right now it could purchase a measure of comfort for someone else. There was a small degree of consolation in that.

The ensuing arrangements took far longer than they should have. There was Shannon's sister to be called, and the explanation given.

They went to the family room where Claire got on the computer while Shannon spoke to the other woman and started looking up flights. After much back and forth, a flight time was selected for the following day. And when Shannon finished saying tearful goodbyes to her sibling, Claire smiled at her reassuringly. "Having your sister with you won't change what you're going through. But it might make it easier, not being alone with your own thoughts all day."

"That's the worst part." Shannon shuddered. "My imagination . . . I try to be positive. That's what the BCI agent suggests. Stay focused on Whitney coming home safely. But sometimes my mind is flooded with every bad thing I've ever heard can happen to kids. And you know what I do to make myself feel better? I tell myself that maybe she's with your daughter. Maybe she has someone there with her so she won't be so afraid. And that the two of them can figure out a way to come home together."

Something inside Claire simply shattered. The violent sobs started in her chest. Clogged her throat until they burst from her lips, loud and keening. They fell into each other's arms, clutching tightly. Claire didn't consider the oddity of two near-strangers hugging as though they'd never again not become entwined.

Because they weren't strangers. Not really. Both of them were unwilling visitors in a horrifying nightmare. One from which there was no escape.

David Willard

November 11
10:15 a.m.

"David." Kurt Schriever pushed open his door. "Do you have a minute?"

Squelching a flicker of irritation at the interruption, David pasted a welcoming smile on his face. "Of course."

The older man crossed to David's desk and handed him a file folder. Mystified, he opened it and quickly saw that it held real-estate listings. "I've dithered over this decision for too long," Schriever said, dropping into a chair. "I've finally decided that I'm opening another office in Columbus." A quick sprint of excitement raced up David's spine. The man had been mulling over the idea for years. David had given up believing he'd ever act on it. "I think the increased client list will more than make up for the additional overhead. I figure we can share staff between the two offices, but I'll want someone stationed there full-time." He made a face. "God knows it would take a stick of dynamite to blast Linda out of this town, but it doesn't necessarily have to be management assigned there. How about you? What are you and Claire's plans after Janie goes away to college?"

It was an effort to keep the elation filling him from sounding in his voice. "I'd describe them as flexible. And it's not like Columbus is all that far from West Bend." It was only a ninety-minute drive, slightly more to the downtown area.

"Other side of the world, according to Linda," Kurt muttered. Then he stopped. Frowned. "Almost forgot. I got word from the hotel we use there. They were served with a warrant this morning for our company receipts for the last six months. Probably weren't supposed to tip me off, but we do a hell of a lot of business there. I've put a call in to our attorney. Damn glad we keep clean records."

David's earlier excitement was replaced with foreboding. "IRS?"

"No, that's the hell of it. BCI." Kurt shook his head. "Can't for the life of me figure out what they'd be interested in, but you can be damn sure I'll find out."

BCI. Acid churned in his gut. "It's not the company, it's me." David figured the attorney would ferret out that much information at any rate. He made no attempt to keep the bitterness from his tone. "You've heard about the girl from Saxon Falls who went missing?"

"Of course." Kurt's voice was gruff. "I didn't want to mention it because—"

"At this point, they're looking for connections to Kelsey's case. And just like seven years ago, the first thing they do is look at the families. They're checking out my alibi for October 30. I was in Columbus that weekend with Martin. We had dinner with Joe Beasley and his wife."

Exactly what was in that warrant? His heart began to hammer. And how much information had the hotel turned over? If it covered only charges to the business, there was no problem. If, however, the agents had inquired about all of David's reservations . . .

His panic was mixed with bitterness. The parents of the victim should feel like they were on the same side as the investigators. But it hadn't ever felt like that for David. He'd always had the sense that every word he uttered was weighed for possible dishonesty. And he'd *been* truthful with them. He'd told them everything they needed to know.

"Your *alibi*? Sons of bitches." Schriever's face clouded, one big fist clenching on his lap. "Like you and Claire haven't already been through enough."

David's smile was forced. "I guess it will all be worth it if they manage to find a link to Kelsey through this new case. But as you can imagine, Claire's pretty stressed out over this."

"I'll bet. And how's Janie doing with it?"

The question hit David like a well-placed punch in the solar plexus. How *was* Janie doing with it? "We've managed to keep the cops away from her." But that wasn't enough. It never would be. There'd always be some little asshole at school bringing it up, like that bitchy Miller girl had. He and Claire often made the mistake of believing that they could keep Janie sheltered from it all, but they were lying to themselves. He made a mental note to sit down with his daughter tonight and have a long talk with her. Try to figure out how much damage all this new coverage had had on her. She wasn't like Kelsey. Happy, sad, angry, their oldest daughter wore her emotions for all to see. Janie spoke freely at home—her anxiety had never been an issue there. But she rarely shared anything personal. At least, not with him.

A stab of guilt arrowed deep. *Father of the year*, an inner voice jeered. Like going to parent-teacher conferences once each semester gave him a clue about what was going on in his youngest daughter's head.

Just like he hadn't had a clue with Kelsey. Until it'd been too late.

◆ ◆ ◆

Glancing at the clock on the wall, David shoved away from the desk and stood. He hadn't been as productive as he would have liked after the meeting with Kurt. So he'd leave on time for once. Have dinner with the family, and spend some time with Janie. Try to get an idea about how much she'd been impacted by the DeVries case. He was ashamed to admit that he couldn't recall the last time he'd had a conversation with his daughter that had lasted more than a couple of minutes. And he knew exactly what that said about him.

Troubled, he crossed the room to collect his coat. Opening the door of the closet tucked into the corner of the room, he noticed one of his gloves on the floor. He bent down to retrieve it and rose, rapping his head painfully on the overhead shelf, knocking it from its brackets. Colors burst behind his eyelids as pain exploded. The shelf and contents tumbled down on top of him. He raised his hands in a delayed response that was too sluggish to stem the avalanche. It all fell to the floor, the shelf with a thud, followed by a tinkle of glass.

Damn it. Gingerly David touched his head where a bump was already forming before squatting down to deal with the mess. He found the brackets and readjusted them before affixing the shelf again. He crouched to dig through the pile. Scrolls of old campaign ads, a ball cap he didn't even recognize, a briefcase he no longer used . . . All were covered with tiny shards of glass. His fingers slowed as he pulled a large framed picture from the bottom of the heap. With hands that had started to shake, he turned it over.

A crayon drawing of their family. No, he corrected himself immediately as his gaze traced over the sketch, not crayons but colored pencils. Kelsey had graduated from crayons years earlier. She'd been eight when she'd presented this to him and told him gravely that he was to hang it at work.

In it, he and Claire flanked the two girls, all of them holding hands with big smiles on their faces. He liked to think Kelsey had gotten her artistic side from him. She'd captured their features with a talent far beyond her years. He'd framed the picture, and it had hung on the wall of his office until several months after she'd disappeared. When looking at it had become an agonizing reminder of everything he'd lost. He'd had to hide it away because each time he passed it, he was sucked back into that emotional maelstrom with its sticky tentacles of grief that could entrap him if he let them.

He carried the picture to the waste can, carefully brushing the broken bits of glass from it. David hadn't thought about it for years. But seeing it again was a reminder of the vagaries of time. How it rushed and ebbed in a rhythm more random than any of them wanted to admit. Had he known how finite the years with his daughter would be, he liked to think he would have worked less. Played more. Listened better. He would have tucked away every moment with her to guard against the day when memories were all he had left, to be taken out and pored over like a miser fingering his gold.

He could feel his eyes misting as he strode back toward the closet, the symbolism not lost on him. It was a tangible representation of how he'd locked away every painful memory in a simple quest for emotional survival.

"Hey, David, glad I caught you."

He froze, glad his back was to the door as he surreptitiously wiped his eyes. "Wow, looks like you've got a mess on your hands. Odd time for spring cleaning." A hearty laugh. Grayson. "How 'bout that celebratory drink you missed out on the other night? My treat. Meet me at the Golden Bucket in ten?"

"Sounds good." Anything to get rid of the man. He rose, replacing the picture on the shelf quickly. "I'll see you there."

"You need some help with any of this?"

"No." The word was more emphatic than necessary. Quickly he moved to replace the briefcase, scrolls of paper, and odds and ends that had been dumped. "No, I can handle this." The same way he'd been handling things for seven years. Tucking them away out of sight in hopes that the painful recollections could be dismissed as easily.

◆ ◆ ◆

"I can't stay long." David slipped off his wool overcoat and draped it over the back of the bar stool next to Steve Grayson. "I want to get home in time to have supper with my family." He'd regretted accepting the man's invite the moment the words had left his mouth. A quick drink, no more, he promised himself, and then he'd be on his way. He caught the bartender's eye, and the man ambled his way. Scanning the bottles arrayed behind the bar, David said, "Lagavulin Sixteen. Neat."

"I've got dinner plans myself." Grayson flashed his trademark bright smile. "Seeing someone new." As the man went into detail about his flavor of the month, David's mind drifted. A sense of despondency had seized him, and he knew exactly what had caused it. Putting the picture away again was less about avoidance and more about self-preservation. He accepted the drink from the bartender gratefully, lifting the glass to his lips and taking a swallow. The scorch of the liquor sliding down his throat was welcome.

"I saw Schriever coming out of your office today." Grayson's tone was studiedly casual. "Rumor is he's finally ready to open a place in Columbus. I'm single and willing to relocate, if that's what Kurt decides. In fact . . ." The other man drained his glass and raised it in a silent signal to the bartender for another. "I'd give my left nut to be the one assigned there full-time."

That was too damn bad, David mused, as he tilted his glass to his lips again. Because *he* was determined to be the one in that position, should it materialize. "That seems unnecessarily self-destructive." Just like it would be self-destructive to surround himself with reminders of the tragedy that had befallen their family. The thought did nothing to assuage the guilt that lingered. It wasn't a betrayal to his daughter to tuck away her mementoes when doing so had helped him heal. That's where he and Claire had always differed. Sometimes violently so. His wife insisted on keeping Kelsey's room a shrine. That was a battle he'd lost. But when he'd found her hidden copies of the age progression sketches of Kelsey that had been done every couple of years, David had destroyed them over his wife's tearful protests. She seemed to lack even the most basic instinct for her own emotional health, as if steeping herself in misery somehow drew her closer to the daughter they'd lost.

"I know exactly what you're planning, you know."

Somehow David had lost track of the conversation. "What's that, Steve?" He downed the rest of the Scotch and set the glass on the bar, then picked up his coat.

"You'll probably advise Kurt against the expansion." There was a dull flush on Grayson's face and no sign of his signature smile. "A couple of weekends a month in Columbus works right into your plans, doesn't it?"

David slipped his arms into his coat. Buttoned it. "And what plans are those?"

"You tell me." The man's look was knowing. "More than once I've been in town with Kurt or Martin to meet with clients, and I ask at the desk about the second room on the firm's account."

Unless the hotel was fully booked, it kept two rooms set aside for the firm's use. Kurt infrequently spent the night, preferring to commute. Which meant that the extra room was rarely needed, since the men doubled up. Trepidation clutching in his gut, David gave the other man a knowing look. "Stinson's snoring get to you, or were you looking to get lucky those nights?"

"Doesn't matter. Because sometimes that room wasn't available. You'd reserved it."

The blood in David's veins solidified. "You're delusional. How many drinks did you have before I got here?"

His words had no discernible effect on the other man. "Know what else I discovered? A couple of times I went to your room, knocked on the door. Called the room phone several times. And there was never any answer. You didn't charge the company for the room on those days, though. I checked. So what were you doing in the city, Willard? And where the hell were you?"

"You checked?" David shoved his hands into his coat pockets where they fisted. "You seem to have a lot of extra time on your hands. I took Claire to the city for our anniversary once. And we went as a family a couple of times to a concert. You really need to get some help. Your imagination is working overtime." Without waiting for the other man's reaction, he turned and made his way out of the bar.

First the BCI warrant and now Grayson. David's jaw clenched as he strode rapidly toward the door. His chest was tight. His throat closed. Fresh air. That's all he needed. He elbowed through a cluster of customers gathered near the entrance and pushed the door open. Filled his lungs with a single greedy gulp. But that didn't completely negate the sensation of walls closing in around him.

Special Agent Mark Foster

November 11
6:45 p.m.

"I appreciate your seeing me, Reverend."

The Reverend Thomas Mikkelsen was tall and lean to the point of skeletal. He engulfed Mark's proffered hand in his two bony ones. "Welcome, Agent. I'm sorry my schedule wouldn't allow a meeting before now. Bless you for the work you do to assist the victims in our society." His dark eyes were intense and strangely hypnotic. Mark had the fleeting mental image of a swaying cobra, gaze fixed on its prey. "It's God's work, as surely as mine is."

"Thank you." Mark gave a small tug to free his hand. "Is there somewhere we can go to talk? I promise I won't take up much of your time." He'd been trying to set up a meet with the man since the day after speaking to Sims, but the pastor had been out of town, according to the church secretary.

"Of course. Please follow me." Mark shut the door behind him and trailed behind the man through a door to their immediate right. Mikkelsen snapped on the light switch. "Our secretary has an office next to mine. Cindy Long. I believe you spoke on the phone."

"We did." Mark looked around at the small cramped space. It was dominated with file cabinets and bookshelves, all of which were crammed to overflowing. A large cross hung behind the pastor's desk, next to a particularly gruesome picture depicting the crucifixion.

"As you could see when you drove up, our work spaces connect the church to our living quarters. There's a social hall behind the offices that doubles as a conference area." The pastor cleared off a chair in front of a battered metal desk and repositioned the file folders and books atop an already teetering pile on a scarred wooden end table. "But there never seems to be enough space. I apologize for the mess." He waved Mark to a chair before rounding the desk and seating himself. "I'm trying to put the Christmas curriculum together for our Wednesday Worship groups." Catching Mark's eye, he added, "That's like Sunday School during the week for kids, in case you're not a churchgoer."

He wasn't, although Kelli occasionally took Nicky. Maybe that was something he should rethink once his wife was back home. A trusted pastor might be able to recommend resources for them. Although Mark was speaking to Kelli and his son nearly nightly, he wasn't communicating in any significant way with his wife. There was a stiltedness between them that only seemed to grow with each passing day. Damned if he knew how to fix it.

Reaching into his pocket, he withdrew a notebook and pen. Some of the agents had embraced technology and used a portable digital tablet for interviews. It probably would save time when it came to completing reports, but Mark preferred writing to tapping keys. He'd stick to pen and paper until forced to make the change. "As your secretary probably mentioned, I'm investigating the Whitney DeVries disappearance. I'm told she attended services at your church."

Mikkelsen nodded. "Occasionally, although her family aren't members. Well," he corrected himself, "at least not her parents. She would sometimes come with her grandmother, Helen DeVries."

"When is the last time you saw her?"

Pursing his lips, Mikkelsen thought for a moment. "I'm afraid I'm not going to be able to be very exact. Three months ago, perhaps? Maybe a bit less. She's here more often in the summer. I assume she spends more time with Helen then than she does during the school year."

"So she doesn't attend Wednesday Worship?"

"No, that's only for church members, I'm afraid."

"What about church camp?"

"She attended twice." Mark's head swiveled toward the new voice. A stout woman entered the room balancing a loaded tray with remarkable ease. She made her way over to the pastor with a cluck of disapproval. "That mess on your table is going to end up on the floor," she scolded the man. Setting the tray down on his desk, she proceeded to pour coffee and load cookies onto plates. "Not last summer, though. Probably not the one before that, either. Once the girls start thinking about nothing more than boys, clothes, and Godless music, we tend to lose their participation."

"Laura," the pastor admonished. "'A gentle tongue is a tree of life, but perverseness in it breaks the spirit.'"

"The mouth of the righteous utters wisdom, and his tongue speaks justice," the woman retorted. She turned with a grace belied by her girth and thrust a coffee cup balanced on a plate toward Mark.

"My wife, Laura," Mikkelsen said belatedly. "She helps a great deal with the youth groups."

"We established a tri-county church camp for children the year we arrived here." Laura Mikkelsen wore her graying hair wound tightly in a bun, and her high-necked dress hit her at midcalf. "With so many small towns in the area, it's almost impossible for each church to put on its own activities. By pooling our resources, we can serve more children and offer a greater array of services."

"We can look up the exact dates that Whitney attended." The pastor picked up a cookie and bit into it with relish. "Laura keeps very exact records. The partner churches send out invitations to youth events to all the families in the area with kids ages five to eighteen."

Under Laura Mikkelsen's gimlet stare, Mark set his notebook down and picked up the coffee. Sipped. She gave a sniff as she added, "Not that we have many camp participants as the children get older. They're involved in sports and clubs and running around, the likes of which we never saw growing up. Time better off studying a Bible, if you ask me."

Because it seemed expected, Mark exchanged the coffee for a cookie. "Family life has certainly gotten busier."

"But not Godlier."

"Thank you for the refreshments, Laura." Although the pastor's tone was mild enough, it also held a command. "That will be all."

With another loud sniff, the woman headed for the door. "I'll be back for the dishes later."

"Before you go . . ." Laura Mikkelsen stopped at Mark's words. Turned. He shot her a smile, one that didn't soften her grim visage appreciably. "I'm interested in your observations about Whitney." His gaze shifted to the pastor. "Both of you."

"A sweet girl," the reverend began.

"Quiet enough," his wife added grudgingly. "But she could be impertinent when surrounded by a gaggle of her friends. And easily distracted."

"Did you ever notice anyone hanging around her? An adult paying her more attention than the rest of the children?"

"Pastors and volunteers from other participating churches would be present on a revolving basis," the reverend said. "We always have several different age groups to cover. And some of the older children would also help out."

"Between the two of you, perhaps you can make a list of everyone involved with the camp the years Whitney attended." It was a long shot, but Mark couldn't ignore the fact that both Whitney and Kelsey Willard had attended the church and camp at some point. It was one of the few connections between the girls that he'd discovered. There was also Sims's reference to Mikkelsen's lack of alibi for the night Kelsey had gone missing. Mark had double-checked the case files. They corroborated Sims's assertion.

"Oh, dear." The pastor shrugged helplessly. "That was so long ago. I'm not sure I could recall . . ."

"Most of that information would be in my files," Laura asserted proudly. "As well as the attendance for volunteers and other campgoers. An adult who couldn't be counted on to show up wasn't asked to help again."

Interest pinged. Mark asked, "How far back would those files go?"

"Since we arrived, as I noted earlier. I'll get them for you. They're in the church office." She flicked a disdainful glance around her husband's space. "I share it with the secretary, but it's much more organized." Without waiting for a response, she bustled out of the door.

"Laura's organizational skills are one of her gifts." Polishing off the last of the cookie, the reverend wiped his hands on a napkin. "I'm so glad we're going to be able to help you, after all."

"Do you remember where you were on October 30, the night Whitney DeVries went missing? When did you hear about it?"

Mikkelsen thought for a moment, then leaned forward to consult a desk calendar that looked as untidy as his office. Flipping through the pages, he finally settled on one. "October 30. That was a Friday. Ah." He tapped a bony forefinger on the page. "Yes, I received a crisis call that night at about seven thirty."

Mark set his plate and mug on the tray before leaning back again and picking up his pen. "A crisis call?"

"The police station had responded to a domestic disturbance at the home of one of my church members. Fortunately, they allowed the couple to phone me, and I was able to go and help."

Mark jotted down this information. "You went alone?"

"Oh, no." Mikkelsen sent a quick look at the doorway before selecting another cookie. "Laura frequently accompanies me on home visits. The members find her such a comfort in times of need."

Comfort? Mark schooled his features to impassivity. Somehow he couldn't imagine the woman as a calming influence. "So you and your wife went to help one of your congregation members. Do you recall when you returned?"

The man took a bite of the cookie and contemplated as he chewed. Swallowing, he answered. "It was several hours later. But we were home before eleven thirty. Then we said some extra prayers before bed, as we always do when one of our members is in distress." He took another bite.

Whitney DeVries's cell phone records had indicated the last communications on her phone had been after midnight, on October 31. One number had belonged to her friend Macy Odegaard. The other presumably belonged to her kidnapper. Which meant that just like in the Willard case, the pastor had no alibi, other than his wife.

"Do you recall when you heard of Whitney's disappearance?"

"Oh, I'm sure Laura would have told me. She has her finger on the pulse of everything that happens in the area."

An interesting choice of words for what some might describe as a gossip. Mark decided to level the same question at the man's wife. "Do you also have lists of other people who might not have been directly affiliated with running the church camps? Repairmen. Groundskeepers. The people who clean the church."

"We work with volunteers as much as possible to keep costs down. But several churches in the area employ the same janitor." He set the cookie on his plate and pulled open his center desk drawer, withdrawing a notepad and pen. "We still hire someone to push snow, but we no longer pay for lawn care." He began to scribble down some names. "Years ago, we employed Whitney's father to take care of it for a summer, though I tend to think his mother might have pressured him into agreeing to do it."

Everything inside Mark stilled. "Brian DeVries worked for you? Or all the area churches?"

"All of them." He smiled. "It was a big job for one person. Now we have volunteers share the duty."

"What year was that?" It had been seven years ago in September that Kelsey had been snatched.

The reverend looked confused. "I really couldn't say. He'd probably recall it better than me."

Mark's smile was grim. "I'll be sure and ask him." Because that was yet another thing DeVries hadn't bothered to share. "If you recall any other volunteers that might have been helping on a regular basis, I'd appreciate their names, as well."

The pastor looked pained but dutifully began writing again.

Laura Mikkelsen returned with the lists she'd promised, and after taking them, Mark asked her several of the same questions he had of her husband. She'd learned of Whitney's disappearance from the girl's grandmother, the woman asserted. She verified her husband's account of their whereabouts on the night the girl disappeared, as well as the timeline. And her memory appeared much more accurate than her husband's when it came to volunteers—including DeVries—as she added several names of people who worked in the kitchen and on various fundraisers. Collecting the papers from her and her husband, Mark rose after jotting a note to check with the Saxon Falls Police Department to corroborate their account of the domestic dispute the Mikkelsens claimed to have been called to.

An undisguised expression of relief on his lean face, the pastor walked him to the door. "I hope we've been of some help."

"I appreciate your assistance." Mark turned slightly to include Laura, who was following closely behind him.

She nodded serenely. "Do not withhold good from those to whom it is due, when it is in your power to act."

Mark couldn't rely on any personal knowledge, but given her pious tone, he assumed she was once again quoting the Bible. When Reverend Mikkelsen pulled open the door, Mark stopped. Stared. Pinpoints of light punctuated the darkness in a semicircle in front of the structure. A murmur of voices could be heard chanting, but the words were indistinct.

"What's this?"

"Some of our members have joined together in the evenings to pray about the evil that has touched our church twice now in the last few years. Two young girls have been sacrificed so far because of the growth of feminism in our country. We pray to God for his forgiveness, and to show us a way to promote the proper role for men and women in our society."

Mark stared hard at the man. "The only one responsible for the evil visited on those two girls is the offender. He alone is responsible for the crime, and we don't know his motivation." If they did, they'd be a lot closer to catching the man.

"God has shown us his motivation." The dim lighting gave Mikkelsen's face an unearthly glow. "It's our responsibility to right the societal wrongs that led to these crimes."

◆ ◆ ◆

Mark paused in the doorway of the hotel. Sloane Medford was bent over her laptop, which was placed in the center of one of the folding tables in the room that Ben Craw had last occupied.

"I got subs. Yours is in the bag." Sloane didn't look up as she uttered the words.

Mark had added a table since Craw had left, as the files and reports had slowly grown. With the other man in it, the room had always seemed more work space than personal. Sloane's occupancy had changed all that.

Her boots were sitting just inside the door. Functional snow boots, but tall and fur-trimmed; decidedly feminine. Her red, fitted wool coat hung over the back of one of the desk chairs. She'd discarded her suit jacket on the bed, revealing a silky white blouse.

"In or out, Foster." She didn't look his way. "You're letting the cold air in."

Blowing out a breath, Mark stepped inside. Any trepidation he felt from working with her again seemed to be unreciprocated. She'd been nothing but businesslike since her arrival.

Locking the door behind him, he went to the fast-food bag and withdrew the remaining sandwich. Unwrapping it, he took a bite, then set down the files the Mikkelsens had given him and struggled out of his coat while he ate, talking in between bites. "What'd you learn from Dane Starkey's family?" When they'd split up assignments that morning, she'd agreed to contact them.

"Nothing earth-shaking." She looked up then, and her fingers paused on the keyboard. It occurred to him for the first time that she must have been writing her report for the day, something he still had to do. "According to the nine members of Shelley Starkey Koen's extended family that I spoke to, Dane Starkey was telling the truth about the incident twenty-two years ago. The DeVrieses had lived in the neighborhood only for a few months, but Brian DeVries spent some time at the Starkey house visiting Lewis, who was his age. Shelley was Lewis's sister. The alleged sexual assault took place in a bathroom in the basement. Shelley kept quiet for a couple of days until she finally spilled the whole sordid story to her mother. I take it her father went over to the DeVries house, out for blood. From the sounds of things, Brian's mother paid them not to report it to the police, in return for putting Brian in counseling and moving out of the neighborhood." She pushed back a strand of blonde hair that had escaped from the intricate knot at her nape. "A couple of months later, Brian and his mother relocated to Saxon Falls."

"I still can't believe none of this would have shown up in a background check."

She lifted a shoulder. "The DeVries family didn't live at that Columbus address long. Brian probably fudged the dates on his application. The years at his former Columbus address would have matched up even if the exact months didn't. It'd be easy to overlook, even if someone was paying attention."

"You pulled property records for each of the Starkey family members on the list?" Technically, Sloane was now the senior member on the case. She had four years' more experience than Mark. But he had the most time on this particular case, so for now, she was following his lead.

"I didn't find any more than you had."

"Damn it." He finished wolfing down the sandwich and wadded up the wrapper in one fist. Dane Starkey's alibi had been unshakeable. He'd been in a poker game with three other people in Westerville, a half hour from Columbus. Even if Mark had been able to poke holes in any of the three men's stories, footage from traffic cameras had solidified Starkey's claim. He'd been nowhere near Saxon Falls the night Whitney DeVries had been taken.

But his large extended family had even more reason to hate Brian DeVries than Dane did. They were still running down the alibis of each of them, including Shelley's husband. So far, nothing was panning out. And if no one in the family owned any property outside of their family homes, where would they have taken Whitney DeVries if one of them had snatched her?

"Aw." Sloane made a faux purr of sympathy. "I recognize that expression. Your prime suspect isn't looking especially shiny anymore. Don't get discouraged. I still have to check out all their alibis for October 30."

"I'm not ready to pull the other investigators off him yet." But she was right. He'd taken the man apart, figuratively at least. Starkey might have the motive for kidnapping Whitney, but given his alibi, he would have needed help. The man's bank records showed that he hadn't shared any of the money DeVries had paid him. And while making DeVries suffer by kidnapping his daughter might have appealed to him, it also would have interfered with the man's willingness to pay the final installment of the blackmail. Starkey should have immediately come to mind once Whitney went missing. But Brian hadn't given his name to BCI. Mark considered that omission damning.

"Have you faced DeVries with all this yet?"

He shook his head, picking up the files and crossing to the table to pull out a seat next to hers. "I wanted to see where the Starkey thing went first. I'm betting he was the first one DeVries suspected, too. He'd have to. What kind of father doesn't share that kind of detail with the cops when his kid goes missing?"

"One with something to hide. We have to wonder if he ever outgrew his taste for teenage or near-teen girls."

He exchanged a look with her. They were often on the same wavelength. On the last case they'd worked together, he'd thought that quality made them good teammates. Which showed how far off base his impressions could be.

"Today I found out he omitted something else." Briefly, he told her about the man's connection to the church. "We need to discover what year he was doing the mowing and if it was anywhere around where the camp was held." He held up the papers. "These might tell us." He spread the pages out on the table in front of him.

"Did you get anything else from the pastor about the girls? He knew Kelsey Willard, too, right?" Mark had to give Sloane credit; she'd caught up on the case remarkably fast since her arrival.

"He knew her but provided no details that weren't in the report. But our meeting did take a turn for weird before I left." Briefly he told her about his final conversation with the pastor. She didn't appear as shocked as he'd been by it.

"Sounds like one of the radical religious types who blames natural disasters on any social agenda they happen to disagree with. Believe me, they're far more common than you might think."

"Laura Mikkelsen said Brian DeVries had helped out ten or eleven years ago." He flipped through the pages Laura had given him until he found the ones detailing the youth-camp participants by year. Skimmed until Willard's name jumped out at him. "Kelsey would have been . . ." He did some quick figuring in his head. "Ten the last time she went to the camp."

She leaned in to read the list in his hand, close enough that her hair tickled his jaw. Dropping the papers, Mark lurched from his chair as though he'd been scorched. "We need to nail down the date DeVries was there, see if it correlates." Even if the times coincided, it didn't tie the man to Willard's disappearance. Or Whitney's.

But it would be another connection, and add to the mountain of explaining the man had to do.

He pulled out his cell, checked the time. "I have to call home." Even if Kelli wasn't exactly communicative lately, he wanted to talk to Nicky before his son went to bed.

"Go ahead. I'm going to change into something more comfortable. I assume it'll be another late night."

The words gave his feet wings. He practically ran for the adjoining door that led to his room. His hand was on the knob when Sloane said, "Give my regards to your wife."

The words transported him to the last time the two of them had worked a case. When their focus had switched from the investigation to each other. A mental picture flashed across his mind. The two of them on the bed, bodies tangled, clothes pooled on the floor. His last remaining brain cell was all that had prevented him from making the biggest mistake of his life. And as he'd rolled off the mattress, headed to his room, she'd uttered the same remark. *Give my regards to your wife.*

Mark responded the way he should have then. "Go to hell, Sloane."

Whitney DeVries

November 12
6:12 p.m.

"Much better, Whitney. I applaud the way you kept your word and tried harder today."

She kept her head down so he wouldn't see the hatred that would surely show on her face. "Thank you."

"Thank you . . . what?"

Her teeth ground. She had to choke the words out. "Thank you . . . Daddy." A wave of revulsion swept over her. As if she could ever be related to this monster. She'd say whatever was necessary to spare herself another whipping. But still . . . every time she called him by the name he insisted on, it felt like a betrayal to her real family. Who were still alive. Since last night, she'd grown more convinced of that by the minute. The words Kelsey Willard had written had been echoing in her brain all day. Had stoked the growing conviction that the freak had constructed an elaborate lie. One guaranteed to make Whitney feel alone. Desolate. With no one else to rely on.

She hated him more for that than for anything else. Even the beatings.

"I realize that this routine is more difficult. But you're so accomplished, I skipped a couple of films to provide you with a challenge. Had it proven too much for you, I would have moved you back. But your effort today proved that my first inclination was correct. You have a natural ability that's rare. Innate talent can make up for a lack of training, although you had that, as well." A thread of disapproval entered his voice. "I would never have allowed you to squander that by quitting your lessons. But that's a moot point now."

Despair filtered through her. She tried to think about her family. About the people who would be looking for her. Her dad was a deputy. The whole sheriff's office would be helping search. But she had no idea where she was. How long she'd been unconscious before she'd awakened in this place. Had it been hours? Days? She could have been taken across the country. A shuddering breath lodged in her throat at the thought.

"Although film is not as interactive as a live teacher, you can be assured you're receiving the finest instruction."

A memory stirred. *Maybe learning all about* him *will get me out.* Kelsey had been right. The more details she could find out about the freak, the better. Perhaps she'd be able to figure out where they were from something he shared. "Did your mother make these films while she was still in New York City?" He'd said she'd been a ballerina there. Were they in New York now?

"No. She made them so my sister could practice even when Mother was gone. She worked quite hard to provide for both of us. I helped out by doing all the chores around the house. That sort of work ethic is sorely lacking in children today."

If kids are so rotten, why do you keep kidnapping them? she thought mutinously. Two of them at least. What had happened to Kelsey Willard? What was his plan after ripping them from their homes? A trickle of fear snaked down her spine.

"Children these days take too much for granted," he lectured. "Even their families." She watched his shadowy outline, trying to get an idea of how tall he was. How big. If she wasn't able to see his face, it would help to at least observe his general height and weight. But his shadow against the backdrop of lighting from the computer screen and projector was elongated. Narrow. It would be hard to get an accurate idea of his appearance from it.

Somehow she thought he knew that, too. "Once children are old enough, they should contribute to the family unit. Love and acceptance must be earned. If you learn your lessons well enough, perhaps in time you will be given that opportunity with our family."

Our. Her mind seized on the word. Were there others here, then? Perhaps Kelsey wasn't dead or escaped. Maybe she'd "graduated" to another space in this man's house. The thought didn't make Whitney feel any better. It wasn't just freedom from this dungeon she wanted, but escape from the freak altogether. She wanted to go home.

Kelsey had written that she'd been down here for a year. Whitney thought it might have been two weeks or so since she'd been taken. The thought of being here twelve months—or longer—made her want to weep.

"You haven't responded, Whitney." The censure in his voice jolted her from her reverie.

"I'm sorry. I was thinking about what you said earlier." What had he been saying? Her mind scrambled frantically to recall his words. "About kids contributing to the family. I don't know how I'm contributing anything."

"At this point your contribution is your effort. Your cooperation in following the rules I've outlined. And your acceptance of your new life. Your gratitude for the privileges I allow you."

"I am grateful." For allowing her to watch a kiddie show? For chaining her up like an animal? Not for the first time, she wondered if the monster was insane. Somehow that didn't make her feel better.

"We'll see. If you do well tomorrow, you'll earn back thirty minutes of TV privileges. For this evening, I suggest you spend the hours before bedtime in quiet contemplation of how you can prove your gratitude and acceptance."

He turned off the projector but left the computer on. She listened carefully. Could hear his sure steps as he retreated. A slight scraping sound, then a door being opened. Closed. The scraping sound was repeated. The sound of a key in a lock? That would mean even if she got loose from the chain around her wrist, she'd have to get through a locked door to get out of here. Her shoulders slumped dejectedly.

She knew better than to go to the mattress. That wasn't allowed until 9:00 p.m. An alert would beep on the computer, warning her it was time to get ready for bed. Fifteen minutes later, it would switch off. The only hours he couldn't observe her were at night. In the dark. A thread of desolation snaked through her. There was no way out. No escape.

Blinking back the tears that threatened, she remained motionless as if locked in the contemplation he'd demanded. He'd be checking on her while the computer was on, even though the screen was blank, emitting only a white glow. He'd know whether she'd follow his instructions.

Or whether she gave the appearance of doing so.

A thread of defiance returned. What had she learned from his appearance here today? Nothing that would aid in a description of him. But she knew he carried a key with him to let himself in and out of the area below the stage. What else? She thought hard. His steps toward the door hadn't been hesitant, although he'd been walking into shadows. Which meant he had the way memorized, or he didn't have to worry about running into any obstacles, because there weren't any.

She squinted into the darkness but as usual could see nothing. But wait, that wasn't true. The projector would have to be elevated in order to beam the film at the stage wall behind her. So it had to be set on a table or stool of some kind. The space directly ahead of it and around it was empty. The glow of the screen showed nothing in its vicinity.

Whitney wasn't sure how any of that helped. But she tucked away the observations in any case. Because if nothing else, she liked knowing that when he checked on her, he'd see a girl with her head bowed submissively.

He wouldn't suspect that she was filing away details that just might aid in her escape.

◆ ◆ ◆

She'd fallen asleep. Whitney bolted upright on the mattress, rubbing at her eyes. How had that happened? She rolled off the edge, wincing a little as the action pulled at the skin surrounding the fresh wound on her back. What time was it? Impossible to tell, but the light hemming the sides of the curtain told her it was no longer night. Early morning, perhaps.

Damn. She hurried to the shower to retrieve the screw. Retraced her steps to pry up the board again. Took out the papers and carried them over to the window. Unrolled them and tried to find her place from the night before. Reading about Kelsey's experiences might provide ideas for escape.

I try to learn as much about him as I can. His mother was a ballerina. His sister danced, too. And he has a wife somewhere. Is she in this place, as well? Does she know that I'm down here? Because if she does, she has to be as much a monster as he is.

I still haven't figured out why I was taken. What made him pick me? Did he just happen to see me on the road that day? I wasn't paying attention. I was too upset to notice the van until it was too late. Or had he already selected me and had been watching me for a while? That creeps me out even more.

Why am I here? He's hurt me . . . badly. Time and time again. But he's never gotten close enough that I can see his face. The movies would say that's a good thing. That maybe it means he'll let me go eventually. But I know that's not true. He isn't going to release me. He has plans for me. But it's hard to figure out what they are. All he talks about is character and being grateful. Earning my place. As if I want to stay and be a part of whatever sick thing he's running here!

Whitney had to stop reading. It was too familiar. She'd had a similar conversation with the freak last night. Knowing that he was playing out the same scenario with her as he had with the girl he'd taken before didn't make her feel better. It made her feel like a puppet. A thing. Like a piece of clay to be molded into a shape of his choosing.

Kelsey hadn't allowed herself to be molded. She'd just pretended. That was probably smart. But Whitney didn't know if she could be that good an actress for any length of time.

Returning to the sheets in her hands, she moved them on the wall until they were positioned in a dim slant of light.

He lets you earn things for good behavior. And after a while, I started requesting things I wanted instead of the lame stuff he offered. Like a big sketch pad and a pencil. I'm good at drawing.

The words were followed by a small sketch of a girl with long, dark hair with her eyes crossed and her tongue out. But despite the silliness of the picture, it was good. Detailed. It looked like a real person and not the stick figure Whitney would be able to draw.

So I fill the pad up with my artwork. Of my room. My family. Places I've seen. And I carefully tear out a page or two in between to write on. Because he'll look at the pad sometime. Nothing is allowed to be private here. But these pages will be because I figured out a way to hide them.

If only I could find a way to hide myself.

Sometimes I miss my family so much, it's like my heart is ripping in two. I can hear my mom's laugh, or see Janie clowning around in my room with one of the tiaras I won in those kiddie pageants. I remember the way it used to be, just the four of us.

And other times I hate my father so much that I don't want to see him, ever again. He's the reason I left the house that day. He's the reason I was so sad and angry those last few weeks, our secret weighing me down like an anchor. I'm here because of him.

Sometimes I dream that he's the one who brought me here.

Whitney's nape prickled, uneasy at the raw emotion in the words. But an instant later, her attention was yanked away by a tiny scratching sound.

A key in the lock of the door.

Panic speared through her. The day's meals were always on the edge of the stage when she got up. Never had she been awake when he brought them. There was no time to put the papers away. To replace the board beneath the mattress. She had a split instant to consider her options. There wasn't a pillowcase or sheet on the mattress. But the dated nightgown she wore was baggy.

The door began to open. Frantically, she rolled the papers up and sprinted on tiptoe back to the mattress as she shoved them beneath the nightgown. The screw she still clutched cut into her palm as she eased back onto the mattress. Huddled there in a fetal position, trying to control her breathing. Her heart was hammering so hard, she was afraid he would hear it.

How had she slept through his approach every morning? Even the quiet sound of his footsteps seemed magnified to her heightened senses. They drew closer and closer, and she squeezed her eyes shut, praying he'd think she still slept.

She hardly dared to breathe as there was a tiny sound only feet away. The food being set down. But he didn't retreat. Not right away.

Did he suspect something? Or did he stay there like that every morning, listening to her breathe? She forced herself to draw oxygen into her lungs and then release it in a slow, even rhythm. Her pulse was galloping in her veins like a spooked wild thing.

The moment stretched. Finally, she heard him move away. Relief streamed from her, turning her muscles lax. The paper made a tiny crinkling sound against her body. His footsteps stopped. Her heart in her throat, Whitney deliberately moved her arm as if she was changing positions. The chain jangled. Praying he'd think that was the source of the sound he'd heard, she lay still again.

A minute later she heard the key in the door. The sound of it opening then closing behind him. She pressed the hand fisted around the screw to her lips to stifle the sob that threatened.

That had been too close. How much time did she have before the computer turned on and the alert sounded? If she wasn't showered and ready by the time the film started, the consequence would be predictable.

She counted to one hundred to make sure he wasn't coming back and then withdrew the pages, rolled them into a tighter scroll, and moved to the space left empty by the floorboard she hadn't replaced. She stuck the papers inside and refit the board before padding toward the shower, her thumb worrying the smooth, flat top of the screw. She mentally berated herself. If she was going to take a risk, this had been a stupid thing to waste it on. It was going to take brains and cunning to get out of here, so she needed to start using her . . .

Her feet faltered to a stop. She ran her thumb over the top of the screw again. A flat head, it had a single groove running through the center of it. Whitney turned to stare in the direction of the barre. It was clamped to the wall at both ends. The clamp was secured by three screws on top, three on the bottom. Screws just like this one. Flat heads. She recalled that much from her endless warm-up routines. Mindless activity that allowed her to take stock of her surroundings. And she had. Whitney had spent plenty of nights testing the security of that barre, but it held tightly. She hadn't been able to pull it loose from the wall, even using all her body weight.

Her fingers closed around the screw again. It had taken all this time to figure out that it could be used for more than a lever.

It might also work as a screwdriver.

Janie Willard

November 13
4:21 p.m.

"I can do this alone," Alyvia said, sending Janie a sideways glance from the passenger seat of the car. "It'd be no big deal."

"You're not doing it alone." Janie knew her friend was trying to reassure her, but it just made the sense of failure clog in her chest again, tighter and darker than before. It had been her idea to approach Newman about the photo shoot. But on Wednesday, she'd managed to get only as close as the hall outside his office, which was in the grungy storage room where the time clock was kept. She'd stood there, heart racing in her chest like a runaway locomotive. Palms sweating. Body shaking. Even if the man wasn't inside, she'd known all she had to do was press a button mounted on the wall that would summon him.

And she'd realized that even if she saw him, she wouldn't be able to utter a word. Janie was finding it hard to forgive herself for that.

The next day Alyvia had accompanied her. A deep fountain of shame welled up at the memory. Her friend had done the talking. It had been all Janie could do to stay in one place when her mind and body were screaming at her to bolt. Alyvia had had to yank her inside when Newman had insisted they go into his office to talk in private.

I'm sorry, Kelsey. After all these years, she hadn't been able to manage a simple conversation, even if it might help them learn something about her sister's disappearance. The fact that a photo shoot had been set up, one for Alyvia rather than Janie, should have comforted her. Somehow it just made her more miserable.

"Why are we waiting here?" Alyvia leaned forward and took the cigarettes from the glove box. Lit one and handed it to Janie. Her fingers fumbling, she drew deeply from it. But it didn't decrease the anxiety clawing through her. Not this time.

A car pulled up beside them. A shaggy-haired boy got out, rounded the hood with a box in his hands.

"Janie Lyn Willard. You've been holding out on me." Typical Alyvia, she wasn't pissed when she recognized Cole Bogart, just intrigued. Reaching over, she snatched the cigarette back and placed it between her lips. Puffed. "Don't tell me he's going to be our bodyguard."

"No."

Cole opened the rear driver-side door and slid inside, pulling it shut behind him. "This thing's a beauty. It'll take care of all your needs and more." He looked at Alyvia. "I'm Cole."

Janie twisted around in her seat to face him. She hadn't been able to speak to Newman, but she'd managed a conversation with Bogart on Wednesday. She'd figured he'd have the expertise they needed. And if the guy thought he owed her something, he'd be likely to agree to her request without demanding too many details.

She could feel Alyvia's gaze on her. Then her friend drawled, "I'm Alyvia. Why don't you tell me how you figure into this little scenario of ours?"

"Janie said you wanted a listening device. Or something that would record without a person knowing they were being recorded. I've checked out Ohio's law, by the way. It's a one-party consent state, so you're in the clear if you want to use the recording in some way."

Alyvia looked impressed. "Janie's always been the smart one."

"I need to know where you're going to use it."

"No," Janie said clearly. "You don't."

Cole looked impatient. "Look, I don't give a shit what you're doing. But I have to know some details. What kind of distance do you need? Where is the transmitter going to be? The settings have to be adjusted accordingly."

"We'll both be in the same room with the person." From there Janie's plan got a bit murkier. Get Newman to agree to take photos similar to the ones on the website. Once they—rather, Alyvia—had convinced him she was serious about the session, the man had opened up a little. Told them he'd taken "artistic photos" for dozens of girls in the area. Which made Janie even more certain that he was the one who'd taken Heather Miller's photos.

And Kelsey's.

"You have to be really careful with this equipment. I used my mom's credit card for it, and I want to get it sent back before she sees the charge on her statement." His voice grew more animated as he pulled off his gloves and opened the box. "These are sweet devices. Since I wasn't sure how they were going to be used, I got more than one. You can record a conversation while you're in proximity to the person, or you can transmit the conversation to the recording mechanism from thirty yards away. So it makes a difference how you want to set it up." He stroked the contents inside the box with affection.

Alyvia lowered her voice. "That means you could wait in the car, Janie. I'd be fine with him, and you'd still get to hear the whole conversation."

"Wait." Cole looked up, his eyes narrowed. "You'd be fine with who?"

"It's *whom*," Alyvia informed him airily. Then frowned. "I think."

"No, I'll be there with you." Janie wasn't that big a coward. At least, she'd hate to think she was. "You'll be safer with me in the room."

Cole looked from one of them to the other. "Okay, so you're going to be inside and not outdoors? Any chance this guy you're meeting has a jamming device?"

"A what?" Janie asked. She reached for the cigarette again, noticed that her fingers were trembling. Damned the physical responses she'd never had total control over.

"A jammer. If the guy you're meeting is technologically savvy, he might have the equipment to scramble the signal of your transmitter."

Alyvia snickered. "Doubtful. I'm surprised this guy even knows how to run a camera."

"A cam . . ." Concern filled Cole's face. "Hey, you aren't by any chance meeting Herb Newman somewhere, are you?"

Turning more fully in her seat, Janie narrowed a look at him. "What do you know about Newman?"

"Other than the fact that his personal grooming sucks and he can live for a week off the food caught in his beard?" He shrugged. "Maybe I started doing some digging when I found those pictures of Miller on the web. I figured Ferin might have taken them, but I can't see him uploading them to that site I found. At least not while he and Miller are still hooking up. I asked around. Heard Newman's name mentioned. The guy claims to work for some sort of talent agency. Takes head shots and stuff and submits them for modeling jobs." Janie couldn't read his expression. "Is that what he told you?"

"Something like that," she admitted.

"And you want proof he's doing it," Cole said slowly. "So you can . . . what? Turn him in for taking skanky pictures?"

She needed to find out whether he'd taken the pictures of Kelsey. And if he had, she wanted him investigated to see if he'd been involved with her sister's disappearance. But she wasn't going to explain any of this to Cole. Despite the favor he'd done her by obtaining the recording device, she had no reason to trust him. And Alyvia, for once, was keeping her mouth shut, as well.

"So you don't want to tell me." He lifted a shoulder, started lifting equipment out of the box. "That's cool. But here's the thing . . . he's been using that empty lake house on Fuller Road. And since that party got busted there last month, the cops are doing a ton of drive-bys. Even Ferin stopped going there for a while, which hasn't been good for his business."

No one said anything for a moment. Then Cole shook the hair out of his eyes and pulled out his cell. "Janie, give me your number."

Immediately wary, she asked, "Why?"

"Because I'll hang out on the road across from the driveway. Pretend I'm on the phone or something. And if I see a cop, I'll call you. Put your phone on vibrate."

She looked at her friend. Alyvia shrugged, as if to say, *why not*? So Janie obeyed, even though she wasn't certain she wanted to give him another way to contact her. Which made her a bitch because she was the one who'd asked him for a favor, and he hadn't hesitated before agreeing to it. "Thanks for doing this."

Cole nodded and finished punching the number into his phone before looking up again. "What time are you meeting him?"

"Five thirty." They'd had to make it early so Alyvia's story of a group-project meeting at the library would appease her foster parents.

"There's no heat or electricity in the cabin, so he must be bringing in his own sources. I think you'll be okay. He's probably a perv, but with two of you there, you should be safe enough. And if you aren't out after an hour, I'll come to the door."

"Hear that, Janie?" Alyvia took a last drag of their shared cigarette before grinding it out in the ashtray. "Our own personal white knight."

"You don't have to do that." Because the words sounded rude even to her ears, she added, "But thanks."

"Yeah." He put his phone away and picked up two pieces of equipment. "Which one of you am I going to wire with this thing?"

◆ ◆ ◆

"Pull your car up on the other side of the garage." It was the only greeting that Newman gave when he came up to their vehicle. "It'll be out of sight that way. Follow me. You can park next to mine."

"Sort of bossy for a daytime school janitor," Alyvia grumbled after Janie buzzed the window up again.

"He's obviously been here before." Janie waited for the man to pull ahead. The semicircle drive was unpaved, so it had been difficult to know if she was even on it as she'd crept up toward the house. The drive was hemmed with trees and overgrown brush, but without their leaves, they'd provide little cover. The house was far enough from the road, though, that it would take a good eye to see a car parked out front in the dark.

"Who hasn't? In the summer, we usually head over by boats. Party on the little beach out back. That way if the cops show up, we can be halfway across the lake before they even get down to us."

Janie pulled up alongside the man's car. Once again Newman came over to her window. "I'm going to haul in equipment. Here." He handed Janie a flashlight. "Once I get the door open, you can come in, but stay out of the way until I get things set up."

She waited for him to go back to his vehicle and start unloading things from his trunk. Then she turned to Alyvia. "Let's go over this one more time."

Her friend threw herself back against the seat theatrically. "Again? Janie, we've practiced every scenario until my brain hurts. I know our stories."

Fingers clenching and unclenching on the steering wheel, Janie drew in a breath. Then another. But deep breathing alone wasn't going to quell her anxiety. Not this time. "Please."

"Okay, fine." As the man made his first trek to the front porch carrying a heavy suitcase in one hand, Alyvia launched into the stories they'd rehearsed and refined repeatedly since Janie had hatched this idea. The familiar lines provided a measure of calm that the breathing hadn't. They'd thought of everything. Picking up the light, she looked at her friend. "Ready?"

◆ ◆ ◆

Alyvia wasted no time once Newman had arranged the space to his satisfaction. "First, I want head shots. I'm going to send them to some modeling agencies. I heard there's a big demand for alternative looks. You know, piercings, dyed hair, tats." She beamed a big smile at him. "That's right up my alley."

The room they were in must have once been a den. Like the large space they'd entered once inside the door, it had a huge stone fireplace on one wall, but empty bookcases covered two of the others. The spotlights he'd brought were situated in a way that made Janie figure he was going to use the blank wall next to the door as a backdrop. She inched over to the fireplace and sat on the stone step before it, her fingers brushing over the pocket with the tiny recorder inside. Cole had seemed sort of disappointed when they determined there was no need for the earpiece and transmitter. Janie had a feeling that he just wanted to play with the equipment. They'd tried out the recorder, though, and it would suit their purposes just fine. She slipped a hand into her coat pocket. Switched it on.

"Yeah, yeah, the punk look is totally popular right now. I actually could show the shots we take to an agency I'm associated with. They might be able to get you a gig as a tattoo or piercing model."

"Yeah?"

Janie shivered. The propane heaters he'd set up on either side of the fireplace hadn't yet made a dent in the temperature. Newman seemed not to feel the cold. He'd slipped out of his parka and was busy taking pieces out of a suitcase. Screwing them into his camera.

"Yeah. It's a niche market, but last year one of the girls I put in touch with them got some good gigs as a goth model. A bunch of her pics are on stock-photo sites." Janie wondered if the girl was also on the site Cole had found on the deep web. "But it's not enough to just have the right look. You have to have unique photos that catch their eye. That's where I come in."

"So how does this deal work?" Newman brought up a camera and snapped an impromptu shot of Alyvia as she slipped her coat off. She pouted. Posed. He took another. When he lowered it, Alyvia went on. "I mean, how do I make money off this gig? Can I get paid for these pictures?"

She was sticking to the script. Janie's chest eased slightly. And being her friend, Alyvia hadn't even inquired too closely about Janie's insistence on this line of questioning.

"You mean for these shots? Probably not. You make your money once the talent agency puts you in touch with clients that hire you as a model. Strike another pose." Alyvia obeyed, and the camera began to click and hum as he began to photograph her. "The agent is in touch with top advertising agencies and fashion designers. They'll line up casting calls for you. You'll get hired for jobs and make a bundle."

Which was a line of bull if Janie had ever heard one. The thought of Herb Newman having any contact with a modeling agency was as far-fetched as her agreeing to a singing and dancing routine in the school talent show. Then the full import of his words hit her. If no money changed hands for the pictures, where had Kelsey gotten $1,000? According to this man, she would have had to accept a modeling job in order to get paid.

Doubt crept in. When would Kelsey have had time for that? And how would she have gotten to the job location without their mom taking her?

"That's good. I like money."

"You'll be raking it in when those advertisers get a look at these shots. I've seen girls that resemble you in *Teen Vogue*. Not as good-looking, even." Who would have guessed that Herb Newman, with the smelly food-catcher beard, was capable of such lines? He and Alyvia continued to chat as he took several more shot sequences.

"How 'bout you, sweetheart?" It took a moment for Janie to realize he was directing the words at her. "You interested in pictures, too?"

"She probably will be when she sees mine." Alyvia bent forward at the waist, her low-cut shirt showing off her cleavage. Blew him a kiss. He captured the shot. "You took pictures of her sister a long time ago. That's how we knew about you."

"Oh, yeah?" He threw an appraising look at Janie. "Who's your sister?"

"Kelsey Willard."

Alyvia glanced at her, clearly surprised that she hadn't had to speak for Janie. But the words had burst from her throat as if propelled. Kelsey. The reason they were here. The reason Janie needed answers from this man.

"Yeah, yeah, I remember." He studied her closely. "You don't look much like her."

"No."

"But you got your own look, right? And for seventy-five bucks, the price I quoted to your friend here, you can get shots done, too. I'll make you look real good."

He turned his attention back to Alyvia, and they proceeded to take full-body shots. Her friend seemed comfortable in her role. She'd had to pretend to be someone else most of her life, just to adapt to all the crappy situations she found herself in because of her deadbeat mother. Janie actually thought she was enjoying this a little bit.

But Janie wasn't. Especially since the man had admitted that he'd taken the pictures Kelsey had hidden in Janie's room shortly before she disappeared. Now that she'd gotten what she came for, she still had to figure out a way to get the information to the cops. Pulling out her cell, she checked the time and saw they'd been there forty minutes already. She had to get Alyvia home soon.

"Okay." Newman lowered his camera. "But you mentioned a tattoo. And if we're going for the punk look, we need some shots of it. They'll be tasteful," he added. Janie's brows rose. This from a man whose sweatshirt didn't quite manage to cover his ample belly. Every time he brought up the camera, a ribbon of doughy flesh was revealed.

"Oh, I don't know." Alyvia played coy. "One's on my shoulder, but the other is on my butt."

"That's fine. That's perfect. Remember what I said about eye-catching pictures? I'll turn around while you take your clothes off, and you can reveal as much as you're comfortable with." His smile revealed stained teeth. "I've been doing this for a while. I've seen it all. And I'm a master at making you look like a million bucks."

The phone in her pocket vibrated. It took a moment for Janie to remember what that meant. When she did, a streak of urgency zipped up her spine. "We have to go."

Alyvia was quicker on the uptake than Janie had been. She was already grabbing her coat.

"What? Hang on, I really need those pictures if you want to make it on the punk-modeling scene. I gotta have more than the hair and piercings to sell you to the agency I was telling you about. C'mon, I can give you something to loosen up. Then you can shed the clothes and let me get the shots."

"I have to be home for dinner." Swiftly, Alyvia grabbed her purse, took out the envelope of money Janie had given her yesterday, and thrust it at the man. "Maybe we can finish up next week. There'd be no extra charge, right?"

"Another trip out here, another setup." Newman was clearly disgruntled. "I can't do that for free."

The girls headed through the doorway. Without the flashlight Newman had given her, Janie couldn't see a thing in the darkness. "Should we look for a back door?" she whispered to her friend.

Her cell was vibrating again. Two calls? What did that mean? Two different police cars? She ran into Alyvia as the girl turned toward her.

"I think we should just hide until they leave," Alyvia began.

But just as the words left her mouth, the front door swung open. A flashlight caught them in its beam. "Allama County sheriff. Don't move," a voice commanded.

Claire Willard

November 13
7:22 p.m.

Your daughter's been arrested.

The words echoed in Claire's head, but she couldn't put aside her sense of disbelief. The phone call had been a mistake. The deputy had someone else confused with Janie.

Claire backed the car partway out of the garage before slamming on the brake. Janie's medication. Surely she was going to need it. She'd be swamped with anxiety in a situation like this. Did the girl have meds with her? She knew her daughter hadn't been taking them regularly. Claire had discussed the issue more than once with Dr. Drake. Mind racing, she recalled seeing a prescription bottle in the bottom of Janie's purse a few weeks ago when Claire had been looking for her daughter's car keys. But did she have her purse with her?

Driving back into the attached garage, she got out and unlocked the door to the house, racing upstairs to her daughter's bedroom. Flipping on the light, she took a quick look around. Didn't see a purse. But as long as she was there, she continued into the attached bath and opened the medicine cabinet. Maybe the deputy had taken Janie's personal effects. That's what happened when a person was in custody, wasn't it? As long as Claire was here, she'd look for some unused . . .

The thought fragmented as she stared, shocked. Every month Claire dutifully refilled Janie's prescription and set it on her daughter's desk. And here most of them were, neatly lined up in a row. Still full, or nearly so. Six months' worth. Her hand rose of its own volition to turn each bottle so she could read the dates on them. June's was half-full. The October bottle looked to be missing only a few pills. The one she'd just refilled for November was missing.

Dazed, she reached for one of the bottles and hurried back to the garage. Her daughter's therapist liked to say that taking meds was Janie's choice. But how could the girl be expected to go to a strange town next year and acclimate to college life if she was refusing the most effective coping tool at her disposal?

Worry about Janie consumed her as she drove to the courthouse, where the sheriff's office was housed. Throwing the car into park, she fumbled to turn it off and almost ran to the back entrance she'd been directed to by the deputy who'd called.

"I'm Claire Willard, Janie Willard's mother." Claire spoke into the intercom outside the doors of the Allama County courthouse. The thought of her daughter . . . her baby being inside these locked doors had the fear and confusion winding more tightly inside her. "I received a phone call . . . my daughter was brought here."

"Just a moment."

But it was long minutes before someone came to the door. Minutes in which she was very much aware that she was alone on a task that should have required the presence of both parents. Memory of the conversation she'd had with her husband immediately following the phone call still elicited anger.

Janie? What could Janie have possibly done to get picked up by the sheriff's department?

I don't know, David. That's what we have to find out. You need to come home. I'm leaving for the courthouse now, but both of us should be there. Can you imagine what this is doing to her anxiety?

Claire, you know I'm in Columbus. Even if I could leave, it'd be an hour and a half before I got there. You'll have Janie home by then. This is probably all a misunderstanding. You go. Call me when you learn something. And for God's sake, if they want to question her, make sure she has a lawyer present!

There had been more, but the crux was the same. David's dinner with his boss and some clients took precedence over their daughter. Finally, an unsmiling uniformed man came to the door, unlocked it, and let Claire inside. As she followed him down a hallway, a nasty, niggling thought blazed across her mind and wouldn't be banished.

Whenever one of his children needed David, he never seemed to be available.

"I want to be taken to my daughter. Immediately." There was a quaver in Claire's voice. "I told the officer who called. She has an anxiety issue that requires medication. This situation has probably brought on a full-blown anxiety attack."

"I'm going to have you talk to Sergeant Rossi, ma'am." He led her to the elevators, and they traveled in silence to the third floor. Her heels echoed in the silent halls as she trailed behind him, trying to calm her nerves. At least she knew Janie was all right. But the girl had lied to Claire about working tonight. Janie never lied. She was truthful, to a fault at times. Dishonesty was totally out of character for her.

But then, so was trespassing. Claire gave a slight shake of her head as the officer held open the door leading to the sheriff's office for her. Janie rarely went anywhere besides school and work. Where would she have trespassed?

Nearly two-thirds of the desks behind the counter were empty. But a couple of smaller offices had lights blazing. It was to one of those spaces that the uniform showed her. Rossi's name was on the half-opened door. "Janie Willard's mother is here."

"Mrs. Willard."

The man inside rounded his desk and came to greet her. "Thank you for coming, ma'am. Please sit down."

Claire remained standing, twisting the handle of her purse between her fingers. "I need to see Janie. Please take me to her."

He gave a smile that was probably meant to be reassuring. It wasn't. He looked vaguely familiar. Tall. Brown hair with a matching droopy mustache. Had he been at the house when Kelsey's investigation was going on? Claire couldn't recall. There had been so many uniforms at first, before the BCI agents had taken over the case. So many questions asked. So few answers received.

"She's fine. Shaken up, seems like. Hasn't spoken a word since Deputy Brennan found them in the vacant lake house out on Fuller Road." He took her arm and steered her to a chair. She sank into it, uncomprehending.

"I don't understand. Why would she be there? And who is *them*?"

"Your daughter hasn't said anything. Not that we've attempted to question either her or her friend before parents arrived," he added hastily. "But the other girl has spoken freely since being brought in, and her foster parents are with her now."

Foster parents. Alyvia. Claire rubbed at a spot between her brows. Of course, it would be. Was that girl the reason Janie had been somewhere she'd had no right to be? "It would be helpful, ma'am, now that you're here, if we can get Janie's story about why they were on someone else's property."

"She isn't going to be able to talk to you. My daughter has an anxiety disorder. I have to go to her now. She needs her medication. Do you have her purse? She'd have pills in it. Otherwise, I've brought some from home."

"I don't think your daughter had any belongings with her. Her car was parked next to the garage at the lake house. Maybe her things are inside it."

"Then I need to see her now. Immediately."

"That will have to wait until—"

"No, it will not wait! *You* will wait!" Temper blazing, she bounced out of the chair to gaze up at the man who stood when she did. He was a good five inches taller, but he didn't intimidate her. Not with her imagination supplying her a vivid picture of the shape Janie was in right now. She'd be more than shaken up. No doubt she was in the grips of a full-blown anxiety attack, with all the accompanying emotional and physical reactions that came with it. Claire had witnessed plenty of those incidents after Kelsey had disappeared when Janie had regressed. "Unless you want me to press charges for denial of critical care while she's in your custody, you will allow me to give her the medication she's been prescribed for anxiety. Now."

Annoyance was visible in his expression as their gazes did battle. He was the first to look away. "It has to be a labeled prescription bottle with her name on it."

"It is." She dug in her purse, pulled out the bottle, and showed it to him.

"All right. Deputy Krantz is the juvenile officer on duty. He's been splitting his time between the two of them. The story the other girl is telling is sort of far-fetched. A statement from Janie could clear up a lot of things. You should be aware, however, that given their ages they could be charged as adults." The man started out the door.

Charged. A fist squeezed Claire's heart as she hurried after him down another hallway. David was right. She needed to call an attorney. She tried to recall the name her husband had mentioned. Brant Strickland. He'd helped them through Kelsey's investigation.

The memory had her stomach hollowing out. This was nothing like seven years ago, she assured herself. Janie was fine. Not lost to them like her sister.

A stocky man with a blond crew cut stepped into the hallway, pulling a door closed behind him. Rossi spoke to him. "This is Mrs. Willard. Ma'am, Deputy Krantz."

"I need to see my daughter."

"She's right inside here, ma'am. She seemed to be in some distress a while ago, so I brought her a glass of water."

The words torched Claire's fear and galvanized her into action. She pushed by Rossi and rushed to the door. Opened it. There was a small scarred table in the center of the room. Her daughter sat on one side of it facing her, arms wrapped tightly around her waist. When she saw Claire, her lips quivered once before she firmed them.

"Janie." Claire rushed to her side, sank to her knees beside her daughter's chair. "Deep breath. Blow it out. Again. Use your self-talk. *I am not controlled by my anxiety. It's okay to be overwhelmed. I'm strong enough to get through this.*" She'd recited the affirmations with Janie often enough years ago that they were embedded in her brain. She took her daughter's hand in both of hers. Felt the clammy moisture of her palm. And was transported to the time after Kelsey was taken. When Janie's progress had taken a giant leap backward. When the anxiety had produced night terrors, a galloping heart, sweaty palms, and strangled breathing. Habit had her checking the pulse in her daughter's wrist. Was surprised to find it rapid but not racing.

"It's okay, Mom. I'm okay."

"I've brought your meds." Claire set her purse down on the floor and twisted off the top to the small bottle she still held. "I know you haven't been taking them. You need one now."

"No, the worst is over." Janie was turned in her chair to face her, her gaze focused on Claire's face. Recognizing the coping strategy for what it was, Claire nearly wept. Janie could speak if she successfully blocked out the others in the room. Focused on her mother. Pretended there were no strangers present. It meant she was still struggling to keep the debilitating waves of nerves in check.

"Baby." Claire's voice trembled as she reached up with her free hand to brush back her daughter's long, dark hair. "Why won't you just make it easier on yourself?"

In answer, Janie captured her hand in one of hers. With the other, she reached into her pocket and took something out. Set it on the table before her. Clicked a switch.

"You need to be strong." Janie's whisper was nearly lost as voices filled the room.

"Yeah, yeah, the punk look is totally popular right now."

Claire frowned in confusion. "Who's the man talking?"

"Shh." The admonishment came from Sergeant Rossi. Glancing his way, she saw his brows furrow. He and Deputy Krantz appeared to be listening intently.

"So how does this deal work? I mean, how do I make money off this gig? Can I get paid for these pictures?"

Janie's hand tightened on hers. A terrible wave of déjà vu swept over Claire. "Oh, Janie, no." Her voice trembled, and for a moment, she thought she'd be sick, right there where she knelt next to her daughter's chair. It was like being frozen in place on the tracks as a runaway locomotive hurtled toward her. She could do nothing to prevent it. There was no way to stop the inescapable collision of the past and present.

"How 'bout you, sweetheart? You interested in pictures, too?"

"She probably will be when she sees mine. You took photos of her sister a long time ago. That's how we knew about you."

Claire pressed the hand that still held the prescription bottle to her lips, but couldn't prevent a tiny moan from escaping. *Oh, Janie.* An inner wail echoed in her brain. *What have you done?*

"Oh, yeah? Who's your sister?"

"Kelsey Willard."

"Yeah, yeah, I remember. You don't look much like her."

Janie switched off the recorder. The contrasting silence in the room was deafening. Gaze still locked with Claire's, she said, "You told the investigators back when Kelsey went missing. You'd heard something about a man photographing young girls. But it never led anywhere. At least, not that you ever heard."

Claire stared at her, recognizing the lies she'd told her daughter only days earlier. Now they were a lifeline, an offer of rescue from her own sea of dishonesty. "I don't know if they followed up. But we never heard anything more about it." The words were for the deputies' benefit. How humbling that her seventeen-year-old daughter had found a way to free Claire's secret after all these years. How humiliating that she'd had to do so at all, and in a way that left her mother blameless. Claire had an overwhelming urge to reach into the bottle she still held and swallow a couple of the pills inside. The one she'd taken after the call from this office had done little to quiet the apprehension that was spiking and careening inside her right now.

"Is there more on that recording?"

Janie switched it on again, but the words tumbled over Claire with no meaning. The old fear she'd lived with since she'd made that fateful decision to destroy the photos was a fanged beast, and it was devouring her now. What could the police have learned from the pictures themselves that they couldn't have discovered from the lie she'd given them? Nothing. She still believed that. But she was well versed in the art of self-delusion. She knew she couldn't rely on her own rationalizations for the truth.

"Who is he?" Her words sounded rusty. "Who's the man on the tape?"

"His name is Herb Newman, ma'am. He's a janitor at West Bend High School."

A distant ping of recognition sounded, but Claire's thoughts were too scattered to pursue it.

"Alyvia heard a rumor from someone at a party she attended a few weeks ago. About Newman taking pictures of Kelsey." The tightness with which Janie was squeezing Claire's hand had her wincing a little. "We wanted to find out for ourselves. Hear him admit it. I figured if I had proof, the police would have more to go on this time. They could question him about his contact with Kelsey. Maybe he'd never been questioned before."

This close to her daughter, looking into her eyes, Claire knew the girl was lying. Her expression was too determined, a glint of warning alight in her gaze. Despite the disability that still took its toll, Janie had an indomitable will. Hadn't Dr. Drake said as much many times over the years?

Slowly Claire rose, using the edge of the table to support herself. She looked at Rossi. "What will you do with that man? You can't let him go free. Not without discovering—"

"We're still holding him, ma'am." If Claire hadn't found the sergeant intimidating before, his expression now was positively forbidding. "You can be sure we'll take all steps to learn what he knows. We'll also turn the information over to the BCI."

"I'm taking my daughter home." Her only remaining daughter. The one who'd taken a bold, reckless risk to aid the investigation into her sister's disappearance. Claire teetered between pride and fear.

The two deputies exchanged a glance. "Under the circumstances . . . the recording has corroborated the other girl's story. I need Janie to write up a statement about the events of tonight before she goes."

"And the charges?" Claire didn't know where she found the strength to look the man in the eye. "They did your office a huge favor by bringing this information to you."

"Information that could have been shared with a phone call instead of engaging in an entrapment scene out of a Hollywood plot."

She heard her daughter snort, and the sergeant's mouth twitched beneath the mustache. "But admittedly, the recording carries a lot of weight. It's possible that the girls won't be charged in return for your daughter's promise not to engage in unlawful activity again."

Deputy Krantz approached Janie with a legal pad and pen. "Be sure to include how you gained access to the lake house this evening," he instructed. After a moment, Janie picked up the pen and began writing.

"I have other concerns to attend to. I want to assure you, Mrs. Willard, that this matter will be investigated thoroughly." Rossi's words held a note of sincerity. But it was Janie that Claire was focused on, bent over the notepad and scribbling away with a freedom denied her with the spoken word.

"I believe you will. But that's all thanks to my daughter, isn't it?"

David Willard

November 13
10:36 p.m.

As silently as possible, David crept out of bed and tiptoed toward the front door of the town house, where he called Claire again. Waited impatiently while the cell rang four times and went to voice mail. Frustration mounting, he called his daughter's phone. Same result.

He stared into the shadows, a hundred different scenarios circling in his mind. Claire should have called by now. It'd been nearly three and a half hours. He shouldn't have let her handle Janie's situation alone. His wife could handle little on her own these days.

And Janie . . . what the hell had gotten into his daughter? Trespassing? Or had Claire gotten that wrong? The girl barely went anywhere outside of school, the Dairy Whip, and the library. Nothing about the few details Claire had provided made sense.

The questions had echoed in his mind for hours, making sitting through the dinner with the execs from Ralston Electronics interminable. Somehow he'd managed to say the right things. Laugh on cue at Kurt's jokes, all of which he'd heard a hundred times before. The whole time he'd been expecting to have to excuse himself for a phone call that had never come. Twice he'd surreptitiously texted Claire with a similar lack of response.

Maybe he should call the sheriff's office. David considered the idea, found it unappealing. He'd had his fill of law-enforcement types recently, after fielding another call from that fucking Foster. The memory had his gut churning. He'd have an ulcer from that prick before all this was done. Just as David had feared, the agent must have gotten all of David's reservations from the hotel, not just the ones under the company's name. And he'd had some not-so-innocent questions about them, too. David hadn't given him the same answers he'd offered Grayson. He couldn't risk having the man corroborate his story with Claire. Instead, he'd spun a story about meeting potential clients on his own, which was frowned upon by the company. That job fell to Kurt and Martin, and while David had done exactly that in order to get the Bonner Nursery account, he'd woven an elaborate cover story, making his initial meeting with Bonner seem accidental.

David was very adept at cover stories.

He tried Claire again. Then his daughter. No response.

At a loss, he scrolled through his contacts until he found the attorney name he'd given Claire.

The call was answered on the second ring. "Brant Strickland."

"Brant." David kept his voice hushed. "It's David Willard."

"Yes. How are you?" The man's circumspect manner gave nothing away. David heard him murmur, "Deal me out this hand."

"I'm sorry to take you away from the poker game." The man played every Friday night. "I'm in Columbus, and there's been some trouble with my daughter tonight. I told Claire to call you, but I haven't been able to reach her. Have you heard from her?"

"From your wife?" The surprise in the attorney's voice sent David's spirits even lower. "No, I can't recall the last time I've spoken to her. What kind of trouble?"

"Some sort of trespassing thing. I'm afraid I don't have many details." And now that it was clear that Strickland didn't, either, David was eager to end the conversation. "I'm really sorry to have bothered you. Looks like I'm going to have to drive home and handle this myself."

"Well, give me a call when you get more information if I can help out. Unless there was vandalism involved, a simple trespassing charge won't be difficult to get dismissed."

"I will, thanks. I'll let you get back to your game."

"No problem."

So Claire hadn't called Strickland. Because she hadn't needed him? If that was the reason, why wouldn't she have reported that to him? The cell in his hand vibrated. An incoming text. Finally. David opened it to read it. From Janie, and maddeningly cryptic.

Everything will be fine. Taking care of Mom.

Will be? Damn it, what was that supposed to mean? Were they home, then? They'd have to be, in order for Janie to access her phone, wouldn't they? He called his daughter. Felt his blood pressure rise when once again it went to voice mail.

Fuming, he considered his options. He was going to have to drive back to West Bend. There was another get-together set here for tomorrow night, drinks this time with a client Kurt was courting. It could be done without David, but he was loath to miss out. It was unusual for him to be included at this juncture in the process. The invitation made it likely that if the account was won, it would be added to David's roster. He wouldn't miss it, he decided in the next moment. With any luck, he could drive back tomorrow evening after dealing with whatever was going on at home.

Decision made, he rose.

"What are you doing up? Who were you talking to?" He looked over his shoulder at the woman silhouetted in the hallway. Just the outline of her figure in the filmy nightgown was enough to have desire stirring.

"I have to go." The regret in his voice was genuine. "Something's come up that I have to deal with. Hopefully, I'll be back tomorrow."

"David, no." There was a pout in her voice. "You just got here. Surely it can wait until Monday."

"If I had a choice, I wouldn't go, believe me."

He crossed to her and drew her into his arms, pressing a lingering kiss on her mouth. After a moment's hesitation, she returned it with enough heat to get his pulse racing. "I'll make it up to you," he whispered against her lips. "I promise."

Special Agent Mark Foster

November 13
10:48 p.m.

"Are my eyes bleeding? Check and tell me if my eyes are bleeding." Sloane pushed away from the table and yawned delicately, stretching her arms over her head to arch her back. After a rundown of their respective days, they'd worked largely in silence, transcribing their reports and reading over those submitted by the various law-enforcement entities partnered on the case before turning their attention to the seemingly endless information from the Willard and TMK investigations.

Ignoring her remark, Mark sat back in his chair, staring broodingly at the computer screen. "Did you know the agency has another profiler? I hadn't heard they'd replaced Luther Sims in that position."

The woman moved her shoulders tiredly. "Who, Greg Larsen? I knew he'd been taking some extra training. I haven't ever worked with him in that capacity, though. Why?"

"Because my SAC mentioned that Larsen is familiar with the Willard case. If he's acting as agency profiler, I'm guessing he's pored over the TMK files." He tapped the screen, indicating the e-mail he'd been reading. "Might not hurt to get his perspective on the offender. I talked to Sims and got his."

"You did?" Sloane eyed him. "You didn't tell me that."

Mark shrugged, avoiding her gaze. It probably wasn't necessary. She'd reverted to a casual businesslike persona that he already knew could be turned on and off at will. For the first time, he wondered if he'd been the first colleague she'd come on to during a case. And if he'd been the first to turn down her offer. Sloane Medford was a tenacious investigator and an assertive agent. She was doing a fast rise at the BCI. A year ago, he wouldn't have doubted that her ascent was based solely on merit.

Now he was questioning that perception. But not as much as he was questioning himself. His conversation with Kelli last night had been stilted. They'd been fine as long as they'd stuck to Nicky. But when she'd asked about the older agent's replacement, Mark had frozen. Finally muttered something about Kelli not knowing him and changed the subject.

Him. A lie, because Sloane Medford was definitely not male. He'd deliberately worked past the time for a call tonight. It was getting harder and harder to rationalize the omissions and half-truths.

He hadn't cheated five months ago. Mark's face flushed as he shoved aside the memories that threatened. Yeah, he was ashamed at how close he'd come. In bed. Both half-undressed. Hands racing . . . everywhere. But he'd come to his senses. He'd walked away. Eventually.

The memory was uncomfortable. Shunting it aside, he refocused. "I wouldn't mind comparing Larsen's take to Sims's." In fact, it might be interesting to see where the two men's views on the case intersected and diverged. Before he could forget, he quickly composed an e-mail to that end and sent it to Larsen. Since it was the weekend, he probably wouldn't hear back from the man until Monday.

She shrugged disinterestedly. "I don't put a lot of stock in that kind of thing. Evidence is what solves a case."

"Yeah, well, you may not have noticed, but there's been a shortage of that so far in this investigation." They had plenty of unanswered questions. Lots of potential subjects of interest. But they'd struck out with the Starkey family, and they hadn't yet landed on the one solid lead that would put this case to rest. And until they did, Whitney DeVries remained in the hands of a monster.

"Do you think she's still alive?"

He was getting used to the way Sloane could fix onto his thoughts. "Yeah. He keeps them for a while, according to Sims." That had also been documented in the infinite TMK files. "No evidence of sexual assault, but plenty of signs of physical abuse. Some torture." Had that come from Sims or the files? Mark couldn't recall. All the details of the past serial cases were starting to run together. "But we're at the two-week point since the girl was taken. She's almost definitely still alive."

What she'd endured to this point, Mark thought grimly, was another matter.

"So." The topic seemed to have refueled Sloane's energy. She inched her chair up to the table again. "There's been nothing new from cyber forensics?"

"No." And there wouldn't be, Mark knew. The offender was too wily for that. Patrick Allen's hacked Facebook persona had been used only long enough to get Whitney to give the man her phone number, when their communications had switched to text messages at his suggestion. "You can bet he's destroyed the burner phone." This offender was too smart not to do that. If indeed they were dealing with the TMK, he'd evaded capture precisely because he didn't make rookie mistakes.

"One thing Sims mentioned during our conversation has stuck with me." He swiveled his chair to face her as he spoke. "Something about a victim they were able to prove was the work of a copycat. With no body for Willard, and DeVries taken so recently—"

"There's no way to be certain if either of them were indeed TMK victims, or the work of someone wanting us to think so." Sloane tapped a finger on the table before her. "Which is why I think it's a mistake to get too tied up in what the profilers say about the Ten Mile Killer. We have no way of knowing if that's who we're dealing with."

That was only one of the sources of the frustration that was starting to eat at him a little more each day. "And no way to know if we're not." He used his phone to check the time and stood up abruptly. "I've got to go. I'm meeting Brian DeVries. I'm going to hit him with everything we've discovered on this Starkey thing."

"He's had plenty of time to get his story straight," she observed, rising as he did and grabbing her coat. "Want me to go at him? Maybe he'll respond better to a softer approach." She buttoned her coat.

Mark shrugged into his coat. "We'll play it by ear." On the way out the door, his cell rang.

"Agent Foster, this is Sergeant Rossi of the Allama County Sheriff's Office. I've been meaning to give you a call to apprise you of a situation that occurred this evening. Just now got the chance."

They reached Mark's car, Sloane meeting him at the driver's side, her hand out, waggling her fingers for the keys. He moved the phone away from his mouth. "You drive when we take your car." She rolled her eyes but rounded the hood and got in on the other side. He settled himself behind the wheel, buckling himself in one-handedly while he hung on to the cell. "What do you have, Sergeant?" Mark started the car and nosed it out of the motel parking lot, heading south for the address DeVries had given them.

With each passing mile, Mark focused less on his upcoming meeting and more on the information being relayed. When the officer had finished, he said, "Thanks for the call, and I'd appreciate being kept apprised of your progress."

"You got it."

Disconnecting, he slipped the phone back in his pocket and slowed to a stop at a red light as his mind flipped through a mental Rolodex of names. Came up with the one he was searching for.

"Well?" Sloane drawled. "That was the locals, I gather. My mind reading's a little rusty. You're going to have to share what that was about."

"Do you recognize the name Herb Newman?"

After a pause, she answered. "He was on the list Mikkelsen gave us, right? The janitor shared by some of the churches in the area."

"He's also the daytime janitor at West Bend High School. He must juggle the church jobs on nights and weekends. He was picked up tonight for trespassing."

The other agent turned more fully in her seat to face him. "And we need to know this because . . . ?"

"He was with Janie Willard and another girl. Janie is Kelsey Willard's sister. The guy claims to be some sort of photographer with contacts at a modeling agency. They provided a recording they'd made of the man admitting he'd taken pictures of Kelsey Willard before her death."

The light turned green. Mark pulled out into the intersection. There was remarkably little traffic for a Friday evening. "A link to Willard through the school," Sloane mused. "Possibly to Willard and DeVries through the church. We need to talk to him."

"We will. I want to double-check whether he was ever interviewed seven years ago." If Mark had read a transcript of the interview, he had no recollection of it. "They released the teenagers but have Newman in custody. He had what they believe are Oxy and K2 on him, and he offered it to the girls. Apparently, the county has had a problem with an unknown local dealing drugs, and they started wondering if it were Newman. Deputies went back to the house to look around a bit more, and their search turned up traces of cocaine in one of the bedrooms. They have enough to hold him while they tear the place apart looking for more drugs. The kids indicated he had a key to the place, and the empty property has been a magnet for teenagers and parties for years." Mark was less interested in the man's other pastimes than he was in the link between Newman and Willard. "They've brought in a drug dog for the search. But we can probably wait and talk to him tomorrow."

He slowed, then turned into the parking lot of the Pub's Bar and Grill. "Think this is the same place DeVries met with Starkey a few years back?"

"Only one way to find out." Sloane released her seat belt and opened the door of the vehicle. "Let's go ask him."

◆ ◆ ◆

"You omitted Dane Starkey's name from your list of acquaintances."

"He wasn't—" Brian DeVries started.

"You failed to tell us about a potential suspect in this case. A man with reason to seek revenge on you," Mark continued inexorably. "You lied about why you were paying him off. And when we talked about the church Whitney occasionally attended, somehow you forgot to mention that you'd spent quite a bit of time around it when you took care of the mowing there one summer. When was that, Brian? Did you know Kelsey Willard? Is that where you first saw her?"

"Who?" The man shook his head as if to dislodge the words. "No! It wasn't like I was mowing when kids were outside. That was at least ten years ago."

"He probably just forgot about the lawn job." Sloane's voice was soft. Understanding. "The man has the weight of the world on his shoulders right now. His daughter is missing, for God's sake. Have a little compassion."

"Yes, that's . . . I just didn't think about it. It was a long time ago. And as far as Starkey . . ."

"Yeah, let's talk about him." If Sloane's tone was cotton batting, Mark's was granite. "Or better yet, let's talk about Shelley Starkey, the twelve-year-old girl you sexually assaulted in the basement bathroom of Lewis Starkey's house when you were fifteen."

"That's bullshit!" A couple of men at a neighboring table looked over at Brian's vehement protest. Lowering his voice, he went on, "First of all, she came on to me. I thought she was a couple of years older, and she never said no until . . . until later."

"Until you almost raped her?"

He looked away, a muscle jumping in his jaw. "It wasn't rape, and I stopped when she started struggling. I don't know if she's the one who spun it or if it was her parents to get money from my mother. Because her dad was all about calling the cops when he came storming over, but he shut up pretty quick when my mother pulled out the checkbook."

"You could have told Agent Foster that. Innocent until proven guilty, right? But hiding it . . . you have to know how it looks."

DeVries scrubbed his hands over his face as Sloane spoke. The man looked like he'd aged ten years since his daughter went missing. "And risk having it show up in the official report? I wasn't ignoring the possibility that Starkey could be behind it. I even—" He snapped his mouth shut on whatever he'd been about to say.

Too late, because Mark could already predict the rest. "You even spent your days back at work digging into the lives of the Starkey family, right? Did some investigating of your own, using law-enforcement tools on searches you weren't authorized to perform? What do you think your sheriff would have to say about that?"

"I was desperate! Think I can't tell my office is coming up empty checking on punks I've arrested?"

That had been a task Mark had left to the Fenton County Sheriff's Office. Something he was regretting now. The sheriff had showed a lack of common sense letting DeVries anywhere near the office while the investigation was ongoing.

The man continued. "Like you say, Starkey was a logical suspect, and I took a hard look at him, even though I didn't really think the gutless prick had it in him. But his relatives . . ." He looked from Mark to Sloane. Back again. "You've checked them out, right? Because they could have been in on it with Dane."

Disgusted with the man, with the situation, Mark pushed away from the table. "We haven't come up with a thing on any of them, and believe me, we looked. Here's what you're going to do, Brian. You're calling the sheriff tomorrow. Say you made a mistake going back to work and need some time at home. I don't give a shit what you tell him, but if I find out you're anywhere near that office again without my okay, I'm laying it all out for him. Every lie you told me. You won't have a job to go back to." He might not, anyway. Mark couldn't keep this information from the sheriff indefinitely. It was up to DeVries's employer to weigh the man's circumstances against his illicit use of law-enforcement search tools and databases.

DeVries gave him a terrible smile. "You gonna threaten me now? Someone took my little girl. Losing a job can't come close to a loss like that."

"Of course it can't." Sloane was comforting. "And you can't risk tainting this investigation by being anywhere near it. You're a cop; you know that."

"Tell me you've got something." DeVries's voice was pleading. "At least that you're close. You've got a person of interest. Something."

"Go home, Brian." Mark was suddenly weary. It was possible, he was finding, to have sympathy for the man while wanting to slug him. "Waiting for news on your daughter is the worst kind of torture, but that's what you have to do. We're looking in several areas. We're talking to people with links to both Kelsey Willard and your daughter. In fact, we just discovered another one who we'll be interviewing tomorrow. The best way you can help us do our jobs is to be open and honest with us."

Hope had bloomed in the man's expression. "So you do have a suspect?"

"He's a person of interest until we determine otherwise. And we'll let you know either way. Go home to your wife and son now. They need you."

"I want to know who you've talked to. Everyone you've eliminated."

Already, the man was reverting to form and issuing demands. "We'll tell you what we can," Sloane promised.

The man's chair scraped as he pushed out of it. Without another word, he turned on his heel and walked away.

"Well." Sloane watched the man's exit. "What should we do as an encore? Find some puppies to stomp?"

"He put himself into this situation. He's hardly blameless." Mark was used to treating parents with kid gloves, but Brian DeVries could have derailed this investigation by inserting himself into it. Mark's cell vibrated. He'd turned off the ringer for this conversation, but it was the third time since they'd sat down that it had alerted. Pulling the phone from his pocket, he squinted at the number that showed on the screen. The same one who'd called him at the motel. He answered it. "Mark Foster."

"Agent." Mark recognized Sergeant Rossi's voice, but it'd lost its dispassionate tone. The edge of excitement in it was difficult to miss. "I'm at the lake house with my crime-scene team. The drug dog alerted to a spot in the bedroom next door to where Newman had the girls. Someone had chiseled out a stone from the fireplace, and there was quite a haul in the empty space."

"Congratulations."

"That's why we decided to take the dog through the whole place. We're in the basement now. The dog didn't alert, not with the sit and bark it gives for narcotics. But it kept whining and returning to the west wall."

Mystified, Mark said, "Okay."

"There's a crawl space there covered by a screen." Mark glanced at Sloane, and his expression had her leaning forward in interest. "There's something inside. We're not sure what. Could be some sort of contraband that's been hidden away. But we called the coroner. Because whatever's in there sure looks like it's in a body bag."

◆ ◆ ◆

The address Mark had been given wasn't difficult to find, despite its isolation. The light bars atop the official vehicles parked outside the house were as visible from the blacktop as a beacon. He pulled up the steep winding drive and parked in back of a white van marked *Allama County Coroner*.

Neither of them spoke as he and Sloane got out of the vehicle. They made it up the front steps before the door opened and a uniform stepped out. From his garb, Mark pegged him as a reserve deputy. "BCI. Agents Foster and Medford." The man took their credentials and examined them under the beam of his Maglite, before nodding and handing them back. "They're in the basement. Follow me."

Large spotlights dotted the empty space they walked through. The rough log-cabin walls, stone fireplace, and beamed ceilings provided rustic touches to what had once been a luxurious home. Mark recognized the quality of the polished wood floor, the intricate woodwork around the doors and windows. The kitchen they entered next was similarly well equipped but somewhat dated. He wondered how long the property had been empty.

Then they started down the split-log steps, and all other thoughts vanished. "Sending BCI down," the reserve called from behind them. Mark led the way. The basement had been left unfinished, with the same stone he'd seen on the fireplace upstairs used for the walls. The floor was cement. The space was open and ran the length of the house. But it was full right now. More spotlights were set up. No cords, Mark noted. So there was no electricity in the place. There was a collapsible wheeled gurney in the center of the room. And a collection of men standing around a rectangular cavity high in the west wall. A screen had been removed and was leaning against the wall near the floor. He identified Rossi by the three stripes on his uniform coat. He was standing near a short balding man in civilian clothes. Adrenaline thrummed inside him as Mark made his way toward them.

"Sheriff Jeff Richards." The shorter man introduced himself. "You're just in time. We haven't touched a thing. Waited for the coroner."

Mark and Sloane stood in silence as two individuals, standing on an overturned crate of some sort, worked a wide, canvas-covered board into the opening. With one man lifting the edge of the object inside, the other was able to work the board beneath it, an inch at a time. Minutes later, Mark moved forward with Rossi and Richards to help balance the board and its contents as it was withdrawn and gingerly lowered it to the gurney.

The sergeant had been right. It looked like a black body bag, if an extra-large one. It hadn't been especially heavy. Mark's pulse quickened as they got the bag settled on the gurney. One of the men wearing a flak jacket with *Coroner* emblazoned across reached out a gloved hand to unzip the circular zipper on top. The sound echoed in the silence.

"Jesus," one of the deputies muttered, pressing his nose into the crook of his arm. Mark's stomach plummeted. Not because of the smell that emanated from the bag, but what that smell meant.

Rossi raised his flashlight, catching the bag's contents in its beam. "Ah, shit." Mark's tone was bleak as his gaze traveled from the tip of one black ballet slipper, up the tights-clad legs, the left drawn up to rest alongside the opposite knee. The tulle of the pink tutu had been smashed by the bag. The matching leotard was long sleeved, and the skeletal arms were arranged above the head. He saw something on the bony fingers. Wire. Holding the hands in a clasped position. The long, dark hair was intact. Not much of the facial skin was. But in his gut, he had no doubt.

They'd found Kelsey Willard.

Whitney DeVries

November 14
10:37 p.m.

She lay on the mattress, silently counting away the hours. Whitney had thought about her plan all day. Mentally polished it during every second of the hated practice. It had run through her mind on a constant loop, even while she talked to the freak, who had noted her distraction. Missing her mom and dad had been Whitney's excuse, which was no more than the truth. It had pissed off the freak, she could tell, resulting in another one of his lectures about gratitude and her good fortune for having the opportunity for a new *family*.

Every time he used the word, she hated him a little more.

The computer had gone dark long ago. But she didn't dare move yet. Whitney had no way of knowing if the freak lived on the premises, but if he did, she wanted to be sure he was deeply asleep before she started working on loosening the barre. The clanking of the chain would be difficult to avoid. She couldn't risk waking him.

She was already taking a big enough chance without adding to it.

Maybe this place was soundproofed. That would make sense, wouldn't it? Screaming and crying for help had been one rule she hadn't broken. She was afraid he might always be close by, even though he usually entered early in the morning and the evening. And when the computer was on, he'd know.

According to her mental calculations, it was time, or close to it. Ice crept up her spine, and that had nothing to do with the chilly temperature in the dungeon. She didn't think she could handle it if her plan failed, shattering hopes of escape. Without hope, what would be the use of going on?

Kelsey had, though. The memory gave her strength. The other girl had mentioned she'd been kept close to a year. And although Whitney hadn't finished reading all the pages under the floorboards, it helped her to know someone else had been through this. Maybe survived.

With newfound resolve, she got up and retrieved the screw. Hauling in a deep breath, she made her way from memory to the back wall. To the barre.

The metal was cold to the touch. Whitney slid her fingers along it until she came to the end nearest the window, where the bracket secured it to the wall. The narrow strip of light edging the curtain didn't make a dent in the shadows this far across the stage. She ran her fingers over the bracket, lingering on the screws that held it firm.

She chose the first screw in the lower facing of the bracket. Flat head. Single groove in the center. Tipping the one she'd retrieved from the shower, she fit the top edge inside that groove. Exerted pressure. The screw in her hand slipped, the point gouging her palm. Whitney brought the injured area to her mouth. Sucked at the sting before trying again. In theory, the screw could be used like the flat tip of a screwdriver. Without the handle and shaft, it would be difficult to apply the needed force to turn the stationary screw.

But hopefully not impossible.

An hour into the task, Whitney was becoming frustrated. The threads of the screw she held dug into her fingers, making them swollen and sore. She solved the problem by wrapping the extra fabric of the flannel nightgown around the screw shaft for cushioning. When she tired, she alternated actions by bracing her feet against the wall and yanking outward on the barre, trying to loosen it. The movement sent the chain rattling, so she didn't dare repeat it for long. And then she switched tasks again. With very little result.

She reached up an arm to wipe her forehead on the sleeve of her nightgown, discouraged. The screws in the bracket were tight. The freak probably checked on things like that before he brought a new victim here. The thought was accompanied by a wave of bitterness. There was no reason her idea wouldn't work. She just needed to keep trying. Or like Mrs. Zaner used to say in math class, work smarter, not harder.

But what would be smarter? She considered for a moment. Then she refit the screw edge to the groove again, taking care to keep the contact as tight and close as possible. Pressing forward to exert as much force as she was capable of, she wrenched at the stationary screw again.

And was rewarded when it moved, ever so slightly.

Thrilled, Whitney promptly tried it a second time. In her haste, the screw she was wielding slipped and gouged her palm again. Grinding her teeth, she repeated the action more carefully. And there was another minute movement in the bracket screw.

Panting with exertion, she grinned in delight. Without an actual screwdriver, her range of motion was limited to small half circles before she had to stop, refit the screw in the groove, and restart.

But it was progress. She didn't waste time wondering what she'd do when she got all the screws free, or how long it might take. For now she was going to enjoy the thrill of anticipation. The first step was freeing herself from the barre.

Then she'd figure out how to escape.

Janie Willard

November 15
11:00 a.m.

Cole Bogart parked next to her in the parking lot of a small coffee shop, Home Brew. Janie's pulse skittered as she watched him get out of his car and dash over to her passenger door, pull it open, and slide into the front seat. "Damn, it's cold." He leaned forward to turn her heat up and scrubbed his bare hands in front of the vent where the air poured out. "Would you believe my heater wouldn't work this morning? Piece of shit. It's, like, stuck on defrost or something. I had to stop and scrape the inside of my windshield twice on the way over."

"Gloves might have helped."

He grinned at her. "Your text didn't give me much time to get ready. What's up?"

In answer, she dug into her purse beside her and handed him an envelope. "It took two trips to the ATM to get enough cash. I want to pay you back for the listening devices."

He made no move to take the money. "No, no, I told you we're cool. I'm going to return the whole box; the purchase will be credited back to my mom's account. All I need is for you to give me back the . . . oh."

"Yeah." She didn't know him well. Still had the tightness in her chest whenever she talked to him. But she *could* talk to him. Janie didn't know exactly what that meant. Maybe it was easier because they'd texted a few times over the weekend about what had gone down in the cabin. But more likely, it was because he'd barged into her house a few days back and made it impossible to avoid him.

"So . . . you gave the recorder to the cops?" Slowly he reached out a hand for the envelope.

"I don't know when we'll get it back."

He thought for a minute. "I've got to get the charge taken care of. But if you do get the recorder back within thirty days, I can still return it, and you'd get this money back."

"Yeah, I don't know if that will happen." Janie had no idea how long it would be before the sheriff's office would return it. If they did at all.

"Me, either. Sorry you got stuck paying for it." Cole folded the envelope and shoved it into his coat pocket.

"It was worth it." Getting hauled into the sheriff's office hadn't exactly been in her plans, but the end result had turned out better than she'd anticipated. Newman had been caught up along with them, and she was guessing he'd had drugs on him. At least, she assumed that was what he'd meant by offering Alyvia something to loosen her up. If so, the cops would have even more reason to investigate him.

And when they did, maybe there'd be a breakthrough in Kelsey's case. She was allowed to feel good about that, right? The anxiety had hit pretty hard once she'd gotten to the sheriff's office, but she'd gotten through it on her own. She was going to count the whole day as a success, even if it had led to her first—and hopefully last—arrest.

"You want to go inside for a coffee?"

Surprised, she looked at the building she was parked next to. It was a popular hangout for high schoolers. Janie had never been there. Judging by the number of cars in the parking lot, it was busy. "I don't think so."

"Mind if I do? I gotta get warmed up. Wait here." Without another word, he had the door open and was dashing to the entrance of the structure.

She turned down the heat that was blasting through the vents and checked the dash clock. Forty-five minutes before she needed to be at work. She had nothing else to do to pass the time, but she hadn't considered spending it all with Cole Bogart.

She didn't know him. Janie kept reminding herself of that. And not too long ago, she hadn't had a great impression of him.

But that was before, when all she'd had to go on was hearing about him hacking the school server. Before he'd told her about his brother. She stared at the door he'd disappeared through. His brother's death wasn't like Kelsey's disappearance. Nothing was. But it was a tenuous bond that she didn't share with anyone else, not even Alyvia. Like she and Cole belonged to the same group in the Shitty Circumstances Club. Membership for life, decided by fate.

It's not like she didn't know of other kids in school who'd lost a parent or something. But she'd never talked to them about it. Janie wouldn't have spoken to Cole about his brother, either, if he hadn't come to her house and spilled it all. The scene had been uncomfortable. But it was the first time she'd ever heard anyone else speak about what the loss of a sibling had done to him. The support groups her mom and dad had tried for a while were never an option for Janie. So listening to Cole had been weird. But sort of helpful in a way to hear from someone else going through something kind of similar.

He reappeared, using his shoulder to push out the door, his hands full with two coffees. He saw her watching and held one up, grinning. Reaching over, she unlatched the passenger door, pushed it open. "I got you a caramel whipped-cream espresso." He handed her a cup. "Or we can switch if you want. I've got a vanilla cappuccino."

Janie sipped at her drink cautiously. Then her brows rose. "I may as well be drinking hot ice cream."

"Yeah, it's pretty good." Making himself at home, Cole reached for the lever to move the seat back. "But if it's ice cream you want, we can finish these and then head over to the Dairy Whip for dessert."

"I'll be there soon enough." She drank again. It was good. The place had a drive-through window. She wouldn't even have to go inside to order here again.

"Sorry you guys didn't get out of the lake house in time." It wasn't the first time he'd apologized. "A plain car pulled up beside mine, and the cop inside started hassling me about why I was pulled over. It took me a minute to realize a cruiser had pulled in to the drive. Some lookout I was."

"It actually turned out okay."

"How much trouble did you get in with your parents?"

Janie hesitated. She'd fared better than Alyvia had, who was currently grounded into infinity. Her friend had even lost cell phone privileges. But she was confident her foster parents would relent. By the time she was done going over the story with them, they'd be convinced she and Janie were modern-day Nancy Drews. "They were all right," she said finally. "I was mostly concerned about my mom. Newman admitted on tape that he'd taken pictures of my sister seven years ago. That was hard for her to hear. She hasn't really been the same since Kelsey was kidnapped." And neither, in truth, had her dad. The change had happened so gradually that Janie hadn't even realized how much time he spent away. Maybe he had more responsibility at work. Or perhaps he'd rather be anywhere but home. She couldn't help feeling that it had been more guilt than concern that had led to him showing up at home late Friday night. Janie had already had her mom calmed down by then. She'd insisted Claire take a hot bath. Get into bed. And had sat with her until her dad had shown up unexpectedly.

"Who would be the same?" A shadow crossed Cole's expression. "My dad used to be a teetotaler, but now I see a bourbon bottle in his bottom desk drawer in the den. And sometimes he hits it pretty hard.

It's like he's a different person. Then it occurred to me that he was using the bourbon for the same reason I bought weed. That had me backing off it. I don't want to rely on it to get by, you know?"

"Yeah." The same way Janie didn't want to depend on medication because of her mother's addiction to alcohol and pills. And it *was* an addiction, even if she could go days without them. Her father seemed blissfully unaware of the problem. Or was it just easier for him to overlook it? He'd lost a daughter, too. If there was one thing their family dynamics proved, it was that everyone managed trauma differently. They all had their own ways of getting by.

"My mom stays super busy with work and all these activities and baking . . . she's always in the kitchen doing something. Like, if she just keeps moving she can outrun Garrett's death. I think she's afraid if she stops, it's going to steamroll over the top of her."

Janie listened in awkward silence, sipping at the coffee to avoid answering. It felt too personal to hear about the cycle of someone else's grief. She'd been trapped in her own and in that of her parents since she was ten. But there was a weird sort of comfort in Cole's revelations, too. No one got out of a personal tragedy unscathed. The wounds didn't go away. It was just a matter of how well each person covered them.

"I don't know what I'm supposed to be feeling. It sucks to be wrapped in this crappy mourning period, but whenever I catch myself having a good time, I feel guilty, you know? Like I'm betraying Garrett by enjoying myself. Then I get mad at him for being dead." He shook his head and took a long gulp of his coffee. "How's that for sick? It's been two years. I should be handling things better."

She surprised herself by saying, "Know what I was doing two years after my sister was kidnapped?" His head swiveled toward her. "I had just started back to school. For a year and a half afterward, I couldn't leave the house. When I tried, it was like someone stuck a vacuum down my throat and sucked all the air out of my lungs." She'd felt as though she'd been slowly suffocating. Other times, the tightness in her chest mimicked a heart attack. She'd known that it wasn't real, that it was her mind making her suffer like that. The helplessness of not being able to control her own brain had been the worst part about it. "I was so medicated sometimes, I felt like a zombie. And even that was preferable to the anxiety attacks. So you're not doing that bad."

He looked at her for a long moment. "Thanks for telling me that. You probably don't talk about it much."

"I don't talk about anything much."

He laughed, and although she hadn't meant it as a joke, she smiled, too. "Now I have to go punch in. Doris freaks out if we're not there fifteen minutes early. Thanks for the coffee."

"Not a problem." Hand on the door latch, he paused. "Is it okay if I text you sometimes?"

The knot in her chest was back. But it felt different this time. "I guess."

"Awesome. See you tomorrow." The door slammed. A moment later, he was in his car, starting it up. Not wanting to be caught staring, Janie put the vehicle in gear. Backed out of the lot and headed for the Dairy Whip.

That had been weird. But a good kind of weird. She waited at the end of the drive for the barely there traffic and then pulled across the street. Janie still wasn't sure what to think about Cole Bogart. But she was okay with taking some time to find out.

Claire Willard

November 15
1:15 p.m.

"David, lunch is ready." Claire felt almost normal engrossing herself in daily chores. Normal except for the muzzy-headed feeling that was the result of the pills she'd taken in the middle of the night while David lay sleeping. Two, to banish the endless movie reel of the nightmarish events that had been replaying in her mind since Friday. She'd needed the pills to shake the mental image of Kelsey drifting above her, condemnation in her eyes.

I was just trying to protect you, Claire told her daughter silently. *I didn't want the police to see you that way. To think about you like that. You made a mistake. Acted out. I covered the best that I could.*

The mental picture faded, but the regret didn't. It had been weak to fall back on the medication when Janie had powered through her anxiety Friday night while refusing it. Claire could be proud of her daughter while admitting to herself that she didn't have Janie's emotional fortitude. Or her brains, for coming up with a plan that would have the police certain to check Kelsey's connection to the photographer, without exposing Claire's part in destroying the pictures. She should be ashamed that her youngest daughter had seen through her lie. But she lacked the will to feel anything but a weary sort of gratitude.

"When did this come?" David came into the kitchen, waving a fat envelope. "Why didn't you give it to Janie?"

Claire turned from the counter, two plates in her hand. She nearly dropped them when she recognized what he held.

"It's from Stanford." He grinned, clearly delighted. "Janie's going to be over the moon." He tested the envelope between two fingers. "Thick. This isn't a polite rejection letter. She's in. Wonder what kind of deal they're offering her."

Swallowing hard, Claire forced her feet to continue to the table. She carefully set down the full plates and returned to the counter for the tea she'd prepared for herself. Coffee, of course, for David. "Umm . . . I think it was Friday?" She pretended to be unsure. As if the arrival of the letter hadn't rocked her back on her heels. It had dread pounding through her until that call from the sheriff's office had wiped everything else from her mind. She'd convinced herself that this day wouldn't come. Had spun an elaborate fantasy that the prestigious university would have no interest in her daughter's SATs with the stratospheric science and math scores, her long list of AP classes, and perfect grades. That had been a far easier fabrication to believe than the one she had: that seeing the letter wouldn't cement Janie's college decision.

The thought of her daughter being halfway across the country less than a year from now had her throat drying out, a familiar panic spreading through her.

"I found it in the drawer of the hallway table, when I was looking for a different garage-door opener." David went to the refrigerator and attached the letter to a magnetic clip where Janie would be certain to see it, since the fridge was the first place she headed to upon arriving home. "I don't know why you would have put it there." He turned then, and catching sight of her expression, his gaze turned shrewd. "Claire, you weren't trying to hide this from her, were you?"

"Honestly, David, of course not." She sat down and spread her napkin on her lap. "I don't even recall putting it away. The phone must have rung when I brought in the mail, and I shoved it in there absent-mindedly and forgot about it. Janie didn't come home after school, remember? With everything else that happened that night, it completely slipped my mind."

He took a seat, reaching for his coffee. "Well, I know you haven't wanted to think about her choosing Stanford over OSU. But we have to consider what's best for her future. It's probably time to make an appointment with that counselor, Rimble. She can help us evaluate the best college offers as they come in. Not that Janie will need to consider finances first and foremost." He set down his cup and picked up the ham sandwich she'd fixed. "We have plenty in her college account to afford wherever she chooses, even if the package is stingy."

Of course they did. Claire nibbled at the edge of her sandwich. For the first time, she almost resented the lifestyle David's success afforded them. Although Janie's academic résumé alone would be strong enough for her to snare the interest of most universities.

Her appetite had fled. Instead of eating, she watched David enjoy the meal she'd fixed. In that age-old trick of Mother Nature, he was growing more handsome with the passing years. His hair was flecked with silver, where many men his age were balding or totally gray. He'd shocked her by coming home Friday night after the phone conversation they'd had. He'd attended his meeting first, of course, but he'd been here before she'd gone to sleep. She'd feigned exhaustion, letting Janie be the one to lead him from the room and apprise him of the events of the evening. Claire hadn't been able to relive them again. It had been traumatic enough being in that cramped space with Janie and the deputies. Listening to the recording of that horrid man admit that he'd taken those revealing pictures of Kelsey.

What else had he done? Had Kelsey gone there alone? Those were the questions her mind had seized on to worry about like a dog with a bone. Surely not. Surely she'd had the sense to take someone else along, like Janie had.

But Kelsey had been unpredictable her last few weeks at home. As great as Claire's need was to reconstruct every moment of their daughter's last days in West Bend, she wasn't certain she had the fortitude to face what the interview with Newman might reveal.

With effort, she searched for a topic to take her mind off her daughter. "How's work? I haven't seen Kurt and Linda for ages."

"Fine. Same old, same old." He reached for the newspaper sitting on the table in front of him. "Kurt will never slow down."

And neither, it seemed, would David. She managed to take a bite of the sandwich. Chewed slowly. He'd headed back to Columbus on Saturday, but not until late afternoon, and he'd surprised her by coming straight home afterward. He must have been more worried than he let on about Janie's run-in with the sheriff's office, although they'd barely discussed it. Claire had the feeling that between her daughter and husband, she was being wrapped in gossamer, as though she might shatter with a careless word.

She wished with all her heart that she could assure them their caution was unnecessary.

"I thought we'd have heard something from the sheriff's office by now." Like a tongue touching a sore tooth, her mind circled back to the same thoughts. "Sergeant Rossi promised he would keep us apprised."

"Wouldn't be the first time the police failed to keep that promise." The bitterness in David's tone had her glancing at him. He was scowling at the sports page. "How many times during the course of Kelsey's investigation did—" His words were interrupted by the peal of the doorbell. They both started to rise.

"Stay. Finish eating." Claire placed her napkin on the table and rose to hurry to the front door. She checked the peephole. An instant bout of nausea rose in her stomach as she saw the BCI agent and a strange woman standing on her porch. She pulled the door open. "Agent Foster. Ma'am."

"This is Agent Medford." There was a lazy scatter of snowflakes in the air. They adorned the agents' hair, their coats in artistic randomness. "Is your husband home, Mrs. Willard? We have something to discuss with you both."

Something grim, judging from their expressions. Claire clutched the doorjamb for support, her knees feeling watery. "Yes," she said faintly. "Of course." She and David had just been talking about Sergeant Rossi's promise to inform the BCI agents of the developments with Newman. And then they'd appeared, as if their words had summoned them.

She stepped aside to allow them to enter. While they stomped the fresh powder off their boots, she turned to fetch David. Found him already approaching. "Agents Foster and Medford have something they want to share with us."

"We were just saying that we haven't been updated about Friday's events at the lake house." There was a glitter of animosity in David's eyes that took Claire aback. She'd been as distressed as he was about the lack of communication, but the agents' arrival changed things. Turning back toward them, she waved them into the formal living room. "Please. Come in and sit."

Claire hadn't seen the stunning blonde woman with Foster before. She didn't look much like police. But then Claire didn't remember ever meeting a woman in law enforcement, with the exception of the security guard at the bank. "Can I get you anything? A cup of coffee?"

"No, thank you."

She sank down on the edge of the sofa, barely aware when David sat next to her.

"We've been working closely with the sheriff's office for the last thirty-six hours," Mark began.

"Have you interviewed Newman?" David asked the question on the tip of Claire's tongue. "What does he know about Kelsey?"

"We have spoken to him, yes." The woman answered this time. "We'll be talking to him again very soon. While he admits to taking photographs of your daughter shortly before she was kidnapped, he denies any other knowledge of her."

"When?" David demanded. "When does he say he took the pictures?"

"He claims it was two or three weeks before she disappeared."

Two or three weeks. Claire's mind flashed back to the recording Janie had played for the deputies. There had been discussion of payment for the photos. Newman had indicated any money could be gotten only through a modeling job once he sent the pictures onward. But other than school, Kelsey hadn't been gone for more than a few hours at a time, so she certainly hadn't modeled. Where had the money in the envelope with the photos come from?

"He's lying." David's voice was impatient. "He probably knows far more than he's telling. Where are these pictures? Maybe there will be something in them to prove he's holding back."

"We served a warrant on his home and car and seized his cameras and computer equipment. They've been delivered to the state lab, where cyber scientists will go over them as early as tomorrow." Mark's gaze was intent. "We'll have those answers for you shortly. Unfortunately, there's a more compelling matter we have to discuss with you. While searching the lake house location for evidence . . . a body was found."

The room tilted. Righted itself, still slightly askew. "What?" Claire reached out to grab her husband's hand. "David, what are they saying?"

"I'm so sorry to bring you this news." And the agent did look regretful, Claire thought dimly. So did the other agent, so pretty in spite of the somberness of her expression. "It's a young girl. Age fourteen to nineteen. She's dressed in a ballet outfit. Posed. More testing is required before we can say how long she's been down there, although we know she was moved after her death. She didn't die at the lake house."

"Ballet clothes," David said dully. "The TMK left his victims like that."

"I'm sorry." Mark glanced down, swallowed hard, and then lifted his head to look at them again. "Yes, the victim matches the manner in which the other TMK victims were found, with the exception of the location."

Claire was spiraling away, like a grain of sand whirling in a drain's vortex. She could feel herself fading. The voices growing distant. "That poor girl. Her parents will be so devastated." Having that last thread of hope snapped had to be the worst sort of nightmare.

"Jesus Christ, Claire." David's voice broke as he brought his free hand to his eyes.

"DNA tests will be run tomorrow." The female agent—Medford?—was talking. "But we have a preliminary match on the dental records. We're fairly certain the victim is your daughter, Kelsey."

A loud sob broke from David, and his shoulders shook. Claire slipped her arm around him.

"No, that's not right," she told him certainly. Then she turned to the agents. "It's not Kelsey."

"I know this is unbearably hard," Mark began.

"No. You know what's hard, Agent Foster?" She could hear her voice growing strident. Was helpless to temper it. "What's hard is receiving eight calls from police in different parts of the state telling us they had human remains—that's what they called them—unidentified human remains that they were going to try to match to Kelsey's DNA samples. Eight times in five years, because we haven't had a call in a while." Because everyone had forgotten all about the Willards, wrapped up in their cocoon of misery awaiting their daughter's return. "And every time—eight times—they were wrong. Like you're wrong now."

She gently extricated herself from her husband. Stood. "I want to be taken to her."

Mark looked pained as he rose. "Mrs. Willard, please. The DNA tests tomorrow will be all that's necessary. You don't have to put yourself through this."

"Yes. I do." The words quaked. "Because you're wrong, and I'm going to prove it to you. That girl isn't Kelsey. She's not my daughter. My daughter is alive."

David Willard

November 15
3:06 p.m.

David sat in the back seat of the sedan next to his wife. No one in the vehicle said a word. What was left to say? He'd done his best to talk Claire out of this. But there was no reasoning with her. He was used to dealing with his wife on the verge of collapse. Used to managing her hysterics. But she wasn't hysterical now; she was eerily calm. Fixed in her certainty despite the proof of the dental records the agents had mentioned. That calm was more unsettling than hysterics would have been.

There had been phone calls to make. Arrangements to set in place. The morgue was in the basement of the hospital. He hadn't known that Allama County Hospital had a morgue, although he should have. But no one thought about things like that unless circumstances forced them to.

Years ago, every time they'd gotten one of those phone calls about unidentified remains had been a special sort of hell. Claire would be overwrought, contemplating all the horrible ways their daughter, if it turned out to be Kelsey, could have died. He had never been able to stop his wife from using the intervening time to look up everything she could about the discovered body. Which only fueled her endless cycle of emotional frenzy that had exhausted them both.

No one who hadn't lost a child in the same manner would ever understand. Loss was a fanged beast that could devour a person whole. He'd had to step back from the constant agony, or it would have consumed him. As it had consumed his wife.

But this time was different. They'd finally reached the end of the interminable road they'd been traveling. There was no way to brace himself from the despair that awaited them. It was only at this moment that David realized he'd somehow managed to convince himself that this day would never come.

Mark pulled in to the hospital parking lot. The same hospital where David had welcomed the birth of both of his daughters. First Kelsey, red-faced and squalling, fists pumping as she screamed her displeasure to the world. And then Janie. Quieter even then. Watching the world with wary eyes and a guarded expression.

A sob clogged his throat. He didn't want to go in there. Would have given anything to avoid the next hour of his life. What was the purpose, when he already knew the outcome?

They sat there for a moment, no one talking. Then Mark spoke. "It's your choice. But this is unnecessary. Later today, the body is due to be transported to Madison County Hospital in London, where a pathologist will perform the forensic examination followed by the autopsy. The tests—"

"If it were your child, would you wait?" Claire's voice rang out, clear as a bell.

The agent didn't answer. Turning off the car, he got out and waited for them to join him before leading them inside the building.

Time slowed. The long trek to the elevators. The slow descent. Then their arrival in the basement. Cold, concrete floor. Musty smells. Walls that hadn't been painted in decades. Mark had used his phone to send a text before entering the building, and there was a man standing outside in the hallway with a lab coat on. Waiting for them. Without conscious thought, David slipped an arm around Claire's shoulders as the stranger ushered them into a sterile room with metal gurneys and foreign equipment that he didn't want to examine too closely. The hospital employee said nothing as he led them to a line of metal doors in the wall. Smaller ones across the top. A few larger ones on the bottom. He unlocked a bigger door and pulled out what looked like a long metal drawer holding a dark bag with a small Ziploc next to it. Slowly he lowered the zipper of the larger bag. Parted it.

"That's not Kelsey. It can't be." Claire sounded more desperate than certain. David forced himself to look at the remains for a moment before hissing in a breath and averting his eyes. For the first time he indulged in a brief fantasy that his wife was right. There was nothing recognizable about the body. Maybe this was a mistake. Maybe the matching dental records were wrong.

"This was found with the body." The man held up the baggie for them to see. David stared at the necklace inside the clear bag, the agony of recognition clawing bloody furrows across his mind. A crystal blue butterfly on a silver chain. Just like the ones his wife had bought the girls for Christmas, a lifetime ago. Just like the one Kelsey had been wearing when she'd disappeared.

Claire's scream echoed in the room. Streaked down David's spine, scraping nerve endings that were already raw. He stared at what was left of his daughter. His arms shot out to catch his wife just as she crumpled. Then he turned them both away from the sight that would inevitably haunt his dreams.

"That's Kelsey." His voice was thick was unshed tears. Kelsey, the way no parent should ever have to see their daughter. Claire's wails reverberated in the area, a constant stream of grief that hinted at an oncoming breakdown. He guided her from the room, saying over his shoulder, "My wife is going to require a doctor."

◆ ◆ ◆

David slowly made his way down the stairs, placing one foot in front of the other like an automaton. Claire was asleep, thanks to the sedative the doctor had given her at the hospital. There'd be follow-up visits required, the man had gravely informed David. Perhaps a complete workup with a mental-health professional, given her past history and the current trauma.

He'd nodded, although in truth, he'd barely listened to the man. His mind had been filled with memories of his daughter. A tiny, twisting body that had defied his efforts to dress her in the little rompers and dresses Claire had bought. An attractive toddler, with an outgoing personality and a penchant for getting her own way. A budding beauty in her teenage years, alternating between youthful exuberance and the drama of puberty.

A stranger, with contempt in her gaze hurling insults and accusations. Making demands he never should have met.

He wondered if other parents who'd lost a child had this hole inside them where all their regrets lived. Every cross word uttered. Every moment they'd let their child's chatter slide over them, by them, without really listening. All the wrong decisions made. Each failure that could never be undone. Sometimes at night they rushed forth to swamp him, strangling him with remorse.

His step faltered on the final tread when he noticed Mark seated in the living room. He'd almost forgotten the man had followed him into the house. Helped him get Claire's near-comatose body upstairs. The agent looked up at his approach. Put away the cell he'd been texting on as he rose.

"How's your wife?"

David flushed. It hadn't been just Claire that had kept him upstairs, but the single frantic phone call he'd made to his attorney. "She'll sleep for several hours. That's probably best." *Best.* As if that were a word that could be applied to either of them right now. "Thanks for helping with her. I have to tell Janie . . ." A boulder lodged in his throat at the thought. He took a breath and tried again. "She's at work until seven. I don't know if I should call and have her come home sooner . . . but what's the point of that, right? Why ruin her world before I have to?" A sudden thought occurred. "Unless . . . there's no way this news would get out, is there? I don't want to chance her hearing about it because someone leaked the information."

Mark regarded him somberly. "I'm not claiming a leak couldn't happen. I don't think it will, but if I were you, I'd have your daughter come home as soon as possible, just in case."

Nodding jerkily, David realized the horror of the day wasn't over. Not nearly. "I'll do that."

"I want to offer my sympathy again, Mr. Willard. Is there anything else I can do for you?"

David grimaced. "Not unless you can undo the last forty-eight hours."

"I wish I could. I'll talk to you soon, when I have updates."

He nodded wearily. They always promised that. But the updates wouldn't change anything. They wouldn't bring Kelsey back.

◆ ◆ ◆

"God, David, I'm sorry. I replayed our conversation in my head all the way over here." Brant Strickland unbuttoned his coat, sat down on the leather recliner in the family room. "What a shitty, shitty day. I'd always hoped, like you and Claire did, that Kelsey would be found safely. What can I do? How can I help?"

Funny, Mark had made a similar offer minutes ago. But the attorney was in a much better position to assist him than the law was. "You can advise me on how to proceed from here." David pulled a canister of Scotch from a cabinet in the entertainment center and took out two glasses. Poured a healthy splash into both of them. Crossing to where the other man sat, he handed him one. "I can get ice."

"This is fine." Brant took the glass, watching him carefully.

David took a gulp, his eyes watering. Then another. "Janie's on her way home, so I have to make this quick. I told you that the body . . ." His eyes filled, and he choked on the word. "Kelsey's body was found in the basement of that empty lake house."

"On Fuller Road, yes. I can't wrap my head around it. To have her so near all this time." Brant shook his head and raised the glass to his lips.

"They'll tear the place apart. Do their forensic testing. Dust for fingerprints." He saw the arrested look on the other man's face. Met his gaze squarely. "My prints are going to be there, Brant. I mean, I assume so. I don't know how long they last, but . . ." He finished the Scotch. Wished the liquor could erase the heart-crushing trauma of the day. "I was there a few times about seven years ago."

"It's been empty for ten." The other man frowned. "No way to get inside."

"The woman I was meeting had access. She was the Realtor."

"She . . . ah." Brant mulled that over for a moment. "Well, a Realtor sells properties. Maybe you were interested in buying it. Doesn't hurt to take a look at things, does it? Hell, I've driven by that place a thousand times thinking what a waste it is, sitting empty like that."

David stared into his empty glass. "My prints will be *only* in the bedroom. And I know they have them on file. The police took elimination prints when Kelsey was taken. It's only a matter of time until they start asking questions."

"Questions you don't have to answer." Brant was firmly in attorney mode now. "I'm not saying you can't talk to them. There will be details flowing in as the forensic tests are completed. But if they broach this subject, you call me."

"I don't want to become their focus." He heard a sound on the street. Was Janie home? He walked across the room. Hooked a finger in the curtain to pull it back so he could look out. No. Relief filled him. He had a few more minutes, anyway. Turning back to the other man, he continued. "They've got a new suspect in the case. I'd just be a distraction."

"Is this Realtor still around? In case they start asking questions?"

"No." And he and Tiffany had been careful. That had been part of the thrill at first. The clandestine meetings. The isolated surroundings.

"So she showed you the property. Just because they don't find prints in other rooms doesn't mean you weren't in them. Maybe you didn't touch anything anywhere else. Prints get smudged. We could argue they could be all over; they just failed to find other clear matches. Hell, we don't know that they'll get a clear set in the bedroom."

David had a mental picture of his body pressing against Tiffany's, hands on the wall on either side of her head, while he pounded himself into her. Leaning over the fireplace to build a fire with wood she'd bought downtown. Shutting the door with one palm as he gazed at her naked body stretched out on the air mattress she'd carried in the trunk of her car. He didn't respond to Brant's words. There'd be a match. It was more than guilty conscience that made him certain of that.

"But the more I think about it, the more I think you'd be better off not to play the lawyer card if they ask about the house. Just tell them what you told me. That you looked at it a couple of times, decided not to make an offer. That should put an end to things."

A measure of relief worked through him. "Thanks."

"No problem." Brant drained his glass and set it on the end table next to the chair. "Does Janie know?"

David shook his head. "I have to figure out how to tell her—" His mouth clamped shut. Where the hell would he find the words?

"I could stay, if you want."

David shook his head. "I need to do this myself. Somehow I have to find the words to explain to my daughter that her sister is dead."

Special Agent Mark Foster

November 15
5:58 p.m.

"I know my rights." Herb Newman was decidedly less talkative this time around. He glared at Mark balefully. "You gotta charge me, or let me go."

"You've been charged, Mr. Newman." How had the man missed that? "For trespassing and two counts of possession of an illegal substance. You'll be arraigned tomorrow. Which makes it imperative that you be more forthcoming this time around. Because a large quantity of drugs was found in the room next to the one you used in the lake house. And under the circumstances, you're the first we're looking at as the owner." There were far more serious charges pending. But that was a conversation for later.

"No way." Newman shook his head violently. "You can't pin that on me. I'm not the only one with a key to the place. There's nothing to tie me to the stash. I know that much."

"You don't seem surprised to hear about it, though." Mark set the file he carried on the table while he unzipped his coat. Unlike most interview rooms he'd been in, this one wasn't freezing. He was already starting to perspire, and he'd just gotten there. "Maybe you know who it belongs to. Could be one of the other people who has a key."

The man's mouth twisted. "The cops had one."

"Given to them by the Realtor so they could check on the place from time to time. Seems that it's a magnet for parties. And apparently illegal activities."

"I don't know who else has keys."

"Where did you get yours?"

The big man studied his fingernails. "Don't recall."

"You seem to have a problem with your memory." Damn, it was hot in here. Mark shrugged out of his coat. Newman seemed comfortable enough, but he was dressed in a short-sleeved orange jumpsuit provided by the county. One that was a size too small. The fabric strained over the man's girth. "You forgot to tell us that some of the pictures you took of teenage girls violated child-pornography laws."

"Bullshit. Those pictures are artistic. And they were taken at the girls' request."

It was easy to lose faith in the intelligence of humanity when faced with people this dumb. "Yeah? In the recording I heard, you were the one suggesting a girl take off her clothes. We've got your computer, Newman. We've seen the pictures." Thousands of digital files uploaded over the years. The cyber team would be able to match the most recent uploads to the SD card in the camera. Their findings had been enough to receive a warrant broadened in scope to include his car and the school, in case he'd hidden more evidence there.

Mark opened the file to take out a scrap of paper with a URL printed on it. Held it up for the man to read. "Recognize this web address? I see that you do." Mark lowered his hand. It had been included in Janie Willard's statement the night she'd been arrested for trespassing.

"No." Whether from the heat in the room or Mark's visual aid, the man was starting to sweat. "I don't even know what that is."

"I figured you'd say that." Taking his time, Mark put the paper back inside the file folder. "So before we shipped your computer off to the lab, the deputies did a little investigating. And imagine their surprise when they went to that URL and found a whole site with pictures just like yours, all available for download at a price."

"I don't know what you're talking about." A bead of sweat rolled down Newman's face and was lost in his beard. "You can't prove that, because it didn't happen."

"Oh, but we can." Mark repositioned his chair so he could stretch his legs out under the table. "See, those guys at the lab are computer geniuses. They can track every site you ever visited, even if you tried to hide your tracks. Uploads, downloads . . . everything's an open book to them. It's just a matter of time before they provide me with a detailed day-by-day account of every activity you've taken on that laptop."

"But I'm not the only one who used it," the man said triumphantly. "I've loaned it out a few times to the churches. I do janitorial work for three of them in the area. Sometimes the pastors need an extra laptop if one in the office goes to the shop, or if they have extra help there working on a project."

"And did you give the ministers the password to your picture files?" Mark asked. "Because it will be easy enough to check the dates your computer was loaned out and match those against the dates of the picture uploads from your laptop. Who were the pastors who had access to it?"

"Pastor Jennings at Hope Springs here in town. Reverend Mikkelsen at Trinity Baptist in West Bend. I don't know." The man rubbed his forehead, as if the act of recall pained him. "Maybe Pastor Wills in Blackston."

Mikkelsen. A thrum of excitement started in Mark's veins. He considered Newman, weighing how much to hit him with all at once. They were pressed for time. Once the janitor started thinking about what they had on him, he was going to start screaming for a lawyer. It was a wonder he hadn't already.

"Here's the thing." Mark decided to lay it all out. "We have you with a key to a property you don't own. Your voice on a recording offering illegal drugs to a teenage girl. You've admitted to taking nude or partially nude pictures of underage girls for a number of years. There's your proximity to a large stash of drugs, and as far as we know, you're the only outsider with access to the property. But the most damning thing is the body we found in the basement. The body of Kelsey Willard, a girl that—by your own admission—you photographed. A girl whose pictures were uploaded to that site." The sheriff had shown him the photos his deputies had found while combing the site minutes before he'd started the interview. It was one more damning piece of evidence against this man. "A girl who went missing shortly after you met with her."

The man's jaw dropped. "No fucking way. Are you kidding me?" His eyes widened. "No. Nuh-uh, you aren't pinning that on me. I've used that place for, like, six months. That girl's been gone for . . . I don't know exactly, but a lot of years."

"Where were you taking pictures before?"

"Three-oh-three Ferguson, on the south edge of town. I had the second floor of a duplex. The place on Fuller Road just fell into my lap, and I figured, hey, bigger space, more privacy . . ."

"Someone else's property . . ."

Newman acted as if he hadn't heard Mark's words. "Who the hell knows how many others have keys? But I'm not going to take a fall for the drugs or a dead body. Josh Ferin gave me a key in exchange for some pictures I took for free. He probably swiped it from his mother. She's the Realtor for the place."

◆ ◆ ◆

"Thank you, Mrs. Ferin. Have a good night." Sloane disconnected the call and set her phone on the edge of the bed beside her, sending Mark a smug look. "Karla Ferin is positively irate about people trespassing at one of the properties in the realty's portfolio. She's going to insist on charges being filed. She was quite indignant when I asked about access to the keys for the lake house. According to her, they're kept in a locked case at the realty office. Although they arrange for a regular cleaning service for the owners, an outside service hasn't been used in several months, because—get this—her son is being paid to take care of it."

"Which backs up Newman's story about how he acquired possession of the key. Unfortunately, he's also telling the truth about the place he rented up to a few months ago. Sheriff Richards had put in a call to Police Chief Miller. Apparently, the address of the property had been a bane for city law enforcement for some time, so he's well acquainted with the landlord. I put in a call, and the man verified the approximate dates that Newman had rented from him." Mark rubbed the back of his neck tiredly. It had been a trying day. But in the grand scheme of things, it didn't come close to the day experienced by the Willard family.

His sympathy for their tragedy could blind him if he let it. Could fog objectivity and alter investigative decisions. But he'd have to be made of stone not to feel compassion for parents given the worst sort of closure in the disappearance of their child. If he ever got used to delivering that sort of news to families about their loved ones, it was time to switch jobs.

"And, you haven't heard a word I said."

His attention jerked back to Sloane. "What?"

"Karla Ferin. I asked how long she'd been showing the property. She said she'd only been with the company since she moved to town two years ago. But it took very little coaxing to get her to rattle off the other three Realtors before her who had tried and failed to sell the place."

"Good. We'll need that information when the pathologist narrows down how long Willard has been dead." Speculating about the length of time her body had been at the lake house would be dicier.

Sloane approached the table and picked up a pen to write the names Ferin had given her on a small pad of paper. "I think we need to consider what Rossi told us about the break-in at the lake house three years ago."

A window had been broken out in back near the kitchen, Mark recalled. The deputies had blamed vandals. But had the killer gained access that way? And why the change in dump sites? According to Sims, the ten-mile radius in Wayne National Forest where the other victims had been found had been isolated. Difficult to reach. So breaking and entering to hide a body in a crawl space would be much easier in comparison. It also might signal that Willard's was a copycat killing and not the work of the TMK at all.

Sloane rubbed her eyes. For the first time, Mark noticed shadows beneath them. He quickly looked away. It didn't pay to observe anything about the woman that didn't pertain to the job. But he recalled in that moment that he'd worked two cases with her, and he knew little about her personal life. Under the circumstances, it wouldn't be wise to change that now.

He turned his attention to his e-mail to answer the work-related messages he'd received that day. There would be investigative reports to pore through. His own to write. And the priorities for tomorrow to discuss with Sloane. Priorities that would be shifted accordingly as the forensic results started filtering in from the lab.

For a moment, he was distracted by the array of pictures Sloane had run off from the TMK case file. The top row had photos of the four victims Sims had guessed were the work of the killer, although their bodies hadn't been found. Whitney DeVries's photo had been added, a constant visual reminder of what was at stake. In the next row were the verified victims. Sloane had switched Kelsey Willard to that line of pictures, for the time being. More evidence would be needed to ensure that she belonged there.

She began typing, and Mark started to scroll through his e-mail. Stopped when his phone rang. He pulled it out and glanced at the screen. Didn't recognize the number. "Mark Foster."

"Mark, this is Greg Larsen."

He glanced at Sloane. Larsen, he mouthed. Then he pushed away from the table to stand. "Greg. Sorry to bother you on the weekend."

"Not at all," the other man replied. "Your reports have been forwarded to me by your SAC." Mark's brows rose. That was news to him. "I understand that you have tentative ID on Kelsey Willard's body."

"Positive, as of today. The parents ID'd it."

There was a short pause. Then a long whistle. "Tough day all around, then. How can I help?"

"You know where this victim was found." Mark dove right in with his questions. "A total deviation from the other body dumps. Does it mean we're looking at a copycat killing? Or a killer who has changed his MO?"

"Ask an easy question, why don't you?" the man joked. "The truth is—and you're not going to like this answer—it's hard to tell. We'll have a better idea when the tests are run on the body and we compare victim photos. Luther Sims, the agent who worked the profiling before me, did attribute one victim to a copycat, so it's possible. But it will take time to make that judgment."

Mark had spent a couple of hours going over the digital photos of past victims. He hadn't found a glaring discrepancy between them and Willard's body. But there'd be tests on the fabric they wore. Measurements on the exact angles of the limbs. Comparison on the wire used on the fingers. With luck, they'd even be able to tell if the wire came from the same lot as that used on the others. "What would cause an offender to change part of his routine like that?" Mark paced the room as he spoke.

"A change in his circumstances." He could hear the shrug in the other man's voice. "Maybe he was physically unable to make the dump in Wayne Forest. Pretty arduous terrain, from the looks of the photos. Or perhaps this marks the beginning of a new trend of his. Leaving victims close by their homes. Sort of a last twist of the knife for the parents." Mark hadn't thought about that. What would it do to the Willards, he wondered, knowing that their daughter had been so near?

"Do you think it means he's in the vicinity?"

"With this dump, he's switched from a rugged site to a basement. From outside elements to inside. From hard to find to . . . I saw the photos. It didn't look like great pains were taken to hide the body."

"If it hadn't been for the drug dog, it wouldn't have been noticed. But I'm surprised no one observed the smell." Even that hadn't been overwhelming, however, until the bag had been opened. "The place is empty, but there are showings for the property, a cleaning service, Realtors. Not to mention the occasional trespasser."

"If I had to guess? And like too much of my job, this is conjecture. If this body does turn out to be the work of the TMK, for whatever reason, I'd predict he wanted her found. And there could be all sorts of explanations for that. To increase the family's suffering might be one. Another could be affection for this victim."

"Luther Sims seemed to think that all the victims had a parent who was deficient in some way."

"Yes, I've read his notes. Certainly, he worked more closely with the cases than I have, but from the reports, I don't really get that picture. But like I say, he met some of those people, and I didn't."

They spoke for several more minutes before Mark disconnected the call. Returned to his laptop. "Larsen thinks the killer may have meant for the body to be discovered." He considered what else the man had suggested. That the reason might be "affection" for the victim. Disgust twisted through him. Mark had what it took to follow the evidence, track down offenders. But ascribing the sickest serial offender in the state's history with any softer human emotions . . . that was probably beyond him.

"It also might mean someone is screwing with us and trying to make it look like Willard was a victim of the TMK. Someone in the vicinity who knew about the empty house and saw a perfect opportunity to get rid of a body."

"Yeah. Unfortunately, it's going to be a few days until they complete the comparisons with the other verified victims." He returned to his e-mail. "He did say he's tentatively attributed a couple more victims from years ago to the killer. He's sending me photos." He waited impatiently for the e-mail to arrive. Opened it and clicked on the pictures attached and printed them. Sloane got up and fetched them from the printer tray. Without a word, she picked up the tape and hung them in the top row with the other unverified victims.

Mark zeroed in on the first one, an odd sense of recognition flickering through him. "Does that first picture look familiar to you?"

"Only because they all have a similar appearance."

That was true enough. All the pictured girls were attractive, with long, dark hair and slender figures. Taken with the entirety of the collection, the sense of familiarity faded. He leaned closer to read the identifying information on the two girls in Larsen's pictures. Betsy Graves and Deena Horton. He frowned as he reread the date on the first one. "I don't know," he said doubtfully. "Thirty years ago? That's eight years earlier than Sims thought the TMK had been active."

"I don't pay much attention to the ones where no bodies were found." Sloane returned to typing her report. "That's a good way to head down the wrong path—start chasing after leads that have no evidence to support them."

Mark grinned. "You know, you almost sounded like Craw there for a minute."

"Be sure and let me know if I start looking like him," she retorted, then stopped when his cell buzzed again. "You're Joe Hollywood tonight."

"It's the sheriff's office," he said tersely before answering it.

"Foster, it's Rossi. We've been running the fingerprints we collected from the lake house and matching them against ones we have in city and county files. Pretty sure we've zeroed in on the owner of that stash of illegals we found—Josh Ferin. Local punk who Newman named as giving him a key."

"The Realtor's son."

"That's the one." The sergeant sounded as exhausted as Mark was feeling. "His prints are all over those bags of illegals. But here's the thing—and this one's a doozy. In the bedroom, same place we found the drugs, we discovered latents that matched another set in our system. They belong to David Willard."

Whitney DeVries

November 16
5:58 p.m.

"It doesn't look as though you've eaten much today."

The words had something inside Whitney going still. How would he be able to see the small pile of food he'd set on the stage this morning? It was well outside the glow provided by the computer screen and projector. And now that she thought about it, how did he see in the morning when he brought the food? She'd been awake the one time. He'd arrived without a light of any kind.

"I haven't been hungry."

She hadn't, because excitement and fear were gnawing a hole in her belly. Last night she'd finally loosened the last screw. Her success had filled her with triumph and a newfound fear. Now came the most difficult part.

Each night when she quit working, she twisted the screws in loosely, so they'd be close to the bracket. But easy to unscrew when the time came.

That time was tonight.

Nerves clutched and jumped inside her. Another reason she hadn't been able to eat much since she'd started loosening the barre. Last night before she finally went to sleep for a few hours, she'd fetched the leftovers and stowed them next to the shower. She had no idea where this place was. What she'd face when she got loose or how long it would take to find help. If she could, she'd take some of the food with her.

"You must eat to keep up your strength, Whitney." Here came the lecture. "You have a duty to maintain your own health so that you aren't a burden to others. If you grow weak, your progress will suffer, and if that happens, you will be punished. My mother always said that sickness was weakness manifesting itself in the body. You must not indulge yourself by allowing yourself to get sick."

His mother sounded like a real winner. Whitney nodded obediently, as if she wasn't contemplating the thought that he and dear old mom must be a chip off the same sadistic block. Maybe it took a monster to make one.

"I'm here to help you reach your full potential." That syrupy sweetness was back in his voice. It always had her flesh prickling. "That's something so few people ever attain. With my help, you'll be one of a select number who do. But you must listen. Like most instructors, I can teach, but it's up to you to learn."

"I'll try to eat an apple." Anything to shut him up.

"Fetch a sandwich and an apple from the meals I brought you, and bring them to center stage."

She did as she was told. The food was always set almost out of the reach of the chain. As if he knew to the inch how far it would stretch. Whitney shivered as the tips of her fingers touched the wrapped sandwich so she could pull it toward her. Of course he knew exactly how far it would stretch. Every tiny detail in her prison had been planned with one thing in mind . . . allow no escape.

Retaking her spot in the pool of light provided by the computer screen and projector, she awaited further instruction. *Fetch*, she thought bitterly, *like a trained dog.* He treated her like an animal with everything he forced her to do, and the punishments for failing. Every year her class raised money for the local animal shelter. She'd gone once and never returned. It'd been too hard to see the animals locked up, barking or rubbing up against the cage doors for attention.

But worse had been the ones that had cowered in the back of their cages, shivering, heads down, refusing eye contact. With a brilliant burst of understanding, she realized that was what he was trying to do. Break her down. Destroy her spirit until she'd do anything—*be* anything he demanded.

Tendrils of fear curled up her spine. Maybe he'd succeed if she didn't get out of here.

"Your nightly TV time won't begin until you've finished. Remember, Whitney, healthy body, healthy spirit, healthy mind." She waited until she heard him move away to begin unwrapping the cellophane from the sandwich.

She couldn't have eaten quickly if she tried. Her nerves were too jittery with her plans for later that night. But she forced the food down, a little at a time. He was right about one thing—she needed her strength for what was to come. When she'd finished, she returned the cellophane and apple core to where he left the food for him to dispose of the next day.

The TV show began before she even returned to her spot. He watched that closely, hovering over the image from the camera he must have on the computer and responding instantly.

She sat down on the chilly floor, turned to stare blindly at the silly show on the wall behind the barre. He had to have the projector hooked to the computer the way they did when they presented their group projects to the class. The detail wasn't important, but it had taken her too long to note it. Just like thinking of another use for that screw in the shower should have occurred to her earlier.

It was like her brain had been frozen with terror and grief. But it wasn't numb anymore. And if she was successful tonight, it might be only a matter of time until the freak was in prison. But she wished, more than anything else, that before he was locked up, she'd get a chance to find his whip and use it on him.

◆ ◆ ◆

How much time had passed since the lights had gone out? It was difficult to know because Whitney had been busy. First, she'd collected all the food she'd squirreled away and brought it to the mattress. It took more time than she'd figured to turn the nightgown into a sort of roomy backpack. She'd ended up ripping two seams along the sides to thread the sleeves through, which could be tied together.

No use worrying what would happen to her for tearing the garment, she thought darkly. Trying to escape would bring the worst punishment yet.

Her hands faltered at the thought. What would he do to her if she were caught? Her pulse began to pound as her imagination obliged with clip after clip of possibilities. Would he kill her? Or was there punishment worse than death?

She shook her head violently to dislodge the thoughts. He wanted her like this. Paralyzed by fear of displeasing him. And how long would it take until she became exactly what he trained her to be, like one of those dogs, broken and afraid? The memory had some of her resolve returning, and she continued laboring over her makeshift backpack until it was ready to fill with her meager supplies.

Trying it on, she made a few minor adjustments, but overall, she was pleased with the result. Then she went to the barre and worked as quietly as she could at removing each of the screws she'd loosened.

A thrill of excitement pounded through her when she held all six of them in her hand. Carefully she removed the bracket from the end of the barre with no more than a few clinks of metal on metal. Bent to set it and the screws on the floor. Barely daring to breathe, Whitney slid the thick, metal manacle that matched the one on her wrist down the barre. Off it.

The oxygen leached from her lungs. The bracket on the far end of the barre kept it hanging from the wall akilter. She gathered up the long links of chain and did a fist pump in the air. She was free! She wanted to get started on her escape plan. Right now. But it couldn't be much past eleven. To pass the time, Whitney took out the scroll of papers Kelsey had left. Wrapping the chain around her waist and tucking in the loose end to reduce its jangling, she then carried the pages over to the window, heady with her newfound range of motion.

It was a goodbye of sorts. She unrolled the sheets and tried to find a glint of light to read by. Whitney had gained strength from the girl who had come before her, and she owed her for that. She skimmed over Kelsey's innermost thoughts that so closely reflected her own. Terror. Determination. Depression. Whitney had experienced all of that, too. She wondered if there was anyone else in the world who could understand her feelings as well as the freak's other captive.

Tonight he told me he's moving me. I don't know what that means. I'm ashamed that my first thought when he said it wasn't escape. It was fear. Fear that wherever he takes me will be even worse.

But what could be worse? I haven't had a beating in months, but I can still feel marks on my back and butt. I don't know if they'll ever go away. He's branded me. Made me his even though I won't be. Never. But I've pretended for all I was worth for so long now that sometimes it's hard to remember my plans to get away. To remember who I am.

I'm KELSEY WILLARD. He's been trying to change that all year, but I won't let him. He's given me a new name. He calls me Faith. He wants to destroy the memories of my family and any life I had before he brought me here, but he hasn't. My sister is Janie. She has social anxiety that doesn't let her do everything she wants to, but she's crazy smart. Way smarter than I was at that age. She fell out of the swing once when she was little, and I was the only one who could get her to get back on it. I taught her to pump with her feet, and after a while, she'd let me give her underdogs. Fly high, Janie. That's what I always told her. Fly high, and you'll find your voice.

Claire is my mom. Not some other unseen woman that he keeps telling me will be my new mother. I have a mother. She's pretty and fun, and we go out for lunch and shopping together, just the two of us. I was so mad at her at the end. So mean. I know I hurt her feelings. But it wasn't her fault. I hope I get a chance to tell her that.

And this POS is not my dad, no matter how many times he has me call him Daddy. My father is David Willard. Fathers take care of their families, but they love them, too. They goof around and make their kids laugh and don't get mad when they take their daughter to practice driving and she scratches the car. My dad just made a joke about buying me a junker when I get my license so I can't damage it.

And sometimes dads make mistakes. Truly awful, horrible mistakes. It's taken me a long time to forgive mine. Because if there's one thing this place has taught me, it's that no matter how bad something seems at the time, it could always be worse.

I'm hoping that being moved means the monster trusts me a little. And that wherever he takes me will be easier to escape from. I can keep pretending as long as I have to. All I need is one instant when I'm not being watched. If there's ever someone who reads this, remember that. There might be only one chance. Any risk is worth taking if it gets you home.

Whitney wasn't aware she was crying until the tear traced down her cheek. She reached up an arm, wiped it on her sleeve. *If I get away, I'll send someone back for you*, she thought fiercely. She wanted to believe that Kelsey was still alive somewhere. The thought helped summon the courage to carry out her plan tonight.

Slowly she rolled up the pages. Replaced them under the floorboard and started toward the shower to return the screw. Then she thought better of it. Instead, she tucked it into her bra between her breasts, the flat head secured by the bottom band, the end pointing upward. There was no reason to put it off any longer. Her heart started knocking faster in her chest. Going to the edge of the stage, she turned and lowered herself off it, keeping a tight grip on its edge. It was about three feet to the floor. The utter darkness had her pausing to get her bearings. There was another window high in the wall in this area. But the tiny glimmer of light around the curtain didn't make a dent in the shadows.

There was no use trying the door. Whitney had listened to him turn the lock when he left, as he always did. Instead, she made her way in the darkness until she was touching the table she figured he'd had the computer sitting on. She'd gone through this plan a hundred times in her mind. Pick up the computer and set it gently on the floor. And now . . . her hands searched. Another machine. The projector. There was a neat pile of books on the table that they had sat on, so Whitney swiftly lowered those, as well. Then she reached for both sides of the table and lifted it.

Not so heavy. Awkwardly, she carried it through the darkness to the stage. Leaned the tabletop against it at an angle and then grasped the far legs to lever it upward. Hopping back up on the stage, Whitney carried the table over to the wall beneath the window.

How much noise had she made? She'd been so busy, she'd forgotten to consider it. She paused to listen. Heard nothing. She went and got the backpack she'd fashioned and tied it securely around her neck. Then she retraced her steps and got on top of the table. Moved the curtain aside. Blinked a little at the dim light that streamed in.

The window was a small rectangle, maybe a foot and a half by three feet. The inside was covered with a thick, clear plastic film. But that wasn't what had Whitney's stomach plummeting.

He'd nailed it shut.

Tears of frustration threatened. For an instant, she considered putting everything back. Rethinking her plan. But he'd know. He knew everything. Even if she got every single detail right, the rips in the nightgown would have him wondering.

There might be only one chance. It's worth any risk if it gets you home.

Gritting her teeth, Whitney carefully climbed down and went back to where she'd left the things from the table on the floor. Found the thickest book and carried it to the window. She'd have to break the glass and take the chance that he'd hear it. Which meant she had to work quickly. Maybe she could wiggle through the broken panes before he got downstairs.

First, she ran her fingers over the plastic. Taped on, she discovered. Easy to remove. Rearing back with the arm holding the book, she smashed it against the window, square in the center.

The glass cracked rather than shattered. But even that noise seemed deafening in the surrounding silence. But it wasn't, she assured herself, repeating the action. Not really. The covering helped muffle the sound. She took a moment then to tear away the two-sided tape that kept the thick plastic in place. Then wrapped it around one hand, which she threaded through the hole she'd made. She pressed her palm against the back of the glass as she worked, knocking out the larger shards until there were only tiny teeth left all around the frame.

There was an outside window, as well. Also nailed shut. Whitney worked more quickly now, stifling the noise as she had with the first one. Finally, she was loosening the outside layer of sheeting free from the window. And then frigid air kissed her face. She opened her mouth, taking a greedy gulp. It tasted of freedom.

She set the book down on the table, and then reached up to tear the outside plastic free so she could wrap it around her other hand. Then, palms placed on the windowsill, she gave a mighty jump.

Her arms quivered, and for a moment, she thought she would fall. The screw gouged her skin, and she gritted her teeth against the pain. The muscles in her arms quivered as she struggled to pull herself up far enough to get her elbows on the sill. Used them to leverage the rest of her body as she squeezed herself an inch at a time through the tight space. Until she got stuck. Moving side to side, she tried to free herself. *The backpack*, she thought. There wasn't enough room for it. Whitney used her teeth to pull the plastic off one hand so she could clumsily untie the nightdress. It fell away, its contents dropping to the floor. She heard the apples thud and roll, and somehow they sounded louder than the glass had breaking.

The noise infused her with panic. Turning back to her task, she shimmied through the opening, uncaring of the glass slicing through the thin tights and leotard to cut her skin. She ignored the sharp point of the screw between her breasts. Fear gave her speed, and moments later, she was pushing through the second window to the frigid ground outside.

She struggled to her feet, aware that blood was trickling down her body in several places. There was a sliver of a moon, sheening the frosted grass with an eerie glisten. Whitney started to run. Not toward the front of the building, but away from it. There were trees in the distance, clustered around the property. Some pines. She'd leave a clear path on the grass, so her best chance was to put as much space between her and this place as possible.

Fear lent flight to her feet as she sped across the slippery ground, which quickly soaked her ballet shoes. She didn't feel the sticky blood or the cold. There was only evil behind her, and this was the one chance she was going to have for escape.

She was almost at the tree line. The arctic air slashed at her lungs as she gulped it in, turning her insides to ice. Maybe there'd be a house nearby where she could seek help. Or perhaps a road where she could flag down a passing car.

A howl of rage split the air. Her feet faltered as she threw a look over her shoulder. A shadow was racing through the darkness. Toward her. For the space of an instant, Whitney froze. *No!* A sob broke from her. Not when she'd come so close! She whirled, flying over the icy ground toward the trees where she could find cover. Where a fallen limb would give her a wea—

The tackle from behind took her down. Terror turned her into a flurry of motion. She rolled, her fists flying, feet kicking, teeth gnashing. The iciness beneath her seeped through her muscles. Settled in her bones. But all her senses were focused on the monster above. He had something over his face again. A mask. Goggles covered his eyes, giving him an alien appearance. She landed a punch against his jaw as he tried to pin her arms and screamed, a raw, jagged shriek fueled by fury and fear. She wouldn't go back. She'd rather die, here and now. Whitney bucked beneath him and swung again. Missed. His hands grasped the sides of her head, slamming it again and again against the ground. "Ungrateful bitch! After all I've done for you!"

Shards of agony arrowed through her brain. A brilliant kaleidoscope of colors wheeled in front of her eyes. Whitney's struggles grew weaker as she fought against receding consciousness. She felt herself being lifted, and the action ignited a primitive survival instinct.

"Nooo!"

The denial was ripped from her throat. Every stride he took was another step back toward her prison. Back to complete submission or death. Her arm rose, fingers scrabbling for the screw she'd hidden inside her bra. He pressed her more tightly against his chest to quell her movements, but there was a newfound strength flowing through her as she pulled out the screw and swung it toward his face. Encouraged by his howl of pain, she struck again, this time raking it down his cheek.

"Bitch!" She felt herself falling, landing hard on the frozen ground, the screw flying from her hand. He was on her before she could roll away on the slippery grass, his hands going to her throat, squeezing mercilessly. She couldn't breathe. Her fingers went to his and tried to pry them away. Spots were dancing in front of her eyes.

"Ha . . . te you," she croaked.

His hands tightened.

"I've given you so many chances. And always you disappoint me, Margaret."

Chest burning from lack of oxygen, her fingers loosened. A sense of calm spread through her. The peace was another sort of freedom. Rational thought drifted away. She saw herself rise to float above the two figures struggling below. Felt a tinge of pity for the girl. Then a moment later, she felt nothing at all.

Janie Willard

November 18
9:34 a.m.

"Did I mention yesterday how much I like what you've done to this place since I was last here?"

Janie looked at Dr. Drake, who was straddling her desk chair in the center of the bedroom. He'd turned it around, resting his crossed arms on the back of it. She didn't know who called him after she'd learned about Kelsey's body being found. Probably her dad, since her mom was barely functioning. It was sort of a relief to have him here, an objective party that she didn't have to tiptoe around while she tried to make sense of the unimaginable.

Kelsey was dead. Somehow being aware of the possibility hadn't completely prepared her for the reality of it.

"Well, I was ten when you used to come here, so . . ." She recognized what he was doing. Lightening the moment. Making it seem less like a mental-health visit and more like . . . what? Two old friends discussing her sister's murder? Not a fun subject, even for a therapist. So much easier to cushion it between a little small talk.

"I remember. You were on a huge butterfly kick. Had cutouts hanging from the ceiling. They were actually a little creepy." His gaze was too steady. Probing, like he wanted to take her apart, examine her thoughts and feelings and then put her back together again. She wished that were possible. Put her back together, excluding the anxiety and grief that took turns dictating her emotions.

"They eventually get out of their cocoons. They don't have a voice, but they're beautiful. And they get to fly. I used to think that meant I'd eventually get wings, too." A juvenile hope, one that had withered when Kelsey was kidnapped. Her sister was the only one who had taken part in the fantasy. They'd spend hours spinning in the yard, arms out, pretending they'd already taken flight.

"Have you heard from Stanford yet? Focusing on your future will be a tool in coping with your grief."

"Yeah. They're offering a full ride." She'd found the envelope on the fridge yesterday. Had opened it alone in her room. Her flicker of initial excitement had been instantly squelched. Her world had been upended. Again. College plans seemed a low priority at the moment.

"Janie!" Dr. Drake's delight was evident. "That's awesome!"

"Right." Her voice was flat. He didn't seem to get that she had more important things on her mind right now. Like the fact that her family was in shreds, and this time she wasn't quite sure if they'd get patched back together.

He proved more intuitive than she'd given him credit for by adding, "But there's plenty of time to make college decisions. Let's focus on the now. Did you take the meds this morning?"

She sighed silently. Always the same thing with this guy. "I told you I would."

"And since I know you so well, I realize that isn't really an answer."

"Yes. I took the meds. Yes, I promise to take them regularly for at least a month." She was already regretting that vow. But she could renegotiate it later. "You'll be glad to know I haven't started screaming once at the thought of leaving the house."

"Have you left the house?"

"No." But not because she physically couldn't. At least, she didn't think so. Where would she go? Alyvia had gotten permission to come straight here after school yesterday and later today. Cole had sent her a couple of texts, which she hadn't answered. Maybe she wasn't as ready to deal with the outside world as Dr. Drake hoped, but that didn't mean she couldn't get there on her own.

Besides, there was her mom to consider. She'd barely been out of bed since Sunday. Barbara had come by a few times, but Janie had sent her away. Claire was in no condition for visitors, even from a close friend. Twice Janie had found her in Kelsey's room, sitting on the floor, Kelsey's blue sweater held to her face to soak up her silent tears. Both times Janie had helped her to her feet, led her back to her bedroom, watching helplessly as her mother sobbed. Marta, who'd started coming every day since the news broke, had swooped in on both occasions, closing her out of her parents' bedroom and tending to Claire.

Her dad wandered around like a lost soul. She'd found him at one point scrubbing the kitchen floor, rubbing the same spot over and over for long minutes until she'd tiptoed away. Another time when she hadn't been able to find him, she'd looked in the garage. He'd had the door open, the cars moved out, and was sweeping with a single-minded purpose stamped on his face. He hadn't been wearing a coat, and it was freezing, but Janie had closed the door and let him be. All of them had to search for peace where they could find it.

"If I offered to take you somewhere with me now, would you go?"

"Maybe tomorrow. We can get coffee."

He looked surprised. "You'll go to the coffee shop with me?"

"No. But I'll go through the drive-up with you."

A slow smile crossed his face. "You've always driven a hard bargain. But it's a deal."

She was sitting on the bed, knees drawn up to her chest, fingers plucking the blanket beneath her. She hadn't made the bed today. Unusual for her. But it just hadn't seemed important in light of what was going on around her. "My mom isn't doing great."

"I know. She's under a doctor's care. I'm concerned with how *you're* doing."

She lifted a shoulder. "Seven years is a long time to think your sister is going to come walking through the door." Her mom had never stopped believing. But was that confidence, really, or fear? Fear that if she let go of the last remnant of hope that Kelsey would truly be gone forever. "It's not that I could ever really believe she was dead." She'd never quite been able to formulate the thought. "But I thought I'd accepted a world without her. And now that I know she's gone, I realize maybe I never really accepted it all."

He nodded. "Imagining something isn't the same as being hit in the face with reality. It's sort of like losing your sister twice. First, when she disappeared, and again . . ."

"When they found her body." That was exactly what it was like. "You think I'm going to start that spiral of grief again. Suffer the same sort of setback I did before. But I'm not the same person I was then. Grief is like a stairway, and I've been perched halfway up it for seven years. I'm not starting on the bottom tread this time."

He cocked his head. Maybe she'd said something wrong. But nothing was ever wrong with Dr. Drake. He'd always accepted every emotion, every irrational fear, and talked her through them.

"Closure can be pretty horrible, especially under circumstances like these. But you're right: it can lend an opportunity to put the past behind you. Eventually."

Did she want to put Kelsey behind her? Janie ducked her head, letting her hair shield her face. Sure, she'd figured out somewhere along the way that her sister probably wasn't coming home, but there had still been those times when she'd let herself dream . . . Kelsey *could* be found.

Janie had spun a hundred different scenarios in her mind. But as time passed, they'd gotten harder and harder to summon.

But that was different from hearing how they'd found her sister's body hidden only miles from their house. Knowing she'd been nearby for a number of years somehow made it all worse.

"I heard the BCI agent talking to my dad when he stopped by yesterday. He told him Kelsey had been in the lake house for a while, but they didn't know how long. But she'd been moved from somewhere else."

"Janie, look at me." He waited until she obeyed. "I'd prefer if you didn't dwell on details like that. They're going to be terrible, and not one of them is going to make your grief easier to bear. At some point, you're going to want to know them. But right now you have a pretty big loss to deal with. Give yourself time to manage that."

She nodded. Maybe it made her a coward, but she didn't want to hear all the lurid details. There'd come a time, she supposed, if they ever caught the killer, when the media would display all the juicy facts of her sister's death, and she needed to be prepared for that. But for now Dr. Drake was right. She needed to handle the *now*.

Saying a final goodbye to her sister was going to take every last ounce of strength she had.

"I'm going to go. But I'll be back tomorrow to take you out for coffee."

"Okay." She was always glad to have a session over. But this wasn't exactly a session. And it had really been all right seeing him yesterday and today. She swung her legs over the bed and stood. Walked him to the door. "You're buying tomorrow."

"I never doubted it." He had a nice smile. A quick flash of teeth, but most of it was in his eyes, where it counted.

"I already know what I'm going to order," she said as they descended the stairs. "A caramel whipped-cream espresso."

He made a face. "That sounds disgustingly sweet."

"Just for that, I'm not going to let you try it."

"My arteries thank you." At the front door, he turned to her, all trace of humor absent from his expression. "I really think you're going to be okay this time. You've developed a resiliency that many adults would envy."

Janie made a face. "That makes me think of a rubber ball that you throw against the wall over and over without damaging it. But I guess what you mean is that I'm not losing my mind. Which is always good to hear."

"No. You're caught up in a tragedy that would be challenging for anybody to manage. But sometimes I think you're the sanest person I know."

His words surprised her, lingering even after the doctor headed outside and down the front steps. She closed the door behind him. If this was what passed for sanity, she hoped she never experienced the opposite.

For the first time, she was aware of a murmur of voices. Curious, she rounded the corner into the living room. She never spent much time here. This space and the formal dining room beyond it were meant for entertaining. The decorations and furniture were fussy and uncomfortable. She'd always preferred the family room.

Her dad always had, too. But he was here now, seated across from that agent. Foster.

"Fingerprints? Well, I shouldn't be surprised. I had a Realtor show me the property on Fuller Road seven or eight years ago. I guess I was going through a phase when I thought living in the country would be peaceful. I looked at the property a couple of times, as I recall."

"With your wife?"

"No, I don't think Claire was ever with me. I came to my senses before I mentioned the possibility to her. It's grossly overpriced."

"That would explain your fingerprints in one of the bedrooms."

"Really? They should be all over. We looked at the entire main floor, as I recall. With the number of people that have been through the house over the years, the place must be full of them."

"It is."

Her dad had once thought about buying the lake house? A sick pocket of dread opened in Janie's stomach, although she couldn't say why. She backed out of the room and turned to go upstairs again. Then saw her mom standing behind her in the doorway of the family room, still clad in her nightgown and robe, her expression frozen.

"Mom?" Tentatively, Janie started toward her.

But Claire walked by her. Started up the stairs. "I'm going to take a bath now." Her voice was almost childlike. Her filmy white robe trailed behind her like a wispy wraith. A chill worked over Janie's body as she watched her go.

Her mother was fading away before her eyes. And Janie wasn't quite sure what she was supposed to do about it.

Claire Willard

November 18
9:44 a.m.

Claire sat on the edge of the bed with no memory of how she'd gotten there. Oh, yes, she'd seen Janie downstairs. Had said something to her—what was it again?—before coming back upstairs. But she didn't recall why she'd left the room to begin with. Everything seemed so foggy. There was a knot of tension between her eyes. She should take something for that. Had she already? Claire couldn't remember that, either. But she knew there were new prescriptions, brand-new bottles lining the counter in the adjoined bath. Somehow Dr. Schultz's compassion had kicked in again, now that they'd found . . .

She snatched up a pillow and buried her face in it, stifling the scream that threatened. There was one lodged inside her all the time now, an instant away from being ripped from her throat. Her baby, her baby, her baby . . . how would she ever bear it? Why would a parent *want* to?

There had always been that possibility. Getting less likely with each passing year, but still there. The chance that Kelsey would be returned. Damaged by her experience, whatever it might have been. But home safely where they could put all their effort into helping her mend emotionally. They'd heal together as a family. All the pieces inside of them that had grown brittle and broken with despair would be cured given enough time. Enough love.

And now even that distant hope had been snatched from them. Claire began to rock, tears dampening the pillow. Everyone had been wrong. Closure didn't help you heal. It just stole away your last reason to live.

She knew from experience that the day would come when the well of tears would dry, become impossible to muster. It was around the same time that people would start putting on those determinedly cheerful expressions. *Look, I'm moving on. Just follow my lead. I'll show you how it's done.*

A hole had been drilled in her heart the day Kelsey disappeared. She'd drifted through seven years waiting for it to be filled again. Now it never would be. Claire knew she didn't have another seven years left in her.

Last night, she'd lain awake for hours, staring at the ceiling. She'd thought David had been asleep. The words had burst forth, a brutally raw truth. "I want to be with her."

"Claire." The pain in her husband's voice had registered. But she'd had no comfort to offer. "That's unhealthy talk."

It might be unhealthy. But it was utterly honest. She couldn't do it again. This time the grief would surely suffocate her.

There was a tiny sound at the door. The knob turned. It was locked. She waited for David to call to her to open it. When no voice came, she knew it was Janie hovering out there, her expression stamped with worry.

What had her youngest daughter thought when she'd heard her father speaking to the agent downstairs? The shock of her husband's lies was buried somewhere deep inside Claire, but she couldn't really feel it on any level. Seven or eight years ago, they had not been in the market for a lake house. The idea was laughable. That was the time period when she and her husband had made a loan to her mother so she could avoid foreclosure. A loan that hadn't been repaid, just as David had predicted. Things had been tight for a while, until he'd gotten a substantial raise at work. And then another. Just the idea of a home outside of town was ludicrous. David's idea of country living was driving a golf cart around eighteen holes.

But Claire had no doubt that he'd been in the lake house. Likely more than once. Tiffany White had been the young Realtor in charge of it then. In her early twenties, the girl had babysat for them several times when they went away for the weekend. Pretty, lithe Tiffany, with the sparkling green eyes, husky laugh, and long, blonde hair. Odd, with her thinking so muddled that she could be so clear about this. David and Tiffany had had an affair.

A fist squeezed her heart. So perhaps she wasn't completely numb inside, after all. Tiffany had left town years ago, for a bigger realty agency in . . . Cincinnati? No, Columbus. Claire's stomach did a neat flip. It *was* possible to feel more pain, she discovered. Even when she'd thought the layers of agony couldn't get worse.

She threw herself back on the bed. Straightened her gown and lay very straight, arms at her sides. Was he still seeing her? David was in Columbus an awful lot. At least eight days a month. Sometimes more frequently. *Something's come up. A major wrinkle with one of the Columbus accounts.* She'd been so easily fooled. So lost in the effort it took to get through each day that she'd never questioned his absences. Never stopped to wonder if it was normal for a husband and wife to remain married for seven years and not have sex once during that time.

Nothing had been normal since Kelsey had been gone. Nothing would ever be normal again.

She thought again of the new prescriptions. No need anymore to hoard pills in secret places. No more shopping for doctors. There were also all those unused pills in Janie's room. Claire's own medication would flow freely again, at least for a few years.

She wouldn't need it for that long.

A sense of calm settled over her. She'd wait until Janie was at college. She owed her youngest that. She'd help her through the hell that the rest of this year would be. Accompany her on the college visits. Remain stoic when Janie chose the one across the country. She'd wait for a morning next fall when Marta wasn't coming.

And then Claire would swallow every last pill in the house. It wouldn't take long. A brief bout of unpleasantness, quickly over.

Then she'd be with Kelsey for eternity.

David Willard

November 18
9:50 a.m.

"We don't have to talk about this now." It was at least the third time Agent Foster had made the suggestion. "It can wait . . . until later."

"Some time when it's easier?" David sat on the couch in the formal living room, bent at the waist, his forearms resting on his thighs. He raised his head to look at the other man. "When will that be? God, I wish someone would tell me when it gets easier. I've been waiting for that day for seven years."

"I know." The agent looked miserable. "But I don't think hearing all the forensic details right now will help."

David wanted to tell him that nothing he learned could make it any worse. But that was probably a lie. Hell had infinite depths, and just when he thought he'd explored them all, he was plunged deeper into the pit. He'd struggled out of it once. Somehow. He didn't know if he had the strength to do so again. "Just tell me," he said dully. "What have you learned about my daughter? You promised us that much."

The agent released a breath. "We still don't have an approximate time of death. There are so many factors to consider given the body's state of . . ." He seemed to think better of what he'd been about to say and switched tacks. "There will be more tests. If necessary, we'll get a forensic anthropologist to help. At this point, we are certain that she was a TMK victim."

Puzzled, David stared at him. "Well, of course. That's obvious."

"There's been at least one copycat crime." Mark looked ill at ease, as if he'd rather be anywhere but here. David couldn't blame him. He'd prefer to be elsewhere, too. But that relief was going to be denied him for the near future. "And the body wasn't found in the location where other victims were left. The wire used on her fingers and foot to pose her, however, is exactly the same as used on the others. It may even have come from the same roll."

"You can tell that?"

Mark nodded. "The scientists at the lab can. The DNA tests on the body, of course, positively identified her."

"Do you think the same person took the girl from Saxon Falls?"

The agent hesitated, then said, "It seems likely at this point."

"What about the photographer?" David wanted this over. Really over. And that wouldn't happen until someone paid for his daughter's death.

"We've been focusing on him for the last few days." The man seemed to be more comfortable with the conversation since it had drifted away from Kelsey. "We found pictures of your daughter on his computer. He was questioned after she disappeared, because a couple of kids at school reported seeing them talking one day. But he gave a plausible story at the time about her asking about a locker that stuck. There was no reason then to look harder at him." The man clasped his hands, the fingers lacing loosely. "He also has a connection with the church Kelsey used to attend with your wife. This individual worked part-time for Pastor Mikkelsen."

"So he could have seen her there. Maybe at youth camp or activities." David stared at the floor. "He could have encountered her years before she ever went to the high school. She was just fourteen when she . . ." His throat closed for a moment, making further words impossible. It was a minute before he could continue. "She was a beautiful girl. Got a lot of attention wherever we went. Ever since she was a baby, really. Claire used to take her to these silly pageants, but Kelsey did well in them. She loved dressing up and getting makeup and hair done." He smiled a little to himself. "So different from Janie in a lot of ways."

"I've been through the files," Mark said quietly. "The pageant lead was exhaustively investigated."

"According to your colleagues, every lead was exhaustively investigated." It was so much simpler to feel anger than grief. To let it channel into a fury that could be wielded like a weapon. "But seven years later, my daughter's dead. And you still don't seem any closer to locking up her killer."

◆ ◆ ◆

"Mom's still in her room."

David looked up from making himself a bowl of soup he didn't want. "Have you eaten?" he asked Janie. He should have thought of that before now. He had to get better at remembering he still had a daughter, and she was hurting every bit as much as he and Claire were. Shame stabbed through him at the reminder. Too often, it was Janie checking up on them. Cooking a pizza to tempt them. Calling their attention to a favorite show on TV. Her efforts had largely been in vain, but he appreciated her thoughtfulness. All he'd managed to do for her was to make the initial call to her therapist to apprise him of what had happened.

"No. But neither has Mom. Not all day. The door's locked. I think someone should check on her."

"Have this soup." He thrust the bowl at her. "I'll go up and unlock the door. I'm sure she's asleep. Probably took another sedative."

His daughter's gaze was anxious. "Is anyone keeping track of what she's taking? And how often?"

Something inside him softened. "It's going to be okay, baby. I don't want you feeling like you're the caretaker around here. These are hard times—the hardest. But we'll get through them."

"We have to take care of each other." She pulled out a drawer and got a spoon as he headed out of the room. "And Dad? Count the pills in her bottles every day, okay?"

He managed a reassuring smile that faded as he left the room. Poor kid. As if losing her sister wasn't enough trauma, he and Claire were adding to her worry. He took the steps two at a time, careful to remain quiet. He'd look in on his wife, but he was hoping that he was correct and she was asleep. Dr. Schultz said that was the best thing for her now. Give her mind a chance to empty of the horrors visited upon them until she was strong enough to deal with them. David wondered if that day would ever come.

If he were honest with himself, he really wasn't up to dealing with his wife right now. He knew his role as head of the family, but there were times that role felt like a paper façade, too close to crumpling. If only he could sleep. Just for a few hours to clear his mind. But every time he closed his eyes, images of Kelsey flashed through his brain, morphing and melding so rapidly, he could barely get a glimpse of one before it merged with another. Her voice would ring through his head clearly. Accusing. Filled with contempt. *This is your fault. This is all your fault.*

If Claire's pills could wipe his mind clean—just for a night—maybe he should try a couple. Just once.

They kept the key on top of the doorjamb. He was the only one in the household tall enough to reach it without a stool. They'd placed keys above any room with a lock back when the kids were small enough to occasionally lock themselves into a room and then shriek until someone got them out. It took only a moment for him to reach up and find the key. To unlock the door and ease it open.

There was a kick in his chest when he saw her stretched out on the bed lying so very still, arms at her sides. But as he stepped into the room, David could see that her eyes were open, although she wasn't looking at him.

He pulled the door shut behind him. "I'm warming up soup. You should come eat something."

"Are you still seeing her?"

Her voice was so low that David stepped closer to the bed in order to hear better. "What?"

"Tiffany."

He froze, a paralysis brought on by shock and remorse. Her head turned as if in slow motion so she could look at him. Her pupils were dilated. But Janie's earlier concern for her mother was the furthest thing from his mind right now.

"Tiffany who?" He was stalling, buying time. But he already knew that in this instance, time had finally run out.

"Tiffany White. You had an affair. At the lake house. Are you still seeing her?"

A torrent of guilt flooded through him. It rose higher and higher, threatening to submerge him completely. It wasn't that he'd thought this day would never come. But somehow he'd never considered he'd be faced with it while he was already frantically treading the churning waters of grief. David couldn't handle this conversation right now. And frankly, neither could his wife. "Claire, that's the medication talking."

"We were never looking to buy a lake house."

So she'd overheard his conversation with the agent. His mind raced, like busy little ants. What else had she heard? "We don't need to talk about this now."

"I think you are." Her monotone, along with her utter stillness, had the flesh on his arms rising. "I remember that she went to Columbus. I wouldn't even have blamed you, if it happened after Kelsey disappeared. We take comfort where we can find it. But this was before, wasn't it? Seven or eight years ago. You were seeing her then."

"Claire, whatever you're on has your imagination working overtime." *Weak, but God, not now.* He couldn't have this conversation now. Not when he felt like a stiff wind could flatten him.

"Do you know what else my imagination is telling me?" She placed a hand on the bed beside her. Struggled to sit up. "It's saying you were with her when I called you to help look for Kelsey. And that you lied when you said you'd driven around for hours afterward, searching. I don't want to hear you admit it. I don't think I could handle that." The shadows under her eyes made them look like huge bruises in her face. "But if it's true, I hope that's gutted you every day since. I hope your life's a misery knowing that when Kelsey needed you most, you were fucking a twenty-two-year-old and too busy to go look for her."

Her words were daggers, slicing at his biggest regret until it was raw and bleeding. One decision made for all the wrong reasons had resulted in a lifetime of remorse. He was unable to ask for forgiveness. He'd never managed to forgive himself. Instead, he turned and walked through the door. Better to leave the words unsaid. Hopefully the pills would erase this scene from her memory. Then she could go back to being the martyred wife cocooned in anguish, who drifted through the days with only surface awareness of what went on around her. In an ironic twist of nature, this final tragedy had restored to her a measure of insight.

Because Claire had guessed some but not all. Only he knew the enormity of how badly he'd failed his little girl.

Special Agent Mark Foster

November 18
1:30 p.m.

"I'm just saying, I think we need to be careful what details we release, including to the victims' families." Sloane didn't look away from the report she was reading on her laptop.

Mark felt a flicker of irritation. Being a linear thinker, he worked best when he could outline a lead with all the various directions it could take, then fill in the information derived from following each branch. Sloane was a broken record, distracting him from the task.

"You're not speaking to a rookie." His tone was testy as he stepped back to study the sheets he'd fastened to the wall of the motel room where he was adding his notes. "There's a balance to be struck between keeping parents informed and withholding some evidence only for law-enforcement officers. I handle the families. We agreed on that from the start. You deal with the media."

Her silence sounded like dissent. He glanced at her, saw the disagreement stamped on her face. He decided to ignore it. And her.

He stared hard at the spiderweb of lines and boxes he'd drawn. In one box was Newman's name. In the other, he'd written Mikkelsen's.

Each line represented discovered connections between the men. Off to the side, he'd written the other two ministers' names Newman had given them. Jennings and Wills. He hadn't explored the janitor's relationship to them yet. They'd spent the last few days going over the evidence from the crime scene, delving into Newman's background, and juggling the incoming lab reports with their next line of inquiry.

While he preferred outline arrays, Sloane immersed herself in the reports and case files, highlighting info and somehow managing to extract even the most insignificant of facts to be recalled later.

He checked the time. They should have more test results by the end of the day. While there had been a flurry of lab activity since Kelsey's body had been found, Mark was constantly aware that they weren't much closer to finding Whitney DeVries. A fact that her father pointed out to him in every conversation they had.

His gaze shifted then, as it often did, to the rows of victims, verified and unverified. There was still that odd catch in his focus when he saw the first one Larsen had sent. But Sloane was right. They all looked enough alike to be related. His glance flicked to the photo of Kelsey Willard. Prettier than the rest, with a vibrancy that was faithfully reflected by the camera's lens. But the victimology reports had revealed that the likenesses went beyond the physical. The observations from people who'd known them were repetitive. *A good girl. A sweet young lady. Never a problem in class.* And when it came to Kelsey, *Spirited, but a pleaser.*

So the victim selection was based on something besides looks. Compliance? Girls less likely to cause trouble for the offender? Mark was veering too close to speculation for his comfort. All the remarks describing the previous victims were also true for Whitney DeVries. He hoped, for the girl's sake, that she turned out to be less agreeable than the killer had predicted. Because it would take a strong spirit to survive what the TMK had in store for her.

Newman also liked attractive young girls. The images on the man's computer and the web address was proof of that. But they'd found nothing so far that definitively tied the custodian to Willard's homicide, although they'd spent plenty of man hours on him. His former landlord had balked at letting them look at the place he used to rent until served with a warrant, which they were still waiting on. But they'd been through the rat hole Newman lived in now. Rental properties were like motel rooms in that they made for crappy evidence gathering. There'd been a mess of latent prints. Alternate light sources had shown a high number of stains behind the latest coat of paint on the walls, on the carpet, and furnishings. A few had even turned out to be bloodstains. There had been DNA galore. Too much. There was no way they could get authorization for testing all of it. Not until they got conclusive evidence that Herb Newman was the offender they were searching for.

It was time to start exploring the man's links to others who were even loosely linked to the case. It was just a matter of finding the right connection.

"Okay, that's it," Sloane said. "I've got no properties in the Mikkelsens' names, or in those of the other two pastors. I'm printing out a list of every parcel owned by the people listed as volunteers, workers, or instructors at the three churches."

Mark turned to retrieve the results from the printer tray. Three pages. His heart dropped with a thud. "We'll split these up among the Fenton County law enforcement and our investigators at the London office." He scanned them. "The ministers listed may not own any real estate. But they all have access to some."

The other agent looked up. "The churches?"

"Especially Trinity Baptist. That's where Newman could have come into contact with both Willard and DeVries."

"I thought you'd been there before."

"I have. But it was dark, and I was only in Mikkelsen's office." Mark remembered the eerie sight of the candlelight vigil that had greeted him when he'd been leaving. "It wouldn't hurt to get a closer look at the property. Outbuildings."

She shrugged. "All right. I'm going to send out assignments on these property searches first, and then I'll be ready to go."

In the meantime, Mark recalled, there was one person who might be able to start filling in some background on the Reverend and Laura Mikkelsen.

◆ ◆ ◆

"Drive around the property," Mark ordered.

"Such as it is," Sloane murmured. They'd taken her car because, he was discovering, she liked being the one in the driver's seat.

There wasn't much to see. The white-clapboard church was a sprawling structure, indicating additions had been added over the years as the needs of the members had changed. Built in 1938, according to the conversation he'd had minutes ago with Barbara Hunt. Modernized over time, the woman had noted, but most of the fund-raising went toward youth activities.

There was a double garage detached from the main building, with another smallish outbuilding set a distance away, not large enough to house much more than the mower and lawn tools that Hunt had said were kept there.

Sloane circled back and pulled in to the parking lot. "So this woman you talked to hired Mikkelsen?"

"She was on the selection committee, yes. She said he had an impressive résumé of church leadership in various communities, mostly in the state."

"Is it usual for these guys to move around a lot?"

Mark had little experience in the area. "No idea. But he left his last position because the congregation had voted to dissolve."

They got out of the car. Started up the walk that would lead to the offices Mark had visited before.

"Think this guy will give us any problems about looking around?"

"I doubt it." He stabbed at the doorbell with one index finger. "Although I wouldn't be surprised if his wife insists on being our tour guide."

As it turned out, his prediction was wrong. The Mikkelsens were both out, they were informed by Cindy Long, the harried secretary. The pastor and his wife were at a Tri-County Ministry meeting, and the woman wasn't sure when they'd return.

"They seemed quite proud of the facilities here when I spoke to them." Mark gave her a smile meant to disarm. "Thought I'd come back to get a tour. Do you think it'd be possible for us to look around?"

The woman looked uncertain. "I really don't have time to show the place to you. I have the Sunday bulletin to put together and a hundred other things that Laura left for me to do." As if hearing the complaint in the words, she added piously, "I'm always happy to be of whatever sort of service I can be, of course."

"Is the church open? Because we can just peek in ourselves." Sloane spoke up for the first time. "There's no reason to pull you away from your work. We'll be in and out."

"We-ell . . . that would probably be fine," Long decided with an air of relief. "The church is always open during the day, for anyone who needs a quiet place for solace and contemplation. You're welcome to go inside. We're especially proud of the old stained-glass window that was found downstairs and restored. It's hanging in the vestibule. But don't go in the basement, please. It's cordoned off because the foundation isn't in good shape, and the steps are something of a hazard."

"No problem." They both remained in place as the woman hurried back to her office.

"Split up?"

"Yeah," Mark responded. "You take the social hall and living quarters. I'll check out the church. Look for an electrical room or anything that would serve as a janitorial closet." They'd gone over Newman's office in the school with the permission of the superintendent and turned up nothing. "I wonder if the basement is confined to the church or if there's an entrance somewhere around here."

"I'll find out." Sloane moved away.

Losing no time, he headed toward the church. And the basement he'd been warned away from.

Two doors dotted the hallway. One was a large coat closet that also held a couple of mops and a bucket. The other was locked. Sending a glance over his shoulder, Mark took out his wallet and extracted a credit card. He was able to fit it in the seam between the door and jamb, but no amount of jiggling could pop the lock. Intrigued, he put the card away. The space could be no larger than the closet he'd just looked in. He wondered what Mikkelsen considered valuable enough to lock up.

At the end of the hall, he ascended a half set of stairs and pushed at a door that swung inward to the vestibule of the church. To his right were more steps, with cords roping across them and a *No Entrance* sign attached. Mark stepped over the barrier and made his way cautiously down the stairs.

The place was in as bad shape as the secretary had indicated. It was more cellar than basement and looked as though it extended only beneath the church. The walls were cracked and crumbling in places. It took just a few minutes to ascertain that he was probably the only person who had been down here in years.

He made his way to the stairway and climbed up to the vestibule again. Where Laura Mikkelsen confronted him.

She made an imposing figure in her long, dark dress, arms folded across her wide chest, chin jutted like an army general ready for battle.

"Mrs. Mikkelsen." Mark stepped over the cords. "The secretary mentioned that we wouldn't have the pleasure of seeing either you or your husband today. I'm happy she was proven wrong."

"I'm sure Mrs. Long also told you that no one was allowed in the basement."

"I thought maybe there was a restroom down there."

She half turned and pointed in the opposite direction. "That way and well marked."

Mark's gaze followed the direction she was indicating. Sure enough, there was signage on two doors behind her. "I know what you're up to, Agent Foster." The woman's lips were tight. "We're aware that poor Herb Newman is sitting in the county jail with the sheriff refusing him even the most basic consideration."

"That's not true, ma'am. Mr. Newman has been afforded all his legal rights." Which included access to counsel and a speedy arraignment. The judge had sided with the prosecutor's argument that the man was a flight risk and set bail at a level Newman still hadn't been able to meet. Hence his continued guest status at the Allama County jail.

She shoved her face close to his. "We've seen this sort of thing before. Godly people being persecuted by nonbelievers. Our Tri-County Ministry is even now trying to come up with the funds to free Mr. Newman so he may return home."

"I'm sure he'll appreciate your efforts, ma'am. I know how much he's helped out around here. He told me about the times he's loaned the church his laptop when you needed an extra one."

He'd managed to surprise her. "I'm sure he would loan it, if asked," she said finally. Easing away, she added, "Fortunately, our circumstances have never required such a generous sacrifice. Now, I think it's time for you to leave."

Interesting. Mark headed toward the front door of the church. Either Newman had lied about that, or Laura Mikkelsen was lying right now. Which meant one of them had something to hide.

Or both of them.

◆ ◆ ◆

"That was a bust." Sloane turned the key in the ignition. "The spaces I looked through were cramped, and if there's a janitorial closet, I didn't see it."

"I found a couple of buckets in a coat closet. And another one that was locked." Hard to believe that only Newman would have access to the area, though. "Laura Mikkelsen caught me coming out of the basement, so that conversation went as expected."

She began backing out of the space. "I'm sure my discussion with the church secretary was more illuminating. She verified that Newman had allowed them use of his laptop. But she said it hadn't happened in the last few years. Most of the students have school-issued notebooks, so if they need extra computers, they call the kids to help out."

So he'd been right. Mark narrowed his eyes. Laura had been lying. But why?

The alert for an incoming text sounded. He pulled out his cell. "Newman's financials have come through." The bank had taken their time complying with the warrant. "I want to get back to my computer and start going through them." Mark was hoping the data would show where the custodian spent his money. The man had no credit cards. Few clothes. His car was only a few years old, but a dog would turn up its nose at Newman's home. For someone working a full-time and a part-time job, he should have more disposable income.

"I think one of us needs to take a look at that empty church where Reverend Mikkelsen used to be pastor." Sloane straightened the car on the road. Braked to a stop.

"How do we know it's still there? They may have torn it down after the congregation dissolved."

"It's still standing," she explained smugly, "according to Cindy Long. 'Boarded up and empty, which is such a shame because the building wasn't in that bad of shape. A lot better shape than their church, according to what Pastor Mikkelsen says.' Cindy and I bonded over our fifteen-year-old daughters' attachment to their cell phones and disreputable boyfriends."

Shocked, Mark stared at her. "I didn't know you had a daughter." Would never have guessed it. Sloane was the least maternal female he knew.

"I don't. But Cindy opened up quite a bit when she thought I did. She said the church is about a mile outside of Tillgy Springs. You and I have been looking for isolated properties connected to someone of interest in this case, so . . ."

Mark did a rapid mental calculation. "That's two hours each way." Could Newman have heard about the property from Mikkelsen? Sloane was right; it needed to be checked out. "Okay, I'll take Newman's financials, and you go look at the old church."

"I'll do some calling on my way down to the county sheriff and the editor of the newspaper."

"Why the newspaper?"

"What better way to get the dirt on Mikkelsen and maybe learn the names of some former members of the church to talk to?" She made a shooing motion with one hand. "You can get back to West Bend on your own, right?"

She was actually pushing him toward the door. "With my Superman cape?"

"The mental image of you in underwear and tights is amusing. But I don't have time to run you back to town."

Disgruntled, Mark got out of the car. "I suppose I can call . . ." She was pulling away before he'd finished shutting the door. "Rossi," he finished, staring after her taillights.

◆ ◆ ◆

Interesting. Mark leaned back in his chair in the motel room, still studying the spreadsheet on the computer screen. According to Herb

Newman's bank records, the man was receiving income from only one source: West Bend High School. Cyber forensics weren't finished with his phone yet, but they'd learned he had a mobile bitcoin wallet, where he received a few hundred dollars a month. Mark was willing to bet they'd discover it was payment for downloads of the photos he'd uploaded to the web. The bank records showed that until four years ago, he'd received a salary from Tri-County Ministry. Newman and Mikkelsen had both indicated that the custodian worked for three churches. So he was volunteering his services?

Mark speared a hand through his hair as he considered the monthly notations for checks in the amount of $500 to Trinity Baptist Church. Despite Laura Mikkelsen's assertion, Newman didn't strike him as the altruistic type. And her husband had even indicated that the churches paid for janitorial services. So who was lying? And why?

Because he thought better on his feet, he rose. Walked the length of the motel room. Back again. Sloane had said the secretary had indicated they hadn't needed to borrow Newman's computer for years. Maybe there was a reason for that. Could someone have gotten into the man's locked picture file? Or even discovered the link to the web address Newman uploaded them to?

That would mean Newman had agreed to clean the churches for free in return for silence on the issue. Or, given the monthly checks to the church, that he was being blackmailed to do so. Either way, the Mikkelsens must know about the man's pastime but hadn't reported his crime.

Checking the clock, Mark grabbed his coat. He had time for another visit to Mikkelsen's church if he made it quick. Shoving his arms into the sleeves, he shrugged it on. Zipped it up. If the pastor wasn't there, he'd level the questions at his wife. He was pretty sure she knew everything that . . .

His cell rang. Checking the screen, he saw it was his SAC, Todd Bennett. Two hours earlier than their scheduled conference call about the day's lab results. Adrenaline surging, he answered. "Foster."

"Mark." The note of excitement in the man's voice sparked his own. "I know we have a phone conference in a couple of hours, but another lab result just came in. During the forensic examination of the victim's body Monday, the pathologist found a hair on her clothes. The lab ran the DNA. We've got a positive match."

◆ ◆ ◆

Mark got out of his car and walked to the sidewalk, where the local police chief and another uniform joined him. Silently, they walked up to the house. Rang the bell. It was best that night fell early this time of year. He'd ordered the cruisers to roll up silently. At least the family would be spared the additional trauma of the neighbors witnessing the upcoming scene.

The suspect opened the door. Looked from one of them to the other, trepidation on his face. "Do you have . . . is there more news?"

"I'm afraid you're the news," Mark said grimly. The police officer stepped forward, cuffed one of the man's wrists. "David Willard, you are under arrest for the murder of your daughter, Kelsey."

◆ ◆ ◆

"How can you be a buzzkill even after breaking the biggest case in BCI history? C'mon, look lively." Sloane snapped her fingers in Mark's face, then danced away as airily as a full-size Tinkerbell. "We just brought down the Ten Mile Killer, responsible for nine homicides that we know of." She waved her hand at the row of pictures on the wall. "And maybe these other six, as well."

Mark couldn't summon her level of euphoria. The initial adrenaline that had preceded the arrest had drained, leaving only bleak sobriety. After the first few initial protestations of his innocence, Willard had fallen silent except to ask for his attorney. He wouldn't be answering any questions, Mark knew. They'd build the case against the man piece by piece.

But the one bit of DNA evidence found with Kelsey's body would be impossible for even the most talented defense attorney to explain away.

"This isn't done." His stomach rumbled, and for the first time, he realized he hadn't eaten that night. Neither of them had. "We need more to tie him to this case. And then we have to start linking him to the others." And that would be the real challenge, Mark knew. Memories faded. Witnesses moved away. "He's got a bargaining chip in Whitney DeVries." At the mention of the girl, Sloane's expression sobered. "If we have him in custody, how long does she stay alive? And what kind of deal will the special prosecutor be willing to make, in exchange for him telling us where he's keeping her?"

She dropped to the edge of the bed, considering. "They might deal on DeVries if she's found alive, but he'd still go down for killing his daughter. And if he gives us the girl, we'd have his place of operation. Probably plenty of DNA there from his other victims."

And if he didn't give up the girl, she'd die of thirst within days. His gut twisted. David Willard had likely been lying to him all along. About the hotel-room reservations that hadn't been turned in as charges on his company's account. About how his fingerprints got in the lake house. About his nonexistent alibis when Kelsey and Whitney had gone missing.

Willard and Mikkelsen. The two men Luther Sims had mentioned. The profiler had never been satisfied with either of their stories. They'd been loose ends. Except now one of those loose ends had been clipped.

"I'm sort of sorry that I'll never get a look inside that old church in Tillgy Springs. If ever a place looked perfect to house a serial killer, it was there. Most of its windows are boarded up, but the ones in the basement look like there are still curtains on them. No one seems to be taking care of the property. The grass and brush are overgrown."

She'd told him about her unsuccessful mission there on the way back from the police station, but his focus had been elsewhere. "You couldn't find out who had the keys to it in town?"

Sloane shook her head. "The sheriff didn't have a clue. The owner of the newspaper is making more calls. But I told you that already."

He looked at the pictures again. Whitney DeVries, whose precious remaining time was ticking away. The other unverified victims who might never get closure.

"Maybe Mikkelsen knows."

She made a scoffing sound and got up to put her boots on. "And he'd be happy to tell us, right?"

"Possibly. I think he knew about Newman's photography sideline. That he used the knowledge to blackmail him into a monthly payment and doing the custodial work for free."

"From what you've told me, that sounds less like the pastor and more like his lovely wife. I got a look at her watching us through the window as we left the church." She slipped into her coat and buttoned it.

"You going somewhere?" Mark asked.

"*We* are." She sent him a blinding smile. "Out to a celebratory dinner and at least one White Russian. We deserve that much."

He wanted to refuse but from the feel of it, his stomach lining was devouring itself. "I could eat." He got his coat. Started toward the door.

"She reminds me of that hatchet-faced movie actress that was in all those oldie horror shows I used to watch. Older, of course. I can't place which one, though."

Mark stopped midstride. "Who?"

"Mikkelsen's wife. She looks like she might have been pretty once before she got joyless and bitter, you know what I mean?"

He turned back to look at the picture of Betsy Graves. And something buried deep in his subconscious clicked. "I think so." Because he now knew exactly why Graves looked so familiar. He couldn't place her before because he couldn't recall the context, but he did now. He was almost certain of it. *Almost.* "I'll drive. And buy," he squashed Sloane's protest. "But first, we take a side trip."

◆ ◆ ◆

"Agent Foster." Luther Sims looked surprised when he opened the door, before swinging it wider in invitation. "Come in."

Mark stepped inside. Wiped his feet on the hooked rug he remembered from his first visit. He saw the man glance beyond him at the car in the drive but knew he couldn't see Sloane inside it. "I'm on my way to Columbus, and you're not far out of the way. Thought I'd stop in to give you a quick update on the case."

Pleasure spread across the retired agent's face. There were two large Band-Aids on one of his cheeks that hadn't been there the last time they'd spoken. "I appreciate that. I don't get many opportunities to talk shop anymore. You know your way back to the kitchen. Let me just shut my wife's door so we don't disturb her." As he moved to the right side of the hallway, Mark threw a quick glance to the left where the family room was. The TV was off, but there was a book lying across a closed laptop next to the recliner. The array of pictures was still on the wall.

Including the photo of Elizabeth Sims. Young. Unsmiling. But nearly identical to the one of Betsy Graves.

As certain as he'd been earlier, it was almost a shock to see the verification. Greg Larsen had been right. Betsy Graves *had* been the TMK's first kidnap victim. Her body had never been found because she was still locked in hell with the Ten Mile Killer. A mental image flashed through Mark's mind of the glimpse he'd gotten of the woman's gnarled hands the last time he was here. Rheumatoid arthritis, Sims had said.

Or maybe the result of systematic torture.

Tension shooting up his spine, Mark headed toward the kitchen, hyper aware that a bloodless killer followed a step behind him. With new eyes, he observed the locks on all the cupboard doors and drawers. Not to protect a woman in the grips of Alzheimer's, but to protect Sims from any weapons she might get her hands on. A ball of hot fury lodged in Mark's chest, and it took every ounce of effort he possessed to not turn and grab the man by the throat. He drew in a silent breath. Released it slowly. And prepared to play the role of his lifetime.

"We found Kelsey Willard's body last weekend," he started conversationally. "The TMK case was sort of your baby while you were at the agency. I thought you'd like to know."

"Kelsey Willard. After all this time. Did you find the remains in Wayne Forest?" Interest threading his voice, the man took a seat at the table. Mark followed suit.

"No, believe it or not." He unzipped his coat partway as if at ease, but his muscles were spiked with knots. "She was found just outside West Bend city limits in the basement of an empty home. Which brings me to another reason for stopping." He manufactured an abashed grin. "Wouldn't mind picking your brain about what this means. I've gone through the files. He's never changed dump sites before."

"No, never." Sims pulled at his bottom lip as he considered. "First thing that comes to mind is questioning whether she was a victim of the TMK or a copycat. But I assume you've verified that."

"With every test possible." For a homicidal maniac, the man was a masterful actor. But he'd already proven that with the bullshit story about the picture of ballerinas that had calmed his nightmares about the victims. Did the print represent the source of Sims's motivation, or the result of his crimes? Either way, it was yet another reminder that this man had fooled trained agents for years while he'd consulted on the case. Mark just hoped he could match the man's acting abilities. Everything depended on it. "It's the same killer."

Sims frowned and drummed his fingers on the table. "It'd be tempting to say that the TMK has switched his location. We had speculated before that his familiarity with the forest could mean that he lived around that area, or had at one time. Or that he was an outdoors enthusiast. His use of the remote area there told us that the offender didn't want the bodies found, or he was attempting to slow the process of discovery. But West Bend doesn't have a similarly isolated area where he could hope to discard his future victims, so in the end, this body dump represents more than just a change in MO. I think, for whatever reason, he wanted this body found."

"That was our conclusion, too," Mark said with feigned relief. *Cunning bastard*, he thought. All this time offering his insights for his own amusement. A sliver of truth here, a red herring there to massage the focus of the investigation. "So is it a onetime thing, or is this what we can expect from him in the future?"

"You mean with the latest victim?"

Mark nodded. "The agency's profiler seems to think that the killer's affection for Willard led to him wanting her discovered."

"That's a plausible theory and might explain why the offender took additional risks this time. By not leaving the body where it was exposed to the elements for years, there was an increased possibility of him leaving prints or DNA."

Mark shook his head. "Unfortunately, the forensic tests came up zero on that end. But we do have a strong person of interest in custody at the moment. He'd been questioned before in Kelsey Willard's case." He paused deliberately. Noted the man's shift in weight to lean forward in anticipation. "Herb Newman, the school custodian. He was found trespassing on the premises where Willard was found. It's only a matter of time until we cement the case against him."

If he hadn't been observing so closely, Mark would have missed the slight tightening of lips. The flicker of disdain in the man's gaze. "That's quick work. Congratulations. I assume there are more tests to be completed. I recall just how long that process can take."

"No." A small thud sounded nearby. Both of them looked in the direction of the front door.

"Elizabeth must have dropped something. Her arthritis makes gripping things difficult. You were saying the lab would be running more tests."

Planting a subliminal suggestion there, Luther? "No, I'm pretty sure they ran everything we submitted. We're confident we've arrested the right guy."

A tinkle of crashing glass had them both jumping. Sims got up abruptly. "I'm sorry, but I must go help my wife. She's probably tried to get out of bed by herself. Thank you for coming, Agent Foster. I hope you'll continue to keep me apprised of further developments." The man was already up, striding rapidly down the hallway. "If you wouldn't mind showing yourself out?"

"Not a problem." Mark waited until the man had disappeared into the bedroom, partially closing the door behind him before getting up to snap off the light switches. He headed swiftly toward the three doors at the end of the room. One was a bathroom. Empty. Another would lead to the attached garage. But the third bore the same lock as the kitchen drawers and cupboards. Mark tried the knob. It wouldn't turn.

Retracing his steps, he strode silently to the front door. A sliver of light showed between the bedroom door and the jamb. Reaching for his cell, he used the camera app to zoom in for a picture of the young Elizabeth Sims before replacing the phone and moving toward the door, one hand inside his half-opened coat resting on the butt of his weapon.

Two more steps to the entrance. One.

Then the wedge of light at the bedroom door widened to show the shadow of a long, narrow barrel. Gun.

Mark reacted instinctively, throwing himself to the ground. Rolling into the family room. The rifle shot took a chunk out of the Sheetrock on the wall beside him, spraying him with tiny splinters and dust. Sims had the advantage. Mark was exposed in the light while the other man remained hidden. He fired twice in quick succession, taking out the lamp in the room and then the overhead fixture in the hallway. Now there was only the backdrop of light coming from the bedroom, which was quickly doused.

"You're a clever man, Agent Foster."

Mark pressed his body against the wall of the family room that bordered the hall, crawling until he had a clean view of the bedroom door.

"But I have too much faith in the scientists in our state crime lab to believe they didn't find DNA evidence with Kelsey's body. I took such great pains planting it."

He couldn't fire into the bedroom knowing there was an innocent victim inside. But he could draw the man out. Rising, he called, "You mean that hair? A little too obvious for someone of your talents, wasn't it?" And then he stepped around the corner and dove into the hallway, a bullet zinging over his head.

"I had to be obvious." The door opened as Mark was scrabbling for the cover the kitchen would provide. Sims emerged, rifle pointed. He fired a shot that lodged in the woodwork of the counter island as Mark lunged behind it. "The TMK has been outsmarting the BCI for three decades." His next shot shattered one of the windows in the wall beyond Mark. "And justice must be served."

Mark squeezed off two shots. Heard a slight grunt of pain and hoped that meant he'd wounded the man. "That's what I'm here for, Sims. Justice. And it doesn't much matter to me whether you go out the door in cuffs or in a body bag."

"You think you can come to *my* home and disrupt *my* family?" Fury throbbed in the man's voice. "You have a small son, don't you, Agent? It's a shame that he'll soon be fatherless."

Nicky. There was a quick stab of panic, even as Mark realized what the man was doing. Introducing Mark's personal life to divert him from the present. Destroy his focus. And for a moment, it worked. The faces of his wife and son swam across his mind. His heart clenched at the thought of not seeing them again. But if Sims thought he could distract

Mark, he was wrong. Thoughts of what he had to lose merely solidified his resolve to take the man down by whatever means possible.

Sims spun into the room, releasing a volley of shots that splintered the cupboards behind Mark. Jagged slivers of wood sped through the air like tiny missiles, several lodging in him. Gritting his teeth against the pain, he remained silent. Listening. Where was Sims now? Had he ducked back into the hallway, or advanced into the kitchen? There was a slight sound. Glass crunching beneath a shoe. It was enough to peg the man's position in the room. Mark silently slid in the opposite direction, guessing Sims's intent. He'd round the corner of the island, expecting to find his quarry. But by the time he did, Mark would be behind him. And the next time Mark fired, he vowed grimly, it'd be a kill shot.

"Drop your weapon, Sims!" A woman's voice rang out.

The man whirled to face the kitchen entrance. "Get down!" Mark shouted as he stood, sending a shot to the man's shoulder. Sims's weapon sagged. But not before he fired in Sloane's direction. Her bullet caught him in the leg, and he fell back against the refrigerator. Slid slowly to the floor. They both approached the man carefully, Sloane kicking the rifle away while Mark, his weapon still trained on the man, quickly frisked him. No other weapons. But there was a small ring of keys in his pocket. Mark confiscated them and looked at Sloane. "The last time you provided backup you had a better sense of timing."

"I was waiting for you to draw him away from the front door."

Switching his attention to Sims, Mark demanded, "Where's Whitney DeVries?"

The man grimaced, clutching his leg. "Dead. You're too late, Agent Foster. BCI has always been a step behind."

Too late. A hot ball of dread twisted in his belly. God help him, if it were true, Mark knew he'd never forgive himself.

The man is an accomplished liar, Mark reminded himself. "I'm sure you won't mind if I check for myself." He caught Sloane's eye. "I'll see to his wife."

"I've got this." Sloane's eyes were hard, her legs slightly spread. Sims was a dead man if he so much as moved. "I called the local sheriff when the first shot was fired."

First, Mark went to the bathroom he'd seen earlier and returned with an armful of towels. He reholstered his weapon so he could bend and wrap one around the man's leg wound. Another was wadded against Sim's shoulder. Then, the man's keys in one hand, he rose and drew his weapon again before making his way cautiously to the man's bedroom.

Nudging the door wide with his foot, Mark switched on the light switch and took in the scene. The shade from the bedside lamp was off. The lightbulb had been unscrewed. It probably accounted for the shards of glass on the floor, surrounding a book there. His gaze traveled to the woman crouched in the middle of the bed, one cheek aflame with the imprint of a palm. Mark recalled the earlier thud he'd heard. The tinkle of breaking glass. Sims's obvious temper. His "wife" had been trying to call for help.

He entered farther into the room, eyes trained on the woman. "Betsy Graves?"

Her eyes widened. She opened her mouth. The croak that emerged sounded more animal than human. She raised one hand to her throat. Gave a jerky nod.

"Betsy." His voice gentled. "You're going home."

A fat tear slid down her cheek. She remained still while he quickly frisked her for a weapon he already knew she wouldn't have. He may have had thirty years to indoctrinate her, but Sims didn't trust her enough to leave an unlocked kitchen cupboard or drawer. Up close Mark could see the dark roots in the part of her long, gray hair. Her mouth was bracketed with creases of pain, but she was clearly decades younger than Sims had tried to make her appear.

He spied the wheelchair in the corner of the room. "Can you walk?" He half expected that Sims's claim was yet another part of disguising the woman. But Elizabeth—Betsy—pulled her worn flannel nightgown away to show her bare feet. A vise tightened in Mark's chest. Her toes were bent at weird angles. The bones on the arches on the tops of her feet appeared flattened, the skin puckered and purplish. Jesus Christ, had Sims taken a hammer to her feet? Mark swallowed a surge of nausea. His gaze rose to the print above the bed. The graceful dancers were a macabre contrast to the way TMK discarded his victims.

I always promised myself that picture would come down when the killer was behind bars. Sims's lie sounded in Mark's mind. He'd make sure that it did, Mark vowed, as he reholstered his weapon and carried Betsy Graves to the wheelchair. Because once the crime-scene team was done with this place, he'd take that damn picture down himself.

Moments later, he wheeled the woman into the kitchen. Sims was slumped over. Unmoving. "Everything okay?" he asked Sloane.

Sloane's gaze went beyond him, and sympathy flashed across her expression. A person would have to be made of stone to be unmoved by the appearance of the woman once known as Betsy Graves. "He's not going anywhere." In other words, she could keep an eye on both of them.

Sirens were sounding in the distance as Mark strode to the locked door, sorting through the keys on the chain until he found the one that opened it. Unlocking it, he found a stairway. Heart hammering in his chest, he descended, only to find another secured door at the base of the steps. And yet another five yards beyond that.

There was a knot in his gut the size of a boulder when he swung open the last one to reveal a wide space that likely measured the remaining square footage of the cabin above. He searched for light switches, but when he found them and turned them on, nothing happened. Taking out his cell, he used the flashlight app to take a careful look around as he entered the area.

It was empty save for a table in the center of it piled with . . . He drew closer. Shone the tiny beam over the objects. Another laptop. What looked like a projector. Both were balanced on piles of books.

There was one window on the left, high in the wall, which gave no light. Same on the right. But ahead there was a dais of some sort that took up a full third of the space. Heavy curtains hung on either side of it, but when Mark approached at an angle, he could see something lying on the stage. A mattress.

And on the mattress, a still, unmoving form.

Oh, God, no! A quick spear of despair stabbed through him. They couldn't be too late. He closed the rest of the distance in a near run. "Whitney DeVries? Whitney, we're here to help."

No response. No movement. Mark jumped up on the stage. He'd been steady enough exchanging gunfire upstairs, but now his pulse was galloping through his veins, and dread pooled in his belly. He knelt beside the mattress. Reached out an unsteady hand to turn the body over.

Whitney DeVries. Her face was a mottled assortment of bruises, and there were matching bruises around her throat. Mark reached out to check the pulse at the base of her neck. Faint but there.

"Whitney." Relief flooded him when the girl's eyes fluttered open. Blinked uncomprehendingly. "It's over. You're safe now."

Whitney DeVries

November 21
8:32 a.m.

"Whit's got a busy morning." Whitney thought her dad looked like a stubborn bulldog, blocking the door of her hospital room so Agent Foster couldn't come in. "She didn't have a great night, and they're planning more tests to check for internal injuries."

"Dad." Her voice still sounded like a frog's croak, even when she was trying to yell. "I need to talk to him."

Her mom looked up from straightening the bedcovers. "Brian, don't be rude. Whitney asked me to call Agent Foster last night and have him come by this morning."

Her dad backed away and let the agent inside. "Keep it short. She's told you guys every detail she knows by now."

Whitney could already see how this was going to go down. Her parents meant well, but they really couldn't handle it when she started talking about what had happened to her in that basement. And okay, maybe she *was* still having a hard time, since she burst into tears at the drop of a hat, even when Ryan had brought her a crumpled picture he'd drawn for her. There was no way she'd be able to get her mom out of the room, short of dynamite. But her dad . . .

"Dad, would you go ask the nurse if I could get some more cherry Jell-O? It really helps my throat."

His face always got soft when he looked at her now. The sight had her blinking away tears. "We'll just use the call button, honey."

"It comes faster if someone goes and gets it, though."

He didn't want to, she could see that by the way he hesitated, but pretty soon he nodded. "Sure, honey. I'll be right back." Once he'd left, she looked at the agent, a sudden shyness coming over her. She had a vivid memory of being lifted in strong arms. Opening her eyes to see him holding her like some white knight in a kid's fairy tale. *You're safe now.* She hadn't believed it at first. But when he'd carried her upstairs, the place had been full of cops and ambulance attendants. There'd been blood all over the kitchen he'd whisked her through, and she'd prayed with everything inside her that it belonged to the freak.

That part was all a bit hazy, but it got clearer every time she saw Agent Foster. Despite what her dad said, she didn't mind talking to the man. He was the only one she could speak to freely, without worrying that she'd upset him. And it didn't hurt that when he smiled, he looked a bit like Orlando Bloom. "Thanks for coming, Mr. Foster." She was suddenly aware that her hair had been washed only once since she'd been rescued, and her face and arms were still a rainbow of bruises. "I had my mom call you because I think I remembered something else."

Her mom smoothed back her hair. "It's Agent Foster, honey."

"Hi, Whitney." He approached the bed and smiled down at her "And I'm a mister, too, so it's okay."

"I was sort of dozing yesterday afternoon. They wake you up all the time at night, so you can't really sleep for long. When I was dropping off, I half dreamed about when I escaped. When he caught me."

"Oh, Whit, it's okay." On cue, her mom reacted. Took her hand. "Don't think about that. You're safe now."

"I *know*, Mom." With a mixture of love and exasperation, she squeezed her mom's hand. "But you have to let me talk. It's probably not good to keep trying to get me to bottle things up, right?" At least that sounded like something the therapist on staff had told her when she'd talked to the woman. Whitney saw the agent's mouth twitch, as if he was trying to hide a smile. "But I remembered something the freak said when he was choking me. 'I've given you so many chances. And always you disappoint me, Margaret.'"

"Margaret? You're sure?" Agent Foster's expression had gone still.

"I'm sure. I just didn't remember it until last night. Does that help?"

"It really does."

Whitney pleated the sheet with her fingers. "Do you . . . was Margaret another girl he kidnapped?" No one wanted to tell her anything, but she'd overheard the nurses whispering a couple of times when they thought she was sleeping. Whitney and Kelsey hadn't been the only ones the monster had taken. There had been a lot of them. A chill skittered down her spine, and she was suddenly glad her mom was by her side.

"No, Whitney, Margaret was his sister. The one you told me about, remember?"

She'd repeated all the personal revelations the man had made in their conversations. "So he was thinking about her when he was choking me?" Her mom looked like she was going to cry at the reminder. Whitney heard her dad's voice in the hall. Knew she didn't have much more time. She met the agent's gaze. "Will you tell me the truth about something?" She saw his gaze flick to her mother. Back to Whitney. "Did you find Kelsey Willard? Is she . . . is she okay?"

His silence and that of her mom was all the answer she needed. Whitney raised a hand to wipe away the tears that sprang up as the realization hit her. "She's dead?" She honestly didn't know if she would have had the courage to escape if she hadn't found the other girl's writings. She'd told her mom all about it, over and over again. Knowing that another had experienced the same thing she was going through . . . and hadn't broken had given Whitney strength when she'd needed it most.

"Yes." Agent Foster's voice was gentle.

She sniffled like a little kid, and her mom handed her a tissue. It was hard to sit here and wonder why she got to go home again and Kelsey had never gotten the chance. Whitney knew it would be a long time before she stopped feeling guilty about that. "She was really brave."

"Yes, she was. And so were you."

She wiped her eyes again at the agent's words. She'd always be sad about Kelsey, even as she was grateful about being rescued. "Thanks again for finding me."

Janie Willard

November 21
9:30 a.m.

"Janie?" When the dark-haired man paused next to her table in the coffee shop, Alyvia and Cole got up from their chairs across from her and beelined for a nearby booth. She stifled a feeling of abandonment and sized up the agent addressing her. Recognized him from a couple of glimpses she'd gotten when he'd been in her home.

"Yes."

Agent Mark Foster pulled out one of the chairs at the table. Sank into it. "Thanks for meeting with me."

"How'd you get my number?" She hadn't recognized the caller on the screen of her cell last night, so she hadn't answered it. When she'd listened to the voice mail he'd left, she'd been shocked. But intrigued, too. He hadn't given a reason for wanting to speak to her. He hadn't needed to. Because she needed to talk to him as well and see if she could get some answers no one else seemed willing to give.

"I got it from Sergeant Rossi at the sheriff's office."

That figured. She'd had to put all her contact information on the statement she'd written out for them. Janie clutched her large plastic coffee cup and raised it to her lips, requiring fortification before she could even formulate the questions she had. But he spoke first.

"I wanted to apologize to you personally."

It was the last thing she'd been expecting. "For arresting my dad?" She wasn't sure it was in her to forgive the man for that. They'd still been reeling from the discovery of Kelsey's body. To watch her dad taken away in handcuffs for her murder had been devastating, even though he'd been held only a short time.

The agent nodded soberly. "We've offered an official apology to him, of course. There was evidence planted that made him look guilty. I'd like to speak to your mother, too."

"Don't. She's . . . not well." Janie wasn't certain how much more her mom could take. "I'll tell her for you." As shitty as things had been at home after Kelsey's body was discovered, they'd deteriorated even further. The last couple of mornings when she'd gone downstairs, she'd found her dad sleeping on the couch in the family room. It was like a huge black cloud had parked itself over their house. And it hadn't finished storming yet. "Dad said you found the real TMK. And that Whitney DeVries was still alive. You saved her."

Mark gave a slow nod. "I wish we'd been able to save Kelsey."

She ducked her head. Shot a sideways glance at Alyvia and Cole, who were studiedly pretending not to be interested in their conversation. Mark followed her gaze with his own. "Friends of yours?"

"Yeah." She drank again. "Did Herb Newman have anything to do with Kelsey's kidnapping?"

"No." Janie's shoulders slumped. Foster went on. "But what he was doing is illegal, and he needed to be stopped. He's facing prison time. We have you and your friend to thank for turning that information over to the sheriff's office. It was a gutsy move."

Not so gutsy, she could have told him. More desperate. Determined. She would never have forgiven herself for not pursuing what could have represented a lead to Kelsey's killer.

"I want you to remember, though, if it hadn't been for your meeting with Newman, the lake house would never have been thoroughly searched. Kelsey's body would never have been found if not for you and your friend."

Janie rubbed her thumbs over the cup she held, her gaze fixed on its plastic top. His words brought mixed feelings. So she was responsible for bringing closure to her family. Finally. But based on her experience the last few days, closure was overrated. It meant snapping that last tenuous thread of hope and living forever with a brutal reality. Being certain of Kelsey's fate reframed everything. And she wasn't any too sure her family would survive it intact.

"I can't even imagine how bad it is for you and your parents right now." It was one of those things people said at a time like this, but there was a note of sincerity in the agent's voice that drew Janie's gaze. "I'm not going to pretend that I can. But I wanted to give you a few details about Kelsey's case that might . . ." He seemed to search for the words. "It might give you a tiny piece of your sister back. She discovered a way to write some messages and hid them away."

With a flash of insight, Janie said, "And Whitney DeVries found them?" Foster nodded.

She sipped from her cup again. Every time she heard the other girl's name, it was like someone carved away another sliver of her heart. She could be glad the girl was safe and still mourn the fact that it had been too late for her sister. She doubted that would ever change.

"I wanted you to know that Kelsey was smart. Shrewd, even. And she never stopped planning a way to come back to you and your family."

Her eyes welled, but the tears didn't fall. Maybe someday she'd want to see everything Kelsey had written. Learn every detail of her sister's captivity and death. But Janie knew she didn't have it in her now.

"And I wanted to give you this." Foster smiled a little. "It's not strictly by the book, but sometimes the book is missing a few pages."

He reached into the inside pocket of his coat. Took out a folded slip of paper. "It's a copy of what she wrote about you. *To* you."

He slid the paper across the table toward her. Janie stared at the note, panic fluttering in her chest. She wanted to reach for it. Couldn't force her fingers to move. There'd been a time long ago when she'd been convinced she'd see her sister again. Talk and laugh and fool around with her the way they used to. The certainty had faded over the years. Had died completely at the discovery of Kelsey's body. This, then, was what was left of her sister. A few words scribbled on a small creased paper.

"Maybe this isn't the right time."

His words shattered her paralysis. Reflexively, she snatched the note from the table. But she had to consciously summon the will to slowly unfold it. *My sister is Janie.* Kelsey's voice rang in Janie's head, narrating the words. *She has social anxiety that doesn't let her do everything she wants to, but she's crazy smart. Way smarter than I was at that age. She fell out of the swing once when she was little, and I was the only one who could get her to get back on it. I taught her to pump with her feet, and after a while, she'd let me give her underdogs. Fly high, Janie. That's what I always told her. Fly high, and you'll find your voice.*

She stared at the words, but her gaze was turned inward. A montage of moments coalesced into a mental film clip. Of Janie on the swing, squealing with laughter with Kelsey behind her, pushing her. Of the two of them, arms spread, spinning in circles beneath a brilliant blue sky until they collapsed in a dizzy pile on the soft emerald lawn, giggling uncontrollably.

A minute ticked by. She must have made a sound because the agent got that half-panicked look men got when they were afraid they'd have to deal with tears. But the smile on her lips was the opposite of what he seemed to expect. "You know, I didn't fall out of that swing on my own. She pushed me."

His lips curved. "Yeah?"

Janie nodded. "She was mad because Mom gave me the last slice of banana cream pie. So when we were swinging that day, she applied a little extra force."

"I have an older brother. I can relate."

Her fingers traced over the words. *Fly high, Janie.* "But she was sorry. Kelsey could be careless, but she didn't have a mean bone in her body. I never would have gone near the swing set again if she hadn't spent weeks coaxing me."

Silence stretched between them for long moments. "Your dad told me once you planned to go to Stanford."

Her earlier amusement fled. College decisions were suspended indefinitely. How could she think about moving across the country with her family shattered? "I've been accepted. But . . . probably not. I might take a year off. It depends on how Mom is doing."

"We can put our lives on hold for only so long. Who knows? Maybe you could convince your mom to visit you regularly in California."

She was struck by the suggestion. Why hadn't she thought of that? "Maybe."

He glanced at his watch. "I've got another appointment, so I'll let you rejoin your friends. Thanks again for meeting me."

She picked up the note he'd given her. It was still just words scribbled on paper. But it represented far more. Her final link to her sister. "Thank you for this."

Claire Willard

November 21
10:02 a.m.

There was a knock on the bedroom door. "Mrs. Willard. You have a visitor."

Marta's voice had Claire lifting her head, confused. She was still sitting on the side of the bed, where she'd sat talking with Janie earlier. It was Saturday. Janie had mentioned that when she'd told Claire she was meeting Alyvia at the coffee shop. Why was Marta here on a Saturday?

The woman's voice lowered on the other side of the door. "I'll send her away."

"No." Claire was surprised at the answer that burst from her lips. Maybe it was Barbara. It probably was. And with Janie out of the house, she wouldn't mind having her friend here for a bit for company. She'd stay with Claire for an hour at a time, holding her hand, saying nothing, her presence speaking volumes. The woman seemed to realize that sometimes there were no words. "Send her up."

There was a pause before she heard the woman move away. Claire stood, swayed as a wave of dizziness hit her before making her way to her dresser. The mirror faithfully reflected what others would see. A too-thin woman still in her robe and nightgown. Hair brushed, thanks to Janie's reminders this morning. Even light makeup applied. But few would guess that the reflection represented only an empty husk. Claire felt completely hollowed out. There was nothing of substance left inside.

She heard the knob turn. Froze when she saw the woman framed in the doorway. It wasn't Barbara at all. It was Shannon DeVries. Claire sagged against the dresser, one hand going out to brace herself.

"Maybe I'm the last person you want to see right now." The woman wore a mask Claire recognized all too well. That of someone who wished she were anywhere else but here. Shannon took a cautious step inside the room. "I know how I'd feel if the situation were reversed. But you helped me. You understood better than anyone else could what I was going through. My sister is leaving tomorrow. I couldn't have made it through this without her. I have your generosity to thank for that."

Claire closed her eyes for a moment. If she possessed a fraction of the generosity Shannon credited her with, the words wouldn't have been so hard to muster. "I'm so happy . . . for your family."

The woman approached further. "Having Julie with me helped, but when things looked bleakest, I thought of you. How you came through the worst thing a parent could suffer. It gave me hope. And Whitney . . . all she talks about is Kelsey. How her writings helped her hang on."

Shannon's last words managed to pierce Claire's blanket of misery. "Kelsey's . . . writings?" Her knees threatened to buckle.

The other woman sprang forward, taking her by the elbow. "Why don't we sit down?"

She walked her to the two easy chairs facing the TV in the corner. Gratefully, Claire sank into one of the seats, her mind still grappling with Shannon's meaning. "I'm afraid I don't understand." She wished now that she could claw away the fog that had settled in her brain. "I haven't been up to speaking with the police or BCI since . . ."

"I understand." Shannon sat in the other chair, impatiently brushing back a stray strand of hair, her dark gaze fixed on Claire's. "Whitney found some things Kelsey had written and hidden away in that basement. Several pages, actually. About . . . her experience." The other woman swallowed hard. Seemed to find it difficult to go on. "But Whit says most of it was talking about how she planned to outwit her captor. How she managed to stay strong until she could get away."

Claire's eyes filled on cue. Kelsey. She'd been born with an engaging combination of charm and sass, which had masked an iron will. Shannon's revelations were accompanied with the customary pain. But as usual, she couldn't resist clutching at each nugget of information about her daughter. "Thank you for telling me this."

Shannon gave her a watery smile. "Whitney's told me over and over how Kelsey's words gave her strength in a terrifying situation. I'm so grateful to your daughter. She must be very like you. Because you kept me strong, too, with your example of how to withstand the worst life could throw at a parent." She stood. "I'll understand if it's too painful . . . but I'd like to come back some time. If you want me to."

Claire looked at her through a film of tears. They shared a horrifying experience, with very different outcomes. One girl rescued. The other gone forever. Claire knew that every time she saw Shannon, she'd be flooded anew with the agony of loss. But they were intricately linked by a terrible bond no one else could truly understand. "Yes. I'd like that."

The woman's hug threatened to shatter the fragile shell around Claire's emotions. She watched Shannon walk away, thinking about what she'd revealed.

That Kelsey had somehow found strength despite the darkness of her circumstances was a bittersweet revelation. But Shannon was wrong thinking that Claire shared that quality. Somehow her daughter had survived for some time at the mercy of a madman. In the entire time Kelsey had been missing, Claire hadn't taken one action that displayed a modicum of her daughter's courage. Perhaps, even in death, Kelsey had one last lesson to teach her.

David Willard

November 21
12:14 p.m.

David sat on the muted-plaid couch in his finished basement, his cell clasped in one hand as he mentally replayed his recent conversation with Kurt Schriever. It had taken two days for the man to return his calls. And though his boss had offered up excuses about respecting his privacy, David could read between the lines. In marketing, branding was everything, and he was damaged goods. Schriever had probably been waiting until he could separate gossip from fact about David's false arrest. And then worked overtime reaching out to pacify David's clients, jittery at their brush with notoriety.

Son of a bitching Foster. The simmering fury at the BCI agent was always there, ready to ignite. David had asked Strickland about suing for false arrest. The attorney had cautioned against it. The evidence found with Kelsey's body had been damning. The cops had had probable cause for arrest. But the hell with that. What about his reputation?

Kurt's suggestion to take a few weeks at home could be interpreted as compassion. David was cynical enough to believe the man wanted to keep him as far away from his business as possible for a while. And who knew what would await him upon his return? Clients jumping ship. Accounts reassigned. David's career torpedoed.

The cell rang in his hand. He checked the number. Not linked to a contact. He was too cautious for that. But familiar. David let it go to voice mail, just as he had the last several times Tiffany had called. Once she'd represented a haven to escape from stresses at home and at work. Now she was yet another complication in a life fraught with too many of them.

He stared dully at the opposite wall with its array of old family photos. Many of them were of Kelsey, taken at the pageants Claire had loved so much. Two-dimensional depictions of his daughter were all he had left. That, and the growing realization that he'd been lying to himself for seven years.

He hadn't reached any magical pinnacle in the grief process after his daughter had been kidnapped. He'd simply done a stellar job of outpacing the swamp of guilt and sorrow that had threatened to suck him in. Devour him whole. But he was mired in it now. Trapped. He wasn't sure he'd ever truly get free.

Maybe it was because they hadn't lost Kelsey all at once. They'd lost pieces of her over time. The kidnapping. The first weeks and months when every new lead seemed to stall. Then the anniversaries that had brought knifelike sadness. The first Christmas without her. Kelsey's birthday. The initial family vacation with just the three of them.

Was it easier to get over it all at once, he wondered. That single shock, a swift blade ripping your child away with a brutal finality? Or was the death by a thousand cuts harder? The constant pendulum swings between hope and despair; the endless grind of an investigation that went on for years, with he and Claire scrabbling for pieces of information the way a starving person gathered up crumbs. David had long left such deliberations behind him, setting aside the memories that threatened to snag him with skeletal fingers.

His cell rang again. This time he didn't even look at it. A therapist at a long-ago support group had said that guilt magnified grief. That had resonated with him, because he lived with both. Every time he closed his eyes, he saw Kelsey, her face stamped with disbelief. Rage. Hurt.

Stop denying it! I followed your car. I went inside and saw the two of you. Does Mom know you're cheating? She will now. Because I'm not going to be part of your lie. I'm going to make sure you pay!

And he had, David thought dully. He'd paid and paid. He knew now that there could be no restitution.

He didn't know how long he sat there before rousing himself to go upstairs. Check on the others. Reach out to Foster, that bastard, and see what the timeline was for Kelsey's body to be released. The tedium of planning a funeral would lend focus to his days. Force him to move forward. If he moved fast enough, long enough, maybe he could escape the desolation.

He poked his head into the family room, then walked through it to the kitchen. Didn't find Janie. Opening the door that led to the garage, he saw her car was gone. That was unusual enough to have him frowning. There was no way she'd be working. Maybe Claire knew where she'd gone.

He closed the door and headed to the stairway, meeting Marta halfway as she made her way down. The woman had been hovering around Claire since the news broke. Averting her eyes, she brushed by him. As he finished his ascent, he heard the sound of the coat closet opening. Moments later, the front door closed.

The door to the master bedroom was ajar. David paused outside it, steeling himself to deal with his wife before pushing it wide. And stopped in his tracks. "Claire. What are you doing?"

Suitcases were everywhere. Both garment bags laid across the bed, bulging and neatly zipped. Claire was crouched beside one bag, but at his arrival, she stood. Still in her pajamas, he noted dimly. "Packing."

He took a deep breath. Reached for reason. "You're emotional. We all are. But it's not a good time to be making decisions like this. Besides, where would you go?"

She walked toward him, stopping a few feet away. With more life in her voice than he'd heard in a long time, she said, "I'm not going anywhere, David. You're moving out."

Special Agent Mark Foster

November 21
1:00 p.m.

"You're a busy woman to get in to see." Mark followed the nurse pushing Betsy Graves's wheelchair down the hallway and into her hospital room. Betsy smiled up at him, and he was struck by how much younger she seemed in the last few days, despite the long dyed-gray hair framing her face. Freedom probably had that effect on people.

"Looks like your dad and sister must have gone out for a bite," the nurse said chattily as she wheeled the woman to the side of the hospital bed and helped her into it. "That's the last test for the day, although the gal will be around in an hour or so for more bloodwork."

Betsy rolled her eyes and nodded, reaching for the iPad sitting on the table. Her family had brought it with them when they'd arrived the afternoon after her rescue. It had been an invaluable method of communication, as the woman had laboriously typed a statement and all her answers to their interview questions. She'd never speak again, her doctors had agreed. Luther Sims had almost killed her when he'd come home one day and heard her shouting for help. Her vocal cords were crushed.

Someone—probably her sister—had brought her pink silky pajamas to wear instead of the patient gown. Maybe she'd understood what a luxury they would be to a woman who had been relegated to wearing only the garments her kidnapper chose.

Betsy typed something painstakingly on the tablet and then handed it to him.

Where's your sidekick?

He grinned and pulled up a chair. "Agent Medford headed back to London this morning. I have a few more loose ends to tie up." Sloane had left before Mark had spoken to Whitney. The girl's revelation about Sims's statements when he'd attempted to strangle her had lent a whole different slant to the man's past, and things had been moving at warp speed since, especially for a weekend. He'd been on the phone half a dozen times with the BCI profiler, Greg Larsen, and SAC Bennett.

"Your statements have given us real insight into Luther Sims." Her expression darkened at the name of her former captor, like a light abruptly extinguished. "They've actually driven our investigation into his history." He'd forwarded copies of Betsy's statements to Larsen. They made for difficult reading. Decades of emotional and physical abuse as Sims's "wife." She'd faced numerous surgeries on her hands and feet, which had borne the brunt of his torture. And it was after years of his failed attempts to impregnate Betsy that the next kidnapping had occurred, starting the longest string of serial homicides in Ohio's history.

It was all tied up in the man's warped idea of family, Mark had told Larsen. But whether the man was re-creating something he'd lost or something he'd never had remained unanswered.

Until he'd spoken to Whitney this morning. Now he was here, seeking verification. "I need to ask you one last question. At least for now."

Betsy nodded grimly, her mouth a firm straight line.

"I want you to remember back to a difficult time. When Luther Sims choked you and nearly killed you. Do you remember him saying anything as he did so?"

In what seemed to be an unconscious movement, one of her hands moved to her throat. Her lips quivered, and she bowed her head. Her fingers remained motionless on the keyboard. But just when he thought she wouldn't answer, she began to type slowly, one key at a time. When she was done, she held the tablet out to him.

Damn you, Margaret! Always you disappoint.

The quick lick of adrenaline up his spine was tempered by the haunted look in Betsy's eyes. "I know that was hard," he told her. "But with your help, we're going to put him away for the rest of his miserable life."

◆ ◆ ◆

Mark stepped into an empty hospital waiting room to take the incoming call. "Where are you?" SAC Todd Bennet demanded.

"Still at the hospital. Betsy Graves just verified Whitney DeVries's story. Sims said much the same thing when he attacked her, calling her Margaret."

"Called them both by his sister's name. Have you shared that with Larsen yet?"

It sounded like a lumber wagon was going by the room. Mark checked the window to see an orderly pushing an overloaded laundry cart. "I just texted him. Any updates since the last time we talked?"

Bennett gave him a rundown of the events of the last few hours, ending with, "Sims is being transferred Monday."

That was news to Mark. The plan had always been to move Sims to a more secure jail location in Franklin County with in-house medical care, but from the way the man's doctors had talked a couple of days ago, that time was at least a week away. "That's a welcome development."

The man had been out of surgery for two days, and between over-concerned hospital staff and the man's steadfast refusal to speak to anyone, no one had gotten a word out of him. Several from BCI had tried, Mark included.

"I just got a call from one of the guards we have stationed at his room. Sims has been asking for you for the last hour. Only you. He made that clear. You ready to take another run at him?"

Anticipation raced through him. It would be a pleasure to hit the man with everything they'd learned that day. "I just need to go out to my car to get the recorder."

"You do that. And Mark? We've already got him wrapped up pretty tight. Put a bow on it for us."

◆ ◆ ◆

"Foster."

Mark pushed Sims's hospital door farther open and walked into the room. "Luther. I hear the operations were considered successful." The man looked stronger than he had a day out of surgery. But heavy bandages showed beneath the hospital gown, swathing his torso and shoulder. Mark guessed the man's thigh was dressed similarly.

The links manacling one of his wrists to the bed rails jangled as he raised a hand, making a dismissive motion. "They say there will be some permanent damage." His tone didn't indicate interest one way or the other.

There was a certain satisfaction in seeing the man in chains, much the way he'd secured his victims. As much satisfaction as he got from looking at the two wounds Whitney DeVries had inflicted on his face a week earlier. He was hoping they'd scar, leaving the man with a permanent reminder of his sins.

Mark had left his coat and weapon outside the room with the guard stationed there. He set the tape recorder on the small table between the bed and a straight-back chair. He turned it on, stating the date and their names.

Sims's mouth twisted. "You aren't going to need that. This isn't an interview. I just wanted to ask you a question."

"Okay. And then you'll answer one of mine."

Ignoring Mark's response, the man said, "What happened to David Willard?"

"He went free. You admitted to planting DNA on his daughter's body to incriminate him. It's the reason you changed dump sites. It's even why you chose to place her in a body bag instead of exposing her to the elements. You wanted to make sure the DNA didn't erode or blow away." He pulled out the chair and sat. "It's why you put the necklace in the bag. You wanted Kelsey Willard found and ID'd."

"I didn't admit to anything. You fabricated that, and there were no witnesses to our conversation to prove otherwise."

That was true enough, Mark silently acknowledged. But the word of a current BCI agent weighed a lot more heavily in a court of law than that of a former one who'd been found with a badly abused missing girl locked in his basement. Another kidnap victim confined in his bedroom.

"There was a break-in at the lake house three years ago. That's when you hid the body, isn't it?"

"It's obvious that Willard attempted a copycat crime. He deserves punishment." There was a glitter of hatred in the man's gaze. "Men who betray the trust of their families don't deserve to have them."

He'd said something similar once, Mark recalled, at their first meeting. That all the victims had a parent who was deficient in some way. After long conversations with Larsen, Mark realized the talk was all part of the man's rationalization for a decision he'd already made when he'd selected their daughters. Using his own twisted logic, he was rescuing the girls from his perceived failings of their parents. But there was more at work than that. Paraphilia often had its roots in childhood. And Sims's childhood had apparently had some very dark corners.

"Maybe so, but the law doesn't always provide for punishing people's bad choices."

"So flippant." Sims pressed the button that would raise the head of his bed more, wincing at the changed position. "The man's a liar and a cheat. Ask him about the lake house and how he used it to meet up with that young Realtor he was banging. While you're at it, ask him about the time Kelsey followed him on her bike and walked in on the two of them."

Mark struggled to keep his face impassive, but something in his expression must have given him away. Sims gave a nod. "You swallowed every line of BS he spun, didn't you? He gave her money when she threatened to tell her mother. A thousand dollars. What kind of man hangs that kind of guilt on his kid for something he did?"

"A shitty father," Mark allowed. "A cheat and a liar. But then again, you lied, too, didn't you? About being at Berlin Lake when Whitney DeVries was kidnapped. Clever to leave the SUV out with the canoe on top, even though there was plenty of room to park it in your double garage." A garage where they'd found a black van matching Kelsey's and Whitney's descriptions. Between the DNA they gathered from the basement and that van, Mark hoped they'd be able to tie several more victims to the man. "David Willard isn't the criminal here. You are."

The cord in Sims's neck was visibly throbbing. Coupled with his heightened color, he looked to Mark on the verge of a heart attack. "He lacks moral fiber. A man capable of deceiving and betraying his family is capable of any number of things, some of them surely illegal. Do your fucking job, Agent. I guarantee if you dig into Willard's life, you'll discover a law that's been broken. Then make. Him. Pay."

Larsen had been right, Mark realized slowly. DeVries had as many skeletons in his background as David Willard. But it wasn't Whitney's father who was the focus of the former profiler's rage. It was Kelsey's . . . *affection for the victim* . . .

It'd been difficult for Mark to wrap his head around that, but surely it was one reason Sims despised Willard. Sims had wanted to cast blame on Kelsey's father and increase his suffering. His hatred of the man was fed by his own feelings for his captive.

"Besides Betsy, you kept her the longest, didn't you?"

Sims pressed his lips together and looked away.

"Long enough to start to consider that she was yours, right? She was special. Everyone says so. Pretty. Clever. Engaging. You were everything her real father wasn't, and she should have loved you, not him." Unconsciously, Mark leaned forward in his chair, certainty fueling his words. "Family. That's important to you." He had Whitney's recollections of her conversations with her kidnapper. They had Kelsey's writings. Betsy's statement. "What kind of family life did you have with no father figure in it? A single mother would have been scandalous nearly seventy years ago. Maybe a single mother who was forced to abandon her dream of dancing for the New York City Ballet was resentful of the child who caused that." They were still searching for relatives who might be able to fill in some blanks on Sims's childhood.

"Is this an attempt to analyze me? You're out of your league, Foster."

Maybe he was. But Mark sensed he was also on the right track. "And then along comes a sister. Still no father, so there's just the three of you. But your mother isn't so resentful anymore because now she has a daughter to mold into her own image. One she can teach everything she knows about dance. One who might achieve the dream your mother had to abandon."

"We're done here."

"Margaret wasn't really your sister. Half, right?"

Sims glared at him. "Family is defined by more than blood. There's shared duty and obligation. A commitment to the common good."

"So how old was Margaret when she defied that commitment?" Mark sat back with feigned nonchalance, hooking one ankle across the opposite knee. "What was it? Boys? Teenage rebellion? Or did she just stop paying attention to her dance lessons?"

"Dance is an important tool for teaching the merits of discipline. It requires total focus. Margaret ran away because she was spending too much time thinking about a young hoodlum she'd met at school."

"Bet that was hard on your mom."

The man stared at Mark stoically.

"Probably harder yet when your mother discovered that her daughter hadn't run away. You'd killed her."

Sims reared back as if Mark had landed a blow.

"Maybe you didn't mean to. Could be when you choked her, you were just trying teach her a lesson. But she died. And then you hid her body somewhere. Not in Wayne National Forest that time—no, not that first time—but somewhere close to home. We got a warrant a few hours ago for your old home place. I'm guessing they'll find her body in an old well on the property. A barn. Perhaps you buried her. But even as we speak, they're getting cadaver dogs ready to search the place. I'm certain they're going to find Margaret—the sister who disappointed you so."

"Turn off the recorder. We're done here." Sims pressed his call light. A moment later, the door to the room swung inward, and one of the officers stepped inside. "I want him out of here. Summon my doctor. I'm feeling dizzy. Faint."

"Sure, I'll go." Mark stood but made no move toward the tape recorder. "But don't you want to ask about Elizabeth first?"

Sims froze.

"What attracted you more to your first victim, I wonder? The fact that she bore a resemblance to your mother? Or the fact that she danced and bore her name. Elizabeth. But everyone called her Betsy, didn't they? Betsy Graves."

The man's lips were moving silently, as if in argument. Finally he muttered, "She's my wife. We met after my mother died. It was love at first sight. Elizabeth adores me. I've taken care of her."

That's obsession, not love, Mark thought. *Possessiveness, not affection. And a sadistic level of rage when met with less than total obedience.* "How do you take care of her, Luther?" he asked, not even attempting to keep the disgust from his tone. "By surrounding the cabin with motion detectors that would alert you if any of your captives escaped? Or disguising her so she'd look your age? By breaking her fingers for the slightest infraction? Smashing her feet with a hammer the one time she tried to run away? Or by choking her so hard, she'll never speak again?"

"That's not true. None of it."

Mark walked closer to the bed. Bent over the man lying in it. "It's true. Every word. Elizabeth—or should I call her Betsy?—wrote it all out for us. She's in this hospital right now, receiving treatment for your years of abuse. She told us how you'd tell her each girl was a potential daughter for you both, to complete your family. But all ended up disappointing you, right? The same way Margaret did."

"She didn't tell you that." The man seemed surer now. "She would never disobey me."

"Then why do you suppose she threw those things the night I came to see you?" Mark pressed on inexorably. "First the book, and then she unscrewed the lightbulb to smash. She was trying to get my attention. She'd finally worked up the courage to defy you and risk it all one last time for escape."

Sims slowly clapped his hands, a derisive sound of applause. "That is quite a story. Unfortunately, you can't prove any of it."

"I've got Betsy's written statement and Whitney DeVries's testimony." It would be all they needed to put this psychopath away for good. Mark wasn't certain he believed in an afterlife, but if one existed, he hoped that somehow Kelsey Willard knew her killer would be punished. That all the other girls he'd murdered could feel a measure of vindication for his capture.

"I think all your victims would enjoy the irony of you spending the rest of your life in a cage."

"I *saved* them," the man roared, sitting upright, a vein throbbing in his temple. "I gave them a real parent. I gave them purpose."

Mark nodded at the guard who'd pushed open the door to investigate the outburst. The man slowly faded into the hallway again. "In other words, you were the father you never had? And Betsy would be the mother you wished yours had been. Fourteen victims." It was an effort to keep the rage from his voice. Lives lost. Families shattered forever. Sacrificed to one man's delusion. "But two survived. They're all we need to make sure you'll never feel the sun on your face again."

Sims fell back against the bed as if suddenly exhausted. "I'm still holding all the cards, Foster. You think you have undiscovered victims? Guess who can lead you to them?"

Mark snapped off the recorder. Picked it up and prepared to leave. Sims's voice trailed after him.

"Imagine the publicity if the BCI puts its own interests ahead of the families of those poor girls. The state attorney is probably writing my plea bargain as we speak."

The taunt followed him as Mark pushed open the door and started down the hall. There might be a kernel of truth in Sims's claims. Everyone wanted to provide closure to the families of crime victims. But the man was insane if he thought he'd skate on any of his offenses.

Eschewing the elevator, he opted for the stairs. One step at a time. That's how they'd build the rest of the case. And that's how he'd fix his marriage. It was Saturday. Bowling Green was only a couple of hours from Columbus. He could stop by headquarters in London for an hour or so, and then be on his way. Surprise Kelli and Nicky. And when he and his wife put the boy to bed, they'd go somewhere they could talk. Just the two of them.

Mark headed toward the exit of the hospital. He didn't fool himself that the upcoming meeting would be easy. But it was a start.

He pushed out of the hospital doors and walked rapidly across the parking lot. The weather had returned to a relatively balmy forty degrees. Too warm for the winter jacket he wore. He switched the recorder from one hand to the other as he shrugged out of the garment.

It would be a long time before he forgot the names of Luther Sims's victims. Longer still before their faces would stop haunting his sleep. Young girls who'd had their dreams stolen from them. Girls who would never finish school. Fall in love. Have children. But Mark figured the best way for him to pay homage to the victims' lost futures was for him to stop screwing up his own.

At least, he was going to do his damnedest to try.

ACKNOWLEDGMENTS

I'm always deeply indebted to all who come to my aid when research and imagination fail me. A big thank you to Chris Herndon, medicolegal death investigator, ABMDI, retired, who is always willing to discuss corpse decomposition and manner of death . . . with visual aids. Endlessly fascinating to a suspense writer! And to Karl Herndon, homicide detective, retired, for details ranging from how to end my victims' lives to latent prints.

A debt of gratitude is owed to my favorite attorney, Jason Bahnsen, for helping me out every time I have a legal question . . . and on this book, there were a lot of them! (I knew law school wouldn't be a waste.)

And many thanks to Jim Swauger, digital forensics investigator, for answering all my questions on cell phone forensics. I got even more ideas for plots after our conversation!

As always, any mistakes are the author's.

ABOUT THE AUTHOR

Photo © Lee Isbel of Studio 16

Kylie Brant is the author of nearly forty novels and is a three-time RITA Award nominee, a four-time RT Award finalist, a two-time Daphne du Maurier Award winner, and a 2008 *Romantic Times* Career Achievement Award winner (as well as a two-time nominee). Her books have been published in twenty-nine countries and translated into eighteen languages. Brant is a member of Romance Writers of America, including its Kiss of Death mystery and suspense chapter; Novelists, Inc.; and International Thriller Writers. Visit her online at www.kyliebrant.com.